SING FOR YOUR SUPPER

Volume I
of

CLOTHES OF A KING'S SON

A Novel in
Three Volumes

SING
FOR
YOUR
SUPPER

Pamela Frankau

Random House . New York

PZ3
F8513
Cl

FIRST PUBLISHED IN THE UNITED STATES 1964

© Copyright, 1963, by Pamela Frankau

All rights reserved under International and Pan-American Copyright
Conventions.

Library of Congress Catalog Card Number: 64–10541

MANUFACTURED IN THE UNITED STATES OF AMERICA
by H. Wolff, New York

FOR NANNY
With My Love

Part One

JULY

I

The children were in her dream. There they came walking often; not always these children. Sometimes these children would turn into the Hales or the Mattingleys, grown-up long since. Sometimes there would come a blend of all the children, past and present, wearing the wrong faces, changing parents and houses, to plague her in a bright disordered flurry before the dream snuffed out.

This dream had Thomas in it, and trains and luggage; so it was at least concerned with today's children. It was still about when she opened her eyes. What had Thomas been doing? Chattering urgently, then running, down to the end of the platform and away out of sight: gone just as the train was due to leave. She had chased him and lost him behind stacks of luggage. And then? As if it mattered . . . Today was here; here and real:

the calendar day, the date with the frame around it, printed on the air for weeks and weeks. July the twenty-third, 1926.

Blanche Briggs got out of bed. She pulled up the blind and twitched the lace curtains aside for a sight of the weather. There was an ominous sheen on the slate roofs opposite; above the roofs she saw a gray woollen-looking sky. Down on the pavement damp patches still lingered. More rain to come; a pity but—like the dream—of little importance. As she lit the gas-ring for the kettle, her fat alarm clock shrilled loudly; there had been no need to set it at all. Six forty-five. Time, and to spare. Only her night things to pack, only the three parcels to perch on the top of the string bag. That was all. She had sent her trunk in advance. Time, and to spare: but she felt the summons to escape, heard the message of a voice saying, "Out of here—and quickly." "Quickly," it said, and "Out of here!" again, making "here" sound like a prison: which was silly and unkind of it. This was her own small room in her sister's house. This was (but not to-day, somehow) her home.

Blanche put on her dressing gown. She scurried downstairs to the lavatory, bobbed across the passage to the bathroom and washed herself from head to foot with an angry kind of energy, though she could not have felt less angry and had indeed taken a bath just before midnight. She was laughing at herself. "*Anybody would think*—" the reproving phrase began in her head, but she found no end for the phrase. Anybody would think—what? That she was young? That it was her wedding day? Something of the sort. *There*, she said when, back in her room, she saw the steam bubbling furiously from the spout of the kettle: *There . . . another minute and it would have boiled over.*

While she drank her tea she heard the house begin to wake up. First her sister creaking out of bed and stumping across the floor below; then the plug-noise and the taps running; then the banging on Frank's door, the fusillade: "*Frank!* Seven o'clock. Seven o'clock, Frank! Are you awake? Well, don't go to sleep again . . . *Frank!*" Presently Frank lumbering to the bathroom. Just the same as every morning, Blanche thought, fastening her stays with a click.

The oval looking glass, set between its posts above the dressing table, was flecked and worn, giving only a dim picture. As a rule she paid this no attention, being so greatly used to it. Today she peered with determination, as if she expected more of her pink, bony face and blue eyes, her high forehead with the straight gray-brown hair drawn back; but the reflection remained dim and barred. She put in the last hairpins. She put on the pink and gray dress. At the collar she fastened the best brooch, the garnet and pearl, poor Mrs. Weston's last present. Poor dear Mrs. Weston . . . Well, she would be pleased about today if she knew, and she probably did where she was, thought Blanche, reminded now to kneel down and say her morning prayers before she finished her packing.

The door opened just as she was rising from the bedside. Mary seldom knocked. She said, "Lost something?"

"Lost something?"

"On the floor."

"I was saying my prayers."

"Oh. There isn't anything wrong, is there?"

"Not that I know of."

"Oh—I thought—I mean—prayers. Do you say them every morning?"

"No," said Blanche, "I'm afraid not, any more. Only when I remember."

"I say mine at *night*." Mary sounded a little hurt. "You're very early aren't you? I came to see if you wanted an egg."

"No thank you, just bread and butter." She said it automatically. Years of children, threat of train sickness, no eggs before journeys: a rule, an absolute rule; she began to laugh. Not me—*them*, she was reminding herself while Mary said, "What's the joke?"

"I would like an egg. If it's not a trouble."

"Of course it isn't, but you said—"

"I know I did, I'm sorry."

"No need to be sorry."

But there was. Under the huge high shimmering balloon of happiness she was sorry: sorry for Mary, the companion of a lifetime, the pretty one of the two, the married one. Now the set, widowed sister with the little Battersea house, the bearlike son and absolutely nothing to be excited about ever again. It was very sad. There was Mr. Dalbrook. He had a large mournful moustache and accompanied Mary to the Whist Drive. Sometimes he came to supper. But that was all. Mary didn't appear to like him very much, but when the phrase "Someone to look after her" came into Blanche's head it would often conjure Mr. Dalbrook.

"Oh, leave that for now, I'll give you a hand with it after breakfast," said Mary, as she began to strip the bed.

"Do it now, I'd better; I thought I'd go with Frank."

"Gracious, you'll be early, won't you?"

"I've got to leave the nightgowns at Mrs. Latham's."

"But that's just a step from Paddington; you'll still be early."

"Bound to be crowds this time of year," said Blanche.

"But with reserved seats." Mary was a great one for Buts and they always came thicker, faster, at the moment of parting. When Blanche didn't reply she said, "*First Class* too," adding, "Did you ever?"

"No, I never did," said Blanche, cheerfully and truthfully. It was as much a surprise to her as to Mary, who murmured, "All that way—cost a fortune," and getting no response, moved restlessly to the window. "Don't forget these, whatever they are." She was hovering above the table where the parcels lay. "Just the nightgowns, and the children's presents," said Blanche. "They'll go in the string bag."

"Presents . . . You didn't say . . . What did you get?" The smile made her quite pretty again: all the lines went up instead of down; the fair faded looks became appealing. (If you hadn't been so disagreeable last night, you could have seen them before I wrapped them. They were there and you looked and didn't ask; just went on about my room being empty till September and my being silly to leave Mrs. Latham and Mrs. Fothergill just because it was the holidays coming round, and saying, "It's the uncertainty—like," the way you always do. Back to, "I don't know, I'm sure; she's funny, sometimes," the safe slogan.)

"I *love* presents," said Mary.

"They're nothing very special. An Eversharp for Gerald. And Sarah wanted a manicure set, so I got a kind of wallet one that rolls up, pink leather—leatherette really, I expect, but it's quite nice. I don't think they ought to have those spiky things in them, though," she added, putting on her hat, thinking about cuticles and stabs under the nail.

"What did you get for Thomas?"

"Thomas . . . oh, another notebook. All he ever wants is notebooks. It's a fat one, brown; it's got a pencil." She looked severely at the dimmed reflection of her hat; gray straw with roses on the narrow brim. "Is that straight, Mary?"

"Yes, very nice. *Before* breakfast . . ."

"Why shouldn't I put it on before breakfast?" She laid her gray coat and her white cotton gloves on the stripped bed; she shut her small suitcase and began to put the parcels in the string bag. "Give this room a good doing," Mary said wistfully. "Well, I'd better boil your egg."

In the kitchen, the questionnaire, as always. It was one of Mary's tricks to show a keen, last-moment curiosity. For months she appeared to have no interest in the Weston family. Now she let fly.

"Not just rooms this time? A house?"

"Mary, I told you. The house they had before. We were at Sawcombe two summers; the year before Mrs. Weston died, and the year after."

Mary didn't remember. She wouldn't. In the year 1919 she was still removed, fortunate, with a husband, a life of her own.

"Roseclay, the house is called," said Blanche. "Rather a pretty name."

"Is it *big?*"

"I don't know that I'd say big. Quite a good size. Just right. The aunt and uncle will be coming, you see. Part of the time, at least. And the grandmother."

"I suppose they help to pay."

"I haven't asked them," said Blanche, cutting herself a slice from the loaf. Frank, wearing his brown suit, wandered in dazedly, while Mary went on undeterred.

"He'll meet you all, won't he?"

"Sending a taxi for us to the junction."

"Why's that?"

"Something to do with the show. They're rehearsing the new numbers. It's all quite new this year." She had told Mary this before, too. "*Moonrakers 1926*," she repeated. "What they call a new edition. He's very busy."

"I don't know what he'd do without you, I really don't." This needed no answer. Frank's bacon was sizzling loudly. Mary turned it over, then dished it out onto the fried bread.

"I expect he'll be getting married again one of these days, don't you?"

"I imagine he will—when he wants to." She used her hold-off tone. No doubts of hers, and there were plenty, on the subject of the children's father would ever be admitted to Mary.

"That Miss Richmond—is she still with the show?"

Frank said, "You *know* she is, Mum. I was telling you all about her, wasn't I? At Broadstairs. Your trouble is you don't listen." He filled his mouth.

Blanche said, as she had said before, "Miss Richmond's quite one of the family. So are Mr. and Mrs. Whittington. And Mr. Clyde." (Though she didn't look upon Leo Clyde as such, she included him for good measure.) "All been with Mr. Weston since *Hi Jinks*." Mary, who had once unforgivably observed that she couldn't feel quite happy about Mr. Weston being a Pierrot, somehow, returned to the children.

"*What* a time they have, traipsing about to all these different places."

"They're in the same place for nine months of the year."

"I don't mean school. Of course, now they're getting so big—"

She would have to say that. It was the one that could make you afraid, if you let it. Blanche spread a little more butter on the corner of her bread. "Anything decided about Christmas?" Mary asked, refilling the teapot.

"Gracious, we don't need to think about Christmas yet, do we, Frank—need to think about Christmas?" He winked at her as he shoveled down the last of the bacon. Frank agreed with her that his mother was "funny, sometimes."

"She's going with you," Mary said, as though she wasn't there. "I've told her she'll be early." While Frank swallowed his gigantic mouthful and held out his cup for more tea, Blanche glanced at the clock. Now, truly, only ten more minutes, and with the thought excitement choked her: the three months telescoping away, the children prancing near so that their faces and voices became more real than this room.

"Aren't you going to finish your egg?"

Hard to get it down; she treated herself to the chiding she might give to Sarah or Thomas: "Finish it up now, you'll be hungry long before it's lunch time."

Her room again; not hers any more; stripped and done with. The suitcase; the string bag. The hall, with the sad plant on the table by the hatstand; Frank shouldering into his mackintosh; Mary's soft darting kiss on her cheek; "Send me a postcard, dear, just to say it all went off all right." Then the slam of the door; the three steps; the red-tiled path. Frank swore at the latch on the iron gate, the latch that always jammed. Forcing it, he brought down a shower of rain drops from the laurel bush beside the gate. Now she was scuttling beside him along Ramillies Terrace, past all the little houses with the laurels in front and the lace curtains at the windows: Ramillies Terrace for the last time. (Not the last time, of course, a silly thing to suggest to yourself, but it felt like that.)

A reminding jingle sang in her head:

> But just for the minute
> That's as long as we are in it,
> We are walking, you and I,
> On our way to by-and-by.

It meant nothing. It was a funny one to come back now.

> But just for the minute
> That's as long as we are in it, . . .

"There," thought Blanche, "now I shall have it on the brain all day." She tried to hum the tune, but it only went "diddle-diddle-diddle," the way all tunes went if she tried to reproduce them. You couldn't call it being tone-deaf, surely, since the tune was palpable in your ear; it was just your voice that lost it, making a throaty, two-note buzz. Frank began to laugh. He knew her disability.

"Pop Goes the King or God Save the Weasel?" asked Frank.

"One of Mr. Weston's songs. Last year. Him and Miss Richmond, marching round the stage." She tried again:

> "But just for the minute
> That's as long as we are in it . . .

And he carried her off, kicking—that's all I can remember."

"Didn't do that one at Broadstairs," said Frank. "I could swear they didn't. I'd remember her being carried off kicking."

"Oh well, he's always changing the program," said Blanche, sounding a note of ownership. It seemed a little out of order for Frank to have caught the *Moonrakers* at Broadstairs last month: he was more up-to-date than she. Though of course he hadn't seen the new edition, which would, according to Mr. Weston, make all their fortunes. (Well, she had heard that one often enough. But *Moonrakers* 1926 had at least achieved a six-weeks resident season at Sawcombe, and this was one of the lights shining upon the summer.)

"Here's the bus. Step on it, Aunty." He did not mean step on the bus; it was a recent slangy expression from America, meaning hurry. She hurried. Frank hoisted her up and paid her fare despite her protest, adding, "Sorry it won't run to First Class," with one of his huge winks. Then they sat in silence . . .

They were over the bridge: no more Battersea; London beginning. The Number Nineteen took Frank all the way to his work. At Hyde Park Corner, he helped her with the string bag and the suitcase, calling, " 'Bye, Aunty—have a nice time!" before he was gone, carried away, wiped out of her thoughts.

She mounted the next bus (with a hand under the elbow and

"Oops-a-daisy" from the conductor, who looked no more than fifteen, Gerald's age. But that, she said to herself, was the war and her own rapidly-approaching fifties, no two ways about it). She sat for a while staring from the façades of Park Lane on one side to the cloudy greenness of the park on the other side. Then, because Frank had made his strenuous joke about the tickets, she opened her purse to look at them again. There they were, with the vouchers for the four places reserved, folded in the half-sheet of writing paper just as Mr. Weston had sent them. No comment, simply:

Dear Nanny,
  I was in town this week on business and got these to save you a scramble. Till Friday. Can't wait—can you? Love,

The quick, scribbly writing was contradicted by the elaborate signature with all its careful dots and flourishes:

Philip Adair.

He must, she reflected again, be very busy; preoccupied in the extreme. He never signed her letters like that. *Philip Weston* was the rule, still varied sometimes by *Daddy*, which was a leftover from the children's younger days. *Philip Adair*, the stage name, the signature for business letters, had always irritated her. Silly. No need to put on another name with his Pierrot costume, was there? Philip Adair's Moonrakers sounded no better to her ear than Philip Weston's Moonrakers would sound.

Something about that butterfly of a signature made her uneasy: she didn't know what, she didn't know why. There was surely no cause for uneasiness today, of all days. There was only the usual question mark in her mind about money, about the weekly tradesmen's books that would mount up at Roseclay and the old bills following on from other places; nothing new about this, nothing was going to change except the children, grown taller in their school clothes, with their new slang and new crazes and their new names for her: she was seldom Nanny now. She could be Briggo,

Briggers, Tiggy-Winkle, Wiggers, or even Blogs. Thomas always began his letters, "My darling Blogs." Philip Weston alone stayed faithful to "Nanny."

"What's he up to?" was the whisper in her head: she shut her ears to it. There was nothing odd about his extravagance: the tickets were merely a different manifestation of the same thing. Philip Weston had always been lavish with money, everybody's money, including all poor Mrs. Weston's and—after that—a great deal of money he hadn't got. Here Blanche found her lips pressing together, her head shaking at him as if he sat opposite her in the bus. Mrs. Weston's voice came in faint echo: "He isn't a *bad* man, poor darling—he's just hopeless about money."

The bus stopped exactly opposite Paddington Station. Giving the station approach a quick, threatening look as though to remind it to be in its place when she came back, Blanche walked down to Norfolk Square. She could give half an hour to Mrs. Latham, if half an hour was needed. As it probably would be. Of her two temporary employers Mrs. Latham was the more dependent. Mrs. Fothergill, in South Kensington, led a brisk life, full of committees and social work and young relatives coming up from the country to occupy the spare room. Blanche never felt the slightest qualm about deserting Mrs. Fothergill, who would wish her a merry, resigned goodbye and welcome her back with a breezy roar.

Inside this flat, whose front door she opened quietly lest Mrs. Latham were still asleep, gloom predominated; the aimless melancholy of its owner. Blanche left her things in the kitchen and went to the drawing room. Here, as she had expected, she found a certain disorder: ashtrays spilling over; the card table still set up, cards and markers lying untidily abandoned; dirty glasses on the side table where the bottles lived. She went to open a window; in the bay there stood a kind of brass bath on legs, with ferns growing out of it. Over the windows there hung huge velvet curtains, then thick net curtains, making a yellowish light come through.

Mrs. Latham was the widow of an Indian Army officer. His likeness was repeated in various gold frames. Moustache, medals;

topee under the arm: moustache, medals; long shiny boots:
moustache, medals; dress uniform with tight trousers. There were
photographs of the daughter, too, and the daughter's baby.
Where the photographs let up there were water-colors, mostly
seascapes, done by Mrs. Latham, a long time ago. Above the
mantelshelf there hung her one oil painting, torrid in color, the
paint very thick. It was the Isle of Wight, the Solent, quite recognizable to Blanche because the Westons had spent the 1913
summer there. She was folding the card table, having a little fight
with its rickety leg, when Mrs. Latham came in. Pink billowing
draperies with the sad puffy face on top, and the plentiful red
hair piled high, the coffee cup in her hand, the wistful greeting,
then, "I don't know what I'm going to do without you."

"The nightgowns," said Blanche, "are on the kitchen table."

"You're an angel." She always said that. "Sorry about the
mess." She always said that too. "Don't bother, Blanche, if you're
in a hurry."

"I've got a few minutes, M'm."

"You look so smart. I expect you're excited, aren't you? Meeting your babies?"

"They're hardly babies any more."

Mrs. Latham lit a cigarette. "Do they all come to Paddington
together? Or what?"

"Sarah and Thomas come together; it's lucky their schools being so close; they'll be put in a taxi at Marylebone. Gerald's train
comes to Paddington, so he's bound to be there first."

"I remember how excited I used to get," said Mrs. Latham wistfully. She wandered around, picking at things, saying, "Devonshire—*so* lovely," and "I ought to get away, I really ought," and
"It's such an *effort* when one's by oneself," exuding plaintive reproach until, with a little shriek, she remembered Blanche's
money and went to get her bag.

"Well, now I shan't see you till September. You'll let me
know—"

"I'll let you know. Somewhere in the third week. I'll write."

"Don't you dare write and tell me you aren't coming back,
now."

"I've always said, M'm, that if by any chance Mr. Weston wanted me permanent—"

"Yes, I know you have, but he *won't*, will he?"

"I shouldn't think so," said Blanche. "Goodbye, M'm. Look after yourself."

"You've been an angel. Where did you say you put the nightgowns? Oh yes. Oh well, thank you—goodbye, Blanche." She said it in tragic tremolo. When the door was shut, Blanche could still see her trailing about in the yellowish light of the drawing room, picking things up and putting them down again.

("What she does with herself all day . . . ?") But now, as she came out into Norfolk Square, Mrs. Latham was gone, just as Frank had gone. One aspect of herself had gone too. Blanche Briggs, walking briskly up Norfolk Street and down the station approach, suitcase in one hand, string bag in the other, turned into Nanny.

She was, of course, far too early. But the crowds were coming already. Taxis drawing up, children tumbling out excitedly; parents and luggage and porters: the holidays begun. As she walked to the barrier at the head of Number Three platform she was looking out for Gerald. There he was. No, he wasn't. Another boy in gray flannels, with something of Gerald's look, a neat, dark-haired boy walking with a swagger: a forecast of Gerald. "*Mind your back, Miss* . . ." A porter pushing a barrow with a mountainous load: there was a new spade and bucket perched on top: an iron spade, bluish-black, with a white wooden handle, the bucket was red with a gold band round it. Gerald and Sarah and Thomas were too big to care for spades and buckets any more. But these things were still stamped with a trademark of rightness; she smiled upon them.

She took up her position behind the barrier. She set down the suitcase and the bulgy string bag. She began to look all ways, turning her neck like a bird. Little springs of anxiety began to bubble up through the excitement. *Where are they? Where are they?*

A loud voice behind her said, "Pawdon me, Moddom. Pawdon." She paid it no attention until it hissed in her ear, "My

name's Rabindranath Tagore" and she was seized around the
shoulders, her hat knocked forward.

"Good gracious, Gerald. Oh, my dear."

"I crept up on you."

"I should think you did." Laughing, she straightened her hat
and adjusted her eyes to the look of him. At least two inches
taller: bare-headed; no cap: he seemed to have oiled his hair—
the hair was jet black like his father's—his eyes were the same
brown and his skin as smooth and sallow. But he had the tip-
tilted nose, like his mother's, instead of Philip's rather hooky
nose; and the pretty mouth was like his mother's too. Gerald had
been what she called a handsome little boy, and now he had
turned into a handsome young man—or nearly—with a man's
voice—or nearly. The changes of puberty again; she remembered
these changes in the Hale boys, and the Mattingleys: the surprised mind asking Where has he gone? and reason replying Here
he is.

"Look at your *shoes*," she said. They were brown and white
shoes.

"Co-respondent shoes. That's what they're called, Brigstock."

"*Brigstock* . . ."

"That's what *you're* called. Or Brigstraw, if you'd rather."

"I don't know that I like either very much."

"Well, that's terribly depressing of you, I made them up in the
train."

Still looking at the shoes, she said, "They don't let you wear
those at school?"

"First time I've had them on. They were a swop." She mistrusted swops. At Sarah's school and Thomas's school they were
rightly forbidden. At Gerald's school, which she saw as an insani-
tary jungle, with overtones of *Eric, or Little by Little*, they
raged.

"And the banjo—" she said, looking at the instrument slung
across his shoulder.

"Ukulele, Brigstock, ukulele. My uke," said the thick, husky
voice.

"Was that a swop too?"

"No, I stole it. Out of a shop window. Smash and grab. My darling, I'm *entranced* to see you, do you know?"

"It's lovely to see you, too." She continued her examination. "Just that little case? Where's the rest of your luggage?"

"I've lost it."

"No, you haven't," she said firmly.

"Yes, I have. It fell out of the van. What *are* we going to do?"

"Don't be silly, Gerald—did it go in advance, your big trunk?"

"Ages ago. We'll find it at Sawbridge Junction, covered with green mold. That's a terribly pretty hat. Can't you sit on something? Rest your poor old feet? We're awfully early."

"I don't mind standing: one sees better standing."

"How are they coming—by taxi?"

"That's what your father said. They'll be put in a taxi at Marylebone. I hope somebody's in charge, I'm sure."

"And I *do* hope it's not Thomas," said Gerald. "Hadn't I better queue up, Brigstock? All these common people . . ."

"Don't say that, please."

"Well, they are. And they're all getting a head start."

"There's no need to queue. We've got reserved seats. And we're going First Class."

"We're *what? Honestly?*" He stared at her. "How? Who paid?"

"Your father, of course."

"Oh ho ho, I doubt that *vairy* much. Don't you?" said Gerald. He stood grinning at her, raising one eyebrow, assured, it seemed, that she would join him in disbelief. It wasn't right for him to be so certain. On the other hand, he had known the facts for so long . . . She had never been able to protect Gerald: the younger two, yes, but not Gerald. He was far too bright. He was always the one who managed to overhear the agonized little conferences or catch the angry tradesman's voice at the door: Gerald with his quivering curiosity, his casual acceptance, saying, "Summons, wasn't it?" or "Broke again, aren't we?" Almost indecently unmoved, taking it all for granted. Looking at him now she saw that the grin had left his face; his expression was severe.

"*You* didn't pay, did you?"

"Good gracious no—whatever put that into your head?"

He didn't answer; he merely looked relieved and said, "Have a bullseye?" Then he began to look away over her shoulder, his profile pointing like the profile of a dog.

"Is that them? Can you see them?"

"No. It's Mullens. Old Jamjar Mullens. He's traveling on this train." Now he turned his back to the gigantic freckled boy carrying two tennis rackets, as though he didn't want to see this Mullens at all. Mullens, unlike Gerald, wore his school cap. When he came close, Blanche could see small glinting bristles on his chin and upper lip.

"Wotcher, Weston."

"Oh . . . wotcher," said Gerald languidly. "May I introduce John Mullens? This is my aunt, Miss Briggs." Mullens lifted his cap, said, "How d'you do," and moved on. Gerald doubled up, giggling.

"Well, I couldn't very well say you were my Nanny, could I? He's captain of cricket."

"Your old nurse, you could have said."

"*Old* nurse—would you rather I'd said that? Truly, Brigstock? It sounds like old luggage."

"The train's coming in."

"So it is," said Gerald. "No hurry," he added masterfully. "Let all the oicks get on first." He patted her shoulder: "Now *don't* start worrying. They'll be here in a minute." Blanche, listening to the high, panting snuffle of steam from the engine, watching the crowd pack through the barrier, said, "They ought to be here *now.*" She looked this way and that. "*Stop it,*" said Gerald. "Forty minutes to go—well, nearly. Tell about Roseclay. Has it turned itself into a boarding house?"

"*Boarding house*—" Somebody bumped her in the back, causing Gerald to say, "Mind your manners, there. I happen to be Sir Rabindranath Tagore and this is my wife." He put an arm around her: "Not a boarding house?"

"Your father's taken it furnished, didn't he tell you?"

"No—he said we'd probably remember it. *I* remember it as enormous."

"Not enormous. Just big. Mrs. Gale's going to be there—do you remember Mrs. Gale?"

"Was she the one at Sidmouth?"

She couldn't blame him; it must be hard to sort out all the different Mrs. Somebodies in charge of the many rooms: a long line of landladies looping all over the map. "She was the cook that summer. She lives at Sawcombe. You probably *will* remember when you see her. She's very excited."

"A cook? Stap my vitals. Curiouser and curiouser." His loftiness could not conceal his pleasure. She could have no part in it; she was too busy darting her head from side to side, searching, wondering, worrying. The noisy echoing scrimmage, the arching glass of the station roof, the shouts, the smell of steam, these held her trapped: her mouth dried and she could say no more to Gerald. He bent towards her: "What's the form with Uncle Percy—Aunt Flavia—Granny?"

"I imagine they'll all be there."

"Staying in the house?"

"Gerald, you don't think anything's gone wrong? Suppose their train was late—"

"It could be a lot later and we'd still be all right. *Staying?*" he repeated.

"Well—they stayed at Roseclay last time, didn't they?" said Blanche.

"But that was just after Mummy died. It isn't as though—" A train whistle shrieked so loudly that she lost the rest of his sentence. The next thing she heard him say was, "Brigstock darling, why don't I go ahead and find the carriage?"

"You'll have to have this voucher thing."

He took it; he picked up his suitcase and hers. He was lost and fresh eddies of people kept coming, children and porters and barrows and high, joyful voices all around her with the noise of the steam. Stupid to get so panicky, with twenty-five minutes left. But where, oh, where was Sarah—and Thomas—and where, come to think of it, was her string bag? Had Gerald picked it up with the two cases? He must have. Bumped and rocked by the new surge about her she thought, *Oh he must have*, but she hadn't seen him do it and this heightened the panic. She tried to keep it sternly under. She squared her shoulders, telling herself to be sensible, but she felt a little dizzy. She began to reproach herself for leaving the arrangements to Mr. Philip. Why hadn't he let her go to Marylebone, meet Sarah and Thomas, bring them on here in the taxi? She ought to have insisted. But (they aren't babies any more) Sarah was thirteen; Thomas was ten, though that didn't seem possible, and now she could think of nothing but the string bag. With their presents in it. Getting yourself in a proper state, aren't you? said Blanche to Blanche. I won't have it, do you see? Gerald's here. Gerald's putting that bag into the carriage this very minute. There's plenty of time. There's nothing to worry about.

"Mind your back, Miss."

There was the sort of person she hoped and expected to see: a lady in a dark coat and skirt, leading two small girls who wore school uniforms. Well, that was what she would see, any moment now, and the children would be Sarah and Thomas.

❂

In the taxi Sarah was saying to Thomas, "Wake up, you cheese. I said have you got sixpence?"

He looked at her for quite a long time before he said, "Why?" His voice, as their father said, came from his boots.

"Well, why d'you think? It's one-and-three already and Miss Cookman only gave me two shillings. You've got your journey money—you haven't touched it, have you now?"

Thomas said nothing at all, but his expression was obliging and he fished in the pockets of his shorts. He produced a florin, handing it over silently.

"I don't need all that."

He remained silent.

"Have you got a pain or something?" Sarah asked impatiently. He didn't look as though he had. He was as rosy as usual and squarer in shape than ever. She was glad to see him but he had maddened her by being last off his prep-school train and then going back to look for his magazine, which didn't sound like the

sort of magazine he should be reading, though as it was lost forever she could not be sure. He had seemed quite unimpressed by
Miss Cookman (the Goddess Athene) waiting so graciously to
put them in the taxi. And he had hardly said a word since. Now
he smiled at her.

"What did you say?" asked Thomas.

"I said, have you got a pain?"

"No, why? Have you?"

"Of course not."

"Well then?" said Thomas, looking bemused.

"You seem to have lost your tongue, as Blogs would say."

"I was thinking about the carriage."

"What carriage?"

"The railway carriage. It's brown," said Thomas thoughtfully,
"with white lace things all round."

"Railway carriages are red."

"This one isn't."

Sarah had no time for his brown and white carriage. Inside her
head were the harrying thoughts, the end-of-term thoughts: a
blend of excitement, romance and cold fear. She looked out of
the window, saying, "We're nearly late, you know. Can you carry
your two things if we don't find a porter?"

He nodded.

"I could help if I hadn't got my two things."

"It's all right," said Thomas, "I carried them for miles this
morning." They were a wooden box and the old sausage-shaped
canvas hold-all that he loved. Strictly speaking, she should offer to
take the hold-all (though he was always loath to part with it) and
trust him with her blue writing case. The writing case had an unexploded bomb in it—her school-report—and this she would have
liked to lose, but there were treasures in the case as well.

"Shall we have to run?" he asked.

"Oh, we shan't miss the train, but Briggo will have been waiting for hours." She meant, without alarming him, to rub in the
fact that it was his fault for being so slow. He looked as if he
hadn't heard her. He sat with his mouth a little open and his
eyes, fringed with the thick white lashes, staring ahead. His

square, dirty hands hung down between his knees. The pink
school cap was too small—or was his pale straw-colored head too
large? Thomas was the only fair one of the three. Certainly he
needed a haircut. The taxi came down the ramp and he leaned
over to grasp his wooden box so that he bumped his head when
they stopped. The bump knocked his cap off.

"Oh *Thomas*. Did it hurt?"

"Yes." By the tone of his voice he might just as well have said
No. And he followed her briskly enough, leaning back from the
weight of the box and the hold-all stacked up in front of him,
kept steady between his palms and his chin. Every time she
turned he was still there, obediently trotting.

"Let me take the hold-all, do."

He mouthed a No.

Breasting ahead of him she saw the barrier; she saw Gerald,
different again as always: taller, more elegant, more grown-up;
she saw Nanny, Briggo, Blogs, the same again as always, the
small figure in the gray coat and a straw hat trimmed with roses.
She saw them before they saw her. Now Nanny turned her way.
There was the look of amazed delight, the little flush, the beaming bony face. "Here they are—here they are!" she was crying to
Gerald as she ran to meet them. The demons keeping Sarah
company flew off, lost power as she came; and now she was mixed
up in the hug with Nanny, safe as a house (but they would come
back, the demons).

"Poor Thomas, you *are* loaded. I'll take this one," she heard
Briggs saying, while Gerald looked her up and down murmuring
languidly, "How do? My name's Rabindranath Tagore—what's
yours?" before he stretched out an arm and seized Thomas's cap
from his head. "Happy Christmas, mate, can't have you wearing
your cap" was his greeting to Thomas, who grinned and said
nothing. Then he took the wooden box from Briggs, who
promptly took the hold-all from Thomas and they charged
through the barrier. Gerald and Sarah drew ahead.

"You've got a shock coming to you, Madam. Brace yourself.
Enter—by virtue of the spell," said Gerald.

Sarah gazed upon the First Class carriage. There were four

corner seats marked Reserved and nobody else here at all. She saw Gerald's suitcase; the ukulele of which he had written in his last letter; the suitcase belonging to Briggs and the plump, familiar string bag.

Gerald hoisted Thomas's box onto the rack, testing it doubtfully. "Probably come down on Brigstock's head," he decided. "Yes, Madam, you may well gape. Plush, ain't it?"

It was also brown; and there were the white "lace things," antimacassars with GWR blocked into the crochet-work.

"Did you know about this?" she asked Gerald.

"Not till now."

"Well Thomas did," said Sarah, as Briggs and Thomas came climbing in.

"Lost your magazine? What a shame. Never mind, I've got plenty for you to read in my bag. Now—who doesn't mind back-to-the-engine?"

"Oh Blogs darling, we *none* of us mind back-to-the-engine any more. Who told you we were traveling First?" she asked Thomas.

He said indifferently, "Is this First? Oh yes, I see."

"But who told you?"

"Nobody."

"But you said—"

"With any luck," Gerald announced from the corridor, "we're going to have it to ourselves." He hung at the window, shouting, "Not in here, Madam, not in here, please—we're all in quarantine for mumps. I'm from the Red Cross, sir, I'm sorry—casualties only in this carriage. All seats reserved for Rabindranath Tagore!" He was showing off: nobody was there to listen to him and Nanny didn't even tell him to be quiet; she was busy producing copies of *The Scout, Picturegoer* and *Photoplay* from the string bag.

"You said it was brown and white," Sarah heckled Thomas. "Didn't you?"

"Did I? What splendid magazines. Look, Sarah."

"How could you have known?"

"Known what, dear?" said Nanny. Thomas bent his head over *The Scout,* mumbling, "Oh well, I suppose I guessed." And now she was drawn to the sight of her reflection in the strip of looking glass above the seat. She pulled off the ugly school hat and threw it onto the rack. She shook out her hair. *The dark ripple with the coppery glints, the pale, lovely face with the great eyes and the sensitive mouth made an unforgettable picture.* Well, no, not exactly. The coppery glints were missing, for one thing. How did one get coppery glints? She went on gazing, fascinated.

With a shudder and a jerk, the train moved. Triumphantly Gerald returned; he slid the glass doors together, cutting them off from the corridor. Sarah still knelt, absorbed.

"That's the girl I want for the part," said the great actor to the great actress, *"that girl over there, do you see? Wait till you hear her read. Voice like a cello. She could be another Meggie Albanesi."* (She was wearing the scarlet tights and silver tunic allotted to Marjorie Davidson for the school Shakespeare. Oh, damn the report in the writing case, it was breaking the dream.)

"How do you find your face, Madam?" Gerald asked, as she deserted the mirror.

"As lovely as the dawn," said Sarah.

If only she could get the report out now and read it and know the worst. It lay on the top, in its sealed envelope, addressed "Philip Weston, Esq.," in Miss Groome's handwriting. They were all put on their honor to hand over the envelopes: the school policy being, as Miss Groome had reminded her at the last hideous interview, to Trust Every Girl, Even The Youngest. The memory made her want to yell aloud with shame. She had to shout something quickly; she shouted at Nanny:

"Darling Blogs, what would we do without you?" It made an abrupt magic against the demons.

"Well I don't know what I'd do without you all, I'm sure. Very lonely I'd be, wouldn't I, Thomas?"

Gerald said, "Do with a haircut, couldn't you, mate?" and ruffled the hair, bringing the inevitable, "Leave him alone, now," from Nanny.

What would today be like without her demons? Wholly magnificent, Sarah decided. The house, Roseclay, had been a palace; still would be a palace, its splendor mysteriously restored to them and it is, she thought, the first time we have ever gone back to anywhere. This thought became full of romantic interest. She said, "It is—isn't it—the first time we've ever gone back to a place? Since we started going to school?"

"Lord, no. Folkestone—two holidays running," snapped Gerald in his always-right voice. "Year before last. With *Gay Cavaliers.*"

"They were different rooms, though. That's what I mean: we never go back to the same ones."

He leaned across to her, hissing, "Of course we don't, landladies like their bills paid." Luckily Nanny didn't catch it. Nanny said, "You came to Elmo Court twice. Don't you remember Elmo Court?"

"Who could forget it?" Gerald asked, rolling his eyes upward and shuddering affectedly. "Ugh!"

Sarah's memory revived Elmo Court: a big dark, echoing house off the Bayswater Road, with half the rooms shut up. Nanny had one of her temporary jobs there as a caretaker; she was allowed to have Thomas with her. By some arrangement that now seemed peculiar, even by Weston standards, two rooms in the house had been opened up for Sarah and for Gerald at Christmas and Easter. Elmo Court had a gloom attached to its very name. Less pocket money than usual, she recalled; and nothing much to do; and their father appearing only intermittently; the uncle and aunt taking them to the cinema and tea at Buzzard's; seats very far back in the upper circle at a pantomime with Nanny; long hours in the Natural History Museum, which lost its luster because they went so often.

"Elmo Court—oh *yes,*" she said on a groan. And at once Thomas, who hadn't seemed to be listening at all, shouted, "I liked Elmo Court best. Better than anywhere. I simply loved it." He dropped *The Scout* on the floor. He projected himself forward, thrusting his furious face at her; gabbling at speed: "There was the statue of the man holding the lamp in the hall and you could slide for miles in the drawing room and the kitchen smelt beautiful and there were those two peacocks, my goodness, Sarah, you can't have forgotten the peacocks."

She caught a dim picture of colored silk panels on a wall with dust-sheeted shapes below: panels one each side of a marble mantelpiece.

"You loved them—we used to count the eyes on their tails, *two peacocks*, not just a peacock and peahen—they went all the way up to the ceiling—you *must* remember." As ever, when he began to talk, the words seemed to get ahead of him in a confused catalogue. The Aberdeen next door that wore a coat when it went for walks and the oil stove, and Elmo Court was the time, you know it was, said Thomas, when the water pipes all burst in the street and made that splendid flood. "I don't know what you're talking about, I really *don't*." He banged his fists on the seat. It was useless to protest that she had talked about nothing; he was in one of his states. When he was smaller they had ended in tears. Not now; he was scarlet, indignant, tearless.

On and on: "Mr. Cox was the man who hired out the stove and came to trim it, his eyes were different colors—and there was a telephone and the telephone number was four nought nought seven Park—such a *good* number!" he yelled at her and stopped abruptly, seeming to have run down.

Nanny was laughing, saying, "Well, fancy you remembering all that." Gerald, Sarah saw, was repressing his giggles, which made him stutter.

"W-W-Why's it such a good number? I mean," he added courteously—he was always nice to Thomas—"I'm not saying it isn't. I'd just like to know why it is."

Thomas, cooling off, looked at him thoughtfully.

"Better than if it had been five nought nought seven Park?" Gerald persisted.

Here, Sarah thought, one could see Thomas's large pale blue eyes searching for traps. The shortness of his upper lip always seemed to be pulling his mouth open.

"It wasn't five nought nought seven Park," he said at last. "It was four."

"Yes, mate, we know."

Thomas went puddingy.

"Come on, tell us why it's so good. Honestly, old boy, I'm deeply interested."

"Don't tease him, Gerald."

She can't see how maddening it is when Thomas does that, thought Sarah; now he doesn't bawl any more, she takes his side. The thought of Thomas bawling led to the Moonrakers because of the fat, jelly-wobbling Pierrette called Maisie Something who had made them choke with giggles at Eastbourne three summers ago. They had behaved quite badly and Thomas had bawled afterwards and kicked Gerald and said, "I liked her the best" all the way home. He was only seven; it was the first time he had seen the show. (Not the Moonrakers, then, of course: not their father's own company, but Philip Adair had written many of the songs; old numbers from *Hi Jinks* or *The Gay Cavaliers* were still inclined to show up in the Moonrakers program. By special request, Philip Adair will sing . . .)

She considered *Moonrakers 1926* while Nanny bridged over the Thomas situation with some doughnuts. ("Only one now; you don't want to spoil your lunch.") Was it the new edition that had enriched them all at once? She asked Gerald who said, "Can't be. They only opened last Monday. I'm inclined to think it's Uncle Percy and Aunt Flavia footing the bill. Hell to have them in the house," he muttered behind his hand.

"Who said?"

"Brigstock. If it was Granny by herself now."

"It wouldn't be. It never is." With Gerald, she found the grandmother fascinating. But the summer routine brought all three: boring uncle, tiresome aunt, fascinating grandmother. It was in the routine for them to stay at an hotel, usually an expensive hotel, paid for by Uncle Percy. The grandmother was, if possible, poorer than the Westons, despite having won her famous libel action in 1920.

Thomas, also devoted to the grandmother, asked with his mouth full, "Will they be there when we arrive?" Nanny said she shouldn't think so; not till after the Bank Holiday. "Mind you, your father hasn't said they're staying in the house, not definitely. It's just my idea."

"Your ideas are usually right," said Thomas, staring at her with passion and a line of doughnut sugar on his upper lip. He added, "The house is *much* too big for us by ourselves."

"You don't remember it—you *can't*. You were only three."

"I do remember it."

"Perhaps we're letting lodgings to all the Moonrakers," said Gerald. "There's a thought."

Nanny was at the string bag again, with Thomas for conspirator, their heads close together. Sarah said to Gerald, "I suppose we'll be able to go tomorrow."

"Go? I've *been* this morning," said Gerald, "haven't you?" It was exquisitely funny and laughing wildly, she looked across at Briggs for the expected veto on lavatory jokes. "I meant *go* to the Moonrakers, you ass."

Gerald said, "Moonrakers? Be *able* to go tomorrow? Are you mad? We shall be *forced* to go. Not a hope of not."

He astonished her. No, he didn't. Everything about him, from the brilliantine smelling of violets to the brown and white shoes, signaled the arrival of a Gerald who had been hovering near. He disturbed her a little, so she said, "Huntley and Palmer," looking out of the window at Reading.

"And Rabindranath Tagore, Limited. Purveyors of superior Reading biscuits. They read in most superior voices," said Gerald, but he wasn't leaving *Moonrakers* alone. He grimaced at her, seized his ukulele and sang in Cockney; while he sang he cultivated an expression of striving nausea:

> *"Moonrakers, Moonrakers!*
> *Masters of laughter, the melody makers,*
> *Wandering minstrels, the givers, the takers!*
> *Pirates of pleasure and rogues of romance,*
> *Gay buccaneers of the song and the dance!"*

He ended with such a convincing sick-noise that Nanny looked up wearing her emergency face; and afterwards rebuked him. "It isn't funny. You're much too big to do nasty, vulgar things like that."

Sarah glanced at his scornful face. This at least made a change of worry. She had accepted always, without question, the one constant in their lives: "Philip Adair." Concert party, Pierrot troupe, music-hall act, winter job in pantomime, all were part of destiny; as solidly established as the shape of one's nose . . . "Philip Adair" was institutional, like Nanny. She had, she found, no point of view. For Gerald to come out in mockery, hating and sneering, was awful. Wasn't it?

"This is for you, Sarah," Thomas was saying, waving a parcel at her. "For you. We've all got presents and we can open them now. *Now*," he added fiercely, "This minute. Before we go to the dining car."

❂

Gerald had hoped to find Mullens in the dining car. Possibly he was taking the second lunch; or perhaps he had sandwiches with him. Either way there was no sign, and Gerald loitered in the corridor; he was reluctant to go searching down the train; why? From a kind of shame and this he didn't understand because—surely—there was no shame about asking for his own money. Mullens owed him four-and-sixpence. Mullens didn't dispute it. But for three weeks he had met Gerald's reminders with regrets; apologies for being "short just now," promises for the future.

He had, he told himself, been a fool to lend it. He would be a worse fool not to chase up Mullens and get it back. Mullens would have money on him today. Yet he still hesitated. He leaned on the brass rail at the window, watching the roofs of Taunton come near under the rain. Taunton already . . . The journey, in his childhood memory had taken forever. He began to score the Devonshires from the past. There was Sawcombe twice and Dawlish before that: Dawlish in wartime and a Red Cross train full of wounded soldiers going by, to be waved to from the beach; Sidmouth, now—when was Sidmouth? The chase in his head postponed the chase for Mullens. But the look of the money kept haunting him, the half-crown and the florin, shining silver, enormously important. He cheered himself up with a secret, hurried snatch at his wallet, a quick counting of the notes

inside, the hoarded treasure. It was a great deal of money, a hazard to carry around, but he could not bear to part with the lovely
notes in exchange for a Post Office savings book. Nobody knew
he had this amount. Nobody must know. It was his private joy,
come by canny dealings, by much calculation and by many a
brave adventure.

Money, money, money. Without it the world was against you.
He seemed to have known this for a long time, to have been
making—for years—a cold, practical assessment of the family
fortunes. Misfortunes, rather. He saw them now with his routine
mixture of pity and scorn. The struggle had endured since he
could remember: even in his mother's lifetime. ("But, Philip, we
haven't got a *bob!*" wailing through the bedroom door.) Bills,
panics, bailiffs: the sell-up at Scarborough. (Did he really remember that, or was it just a hand-down? He did remember the one
prosperous patch; 1917, when Philip was invalided out of the
Gunners, there had been money, then; a pension or a gratuity. A
boy of five, recognizing a prosperous patch . . .)

After his mother's death it had all become more exasperating
and, with the last few years, more visibly dishonest. One day soon
he would summon courage to tell his father how bitterly he disapproved of Briggs coming to them for nothing in the holidays and
—worse—dishing out money she had earned in term-time. That
didn't always happen, any more than Uncle Percy's reluctant-
savior checks always happened—but it had, and it could again.

It was a mess. Their life maddened him with its sloppiness, its
sentimentality, its absurd "Ladies and Gentlemen" shibboleth:
his father's totem which somehow made the Moonrakers seem
still more idiotic. (Sarah had looked so shocked just now; her eyes
had widened in horror; surely she should know how greatly he
despised "Philip Adair.") A gentleman, Philip Adair, a gentleman even in ruffles and silk cap. (Gunner tie or old-school tie
worn, as you might say, under the domino.) The façade was
strenuously preserved. *Oh*, the upper-class jokes shot out with the
Oxford accent; the little French songs flawlessly, affectedly ren-
dered; the "Don't-forget-I-was-at-Eton" patter. And the utterly
bloody "serious" interludes. (He would not think of the one

where Philip Adair came on in khaki and Sam Browne, he would *not*.)

The Ladies-and-Gentlemen mystique would be his enemy always. He saw it as the root cause of the money mess. The Westons, even in boarding houses, must never forget they were Ladies and Gentlemen. Appearances To Be Kept Up. At the theatre, for example. Not to queue for the pit, so you sat where you couldn't see half as well, in the upper circle. The children you mustn't play with; the words you mustn't use (like "pardon" and "serviette"). The "right" clothes. The rules were laid down by Philip and scrupulously administered by Briggs.

Gerald saw Briggs herself as a sign and a symbol. Loving her dearly, he would never say so. Brigstock believed in "Ladies and Gentlemen" as God was to be believed in. Though she had rebuked him for saying "common people" this morning—missing the point of his satire—she held to that standard: the standard of Philip Adair.

To hell with Ladies and Gentlemen. To hell with this possibly gentlemanly impulse that kept him from chasing Mullens. (And to hell with the notion that he had only lent Mullens the four-and-sixpence because Mullens was captain of the First Eleven. The person Gerald aspired to be, the person he almost was, damn it, sneered from a comfortable distance at the First Eleven.)

To hell with school. He was top of his Form, thanks to the parrot's trick that mastered words and gave the right answer even when he hadn't understood the question. He was a star on the games field; playing the pointless games as though he cared. Would Philip be horrified to know the truth: that he despised all of it, counted himself done with it and leapingly ready for the adult world? Philip after all had skipped away from the same school and joined a touring company at seventeen. But nowadays he made it sound as though this were done in heroic self-sacrifice, to save his parents from expense. Gerald kept his own longing to himself. Uncle Percy might applaud the wish to get out and earn a living. But Uncle Percy, the successful businessman, said there was nothing like a public school education; and that was why Uncle Percy paid the school fees.

Here he cast a speculative eye to the First Class tickets. Ladies and Gentlemen could, in the tradition, travel Third without losing caste. Roseclay was a puzzler, too. What had happened? An authentic turn in the family fortunes? The detached mind, on whose possession Gerald prided himself, remained coldly unbelieving. One solution occurred to him, only one.

Gwen Richmond ("Dear Old Gwen" in his father's voice) might be the solution. Gwen had what she called a Legacy Aunt, obstinately surviving in her eighty-sixth year. Gwen had enchanted him last holidays by saying, "I'll be forced to suggest she *could* be the first old lady of eighty-six to swim the Channel."

"Possible," said Gerald to Gerald. "Highly possible. The Legacy Aunt finally kicks the bucket. *He* makes it all right by marrying Dear Old Gwen. And Dear Old Gwen's cash—in due course —goes the way Mummy's went."

Gwen had been there a long time, the six-foot soubrette, with bright red hair; born in Australia, a natural clown, full of talent: Philip Adair's opposite number. Off the boards, she rated as a kind, capable aunt, but with a special comic significance. He couldn't see her as a stepmother. And now by a peculiar mercy, the door dividing this coach from the next swung open and here was Mullens.

"Wotcher," said Mullens, "been hunting you all over the damn train." He pulled a load of silver from his pocket.

"Couldn't very well hand it over in front of your Aunty, could I?" said Mullens. He selected half-a-crown and a florin, letting the rest rattle back into the pocket. "Sorry I've been so long."

"That's all right. Thank you."

"Any interest due?"

"Ha ha," said Gerald. This kind of joke wasn't, he reflected, in old Jamjar's line at all.

"Where did you get those shoes?" was the next question.

"They were a swop."

"Didn't imagine you'd paid for them yourself."

This, too, was out of character. He met it with "Ha, *bloody* Ha." Mullens leaned on the rail beside him.

"Going to do any odd-job work in the vac?" he asked. He sounded breathless. He was turning pink among his freckles and this gave Gerald the cue.

"Oh I might," he drawled, "You never know. Gigolo, perhaps. Pimp. Or just a waiter."

Mullens was pinker still. Mullens was no match for him. No match for anybody. It was easy to see that one of the smart alecks had primed Mullens, coached him, dared him to challenge Weston and report back.

"What's on your little mind?" said Gerald. "Could it be I was spotted snatching the old lady's handbag after Chapel? Or was somebody snooping when I cut the emeralds off the dead girl's ears?"

Mullens gave a reluctant gurgle.

"Just you tell whoever put you up to this to mind his own ball-aching business."

There was a moment's silence. Then Mullens said, "Must say you've got a nerve. They could sack you."

"That, my dear Jamjar, would suit me down to the ground."

Now he was winning. Mullens sagged. Gerald savored the taste of victory. He wanted the name of the spy. He wanted to know which adventure had leaked into public domain. (He thought the café.) He would lose face by asking. He gave Mullens a slap on his broad back.

"Cheer up, Jamjar. No hard feelings. Just remember who sups with me needs a long spoon." He began to dance a neat little Charleston as Mullens turned heavily away.

Undoubtedly the café. It was within half a mile of the school building and, looking back, he was still surprised at his own courage. He was still surprised, too, that the act had worked: the assumed accent, the carefully tousled hair, the shirt with the open neck. Just one of the brave adventures. Fun, because it was frightening. He had spent two free afternoons washing up the dirty crockery in the café. Who had found out? Was it true, as he had said to Mullens, that he would welcome the sack? Not quite, because of Philip. He began to imagine the scene. Sarah called it the King Lear performance. That was how all their sins took Philip: Philip was hurt, so one dodged, out of kindliness.

He had dodged like that this morning. He had shoveled away his old Eversharp pencil, just in time for Nanny to think his pleasure at her gift wholly genuine. The old pencil safely stowed, he had clipped the new one on to his breast-pocket with a flourish. The current school fashion was dead against this practice; and old Jamjar Mullens might well have remarked on it. Poor old Jamjar; easily defeated by skill and agility. Now the noise of the train wheels went "Skill and agility—skill and agility" while Gerald wondered if he could get ninepence or thereabouts for the dethroned Eversharp. This brought a wispy memory from seven years back. A jeweler's shop in Sawcombe; some row about a brooch that had been his mother's, Aunt Flavia's voice shrilling furiously behind a shut door. Had his father sold the brooch? Here he sighted Thomas, proceeding slowly from the far end of the corridor. Thomas said, "We thought you'd got locked in."

Gerald studied his small brother with a musing, paternal eye. Thomas stood square as a bullock and rolled with the train. He hadn't grown much; he had merely thickened. Nanny had re-knotted his tie and made him comb his near-white hair. The new notebook, too big for his blazer pocket, kept riding up and he kept patting it down. Returning Gerald's stare he wore the smile that looked, Gerald thought, as though it were pinned on him: as though he had smiled at something a while ago and forgotten to stop.

"I was just having a think," Gerald explained to the smile. Sarah would have asked, "What about?" but Thomas only nodded.

"I hope you had a good term."

"It was all right," Thomas allowed in his deep, booming voice.

"Honestly? You don't need to be a little gentleman with me, you know. I hated Puxford. Or most of it. All prep schools are hellholes. I was ragged to death my first year," he offered, being quite sure they ragged Thomas. "And the *smut*," he said. "I assume they've handed you out all the smut by now."

"Oh yes," said Thomas. "I was quite interested at first."

"Not any more?"

"Not really. It's always the same."

Thomas moved up beside him, holding the rail with both hands, then leaning back from it to the full stretch of his arms. "There's a letter," he said, and stopped.

"A letter?"

Thomas pulled himself up to the rail and then went back again; he did this several times: he might have been doing an exercise in the gymnasium. "It's on its way," he murmured.

"I don't catch your meaning, mate. Is this a letter you've written?"

"Not me. Bits of it were read *to* me. I was supposed to say if I thought it was fair. Mr. Appleby wrote it. Was there Mr. Appleby when you were at Puxford?" Thomas asked.

"There was, there was indeed, oh certainly. G-and-G. God-and-Games Appleby. Do you call him that?"

"No, I don't call him anything." Thomas relapsed into silence.

"Well, go on," said Gerald. "Who was he writing to—Father?"

"Um," said Thomas.

"What's the letter about?"

"It's about my ungovernable rages."

"Your *what?*" Gerald spluttered. Thomas repeated, "My ungovernable rages. And quite a lot of other things. He didn't read them all."

Gerald blinked down at the straw-colored head. Thomas had pulled himself up by the rail and this time he stayed there, drawing with his finger on the steamy window. He drew a pig.

"You're in trouble, mate? Really?"

"Looks like it," said Thomas.

Gerald's memories of Puxford were dimmed by the years between. Chiltern Hills, "bracing atmosphere," ugly gables; motto *Adsum et Possum* or some such balls. The main features still outstanding were Puxford's reduced rates for the sons of gentlemen and the hearty atmosphere. He recalled the Boy-Scouting manner of the Head and the thunderous jollity of the Head's wife. The whole staff had been madly hearty and jolly, kind to a peak of cosiness when he compared their behavior with the painstaking savagery of the boys. God-and-Games Appleby, most of all. G-and-G had a habit of telling them not to forget that the man who never made mistakes never made anything. Letters to fathers weren't in his line. It would be exactly like Thomas to have got this all wrong. He said gently, "What have you been doing?"

"I told you." Thomas added a two-curl tail to his pig. "Getting into rages."

"Your states. Old Thomas's old states. You bin getting in your old states, eh? Haven't bin fighting, have you?"

"Oh yes."

"You *have* . . . Much?"

"About three times."

"Who began it?"

"I did."

"Are you sure?"

"Well, of course I'm sure."

"Were they ragging you, I mean? Was that what started you off?"

"No."

"No?"

"Nothing like that."

"All your own work . . . Did you inflict serious damage?"

"A person's nose bled," Thomas admitted, adding, "and then I was sorry."

On the steamed glass the pig was already beginning to dislimn: first its tail trickled down and then its eye. Thomas seemed entirely preoccupied in trying to remedy this with dabs of his finger. He offered no more information.

"What else?" Gerald asked.

The pig was now beyond repair. Thomas wiped it away with his sleeve and said briskly, "Oh well, walking about at night. It isn't allowed," he explained.

"*I'll* say it isn't allowed. What's the idea? Raiding the kitchen? All you'd find would be blackbeetles, in my recollection."

"I was just walking; nowhere special. Don't you ever do it?"

Gerald said, "I used to walk in my sleep. Once I woke up on

the balcony—can't remember where that was. Brigstock would
know."

"What was it like?" Thomas asked.

"Waking up on the balcony? Very cold, I assure you. Brass
monkeys, not to put too fine a point upon it."

"I meant, what was it like walking in your sleep?"

"How the devil should I know? I was asleep."

"Were you dreaming?"

"Look, mate, it's you we're talking about, not me. Why do
you want to walk about that hideous place at night? Don't you see
enough of it by day?"

Thomas, in Sarah's phrase, went puddingy. Gerald, while agreeing with her that this stolid silence made one want to hit him,
still spoke gently.

"Has G-and-G posted this letter of his?"

"I suppose so."

"When did he read it to you?"

"I think it was Monday. Yes, it was. Treacle-tart day," said
Thomas, "I remember clearly."

"Then it's probably waiting."

Here he received a wide grin as if he had made some splendid
suggestion.

"It might be," said Thomas. "On the other hand, it might
not arrive before tomorrow. It could have gone off with the re-
ports, couldn't it? They all get posted today."

"Yes, well, that's another bright thought. Just the thing for
Father at breakfast, won't half help him get his grapenuts down.
Look here, mate, my advice, based on sound experience, would
be to tell him first. *If* the letter hasn't arrived, d'you see? He'll
come up to the house before the evening show. You beard him.
Right away. I'll come with you, if you like."

"You needn't bother," said Thomas. "Thanks all the same."

"It may put him in one of *his* states, you know."

"I suppose it might," said Thomas indifferently.

"Doesn't it scare you at all, Thomas, poor Thomas, Lord
Thomas my son?"

Thomas shook his head. Which bewildered his brother still

more. (I really do believe the poor little bugger's half-witted.) He then patted his notebook down again and set off along the corridor. Gerald followed. Over Thomas's shoulder he saw the carriage, beginning to be the place where they lived: Nanny was reading *Woman's Pictorial,* Sarah had her writing case balanced on her knees; she was hunched over it, secretly examining some treasure inside. She gave him a slanted, hostile look before she shut the writing case. He was made suddenly aware that all three of them had their private lives now, even Thomas.

II

Seven years, Blanche reminded herself, was a long time; time
enough for Sawcombe to grow and be spoiled, though she didn't
say this aloud. From the neat, ugly little houses that began on
the hill where there used to be fields and trees, she saw the
changes come. The harbor and the old town, over to the east
where the river ran out under the cliff, looked consolingly the
same. But there was only a glimpse of these before the big rattling car took them west along the sea-front. She saw a yellow
brick cinema; an ice-cream parlor; a rush of shop windows. The
terrace of private houses on the front had turned into small hotels. They wore their new names in gilt or black lettering; bathing
suits and towels hung out of their windows. The summer crowds
had thickened (the wrong sort of people) and there were too

many cars. The pier was freshly painted in gold and green. Along the beach under the sea wall a brightly colored line of bathing huts strung out. The tide was low and the long reaches of sand, peacefully empty in memory, were dotted with bathers, paddlers, little family clumps; not crowded together but spread here and there in comfortable possession down to the water's edge.

The car came past the corner of Galleon Street. Better. The toy shop was still on the corner; still displaying bunches of pink and blue celluloid windmills on wooden sticks; a variety of spades and shrimping nets. Galleon Street mounted steeply from the parade and at the higher end, Blanche remembered, there were elegant curving houses with bow windows: this end of it boasted the better shops, old Mr. McPhee the jeweler, she recalled, and Crabbe the butcher and—what was the name of the chemist? But Galleon Street was gone. They had come to the end of the parade. Pink, enormous and quite hideously modern, jutting up out of the formal gardens, stood the expected building, the Fundrome. Although expected, it was a shock to the eye. The gardens had in the past held nothing but a wistful, dilapidated bandstand somewhere in the middle. Lawns, palm trees, star-shaped flower beds, Blanche remembered, and a pond where ducks swam. Not any more. The heart of the gardens had gone. The part that was left formed a fringe round the new monstrous palace. At either side of the gate a huge poster announced:

MOONRAKERS 1926!

WITH

PHILIP ADAIR

and the rest of the names in smaller letters. Gerald and Sarah, having shrieked their horror at the building, read off the names. Gwen Richmond, Tubby Whittington; Susie Silva, Leo Clyde.

"Who's Perry Potter? Who's Shirley Ormonde?"

"We seem," said Gerald loftily, "to have collected two new cads."

"That means Joey and Gilly have left," said Sarah.

"And about time too," said Gerald.

(And they used, Blanche thought, to be so excited when they saw the posters.)

Gerald began to chant, "Shirley and Perry are boring, but very—Though rather less silly than Joey and Gilly," which brought giggles from Sarah. They were past the Fundrome, away from the parade, back on old, reassuring ground. The road went up again, mounting the West Cliff; here were trees, solid houses aloof in their gardens. This green, shady road climbing, the children's voices, this particular horse-and-harness smell coming from the old car's gray upholstery struck notes from long ago.

"Thomas, you can't *possibly* remember."

"I do remember. I know it's the last house but one before the top of the hill. On the right."

"Because I just told you."

"I knew anyway. In a minute I'll tell you some more."

"In a minute you won't have to. We'll be there. Who were that *frightful* family in the next house, Brigstock? Four beastly children who wore spectacles and were all yellow because they used to live in India? The father and mother were yellow too."

"That would be the Stevens family. I don't know why you should be so rude about them, they were always very nice to you."

"They were all over the beach—our beach—and we had to play horrible games with them." Gerald peered out on the sea side. "Can't find the path down to the cove."

"It goes between the trees—*there*," said Thomas, pointing.

The car stopped. Two gates in a low wall; a half-circle of lawn with a gravel drive looping it; plump rosebushes on the lawn; the chestnuts grown taller, cutting off the view behind the house. Then the house itself. "Rather hidge," poor Mrs. Weston's voice echoed in Blanche's ear: "hidge" was her abbreviation for hideous. She had liked houses to have flat faces. Roseclay—she had pointed out to Blanche—was Edwardian. Blanche thought it imposing, with the red brick, purplish tiles and white window frames. It had a confusion of gables and a turret. There was a loggia, with red twisty pillars, projecting on one side.

"It's bigger than I remembered."

"No—smaller."

"It's exactly the same," said Thomas.

For Blanche the place was crowding with memories of their mother; and now she could see Mrs. Weston, too clearly for comfort, standing on the step: she could see the white coat and skirt, a ruffled blouse and white shoes. The small butterfly face was smiling anxiously. In memory she was forever anxious, looking ahead to trouble, sure that something would go wrong. (*Are they all right, Nanny?* the ghost-voice asked.)

Had the children forgotten her? Thomas couldn't, of course, be expected to remember. Did Gerald and Sarah, now greeting Mrs. Gale, exploring, discovering, shouting all over the place, give a thought to that first summer when she was here?

❁

"Aren't they grown-up?" said Mrs. Gale. "Goodness gracious!" Mrs. Gale herself had aged (like me, thought Blanche). Each was careful to compliment the other on her appearance before agreeing that they were not getting any younger. Roseclay, in contrast, was rejuvenated. A vigorous wind had swept through it. There were structural changes. The old drawing room was gone from the first floor; in its place there was an extra bedroom with dressing room and bathroom. "Two suites—like," said Mrs. Gale. Mr. Philip was presumably keeping this first-floor magnificence for himself, the Uncle and the Aunt. Gerald had the only other bedroom at the end of the passage. Blanche would have expected the Grandmother to occupy that.

The rest of them were installed upstairs, on the second and third floors, with the turret room allotted to Sarah. A new bathroom up here also, and the warren of attics transformed: a playroom with a ping-pong table, fitted cupboards in abundance, the servants' sitting room and both bedrooms repapered and painted. "They're something in industry, very wealthy," Mrs. Gale explained, not in awe, but with a sniff.

On the ground floor a new drawing room had been built out at the back, across the site of the old conservatory. "It's handsome, but it doesn't quite match somehow," was Mrs. Gale's comment; she opened the door on a startling blaze of orange and rust-color. "Mr. Philip's glad of the piano," she added. "And now just you look here. What it must have cost them . . ." She opened a green baize door this time. Blanche looked upon the new kitchen, long, shining and elaborately equipped like the kitchens in the women's magazines. "The little study's still there —across the hall. Different furniture, of course. And you'll remember the old dining room. They've done a lot to it."

They had. It was blue and white, the blue and white of those vases on the mantelpiece: what were they called? Wedgwood, that was the name. Too grand for a dining room, this. She saw white medallions set into the blue walls; she saw pale-blue velvet on the chairs; pale-blue velvet on the window seats: these windows were deeply recessed. The view beyond, the terraced garden pouring downhill, the trees pouring upward, oak and chestnut, pines and the sky, came to Blanche as a relief. She walked to the window. She looked down. She saw the hydrangea bushes, the lily pond, the lawn. On the level below the lawn they had made a tennis court and that was where the wild garden used to be. Never mind: the children would like the tennis court. The calm garden view reassured her. (For one unnerving minute, the renewed Roseclay had seemed to have something in common with the Fundrome.) She heard Mrs. Gale saying, "The neighbors have been using the tennis court. With Mr. Philip's permission, of course. Do you remember them, Nanny? Stevens, the name is. I've seen them about every summer. They always come back to Sawcombe."

Blanche's reply was deflected by the look of the dining-room table. She had missed its full impact until now. There was a flat dish of floating rose-heads in the middle; a rather strange decoration made up of flags, kewpie dolls and ribbons encircled the dish. She saw two jellies and a trifle; an unsuitable-looking meat pie with a glazed top. A cold tongue; radishes. An iced cake; potted meat; strawberry jam; butter; scones; sardine sandwiches; stewed fruit in bowls and a gigantic cream-jug; the jug had something written on it in Devonshire dialect. Crinkled paper napkins in bright colors gave a hint of Christmas.

"Miss Richmond did the table," said Mrs. Gale.

"They won't want all that," said Blanche, meaning they will want all that and they're not going to have it. Miss Richmond—on these occasions—was subject to a certain loss of head.

"She was here the whole morning. She *would* pick the roses out of the front garden. I did wonder—"

"Miss Richmond," said Blanche, "is quite one of the family. We're all very fond of her."

Mrs. Gale, so instructed, said Miss Richmond had struck her as a good sport and that that kettle would be boiling now. Blanche went to the foot of the stairs. She stood there calling upwards: "Hurry now! Tea's ready! I said just wash your hands and come down! Your father will be here!" The time was already half-past five. Miss Richmond's choice of food might be excused in terms of high tea or early supper. What with the times of the shows and Mr. Philip's preference for eating with the children, the evening meal in the Weston family was, though Blanche deplored this, a highly movable feast.

"Sarah! Gerald! Thomas!"

Sarah and Gerald came running down. Gerald wore a short-sleeved blue shirt and different trousers, paler gray; he had kept on his brown and white shoes. Sarah had unearthed a tennis dress and her red sandals. (Echoes of "Oh *need* I change? I'm perfectly tidy," came back; another milestone had been passed.)

"Where's Thomas?"

"Just bumbling about," said Gerald. He and Sarah shrieked at the sight of the table as they had shrieked at the Fundrome building. "*Darling* Gwen—doesn't that look *terrible.*" "Wot a banquet. Fit for Rabindranath Tagore. Have a kewpie with cream, won't you?"

They slid into their places. Gerald said to Sarah, "What have we there, Madam?"

"What have we where?" she asked defensively.

"Underneath our napkin. On our lapkin."

"That? Only my report." Her voice was almost as husky as his.

"Heavens, you're in a hurry to open it."

She looked at him with an expression of large-eyed loathing.

He said, "A useful term. Good progress in chip-carving and religious knowledge. Sarah must learn to control her tongue."

"Like her elder brother, whose unfortunate habits are well known," Sarah snapped. She was more tense and trembly than ever, Blanche noted. Prettier, perhaps, but with a new shadowy look. Sarah, like Gerald, had gone away and returned in disguise. One had to meet them again, find them again behind the small, puzzling screen that hid them on the first day. Only Thomas seemed unchanged.

"Where *is* Thomas? Gerald, do go and tell him to hurry."

"Darling Brigstock, what would be the use? That's one of the things he can't do."

"I hear a car," said Sarah. They both sprang up from the table and Blanche followed: it was ritual. She was a little slower than they and as they plucked the front door open, the car itself was the first thing she noticed; a hired car, of course, but it looked most impressive, new and shiny, light brown and dark brown in color, with an open top. Mr. Philip leaped out in a hurry, slammed the shiny door and came running like a boy, with great strides of the long, valued Weston legs. (He had irritated her last summer by pointing out that Thomas was the only one of the Westons who had short legs.)

"That's more like it—*that's* more like it," said Mr. Philip. "We're all together again."

❋

He was different. So different that Sarah, gazing upon him, forgot the grim hurdle of the report just ahead. Why was he different? More glossy, more vivid, and he wasn't twitching at all. The little twitch at his cheek, the result of shell shock, came as a rule when he was excited: and he was certainly excited now. He picked her up and swung her around in the air. "Aren't you beautiful?" said Philip. She thought, "So are you." The top of his face was quite beautiful, with the dark crinkled hair, the wide smooth forehead and the big toffee-colored eyes going down at the corners. He had very long thick eyelashes. His nose was just too

long and too pointed, the mouth small and neat, not quite
enough chin. (Gwen Richmond said he reminded her of a pretty
water-rat.) Having catalogued his features, Sarah saw his clothes
—blazer, scarf in regimental colors, white flannels and buckskin
shoes—with a new eye: a new pride. The great actor of her dream
dressed like this, offstage.

"Didn't I have a third child, Nanny? I know my memory's
terrible but it seems to me there *were* three of them."

"Gerald, please go up and fetch Thomas. I can't imagine what
he's doing all this time."

With an arm round Nanny and an arm round Sarah, Philip
said, "I can imagine. Standing quite still in the middle of the
floor, with one shoe off. Heavens—dear old Gwen has really gone
a bit far, hasn't she? Bless her," he added, making humorous gri-
maces, "are we *ever* going to be able to eat all this?"

"Not tonight, sir," said Nanny.

"I can do with some pie. Been in the theatre all day. Never
thought I'd get here on time. Drove at sixty. Don't *click*, Nanny.
I'm the best driver in the world."

"Whose is the car?" Sarah asked; she pulled her chair close to
his, keeping the report under the paper napkin. Philip gave her
hand a squeeze and said, "Wait till the others come. It's to be a
surprise."

"What *sort* of surprise?"

"Wait," he said.

They heard Gerald's laughter in the hall. When he came into
the dining room he was still out of control. "Thomas," he said in
a shaky voice, "is on his way. I told him to come just as he was."

Nanny said, "What does that mean?"

"Well, believe it or not, he'd gone to bed by mistake."

"Gone to *bed?*" Philip put down the knife and fork. He
sounded outraged and Sarah was too late to stifle her burst of
laughter. Gerald said, "One thing led to another. First he washed;
then he undressed; then he put on his pyjamas. He was just lying
there, writing in his notebook. You know I really think the old
boy's what's known as wanting."

Now there were two different kinds of sparky crossness at the table, Nanny's because Gerald had said that about Thomas; Philip's less identifiable. And now here was Thomas, wearing his Jaeger dressing gown, striped pyjamas and flappy Jaeger slippers. He looked quite untroubled.

"Hullo, Father. Sorry, I just wasn't thinking," said Thomas. He moved vaguely into Philip's arms for a hug and then became hypnotized by the tea table. "My goodness. Isn't that splendid?"

"Something far more splendid out on the drive, I assure you," said Philip. Sarah could feel the eager importance of the moment. Thomas, quite obviously, could not. He said, "I can't see the drive from here," and continued to gaze at the pie.

"You *would* have seen, if you hadn't been so busy putting yourself to bed," Philip began; Gerald interrupted him, which was a sin. "The car? The Buick? It's the six-cylinder roadster, isn't it? The Country Club model?" At once it seemed to Sarah that her father resented this knowledgeable line. "Yes, that's exactly what it is, Gerald," was said in a cooler voice; and Philip added, "How do you know?" as Thomas helped himself to pie.

"Mullens' father just got one: old Jamjar Mullens—"

"Well," said Philip, "we've got one now."

He looked all around the table, waiting for their response.

"It's *ours*," Sarah croaked.

"Ours. Our very own. What about *that?*"

Somehow, she thought, none of them gave him the right reception. The instant question in her mind was, "But how can we possibly afford it?" Not daring to say this she found she couldn't say anything, though Philip's eyes besought her. She had never imagined their owning a car. She needed notice of the proper emotion. Gerald gave a Cockney "Coo-er!" that sounded more derisive than anything else. Briggs' startled "Good gracious!" might have been for a calamity. Meanwhile Philip, in his exuberance, had slapped Thomas on the back and Thomas, with his mouth full of pie, immediately began to choke.

Sarah looked at her father. Somehow, she thought, the moment was gone for him and could never be put back, replayed as he would have wished. Though Gerald now took over, firing off volleys of appreciation while Nanny dealt with Thomas, Philip's vulnerable face gave him away. And of course Gerald had to wind up with the wrong question: "What's going on? Have we come into millions?"

There was a pause. Philip said, "I'd like to talk to you later, if you don't mind." The voice had cooled still further. And now he turned his attention exclusively to Thomas. "Strangled you, eh? That's what I did. Sorry, old chap. Drink some more lemonade. Better? Jolly good. How was Puxford? How's the cricket?"

If only Thomas could say something other than "all right." Cricket was all right, work was all right, the end-of-term concert had been all right. His face was still crimson and his eyes watery. He puffed a good deal, drinking his lemonade and presently managed to intrude a question of his own: "Where's Gwen?"

This earned him marks. His father put an elbow on the table, turning to him, talking as though they were alone together. "Gwen won't be long. An old friend of hers turned up at the Marina; she had to stop off and have a drink with him. She was miserable about it, poor darling: the only thing she wanted was to see your faces when I showed you the car."

Thomas rubbed one pinkish eye and said in his devastating monotone, "Well, she still can. You haven't shown it to us, yet, have you?"

All his marks vanished off the invisible, palpable blackboard. Zero for Thomas. Philip looked over the top of his head at Briggs.

"We go up at eight, Nanny. I'll have to be there by half-past seven. I'm taking the car. Shall I send a taxi for Sarah and Gerald or can they walk it?"

"Tonight, sir?"

"Tonight, yes."

Now it was Philip who was losing marks: with Nanny: she said the long journey and getting up so early, she would have thought —and Gerald grimaced at Sarah. Philip, turning plaintively irritable said, "My God," which Nanny never liked and, "They can sleep all the morning," and "The show's *over* by ten. I'll run them back immediately afterwards, I promise. I can't *wait* for them to see it."

Thomas helped himself to iced cake and asked, "Can you wait for *me* to see it?"

"That's different, old chap. You can come tomorrow afternoon."

"Well, in that case Sarah ought to rest for half an hour," said Nanny, thin-lipped.

"*Will* you open my report?" Sarah groaned, thrusting it at Philip. Terrible timing. He said, "Not now, for Heaven's sake. We're all going to look at the car: come on," and tossed the unexploded bomb into the middle of the table, among the kewpies. Nanny raised an objection to Thomas going out in his dressing gown and Philip said, "Rats," another expression of which she disapproved. And now, Sarah thought, the day seemed to have gone past itself. She felt tired, and ominously achy round the middle; she wanted only to read the report and she didn't (was this Gerald's effect?) care if she saw *Moonrakers 1926* tonight or not.

They all stood round the glorious, glittering car with Philip. Gerald soared up into favor: climbing in, knowing about the gears, asking the right questions. His father got in beside him. Thomas, with his dressing-gown cord trailing, climbed hopefully onto the step. Philip waved him down.

"That's all for now, chaps. I want a word with Gerald. Sarah my love, if you'd like to put me back in Nanny's good books, you'll go and lie down." But then a taxi roared through the gate, and Gwen shot out of it, whooping.

❀

Nothing different about Gwen, except the ring on her finger. Sarah went on gazing at it. Had the others noticed? Certainly not Gerald, whipped away to the study with Philip and still closeted there. She couldn't tell about Thomas, who had annexed Gwen on sight for a voyage of exploration through the garden, with the result that Gwen had now joined Philip in Nanny's bad books.

"Damn silly of me," she said, "I thought he was *meant* to be in his pyjamas—I suppose I ought to have realized. And kept him away from the lily pond while I was about it. Cheers!"

"Cheers!" Sarah echoed, still looking at the ring. The minutes were going by. Nearly seven o'clock. She ought to go up and rest. But she stayed on with Gwen in the dining room; the unexploded bomb still lay where Philip had flung it, the thin envelope on its bed of ribbons, presided over by the kewpies. Gwen had added a bottle of gin and some lime juice to the refreshments on the table.

"*Jolly* nice to have you all back," she said, sprawling at ease. She looked hot and happy. She had dyed her hair redder still this summer. Cut short and tightly waved, it looked like a wig. The wig-look was suitable, somehow, to the round white forehead. Gwen had china blue eyes and an up-soaring nose with rocking-horse nostrils. The almond-green dress with its low waistline and the three frills making the skirt, which stopped again at her knees, seemed to lengthen her even more. There was a great deal of Gwen, lengthwise: long neck, long body, long arms, long legs: the whole gave the impression of being precariously held together, as with the cheaper kind of jointed doll. One expected an arm or a leg to come off.

She was, indeed, subject to comic accidents, such as the time when her high heel got stuck in a drain that ran across the pavement at Folkestone: Sarah remembered the squeals. There was the time she had taken them to the Tower and her drawers had fallen down: very pink and clean and silky, but still drawers. (That had really made the outing memorable. Even Thomas, once Gwen laughed too, had been delighted.)

The ring was one of those bafflers. It might be a wedding ring or it might not. Thin as a wedding ring, made of diamonds or paste. She had never worn it before. She seemed quite unconscious of Sarah's absorption; she was filling up her glass, pulling another cigarette from the yellow packet, saying, "You look a bit peaky, darling. Sure you want to come tonight? It ain't all that wonderful, yer know."

"Ain't it?" said Sarah, startled. Gwen winked: "Well, you'll see. Don't quote me to Pa, there's a good kid. Sure you're all right, Sal? You look—what? Beautiful but fragile. Got the curse?"

"I think it's on its way; with stern avenging stroke."

" 'Stern avenging stroke.' The way you all go around reciting
. . . Just like Dad. Gin would help, yer know."

"No thank you," said Sarah hurriedly, "and it isn't only that.
I'm worried."

"What about?"

The return to Gwen differed from the return to Nanny. The
old sense of comradeship reminded Sarah that whereas Nanny
shared top authority with Philip, being in exactly equal collision with him when collisions occurred, Gwen was a little way
down from the top. One would never love Gwen as one loved
Nanny, but she was an equal. The funny, friendly face came closer
and the accented voice ("Not common—Australian" said Philip.)
asked again, "What about?" adding, "Tell your chum."

Sarah leaned over and picked the thin envelope out of the ribbons. Gwen, having seen many such, recognized it at once. "Ho,"
she said, "What *ho*. Got a bad one this time?"

"I may have."

"Well, why don't you open it?"

"We're on our honor."

"I'm not," said Gwen briskly. The moment came too fast for
fear. Hypnotized, Sarah watched the long scarlet nail on Gwen's
forefinger slide under the flap of the envelope. It performed a
neat operation, without a jag or a tear. "There you are," said
Gwen. "Have a squiz."

Feeling the ache around her body become a series of stabs, Sarah
unfolded the single sheet. Her eyes went straight to the last paragraph, Miss Groome's territory: *General Conduct*. (Oh spite, oh
hell, there was more of it than usual.)

*She has worked hard and tries to please. I see signs of
improvement all round. I am confident she will soon master
the difficult lesson that she is one of a community—not just
Sarah. But she mustn't let her emotions carry her away!*

The exclamation mark was like a blessing. No doubt as to the
meaning of the last line. But the exclamation mark, limpidly clear
in school sign language, made a joke of it. Miss Groome, after

the hideous interview, had decided to be amused. Reading thank-
fully upwards, past "Has shown more interest," "Better work this
term," "Always lively and keen," in the varied handwritings, she
heard Gwen say, "What *were* you doing, ducky? Kissing the gardener's boy?" She came back to the new, immediate sin:

"Gwen—I'll have to tell him I opened it."

"You will, will you? Then you'll be lying in your beard. *I*
opened it. I'll tell him. Unless you'd rather we stuck the flap
down again. Lime juice might do it . . . Why worry?"

"He'll be livid," Sarah croaked.

"He will, will he? I'll give him livid. Leave it to me."

This was unbelievable: Gwen shrugging defiantly at the threat
of Philip. No act, either: she pushed the report halfway into its
envelope, then took careless charge of it, putting it down beside
her yellow packet of cigarettes. This done, the clown-face sparkled
with curiosity.

"I take it you've got away with something. You look like the relief of Mafeking. *Was* it the gardener's boy?"

The consequences were off and the demons fled. But the secret
was still a secret. Impossible to say to Gwen, "I have a passion for
somebody in the Sixth Form, and I left her a note with some
flowers I picked for her birthday; and Miss Groome got hold of
the note."

She began to act with all her might. She flung back her head.
*The long white throat, the coppery glints in the mane of dark
hair, the look of secret tragedy in those great eyes. The deep, mel-
low voice was like a cello*—(oh, damn cello for rhyming with mel-
low)—*like a violin.*

Softly she intoned, "I'll tell you someday . . . Someday when
it's all ceased to matter." (She liked that.)

Gwen said, "I sye—got a sore throat?"

The dining-room door opened and Philip came in with Gerald.
Gwen swung round in her chair: "You two have been a hell of
a time, haven't you? Why the great confab? Not that us girls
haven't had some fun on our own." She gave Sarah another of
her enormous winks. "But anyone would imagine there were secrets in this family."

"We never have secrets in the family," Philip had said, shutting the study door. "And there aren't any now. Just a private word between you and me."

Philip Adair in crescendo, thought Gerald. Cliché position Number One, standing on the hearth rug, hunched a little—smiling too much. Cliché position Number Two, the engagement with the pipe and the tobacco pouch (corded silk, regimental colors).

While this process went on, Gerald glanced about him. He had forgotten the study in its old likeness; in its new likeness it was a rich, somber parody of a room seen through the proscenium arch. Dark maroon was the predominant color. There was a Buhl desk of great opulence and ugliness. Glass-fronted bookcases held ranks of unreadable books, heavily and uniformly bound. Two fat leather chairs, twins, were drawn up face to face in stolid enmity across the hearth. A distressing copper fender, with andirons to match, divided them. Two black bronze jungle beasts were killing each other on the mantelpiece.

"What a revolting room," Gerald said gaily as Philip wafted the match to and fro above the bowl of his pipe.

"It's changed, the house. And I'm grateful," said Philip. "The echoes have gone. For me. You wouldn't remember them, thank God." The toffee-colored eyes shimmered. The lower half of his face, the ratlike, the running-away half, tucked itself into his collar—King Lear alone with his grief. "That's why I decided to take it. Good idea, don't you think? We can be pretty comfortable."

"*Not* to say luxurious." He didn't mean to sound so acidly detached, appraising, standing off. It was the way the Philip Adair act took him. His father lifted his chin out of his collar and held his pipe as though for a photographer: "You asked me if we'd come into millions. What made you say that?"

"Just the car."

"Nobody's been talking to you?"

This was a pointer. But a pointer pointing where? Alight with curiosity, Gerald said, "What about?" Philip Adair's beautiful hand waved expansively. "About us. About all of it. About the Moonrakers."

"No. Who could?" (It would be cruel to add, "Nobody at school's *heard* of Moonrakers.")

"Just as well. I'd an idea you might have heard rumors. There are quite a few going round."

The smile, the look of self-gratification, the angle of the head, all suggested a Prime Minister contradicting world-wide whispers. ("That fierce light which beats upon a Fundrome.")

"All I'm going to tell you just now is that we're all right. Money's all right. At last. And the show's more than all right —it's superb." He was away. "Beauty—taste—wit—sophistication —magic—just as I've always wanted it to be: and it's all mine."

Gerald thought, "Well perhaps it *is* less awful." But "All mine" bewildered him. Ever since he remembered, there had been backers, of one sort or another, ranking in his father's judgment as cowards, skinflints and common little cads with no imagination.

"There's no bad patch, however long," said Philip, "that doesn't end in triumph. No great sorrow that isn't followed by great joy. Haven't I always said so?"

In truth he had. Gerald could remember his saying it about the bailiff: the gray, speechless little man who had sat on the sofa in Westgate, while their mother went round the room skirting him, ignoring him, humming and dusting and arranging some daffodils. (Which year was Westgate?)

"You look quite stunned," his father said.

"I am—just a trifle stunned."

"Bless you. There's far more to tell you. But first I want us all to settle down and catch up with one another again and be happy." He drooped his eyelids; his long lashes fluttered. "Gerald, I've rather given Nanny to understand Percy and Flavia will be coming here. In fact they won't. It's unlikely we'll see them these holidays. They've decided to go later than usual. To Wimereux, this time."

Pleasure at the news was tempered, Uncle Percy for all his dullness being guaranteed to tip at least a pound. "Only I'd like you to keep that to yourself, just for the moment."

"What about Granny?"

"Oh . . . Well, they'll probably take her to Wimereux when the time comes—though no doubt she'd be happier staying on in Scotland."

"We're to be *alone*—dwelling in these marble halls?"

"Well, y-yes. And I don't want a lot of talk about it."

(*Where's it come from? Or does one, knowing him, just cut the optimistic outlook by eighty percent?*) Gerald's interior adding machine was busy reducing Philip's rainbow to a more-than-usually-generous backer and a gamble on the season's profits when he heard the word "Cambridge." He came out of his calculations with a blink. Obviously Philip had been addressing him at some length.

"Well. How do you like the idea? There's nothing in the way of it now."

The faithful parrot had somehow recorded the gist of the speech while its owner worked the adding machine. "Would it be Uncle Percy's idea—my going to Cambridge?" Gerald asked cautiously.

"Good God, no. He'd say you ought to start earning your living. I haven't discussed it with him anyway; pompous ass."

"Cambridge would only be school *in extenso*." He was pleased with *extenso*. His father grinned at him: was there a look of sympathy in the toffee-colored eyes now?

"So? Do I take it you're fed up with school?"

Was it the moment to tell the truth; reminding Philip that he himself had once run from the boring and expensive monastery? He thought it might be. Yet his ingrained habit of secrecy held. He murmured, "I suppose one has to take the long view."

Philip's laughter was irritating. So was the comment: "You're exactly like me."

"I am?"

"The artful dodger. Never mind." Philip Adair was in his sunniest ascendant now. "You keep your private dreams to yourself: and I'll keep mine." He glanced at the new gold watch on his wrist: "Just on seven. Time for a drink before I run Gwen

down to the theatre." (He wouldn't, of course, demean himself
by calling it the Fundrome.)

❖

"Anyone would imagine there were secrets in this family."

Unusually bold of Gwen. Gwen, Gerald decided, knew something. Having winked at Sarah she was now winking at him.
Though the wink was on the scale of a slammed door, Philip
didn't appear to notice. Philip was saying to Sarah, "*You're* supposed to be resting, beautiful," and Sarah, looking dazed but
happy, shot past Gerald into the hall. The eagle eye on which
—like the detached mind—Gerald prided himself, discovered her
report lying open at Gwen's elbow.

"You too—out, there's a good fellow," said his father. "Gwennie and I have to run through a spot of business for tonight."

"That's your story and you stick to it," Gwen said with a loud
neighing laugh.

When Gerald reached the first-floor landing Sarah was ahead
of him vanishing up the next staircase. "Come down, O maid,
from yonder mountain heights," he called. He saw her halt, peering at him through the banister rails.

"Why should I?"

"Why shouldn't you?"

"I'm supposed to rest."

"You can rest on my bed. Something I want to say to you."

She came reluctantly, elaborately, acting somebody or other,
all droops and curves. "I'm so ti-ired," she drawled. "So hahpy
—So gloriously hahpy—so gloriously tahed. Ah God—"

"Not God, Madam, please. Brigstock doesn't like him except in
prayers, remember."

Sarah feathered her way to his bed and flung herself down.
"So hahpy" she crooned, pointing her chin at the ceiling.

"Because you opened that report and all your tiny fears were
unfounded."

Sarah came out of the act: "How on earth do you know?"

"Psychic gifts—that's what I have—psychic gifts," said Gerald, sitting on the end of the bed.

"Oh you have, have you? Well I didn't open it, Gwen did." She sat up: "Is Gwen what you want to talk to me about?"

"Why?"

She looked at him slantingly and said, "How are your powers of observation?"

"Flawless. Like my teeth and my complexion."

"*Must* you be so funny all the time?"

"Oh I must. Though my heart break I wear my motley still. I Pagliacci Tagore. I suppose," he added, "I'd better put on a tie for this farting Fundrome: and that means another shirt." Getting off the bed, he began to rummage in the trunk. "I just wanted to drop you a hint, Madam. There's no point in our asking where the cash has come from—he ain't going to tell us."

"Wherever it comes from," said Sarah, "it won't last. What else did he say?"

Gerald, debating between two shirts, hesitated. "Oh—a lot of burble. Amicable burble, most of it."

"Nothing about Gwen?"

"Nothing. Why?"

"I think he's married her."

Gerald dropped the two shirts back on the top of the trunk.

"Look at the third finger of her left hand. Which seems," Sarah added, lying back again, "to have escaped your flawless powers."

He stood staring at her, making the new addition sum. It came out perfectly, with the aid of Gwen's Legacy Aunt.

"She's quite different, you know. So's he, come to that," Sarah was saying. Then she murmured, "Will we mind?"

Gerald was silent, turning away towards the window. A late, tired sunlight had come suddenly, making him aware of this house where he had been before, of this view across the road to the trees and the drop of the sky behind them, the edge of the cliff. He saw the trees grown higher, the undergrowth hiding the track between the trees, down to the cove. He remembered. He seldom thought of his mother, because he had trained himself not to think. But he was back with Gerald aged seven, sitting

at a table, staring at this view under the evening sunlight. There
was a book on the table. The door was opening behind him and
he thought Briggs had come to call him to bed, so he didn't look
round. Two hands, cool and smooth, not Briggs' hands, had
stolen across his face, had covered his eyes. A gentle laugh
sounded above his head. Why that joy—that ecstasy? He did not
know, but he remembered it, and with the memory there was the
color of her dress, the scented air around her, the boy saying, "I
thought you were Nanny."

The older Gerald felt a sweet, sentimental sadness flowing
through him. He had no wish to share it. He said abruptly, "A
stepmother's the sort of thing one can't imagine." He picked up
the first of the two shirts and put it on, having thrown the blue
shirt onto the bed. As he knotted his tie Sarah said drowsily,
"It's made you in a hurry, hasn't it? Why has it?"

He said only, "Excuse me, Madam," and ran out. In the passage
he heard, from below, the slam of the front door. Then, as he
reached the landing there was the noise of the car outside, starting
up, moving away. Gwen and Philip were gone.

Gerald walked slowly down the stairs. He had no idea what he
would have said to them, if indeed he could have summoned the
courage to say anything. Mainly, he supposed, he had wanted
to see the ring for himself. He stood in the middle of the hall,
wondering why he should resent the whole prospect so much,
and Nanny came from the kitchen carrying a tray of milk and
biscuits.

"You wouldn't think," she said, "he'd still be hungry after all
that tea."

"Who wouldn't? Who is? You confuse me, Brigstock."

"Thomas," said Nanny.

"I think he ought to enter for one of those pie-eating contests
in America." (But he wasn't thinking about Thomas. He was
staring at Briggs and realizing that she too would resent the prospect. How could he be so sure of that? She was, after all, recon-
ciled to Gwen; even calling her "M'm" on occasion, as she had
called his mother, as she called Aunt Flavia and the rest of her
chosen élite. Not "Ma'am"; "M'm." But still she wouldn't like it.)

"I must say I'm surprised at Miss Richmond," said Nanny.

"*Eh?*" said Gerald.

"Letting him go into the pond like that."

Oh yes, poor old Thomas in trouble again. He remembered, all at once, the letter from God-and-Games Appleby. Quite obviously this had not yet reached Philip. Had it arrived, poor old Thomas would have been greeted by King Lear. He remembered his own words: "My advice, based on sound experience, would be to tell him first." But now, thinking it over, he was inclined to believe that Thomas had invented—or exaggerated—the letter. Like Sarah fussing and frenzying inside about her report.

"You should have seen his pyjamas," Nanny was saying, "The bottom of that pond must be nothing but mud."

Gerald bent to kiss her. He was not yet used to being so much taller than she. "Good night, Mrs. Tiggy Winkle," he said to the kind blue eyes.

"Good night, dear. Remember me to everybody, won't you? And don't let them keep you up till all hours now."

"I say, Brigstock."

She turned at the foot of the stairs.

"Did you notice Gwen's new ring?"

There was a pause before she said, "Gracious, I've been much too busy to look at anybody's new rings," and went on up the staircase.

III

Behind the pink plushy curtains, Tubby Whittington and Susie had begun to play "Here We Are" on their two pianos.

"Hardly new . . ." Gerald whispered to Sarah.

"Antique. *Hi Jinks*—" she whispered back.

"No, Madam, *Gay Cavaliers*."

"Want to bet?"

The front lights went out, the curtains parted. Tubby and Susie were playing with their backs to each other as usual, but newly dressed from head to foot in silver satin, with pale blue ruffles and pom-poms, pale blue skullcaps. The midnight-blue backcloth carried silver cutouts of moon and stars.

> *"Here we are, here we are,*
> *Riding on a shooting star!*

> *Leave the dull old world behind*
> *All aboard! We're off to find*
> *Moonland, Sunland, Let's-Have-Fun-land,*
> *Laugh Land, Joy Land, Girl-and-Boy Land."*

Everybody on, except Philip. Gerald's grudging eyes picked them up, one by one. He saw Leo Clyde first, because he disliked him the most. Leo, who could see Sarah and himself because they were in the front row, was singing straight at them.

> *"Glad to meet you,*
> *Proud to know you!"*

sang Leo Clyde; and presumably meant it: his striving Jewish face shone with pleasure.

("The ring," Sarah hissed, as though he hadn't spotted it already, flashing on Gwen's finger.)

> *"Just you wait!*
> *We're out to show you—"*

On a crashing chord from Tubby and Susie, the song stopped dead. Philip strolled, tall and exquisite, through the velvet back-cloth upstage center. While the applause came clattering dutifully, Gerald considered the new recruits. The stately brunette, out of Moonrakers uniform and wearing an evening dress of silver lamé, must be Shirley Ormonde. She had brought on a sheaf of red roses and laid it on top of Tubby's piano. She stood like a gracious monument: her silver shoes were long, thin and aquiline. An innovation, Miss Ormonde, obviously in love with herself and already embarrassing. The little fair fat man must be Perry Potter. He had big blue eyes and a dazed look, reminding Gerald of Thomas.

"Excuse me, my name's Philip Adair."

"*His name's Philip Adair.*"

Gwen, facing front, saying, "Adair say you've heard of him," brought a groan of "Oh God" from Gerald's right. Turning, he surveyed his neighbor: a young man with pale wavy hair and a pale face: fattish, well-dressed, holding between his knees a cane on whose top he rested his chin. He was gazing at Gwen with horrified fascination. Gerald gazed too. He saw, in one cold blink, the clown-face, the shelving bosom and the long prancing legs. *I think you've met my stepmother.* Then he hated himself for hating the idea: he, Gerald, the despiser of the snob.

He heard Philip's voice: "What's going on?"

"We're going on."

"What for?"

"Just for fun."

"But look here, I don't do this sort of thing for fun, I do it for money."

Sarah leaned towards him: "She's beautiful, don't you think?"

"Who is?"

"The new one—Shirley Ormonde."

"I think she's a pain in the neck," said Gerald rather too loudly. Leo Clyde was appeasing Philip with "That's all right, old man, we've got their money," leading to the exchange about pirates before Tubby's light tenor took up the recitative.

> *"It's really very simple,*
> *As simple as can be.*
> *A Moonraker's a pirate,*
> *A chap who's all at sea.*
> *(A girl who's all at sea)*
> *At large and living free . . ."*

To the chorus. Gerald found the tune, Tubby's composition, good enough. There was excitement in the phrasing. It dragged and summoned you, like the "Come On and Hear" of Alexander's Ragtime Band.

> *"Moonrakers, moonrakers!*
> *Masters of laughter, the melody makers,*
> *Wandering minstrels, the givers, the takers . . ."*

The pale young man had removed his chin from the supporting cane: he hummed the melody. "Not bad," he said in a thick, superior voice to the girl on the other side of him. "Rather good, in fact. Rather charming."

How long, Gerald asked himself, since the show had become a menace and a private shame? He could remember no exact moment of revulsion. He could, on the other hand, remember the time before it: when he used to brag to the boys at Puxford that his father was Philip Adair. The fall of the hero had not come suddenly but gradually: by way of a creeping discomfort at certain moments.

Gwen and Philip, in song and dance and silliness, took the house with them: they even commanded a snorting chuckle from the pale young man. The cross-talk had acquired some 1926 flavorings.

"I say, Gwen, what did you do in the General Strike?"

"What did I do in the General Strike? I struck a General."

"You struck a General? Whatever for?"

"The beast gave me a lift home in his car."

"Well, why did you let him if you didn't like him?"

"I didn't like him, *that's why I didn't let him.*"

A new song. Gwen had acquired one of the velvety toy dogs, called a Bonzo. (The rhymes were Alfonso, Oxford-Dons-oh! and Carry-on-so.) "I could do without that one, couldn't you?" the pale young man observed, addressing Gerald, giving him a glimpse of heavy eyelids and a smile that twisted.

"Watch your step. Philip Adair happens to be my father."

The pale young man looked disconcerted; he said "Honestly?" and turned away from Gerald's emphatic nod.

An old number, by request: "In the Middle of the Road," with its rather sickening good-pals motif. The two marched around the stage, carrying sticks and bundles, singing:

> *"But just for the minute*
> *That's as long as we are in it,*
> *We are walking, you and I,*
> *On our way to by-and-by.*
> *I'm your burden, you're my load*
> *In the middle of the road."*

Gerald's right-hand neighbor had adopted a pose of severe attention; trying to make amends, perhaps: he clapped briskly when Philip lifted Gwen and carried her off, kicking and waving, looking as long as a ladder and considerably more cumbersome.

"They *like* it," Sarah said fiercely: was she trying to convince herself? She added, "All the same, that number went better with the other clothes. Do you like these clothes?" She wanted him to say Yes. He said Yes and found a yawn coming for the ensemble, "Wish I'd Got a Wishing Cap." It was followed by a sketch, "Poppy-cocktails," with Philip at his most Mayfair and the jokes too risky for this audience, though the pale young man was now at pains to show his sophistication by laughing heartily. Certainly an egg-layer for Sawcombe, Gerald decided; perhaps Philip would have the sense to cut it. He began to wonder what he was going to say to Philip when the show ended. He came out of his bewilderment to realize that Shirley Ormonde was alone on the stage, wearing hoops and panniers with a white wig. The song was called "Telephone-Doll." At the line, "Are you there, Love-affair?" the pale young man bowed over and buried his face in his hands. Towards the end the stage was blacked out. By means of small electric bulbs Miss Ormonde's wig and panniers lit up, and a bell rang.

> *"Hello, Romance!*
> *It's me! It's you!"*

sang the rounded contralto. Shaking, Gerald could feel that the pale young man beside him was shaking too. This made a bond and now they stopped giggling to wag their heads sorrowfully at each other. "Seen her before—on a calendar," said the pale young man and snorted, having broken himself up.

Looking to his left Gerald saw Sarah thrusting her profile at the stage and clapping furiously. "Loyalty, Madam," he said, "is all very well, but one can go too far." She did not seem to hear.

There remained the puzzle of Perry Potter who was, so far, meekly anonymous. The rest of the company pushed him around, bumped into him and fell over him. When he announced that he was going to sing, Leo Clyde said, "Not now, Perry." When Perry sat down again, Susie took his stool away. But he hadn't, somehow, the personality of an out-and-out buffoon. The laugh was quickly quieted for Leo's number, "You Want to Watch Me." All the odder then that Perry should have the spot position on the program coming up now, last before the interval. Philip was introducing him: "Ladies and gentlemen, Perry Potter will entertain you with 'Magic As You Like It.' "

"A conjuror?" the pale young man asked, "How very unexpected."

"He's new—like the telephone doll."

"Perhaps they're married. Love to see them in bed, wouldn't you?" He was friendly now; as he sat back, folding his arms, he was trying to make his shoulder touch Gerald's. One of those, Gerald decided, pulling away.

Perry Potter's face remained expressionless throughout. The innocent blue eyes and the solemn mouth seemed to have no connection with the deceiving hands. The card tricks, the billiard balls, a rabbit and some baby chickens belonged only to the hands. This turn was getting the loudest reception of any tonight. After the chickens, Gerald saw Perry Potter smile for the first time, like a baby smiling, before his face returned to solemnity. The noise died down. Leo and Susie carried his table with his props away, then returned. Was it over? No, it wasn't. Perry Potter came up from his last bow (he bowed jerkily, perfunctorily as an amateur) and said in his rather squeaky voice,

"Well that's nearly all, not quite. I *was* going to saw Miss Richmond in half. But she objects to the principle of two for the price of one. So we'll do something simpler." He whipped a red silk handkerchief out of his pocket, handing it to Susie, who tied it over his eyes.

There was a moment's silence. When he spoke some of the squeak had gone from his voice.

"Mind reading," said Perry Potter. "Quite a pleasant game. Sometimes a little dangerous—all depends on your mind. You may think I can see through this handkerchief. In a way you're right. But my way of seeing through isn't the same as your way. In a minute, I'll turn my back to you. I shall then choose my victims at random. Don't be frightened, anybody." The mouth, be-

low the red silk, puckered in its babyish smile. "Here we go," said
Perry Potter. He took a pace further front. Then he turned his
back. His voice became very loud:

"You, Madam, in the circle, Row C, Number Twenty-one.
Will you please stand up? We're going to turn the spotlight on
you—don't be shy. Now, I want you to think of somebody close
to you: I don't mean physically close: not your next-door neighbor. I mean a friend or a relative. Think hard, get that person
well into your mind, take your time, let me know when you're
ready."

Everybody was twisting and turning away from the stage to
look up at the figure in the spotlight. Gerald kept his eyes on
Perry Potter who stood, quite motionless, with his short arms hanging at his sides. The company were all in drilled attitudes of concentration, knees crossed, every chin on every hand.

"Ready!" called the shrill voice from above.

"All right. Spotlight off the lady, please." Perry faced the audience, still blindfolded, tilting his chin, speaking up to the circle.

"You're thinking of a child."

"That's right!"

"Wait, please. The child isn't your own, but related to you. A
boy. Brown hair. Brown eyes. Age—about eight. Name begins
with—is it A or E? Wait . . . E. Two syllables. Edward, I think.
Your nephew, would it be? It would . . . Spotlight on, please."

With the noise crashing about their ears they were all four saying the same words: Gerald, Sarah, the pale young man and his
neighbor, now revealed as a black-haired girl with a gay, chubby
face. They were saying "But how?" and "It isn't possible," and
"Planted—it *must* be planted."

"He's going to do it again."

"Silence, please. Next victim. The young gentleman in the
front row, seat Number Twelve."

"That would be you," said the pale young man, "Wouldn't it?
Now we *know* it's a fake." He settled comfortably while Gerald
rose and Sarah moaned, "Oh Father *is* a beast—why not me?"

"I want you," said the blindfolded face, "to think of a thing,
not a person. Think of something you're carrying with you to-

night. Something in one of your pockets. Think hard and I'll
tell you what it is. Say when you're ready."

Ridiculous, this sudden heart-thump, this fear. But it was there
all the same. As if he really believed in the magician, Gerald
fought to keep his mind off the wallet and its hoard.

Why was it impossible to think of anything else? He stared
stupidly at Perry Potter's back and limp, motionless arms. Sarah's
voice hissed, "Go *on*—" The pale young man said in a clipped
falsetto, "We're all waiting, dear." "Ready, " said Gerald. Perry
turned. The blindfolded face was smiling again.

"All right," said the magician. "That secret's between you and
me. I mean the one in your left-hand inside pocket. You've
switched to the right side now." He paused. "It's new. You
might only have got it today: a present: narrow, pointed—oh yes.
Silver pencil, isn't it? It is . . . Spotlight on, please."

❀

"Well," said Mrs. Gale, looking at the kitchen clock.

"Well," said Blanche, looking at the kitchen clock. They both
set down their cups in their saucers. The time was twenty minutes to ten. Mrs. Gale picked up the two plates of sandwiches;
Blanche took the fruit and the salad. These they left for Mr. Philip
in the dining room. Miss Richmond's decorations were still on
the table.

"I'll get them off, first thing," said Mrs. Gale. She added, "Nice
of her, though, wasn't it?" Mrs. Gale seemed determined to
thrust Miss Richmond's name forward and wait for comment.

Blanche said, "He'll want a syphon."

"There's one in the sideboard. I'll get it out."

After all, Blanche reminded herself once again, there might be
worse fates than Miss Richmond. She could look back on a string
of horrific little threats. (That tiny dark one in *Aladdin*—what
was her name? Esmé Something.) She could always recognize
them. Nothing was ever said; nothing was ever audible, visible;
she just knew when it happened and who it was. When Blanche
thought "It" her mind made no exact statement. And "It" was

none of her business. Not until Mr. Philip told her would Miss Richmond become her business.

"Am I imagining things?" she asked herself as Mrs. Gale set the syphon with some bottles beside the whisky and said cheerfully, "I expect Sarah and Gerald will want lemonade. You know, I can't get over them being grown-up like this."

"They're not grown-up yet."

"Compared to seven years ago they are," said Mrs. Gale, as though the change were quite unnatural. She added, "And Thomas was just a baby then."

"Thomas," said Blanche, "can still behave like a baby."

"He's your favorite though, isn't he?"

"I don't have favorites." She had snapped, making Mrs. Gale so apologetic that she felt obliged to add some appeasing observation; she said, "I've never had a child quite like him before. He doesn't *mean* to be naughty, he just loses his head."

"You know who he reminds me of? His grandmother. Quite a look of her, he's got."

It was hardly surprising that Mrs. Gale should remember the grandmother. There had been plenty of photographs in the newspapers while the libel case proceeded on its spectacular way. Blanche (with some necessary reservations) was fond of the grandmother: poor Mrs. Weston's mother, the person who had interviewed and engaged her, fourteen years ago. But she could see no resemblance between that face and the face of Thomas. "Something about the forehead and the eyes," Mrs. Gale was saying as they crossed the hall. "I saw it at once. I believe you'll notice it when she gets here."

They went up the stairs together: so many stairs in this house. "I'm getting old," Blanche said at the top.

"Well, you've had a long day."

"Good night, Mrs. Gale."

"Good night, Nanny."

She was tired tonight. She knew it less by her body than by the tangle of thoughts in her head. There, she was still fussing about Gerald and Sarah staying up late, still puzzling about the car, Miss Richmond's ring and the way Mr. Philip, for all his rapturous good spirits, had avoided her eye. She came to Thomas's door; she was instantly hailed from within. "Brigstock!" (The new name was, it seemed, here to stay.) "Come and say good night."

"Gracious, aren't you asleep yet? And how did you know it was me?"

"You walk quite different to Mrs. Gale," said Thomas. He was lying flat, with his arms outside the bedclothes; the new notebook rested on the sheet under his right hand. In the square of light from the bedside lamp she saw the round fair head and the solemn eyes, and at once caught herself looking for the likeness because of Mrs. Gale's remark.

"Why aren't you asleep? It's late."

"I know. I started all right: then I woke up. So I put on the lamp and did some writing. I hadn't done today." Blanche never knew exactly what Doing Today meant: the notebooks were not really diaries; though he made regular notes, signs and drawings in them: sometimes he showed them to her, sometimes not. She said, "Well, couldn't you have done today tomorrow?"

"I might," said Thomas, "but it's better to get it down at the time. Particularly if it's a difficult one."

"What was difficult about it?"

He looked at her thoughtfully before he replied, "All sorts. I'll show you." He sat up. The striped pyjamas, the replacement after the lily pond, looked very clean. "Here, you see," said Thomas, pointing to two drawings in the book, "It's mixed."

"What's that meant to be?"

"Skull and crossbones. But, you see, there has to be a star as well because of no trouble till I fell in the pond. And even *that* was mixed." He grinned at her. "Have you forgiven me?"

"Yes, of course. You said you were sorry," she reminded him.

He shut the book. "Well, I was sorry because you were cross. But being in the pond was much too good to be sorry about by itself. You've no idea how squdgy the mud is at the bottom."

"Oh haven't I? I saw your feet, and your pyjamas."

"But you didn't feel the splendid squdge."

"No, and I'm sure I don't want to."

"Oh well," said Thomas.

"Light out now. Said your prayers?"

"Yes."

"Kneeling down?"

"I keep *some* for lying down," he said severely. He looked as though he were ready to discuss the subject. Blanche was not. Thomas's prayers had been a problem since she could remember. With an obstinate passion for detail, he had long ago rejected the "Bless Daddy, Gerald, Sarah, Nanny and all kind friends" routine. When he was still small enough for her to hear the prayers, he had mumbled and bumbled, on and on: taking in animals, old toys, people he had seen in shops, the characters from Beatrix Potter's books and once going so far as to pray for a kettle whose bottom had burned out.

"You know—" he began.

"I know it's time you went to sleep." She stooped and kissed him, receiving his strangle hug. She put out the lamp. The moment she reached the door there came a loud "I *say*. I *must* ask you something." It was one of the oldest tricks; they had all played it in their time, Westons, Hales and Mattingleys.

"Not now. Good night, lovey," she said firmly.

"It's urgent."

"It can wait till the morning."

"It simply couldn't. I have to know *now*." He switched on the lamp again.

"You put that out at once," said Blanche. "Or I will."

He said, "It won't take you a minute to answer. If you *know* the answer."

"Hurry up now and put it out."

He put it out. He said, "Why have Gwen and Father stopped being friends?"

"I've no idea what you're talking about—and I'm sure you haven't, either."

"You really don't know? I thought perhaps you would. Oh, well, never mind. Good night, Brigstock."

❁

"We wouldn't know why people dance the Charleston!
(*Charleston*)
We'd like to burn that darned old shack in Charleston!
(*Charleston*)

We all gyrate
And agitate
To tunes we hate.
What is the fate
That makes us dance this idiotic Charleston?"

Shirley Ormonde, Sarah noted, took no part in the frenzied
kicking and shuffling. Shirley Ormonde leaned on the piano,
watching the dance; quite alone, in her silver dress, with the
sheaf of red roses beside her.

Sarah went on looking at Shirley. She was conscious of a
quiver in the air, a color coming upon her thoughts. That head,
those hands, were so beautiful. There was the sense of a stranger
met suddenly, a personality impinging, then leading away into
mystery, beckoning her on to wonder who Shirley was and how
she had come here.

With this little haunt in her mind, made of admiration and
curiosity, she found herself looking back to the term just ended.
There in its niche stood her current idol. For a moment the idol
seemed to lose stature, dressed as it was in a gym tunic and black
stockings.

Sarah blinked, unbelievingly, and let the comparison go. She
watched the stage. The Moonrakers never ended on a comedy
note; yet this was surely the last number, the uproarious Charleston ensemble? No. Tubby began to slow the tempo down and,
with a rippling flourish, ended the tune. A waltz now: sounding
like a mixture of all the waltzes there had ever been. Surely Tubby
had stolen phrases left and right? Yes, he had. But she was deflected from them, watching Philip take Shirley as his partner.
Preserving detachment, Sarah could see that Shirley was not so
good a dancer as Philip; but the sight of them together reflected
her constant image: the two, always the two. Great actor and
great actress, romantic lovers unspecified, and the secret sense

that she herself was part of the two, might be one, might be the other or both, in the beguiling dream.

The song dipped and rose and dipped again. The words were concerned with Love's Old Game being Still, Still, Still the Same; insisting finally that the Laugh, the Sigh Would Never, Never, Never Die, before a blue light bathed the circling figures, the curtains swept across to hide them and the clapping began.

Did they take fewer calls than usual? Sarah thought so. Or perhaps she judged this by the small, as yet the very small, pang of not seeing Shirley just once more. The house lights came on.

"Now, Weston, we must ask you to submit to a search," said Gerald's new chum, the grown-up young man with the pale face. He was, she thought, elusive and conceited. He had introduced himself as Morris Ward, and the girl (embarrassingly) as "My henchwoman, Poppy."

"If you don't tell me what's in that pocket, I shall have a relapse. You wouldn't want me to have a relapse, would you?" he went on. During the interval he had told them about his illness: "a severe and highly personal operation, not to put too fine a point upon it, piles." He had something of Gerald's manner, though he was far older than Gerald; the girl was old too, eighteen at least.

Sarah listened to Gerald denying all over again the existence of any secret possession in his pocket. The silver pencil, he said, was easy. He had shown it to Philip and Philip had passed this on to Perry Potter for action. Morris Ward, leaning on his cane, continued to look sceptical. There was some talk of a next meeting. Bored, Sarah tried to hum the melody of "Rose in the Bud," Shirley's last song.

"I don't like that Morris—or the girl, do you?" she said when they were gone.

"Not sure. Let the oicks get out before we move, shall we?"

She sat still beside him, sniffing the cinema-theatre smell: hot velvet, stale tobacco, sweat and face powder; the sharp, sweet stuffiness belonging nowhere else, making the nose forget the air outside.

Backstage territory was familiar to them both. But here at the

Fundrome the door labeled *Artistes* opened upon a bewildering circular passage, a sort of galleried warren, dimly lit and full of echoes; it appeared to run all the way round the building. The first to pop out at Sarah and Gerald was Leo Clyde. It would be. "What ho, what ho, what *ho!* Come into my cubbyhole. Got a kiss for your Uncle Leo?" Always so busy and anxious and hearty that he made you sorry, because you couldn't like him. Why not? He wanted to be liked. He wanted to be one of the family. He took trouble. He noticed everything. Her hair cut shorter: "Suits you, ducky"; Gerald's shoes: "Quite the man about town." He asked after Nanny and after Thomas. In the hooky, beaming mask his eyes moved all the time, sad eyes, watchful eyes. "Daddy's about a mile away; greyhound track, this place; just keep on keeping on. You'll find all your old friends— and the new ones." Here he gave Gerald a leer. "I say, just what *are* you hiding in that pocket? We've all been having bets."

"Why not ask the man who knows?" There was a deceptive sweetness in Gerald's voice.

"Perry? *He* wouldn't tell. Mind you—" But Gerald had had enough of Leo Clyde; he walked on and away. Sarah lingered. Partly because she was sorry for him, partly to inform herself a little about Shirley Ormonde. Leo, besides being a serviceable baritone, was business manager for the company. Hence the honor of the "cubbyhole" to himself. Perhaps it was because he paid the salaries that he always talked about money: he was doing it now. "Mind you, that Perry's worth every penny he gets," said Leo, his eyes flickering over the fact of Gerald's swift departure, "and more. Don't know how he does it. Doesn't do it every night of course: not the mind-reading act."

"Was she planted, the woman up in the circle?"

Leo hesitated, putting on an appalling knitted sports jacket that she remembered from last year. "Well, she may have been, and again she may not. Keeps himself to himself, does Mr. Potter. Like our other new star: our proud beauty. *She* keeps herself to herself all right, all right. Married, though: 'may account for it. Quite the lady, Shirley. Adds tone, doesn't she? What d'you think of the show, Sal? Gone up in the world, haven't we?" He took a drink from the glass on his table. "Expect you've heard all about it. Met our new backer yet?"

A tall figure was sweeping past Leo's door, half-seen, but wearing a pale coat and a small red hat.

"There she goes," said Leo. "Same every night. Has to telephone that husband of hers: or so she says. Don't know which mistrusts which. Or is it love, perhaps it is."

He made it easy to ask, "Where does the husband live?"

"Bristol," said Leo Clyde. "Shirley's at the Wayne Court. Most depressing hotel in Sawcombe, I'd say: but far from cheap, oh *far* from cheap. No such thing as digs for Her Ladyship. Hubby foots the bill, I make no doubt."

Sarah paused on her next question. Ormonde sounded like a stage name. To ask the true, the married name might result in its being something disheartening, like Hogg. Why should she mind Shirley being Mrs. Hogg? (But I would mind.) Leo downed his drink, and took a key from a hook on the wall. "Time for off, ducky. You're all coming to a picnic tomorrow, did you know? *My* picnic. Special welcome picnic. Marina beach. Swim first and guzzle afterwards. Then you can sleep it off. We can't. Kiddies' Show at three o'clock, what a life. Still we're all on the up-and-up, that's the great thing."

As he locked his door, peals of laughter came down the passage: they preceded Gwen, all dressed up in billowing apricot taffeta—with a very small man at her elbow. The small man had a gold tooth and a dinner jacket. Gwen introduced him as Mr. Evans. They were, she explained, going to a dance at the Rivermouth Hotel. She kissed Sarah good night. Sarah gazed after them.

"Take you along to Daddy," Leo said.

She had remembered his earlier question. "Is that the new backer?" she asked him.

"Eh?" said Leo.

"That little man . . . Mr. Evans. You said a new backer."

For a second Leo's face sagged; then he began to laugh; then he cut the laugh short. "No, Sal: Mr. Evans is *not* our new backer."

And now they were at the door of Philip's dressing room, another lighted cave in the warren-gallery; a cave larger than Leo Clyde's; with a little cluster of people spilling out of it. Leo scurried away; the expression of his face as he went puzzled her: he looked slitty-eyed and secretive. Here was the magician, Perry Potter, most ordinary in a wrinkled gray flannel suit; behind him, Gerald and Philip, with Tubby Whittington, and two visitors saying "Marvelous" over and over again.

"I want to *know*," Sarah said to the magician. "I'm Sarah Weston," she added. "How do you do?"

"How do you do. What do you want to know?" He seemed to be in a hurry.

"How it's done—the mind-reading act?"

"Oh—that," said Perry Potter. "Excuse me, Miss Sarah, it's my supper time." He walked off, waddly and short-legged. She was swept into the group.

Philip, shepherding them to the car-park, doing all his waves and Hullos and Bless-Yous, was, she thought, entirely happy. "Pack in, chaps, it's late and I'm scared of Nanny," said Philip. He drove fast along the parade. With the crowds strolling and the chain of lights looped around the bay, Sawcombe became a different, enchanted place. Sarah crooned softly from Shirley's song:

> *"Are you afraid to bloom in cri-imson splendor*
> *Lest someone come and steal your heart away?"*

"That a daughter of mine should sing out of tune—" Philip said plaintively as he had said before. He made up for it by adding "Lovely, isn't she—Shirley?" before he turned his attention to Gerald.

"All right, old boy"—the wooing note—"Perry knows there's something, but he doesn't know what: that's his story." Obviously this had been discussed in the dressing room before she arrived there. "Let's have yours, now, eh?"

"I've told you. My left-hand inside pocket is *virgo intacta*," said Gerald.

Sarah knew what that meant. The words gave her a clue: there was something in the pocket and it was something improper. Here her ideas were vague. She knew too much and too little. (There was a thing beyond the pale, for which a girl named Elsa Parish had been expelled and Miss Groome had later given the Middle House a most confusing talk on Purity. None of those present had seen the point: Sarah was no wiser today. At the other end of the scale of knowledge there were all the resoundingly simple things that happened in the classics; like rape. Somewhere halfway between ignorance and understanding was the hidden murk of Gerald's public school. Boys were familiar with all kinds of unknown obscenities.)

She heard Philip saying in his hurt voice, "If you won't tell me, I'll respect your desire for privacy. But I'd rather you didn't lie about it. Truth is the most important thing in the world."

Gerald went down into a sulky silence; which made it all the odder that he should be grinning from ear to ear once they were alone. Philip in the car had roared off to the dance at the Rivermouth. She and Gerald had the food in the dining room to themselves.

"Interesting character our Papa," said Gerald with his mouth full. "Can't stop lying himself so he's always begging other people not to. Why's that, do you suppose?"

Sarah ate a piece of cheese. "You mean he's lying about Gwen. Well, no, he isn't. He just isn't telling."

"Same thing," said Gerald.

I V

Thomas blinked and knew that it was very early in the morning, and drowsed again. This was the good time for dreaming. It resembled in a way the last moments before sleeping at night, though the process he employed was more deliberate then than now. At night it was a process of letting go, of breathing slowly and steadily; until the breathing seemed to take care of itself, bringing first the gradual gentleness that took him away from his own body; then the true bright pictures just as he thought they would never come. At night they were the gold men marching; going past in their glory with flags that flew on the wind. The white towers shone as they came to the city. And this was the best of all beginnings.

Now he merely burrowed back into the gentleness, still there

and waiting for him. One minute he was conscious of the muted
light all round the room, of the squashy pillow, the sheet tucked
close to his chin; and the next he was looking at a face. It was a
brown face, with cropped hair as pale as his own hair. The blue
eyes were large above bumpy cheekbones, the nose small, the
mouth square and pouting. A child's face, that gazed at him
steadily for its tiny moment of being there. After it came the sea;
a harbor basin of bright water, small boats rocking, and inland
a brown church tower above green trees. He seemed to have
walked right into this picture; away from the harbor, down a
broad dusty road, over a causeway where he could still see the
boats to his left and a marshy pond to his right. A seabird swooped
down in front of him. Wide-winged, it dropped to the road. It was
brownish-white, speckly. As he came towards the bird, it picked
something up from the road with its beak and began to run on
pompous, stilted legs. This he liked, but now he had lost it; the
scene broke up completely, having become too real for him, or he
for it. There was a sequence of disordered grayness that turned to
falling rain. Through the rain he saw Nanny walk and then stand
still. But what had they been doing to her? She was crying. Her
hat was crooked, the new hat with the flowers, it was getting spoilt
by the rain; below its brim, he could see her hair sticking out in
wisps; her nose was all red and the tears spilled down.

"Oh Brigstock, *don't!*" he shouted. "*Don't!* I'm here. It's all
right. *It's all right!*" He fought to get to her, but the rain or
something was solid between them, a wall against which he
hurled himself, shouting, "I'm here, I'm coming!" and still he
couldn't get close. He called to her again and woke himself up.

There she was. Not wearing a hat, of course; ready for the day
in a dark blue cotton dress, with white collar and cuffs; and her
hair net on. "Good morning. Gosh, I'm glad to see you," said
Thomas.

"Were you talking in your sleep?" she asked.

"Talking? I was simply *yelling.*"

"No, you were just mumbling," she said gently. "And it's only
half-past seven."

"Oh, well. Can I get up?"

"Breakfast isn't till half-past eight. Because they were late last night. I'll draw the curtains and you can read."

It was, Thomas decided, the kind of day liable to play tricks. How did one in advance know a tricky day from a non-tricky day? He had no idea. And all the early-morning pictures were gone; except the last awful one, which he would do his best to forget. He refused to put it in the notebook. But it was still there when he came down to breakfast. He was first. He stood in the blue and white dining room that was full of sunshine and the smell of bacon. On the tablecloth, packets of Force and Grape-nuts had ousted the ribbons and dolls. The roses were still in the middle. Not a sign of the Devonshire cream. He went to the window and looked out at the garden; seeing the lily pond he said aloud, "Arriving on the scene of yesterday's activities," which was a sentence that pleased him, though he had forgotten where he found it. He said it several times before the others appeared; and now, as always on the first day, there seemed to be a great many plans. Thomas listened to them in silence, eating hugely and keeping an eye on Brigstock. Leo Clyde's picnic was today, on the Marina beach; Gwen's picnic was tomorrow, Sunday, here at the cove. "Surrounded by the sickening Stevenses, I presume?"

"Honestly," said Sarah, "You'd think they'd have folded their tents *years* ago."

Sarah was different today, Thomas decided: or, more accurately, she was the same today whereas she had been different yesterday; yesterday she had been in a kind of cocoon. Today she was out, all ablaze and chattery. He began to compose a poem that began "Sarah the silkworm has shed her cocoon," but her voice got in the way of his concentration.

She was telling about three girls who had fainted in church on the same Sunday. "Why can't *I* faint? I never can—it's not fair—" on and on; and Brigstock saying, "Whatever do you want to faint for?" and Sarah sighing, "It would be romantic."

"Think again, Madam," said Gerald. "One of the juniors did it in an astronomy lecture and he was sick all over himself at the same time."

"Not at breakfast, Gerald, please."

"If I fainted, it would be very beautiful and quiet and graceful and everyone would think I was dead."

"Sarah the silkworm has shed her cocoon," said Thomas, taking another piece of toast. Nobody answered him and he was deflected by realizing that he remembered the toast rack. It was a collection of bent silver hoops with a small silver ring on top. Why was it still here when so many things were changed in the house? "Why is it the same toast rack, I wonder?" he said. Again nobody answered, because they were now talking of the Moonrakers; something about a magician, which interested him, though he had missed the beginning.

"You ought to go this evening, Brigstock—why not? You can take old Thomas."

"I shall be too busy, I'm afraid; it must wait till next week."

"I don't mind going again," said Sarah nonchalantly, "So I can take Thomas."

"Excuse me, but your father said Thomas was to go this afternoon, that's what I understood him to say."

"But it's the Kiddies' Show this afternoon. He isn't a kiddy any more. He's nearly eleven."

"It's for your father to say."

"Mean poor old Thomas isn't nearly eleven unless father says so?"

"*Poor* old Thomas."

The door banged open and their father appeared, in a dressing gown of peacock colors, crying, "I've dropped my watch and bust it."

This made a change. Thomas was sorry about the watch, but at least the argument was interrupted. The watch was beautiful; its only trouble was that the winding knob at the top went on going round and round. He stared at it ferociously, willing it to behave as it should.

"Mainspring, I suppose," said Philip. "What you do, Nanny, is take it to old McPhee. Galleon Street. Remember old McPhee? You must. Dear old McPhee. Such a character."

"What's a character?" asked Thomas.

"Don't you know?"

"No."

His father hitched a chair to the table beside Brigstock and said, "Now I'm here I'd like some tea. Somebody tell Thomas what a character is," he added fretfully, still fussing and poking at the watch.

"A character is an outstanding personality," said Sarah.

Gerald said, "You're one yourself, mate, if you did but know it," which didn't help him at all. Thomas said, "Oh well," and his father abandoned the watch resignedly to Nanny. "Please ask McPhee to be as quick as he can. It won't be a trouble, will it? You'll be going to the shops."

"Yes, I'll be going quite soon as it's Saturday."

"So shall I," said Thomas. His father looked at him over the edge of his teacup: he had a lot of beard at this time of day. "You will, will you?"

Thomas nodded.

"What d'you want to buy?"

He didn't want to buy anything. He felt, with a purpose cloudy but firm, that he ought to go on keeping an eye on Brigstock. This would not, he knew, come as an acceptable explanation. He was grateful to Gerald for chipping in: "Since we can't tell him what a character is he obviously wants to meet dear old McPhee and find out for himself."

"That's it," said Thomas, "That's exactly it. Old McPhee. Dear old McPhee."

Here he met opposition from Philip, asking if he wouldn't rather go on the beach?"

"I'm *going* on the beach. To Leo's picnic. Aren't I?"

"I meant our beach—here, the cove," said his father. "I thought we'd all do that first. Then we'll drive down to the Marina."

It was a choice; it would be: a choice was his least favorite thing. And the end of breakfast was always shadowed by wanting, or not wanting, to go to the lavatory. (It was still a mystery to him why neither state should be desirable nor, indeed, wholly identifiable.) Gerald said, "Anyone explain why Scotsmen are characters and Jews not?" which led to Brigstock taking a slightly bristly line about Jews as though they shouldn't be mentioned; and Gerald doing an imitation of Leo Clyde, ending with, "I'm a Jew—boo-hoo—why aren't you?" which made his father laugh; Sarah began again about tonight. She was cut short by Philip; "I'd rather Thomas went to the afternoon show. We don't go up till eight-fifteen Saturdays and we're liable to run late."

At least that decision had been made.

So, apparently, had the ruling between the shops and the cove. Waiting for the bus with Brigstock, he saw Gerald and Sarah depart across the road, between the trees. A moment later the Stevenses went trooping across from their gate. They all looked very tall and serious, carrying bags and towels and books.

"Why are the Stevenses so sickening?" he asked Brigstock. "I can't remember them at all."

"They're nothing of the kind. It's just Gerald being nasty." She gave him a doubtful look. "Are you quite sure you wouldn't rather go to the beach? You never used to like the shops."

"Didn't I? *Why* didn't I?" It struck him on occasion that everyone else knew far more about him than he knew about himself.

"Well, you used to hate the butcher's. Here's the bus."

The bus put them down at the corner of Galleon Street. One window of the toyshop faced the street itself and the other faced the parade. Here he lingered, at Nanny's suggestion, while she went across to the butcher's; he kept an eye on her until she reached the opposite pavement.

The toy shop took him back, took him down into a place where he met them all again: the woolly animals, the rocking horse and the golliwog, the painted Noah's Ark procession, the two wooden pigs that ran up a ridged stairway, the yellow chickens (red beaks, one black feather on each side), the tin soldiers in their boxes, a brown monkey with flat, joined toes. These toys were in his head. One or two facsimiles were to be found in the window. His eyes went past them, past a rank of Bonzo dogs, to the penknives.

Nobody could teach him a thing about penknives. Unlike the toys, they were of the present; and of the future: he was, unhap-

pily, between penknives just now, having lost the one his grandmother gave him (steel, with two rings that opened the blades by
turning). But the whole glorious range was here in the window.
Walnut, white, mother-o'-pearl; a fat bone handle that shaded
from black through gray to a whitish color, reminding him of a
goat's fur. The biggest was attached to a card of its own, marked
at 10/6d. The handle was of dark walnut. They had opened
the knife. Against the card it projected its fanged wealth; blades,
corkscrew, file and spike; there was also the long curved instrument for taking stones out of horses' hooves. Of such he remembered his father saying to Gerald, "I can't believe there are
enough horses left to make it necessary," but Thomas accepted
the idea all the same.

Tranquilly covetous, making imaginary choices without pain,
he gazed upon the knives until Brigstock returned. "You have too
much to carry," he said, "haven't you?"

"Only the extra chops. The rest are your bathing things."

"Well, goodness, give those to me."

"I will, directly. We must take your father's watch."

Mr. McPhee was in conference with two ladies about a necklace.
As a character he was, at first sight, disappointing. Thomas wasn't
sure what he had expected, but this was merely a tufty little man
in a yellowish tweed suit. The shop was long, dark and promising: he began to explore while Mr. McPhee talked on to the ladies
and Brigstock sat on a chair.

Presently he found, lying in a tray of rings, brooches and tie-
pins at the far end of the counter, a small silver lion with green
glass eyes. It would do, he thought, for Gwen's birthday. August
the first, Leo: a lion was suitable and he wanted it himself, the
sure test for a present. The lion was on its side. He picked it out
of the tray. Deep depression followed. It had only one green
glass eye; the other was missing: just a cavity where it had been.

He stood, turning the lion in his hand. Mr. McPhee had come
out from behind the counter to escort the two ladies to the door.
At the door he told them an old saying of his grandfather's
about the weather. It was a rhyme with puns in it, which involved some repetition but everybody laughed at last, Mr. McPhee

the loudest. He returned majestically and greeted Brigstock. Thomas shuffled nearer, carrying the lion. He had made up his mind. Gwen might not want a one-eyed lion, but it must be bought or he would have a hideous time worrying about it.

Mr. McPhee had the watch open; he was examining its entrails through a spyglass. He made Hrrmph noises as he did so. Presently he announced, on a note of doom, "This is a *French* watch." He said the word "French" as though it had six *r*'s in it. He then put the watch on the counter and looked at it severely. Thomas leaned over to read the inscription on the inside of the open case. He read the words "My Darling," in what looked like handwriting on the gold. There was a date there too. Mr. McPhee snapped the case shut.

"But it is not beyond my powers to rectify, tell Mr. Adair. I may be aging but I've my faculties about me still. How old do you think I am?" he asked Brigstock, who said she didn't know, she was sure.

"How much is this lion?" Thomas inquired.

Mr. McPhee stared at him: the face, Thomas saw, was knobby and gnomish; and he wore a stiff collar, rather high, suggesting that if you took off his head there might be chocolates inside. He puffed out his lips.

"Well now, laddie, how much do you think it is?"

"I don't know."

"Then you shall guess," said Mr. McPhee.

"Couldn't you just tell me?"

"Aha, I could indeed."

Silence fell.

"If I were to tell you it cost a hundred guineas," said Mr. McPhee, smiling very much, "what then?"

"Well then I couldn't afford it," said Thomas. It didn't seem to be the right answer for Mr. McPhee, though a glance at Brigstock showed him that she looked almost giggly. Mr. McPhee leaned on the counter. "Those eyes," he hissed, "might be a pair of emeralds. Each worth a king's ransom. Might they not?"

"No," said Thomas.

"Why not indeed?"

"It's only got one eye."

Mr. McPhee snatched the lion out of his hand, turned it over quickly and said, "The price, to a wee laddie like yourself will be seven shillings divided by two. How good is your arithmetic?"

"Not good, but I make that three-and-sixpence," said Thomas wearily.

"Rather a lot," said Brigstock. "Do you really want it?"

"*Yes*. It's all *right*. I've got eight-and-threepence." He was beginning to lose his temper with this endless range of obstacles. "*Eight-and-threepence*," he shouted. "*Not* including the postal order."

"A man of means," said Mr. McPhee in a distant voice, staring over the top of his head. Brigstock said there was no need to shout. Mr. McPhee crossly packed the lion in a box with some cotton wool; Thomas counted out the silver. He was not sure now that the lion had been worth the battle, but at least it saved a worry. He stuffed the box into his pocket. Mr. McPhee had gone back to the watch.

"You must tell Mr. Adair that I'll need to keep it at least a week. Not for the repair itself, you understand. But"—he cheered up suddenly—"because—ha-ha—because—ha-ha—this watch will want watching." He laughed all over. "And that reminds one of Mr. Clyde's song, doesn't it? 'You Want to Watch Me.' You'll be seeing Mr. Clyde, I take it?"

Brigstock said yes, she supposed so, she would be seeing them all.

"I am expecting him to make up his mind about the tiepin. I cannot keep a real beauty like that on one side indefinitely, forbye it's a tremendous bargain." Thomas was taken unawares by a huge yawn. Brigstock, thank goodness, now seemed as bored as he was, saying briskly, "Well, I should speak to Mr. Clyde if I was you," and heading for the door.

Outside she said, "Funny old man, isn't he?"

Thomas compromised with, "Oh well."

"Suppose you let me pay for half the lion?"

"No, honestly, thank you. Did you see Father's watch has got 'My Darling' written inside? Why has it?"

She didn't answer. And then Tubby Whittington came round the corner, to greet them with a yell. "Nanny! Thomas! Well, glory alleluia," said Tubby. He was even fatter than last time. Tubby was rosy-faced, black-haired, with eyebrows that seemed to be painted on. To Thomas, he never looked himself in ordinary clothes. Round face and round body alike belonged inside Pierrot clothes; his proper place was at the piano, leaning back from the keyboard, spinning round on the stool, more an outsize toy than a person. "Hail, hail, the gang's all here," said Tubby. "I'm not half glad to see you, not half I'm not. How are you? Are you very well? I'm glad you're very well. I'm very well. I'm glad I'm very well. Comes of *not* going to that party," he added cryptically. "Want to come and swim with me and Susie?"

This idea needed discussion. "I was going to take him on the beach, as soon as I'd finished the shopping—to wait for Mr. Philip and the others—it didn't seem worth his going all up the hill again . . . Only just after eleven now," and a lot more talk while he hopped from one foot to the other, muttering, "Rabbits —Onions—*Owls*," as a magic against waiting.

He was to go with Tubby and Susie. He remembered his dream and said, "Take care of yourself," to Brigstock, adding, "What are you going to do? After the shopping? Aren't you coming to the picnic? Why are you too busy?" And in spite of her brisk replies, he was still disturbed. "I don't know why she *always* has to be so busy," he observed to Tubby, watching her depart up Galleon Street. "All that washing and ironing. All our *things* take her such a time. Particularly at the beginning, like now. When it's a holiday. Doesn't seem to me she ever *has* a holiday. When's *your* holiday?"

"Every day except matinees," said Tubby. "What about an ice? An ice is a nice thing, an ice is. Here's that woman I married."

Susie was very small, next to Tubby: with fair fluffy hair and a pouter pigeon look to the top of her pink dress, and no stockings.

"Swim first—ice afterwards. I'm sure that's the right way round. Or am I just thinking about my hangover? It doesn't half need a dip."

"What's your hangover?" said Thomas.

"Somebody who's staying with me."

"Why?"

As usual the question got no answer and they turned along the parade. Susie pointed out the beach huts annexed by the Moon-rakers: three in a row, this side of the pier. "You can undress with Tubby and I'll undress with me."

"And here's where we aim for afterwards," said Tubby, waving a flipper-like arm as they passed the splendidly painted frontage, all blue and yellow, labeled *Ice Cream Parlour* in red lettering. The parlor was set back from the parade, giving room for three small tables with chairs outside. Thomas halted to look and then bumped into Tubby's bottom. Tubby had pulled up right in front of him.

"*Rab*—" said Tubby, sounding surprised.

"*Rab*—" said Susie, sounding if possible, more surprised.

There was something foreign and odd about the boy at the doorway of the ice cream parlor. He was a little taller than Thomas; he was bony and he slouched. His skin was tanned, making the cropped hair look almost white. The blue eyes were large above bumpy cheekbones, the nose small, the mouth square and pouting. He was dressed in blue linen, shirt and trousers to match. On his leather belt, to Thomas's deep interest, there hung the ten-and-sixpenny knife from the toy-shop window: the purple-dark walnut knife with all its bright equipment folded away. It looked most flashingly new and desirable.

The moment Rab spoke, Thomas realized that this was not a boy, but a girl: certainly the oddest looking girl he could imagine. She seemed very slouchy and shy. She poked her head forward, not looking at Tubby or Susie, looking down while she answered their questions.

"Oh, I just *came* . . . I didn't want to go to Paris . . . No, I'm not alone. Miles is here . . . We're at the Rivermouth." She

scuffled with one foot. What was this all about? Suddenly he was
in it.

"Thomas. Thomas Weston. Thomas, this is Rab. Rab Lee."

"How do you do," said Thomas.

She looked straight at him and up and down him and all over
him, seeming to have lost her shyness. Her eyes became larger
still, finally she grinned. She said, "Hullo," and added, "you don't
look the way I thought you would."

"Are you American?" Thomas asked, bemusedly. It had taken a
few minutes to identify her funny accent.

"Yes," said Rab.

"Well, why do you know about me in advance?"

She gave a grunt and a shrug. Tubby and Susie both began to
talk at once. Rab was saying, "I don't really want to swim again;
I swam all morning. If you're coming here for ice cream"—she
put the emphasis on the word "ice"—"I'll see you later." She
went, swaggering and slouching, looking back now and again
over her shoulder.

"Comic little tough," Tubby said.

V

Rab thrust the spoon into her chocolate-fudge sundae and decided she didn't want any more. An appetite was not her strong point. She laid down her spoon and stared again at Thomas Weston.

Had there been no adults present, she might establish talk with him. Adults and children made, in her view, an impossible mixture. She could cope with one kind or the other kind, but not both kinds. Since Leo Clyde had come up from the beach with Tubby and Susie and Thomas, to crowd the little table outside the ice-cream parlor, this situation was beyond her control. (Great laughs and jokes and comments on the people who passed along the parade.) Sawcombe was not her first sight of an English seaside town; but this section seemed as dully foreign as the rest:

with its pier and its huts and its prim look, so sadly different from
the Vineyard (but, oh, don't think about the Vineyard here,
it hurts too much). Eastward, the old town, the harbor and the
fishing boats were bearable. The East Cliff with its great sharp
outline, green-capped, the stone bluff streaked with red and white,
could remind her, if she tried hard, of the cliffs at Gay Head.
The river curled out under the base of this cliff. The hotel was
built above. From her window in the hotel she looked straight
down onto rocks, pools and seaweed; there were gulls in abundance and, this morning early, the prize of an oyster-catcher. She
would whistle up Miles and go back right now, were it not for
the presence of Thomas Weston.

He was eating a banana split. His hair was all fuzzy from the
swim and his face was pink; just a square little boy with blue
eyes and a short upper lip; babyish in appearance, considering his
age. Nearly eleven, she had understood. Rab was twelve. What
surprised her most was his healthy, well-cared-for look. He was
dressed in a clean white shirt and gray flannel knickerbockers;
she had expected rags, or at least darns and patches.

The first thing she had grasped about the Westons was their
poverty. They were waifs, wanderers, with no home and no background. They were dragged about from place to place in the trail
of the Moonrakers. Between grim lodgings and boarding houses,
they were sent off to hideous schools in cold, far places. Orphanages, she had thought; English orphanages out of Dickens. But
never having got on true terms with Dickens, she had made a
mental picture of Gerald, Sarah and Thomas from the Hummils
in the early chapter of *Little Women*: the poor family to whom
the Marches gave their Christmas breakfast. ("I'll take the cream
and the muffins," said Jo.) She had imagined the arrival of the
three Westons, pale, dirty, whining and starving. A jailer called
Nanny, of whom she had no picture, would be in charge. Her
own nurse, long ago, had been Norah, not Nanny: young, Irish,
fun to be with. A friend, as Miles was her friend.

"I could eat another of those," said Thomas, tinkling his spoon
on his saucer, where no trace of banana or cream remained.

"You won't have any room for the picnic," said Leo Clyde.

"I can eat tons and tons of absolutely everything."

"Have mine," said Rab. Perhaps he was starving, after his fashion. He said, "Honestly? Don't you want it?" and took it over. The adults were all talking at once; show talk: last night's house, Perry Potter's act, Shirley Ormonde's amateur quality. Rab had heard it all before. Under the bridge of noise, Thomas Weston said to her, "I say, could I look at your knife?"

"Sure." She unhooked it from her belt, laying it on the table. He held it lovingly.

"Did you get it from the shop on the corner?"

"Yeah. I bought it this morning."

"It's the best I've ever seen." He turned it over and over.

"Do you have a knife?" she asked.

He blinked; his eyelashes were very white and thick. His fairness surprised her too. She had expected all three children to be dark, like Philip.

"Lost mine," he said.

"Why don't you get another?"

"I'm sort of waiting." He pushed the knife back to her. "If you want one like this there are plenty in the store," said Rab. He must surely have ten-and-sixpence: less than three dollars. But, no, of course he hadn't. The flesh-and-blood Thomas had obscured the Weston poverty for a moment, that was all. She thought of offering to lend him the money. Would he be offended? He said, "Have you seen the Moonrakers?"

"*Me*? Why, yes: lots of times." Above their heads the adult chatter stilled.

"*Moonrakers 1926*, I mean," said Thomas. "That's the new edition."

"Well, not the whole shooting match. I only got here last night. But I saw some of the new numbers at Folkestone, where they first put them in. Two weeks ago, that was. And I've seen rehearsals." Tubby was raising his comic eyebrows at her, which struck her as odd, since Tubby didn't know what she knew. Leo was looking at her with his mouth drawn a little to one side, making his puckered Mephisto face. "Guess I'll go tonight," said Rab. "Miles went last night. I was too sleepy."

"I'm going this afternoon. Who's Miles?" Thomas asked.

Before she could answer him, a boy and a girl stopped beside their table; she knew at once that they were Gerald and Sarah. There was plenty of time to stare. Nobody, for the moment, thought of introducing her because the talk was all about Philip's new car, which had produced a flat tire on the way down from Roseclay, and Philip, "in one of his finer frenzies," said Sarah, had taken it to the garage. Sarah, Rab decided, was as beautiful a creature as could be. She was dark and large-eyed, with a deep, queer voice. She didn't conform to the starvation image, any more than Thomas did, though her face was exquisitely thin and hollow-cheeked, with a dazzle to it like the dazzle that could come on Philip's face. She wore a scarlet blouse with her gray pleated skirt. Under the blouse you could see that she had small, perceptible breasts. Rab had none. Her mother remarked upon this now and then. Her mother, she thought, would approve of Sarah's looks, of the wave in the hair and the graceful body. (*"Do* sit up, Rabby. Don't *yawn* . . . yawning's so hideous it ought to be illegal. *Don't* shuffle. Must you be such a gawk? That's better. I love it when you stand like a Greek boy.") Gerald, she saw, was a better-looking version of his father: a flashing, lounging show-off with a ukulele slung across his shoulder; full of himself, like all people his age. They were gods, Sarah and Gerald, limitlessly far. (Surprise, surprise . . .)

"He said he'd meet us on the beach—in front of the huts. That's right, isn't it, Leo?"

This awoke Rab. Danger. Philip wouldn't expect to find her here. His call to the hotel this morning had been hurried, his voice less fatherly than usual, sounding she had thought, most anxious to get off the line. "Rab, darling—I only just heard . . . You all right? Miles looking after you, ducky? Well, I'll see you. Tomorrow, perhaps—I'll ring again, 'Bye, now."

She scrambled down from her chair.

❁

Miles said, "You could have gone to the picnic."

"I didn't want to. Yes, I did. Kind of."

"What excuse did you give?"

"I said I had a date with some friends at this hotel. They all believed it. No, Leo didn't. And Susie said to come to *Gwen's* picnic tomorrow. That's up on the other beach, their beach. I'd like it if it's okay with Philip."

Miles drank his coffee and grimaced. He put in two more lumps of sugar. He was always complaining about the coffee. In France, too much chicory. In Italy, a muddy syrup. Here, he said, it tasted of nothing at all; well, hot water with a faint flavoring of blankets.

"At an hotel of this quality you would think," said Miles.

Rab stared around the glassed-in veranda, the summer dining room of the Rivermouth, thinking it had something in common with hotel dining rooms everywhere: flowers on the tables, waiters wearing white jackets, too much elaborate food, too many people. She seemed to have been eating in rooms like this for a very long time. Or rather, not eating.

"Look at you," said Miles. "Still dragging that lobster around the plate: it must be getting tired. *I'm* getting tired looking at it."

"I told you, I had some ice cream."

"Probably poisoned yourself."

"Goodness, I don't have to be poisoned not to eat."

"*Is zat so?*" said Miles. He took one of his brown Russian cigarettes from his silver case. Lighting it, he was listening to the talk from the table across the floor, where two snooty British parents sat with two snooty little girls: all were the same color which was really no color, Rab decided; a pale blur.

"What are you laughing at?" she asked.

"They think I'm your father."

She studied him listlessly; she saw the oiled fair hair making a cap above the round grinning face with the pinkish tan; the narrow blue eyes. If there could be a fat skull it would have the face of Miles. He had enormous shoulders, which always looked as though they were padded, even when he wore a bathing suit. At the moment he was wearing a dark blue shirt with his gray uniform trousers. He hadn't shaved this morning: this omission was inclined to occur when they were alone.

"You could be my father. You're old enough," she said.

Miles went on grinning. "*Is it that we're common or are we foreigners?* That's the discussion," he said. "That's what they want to know."

Rab said, "I never heard about 'common' till England, did you?"

"I can't remember. But it's an interesting question." As the colorless four left their table Miles began to talk very fast, in German, then in French, then in Spanish.

"That's fixed them," he said. "Will Madam be wanting the automobile this afternoon?"

The debate in Rab's head was concerned with the Westons. Though she thought nothing to the prospect of the Kiddies' Show, Thomas had said he was going today. It was possible that Sarah and Gerald, or at least one of them, might go too. She was so greatly used to being bored and homesick by turns that this rising flame of curiosity was quite unmanageable: a pleasure and a pain.

"Take me to the Fundrome, Miles. Then you can go off and do anything you want."

"Just what I can't do with you on my hands," said Miles. It was a joke, or meant to be. Miles in Europe was always having adventures. Her mother loved to hear his stories; Paula was a sucker for any story: she would beg Miles for more detail of the fights, the drinks and the ladies; though these were seldom coherently told. Any narrative brought out his variety of languages and accents. Indeed the whole trip seemed to do that. At home (was there, had there ever been, such a place as home?) he talked straight American. Didn't he? Rab was beginning to forget.

"Kiddies Show," he murmured, driving fast. "Whole show's for kiddies, if you ask me. *Furchtbar. Epouvantable.* Stinks. You bet."

"Well, but we don't understand about Pierrots. That's what Paula says."

Miles shrugged. He brought the gray Hispano to the gates of the
Fundrome. He took his chauffeur's cap from the dashboard com-
partment and put it on before he climbed out to open the door
for her. He was insistent about this detail, even on the days when
he didn't shave.

"You really want to spend the afternoon in there?" he asked,
glowering upon the pink walls behind the fringe of garden.

"I shan't *be* in there, dopey. The Kiddies' Show's out back—on
the open-air stage. When fine. And it's fine."

"By British standards," said Miles. As usual, he asked her if she
had enough money. She said yes. He suggested picking her up
when the show was over; and to this she said no, wanting to
leave herself freedom, although she knew she would be too shy to
offer her company to the Westons and it was highly unlikely that
they would invite it. "You go have an adventure. I'll be back for
supper," said Rab.

"Not to be late, now. Your mother's going to call, remember?"

She nodded. He saluted her. This drew some attention from a
cluster of children with their parents coming in through the gates.
She and Miles were in agreement that everybody in England
stared, no matter how one behaved. Now Miles put on the false
moustache he had bought at Brighton. It was a big red moustache. Rab watched the heads turning to see him go. She went
on her way.

A tilted half-circle of hard white benches surrounded the outdoor stage. Having bought her ticket, she stood at the top, spying for the Westons. The benches were filling; with palpably
British customers: little boys wearing floppy gray felt hats, little
girls with pigtails; shady straw hats for the mothers, Panama hats
for the fathers; some Nannies in gray and blue: their hats were
black. Miles had pointed out Nannies all the way from Dover.
He had a passion for them: he was pining, he said, to meet the
Westons' Nanny.

Sitting alone in the middle of the front row, right under the
lip of the outdoor stage, Rab saw Thomas Weston; recognizable
to her at once though she did not know why a round fair head
and a pair of shoulders in a white shirt should so certainly prove

Thomas. He sat very still, leaning forward, hunched up. There was nothing for him to look at except the drawn red curtains. From this height she had glimpses of the Moonrakers dodging about on the grass at the back. Their dressing room was a marquee tent set up on the one remaining lawn of the formal gardens. Though Rab had seen none of this in operation, she had heard the Sawcombe plan discussed. She went down the aisle of steps between the benches to the front row. Here she was attacked with shyness. Thomas had put a bag of candy on the seat beside his, and a small box, tied with string. Was he keeping the place for somebody else? "Hello," she said, slouching up to him.

"Oh hullo." He looked pleased to see her.

"Are you by yourself?"

"Yes," said Thomas, "are you? Oh, good." He moved the candy and the box. "Nobody likes the front row, it seems," he said, "because it's right underneath. You get a better view from the third row and up. That's what Leo says."

"Well then, why do you sit here?"

He looked at her blankly. "*Somebody's* got to sit here," he said in an impatient voice.

"Why?"

Thomas said, "Oh well," and offered her the bag of candy. He added, "If you want to go further up, please do."

"I'll stay here." Sucking the bull's-eye, she asked, "Will your brother and sister be coming?"

He shook his head, saying, "Saw it last night." He then paid her no further attention; taking the lid off his small box and peering inside. He had obviously done this more than once; the string had worked loose and he made clumsy attempts to tie it again.

"What's in there?" she asked.

"A thing I bought this morning."

"A secret thing?"

"No. Show you afterwards, if you like." He twisted round to look up the tiers of seats. "*All* the back rows are empty, aren't they?" He sighed heavily. "I'd like it to be absolutely full, wouldn't you?"

"They don't expect to fill it for the Kiddies' Show."

He blinked those white eyelashes for a moment before he asked, "Who told you?"

"Well, Philip and Leo were talking about it." In mentioning Philip's name she was perhaps making a mistake, but it was hard to know. Had Philip not been in such a hurry this morning, she would have known. Her instruction from Paula was, "Do just as Philip says." And he hadn't said anything. Not that this surprised her. Nothing they did surprised her. For Rab, life with adults was like trying to see over a wall: sometimes the wall was low enough for a glimpse: sometimes there were gaps providing a clear view and sometimes—as now—the wall was so high you couldn't see a thing. What would she say to Thomas if he asked a question on the lines of this morning's "Why do you know about me in advance?" He didn't. He seemed to accept her. The tune "Here We Are" struck up behind the flimsy red curtains.

Thomas departed from her completely: never looking her way. Whether he rolled with laughter, clapped his hands furiously (long after everyone else had ceased clapping) or sat in solemn attention, he ignored her neighborhood. Yet he must have seen much of this before. The proudly-advertised 1926 edition (First Time Ever, according to the posters) had old numbers in it. Some she herself had seen already. Some, she knew, dated from Philip's earlier shows; so Thomas must be familiar with the jokes: but still he laughed till there were tears in his eyes, and he bounced up and down. Just as well he didn't notice her. This was a babyish deal and she was bored. Maybe the evening performance (despite Miles) would live up to Philip's estimate. And maybe not. Maybe the magician was as good as Philip said he was. He looked a funny, ordinary little guy, Mr. Perry Potter.

They were singing "Wish I'd Got a Wishing Cap." Some line changes here, for the Kiddies' Show. (Rab had heard them debated.) In the evening, Philip's

> *"Wish I'd backed the winner, wish my fortunes*
> *weren't so fickle"*

was followed by Leo's

"Wish I'd got a girl who wished to have a slap
and tickle."

For this performance Leo substituted:

"Wish they'd make mosquitoes with bites that
didn't tickle."

There were some special children's numbers: a mock Punch-and-Judy show, with Leo as Punch, Gwen as Judy and Tubby as "Dog Tubby." Afterwards Gwen came on dressed as a Dutch doll and Philip as a golliwog. Thomas continued to have a good time. He even seemed to approve Shirley Ormonde (whom Rab found perfectly terrible) singing "Oh, Where and Oh, Where Is the Rainbow's End?" and wearing a long dress in rainbow colors. The hem of the dress caught in a nail or something as she made her exit. This got a laugh. Miss Ormonde looked savage. Thomas —for once—hadn't joined in the laugh. Now it was Susie, with a monologue about A Day at the Zoo. Rab was still unsure whether Philip had spotted her here in the front row: at least they were less visible from the stage than they would have been further back; but when the whole company came right downstage Philip could surely see her sitting next to Thomas. He gave no sign.

"Perry Potter will entertain you with Magic As You Like It."

Thomas turned to her at last.

"Seen this?"

"No," said Rab.

"It's my favorite type of thing," he assured her.

He was right. Once Perry Potter was in his own act, he became a different person; not just an ordinary little guy, but a sort of spellbound Simple Simon; amazed at his own achievements. His eyes seemed to grow rounder and bigger. He never smiled. The children yelled for him, and still he didn't smile. At the evening performance, Rab knew, the Moonrakers sat around him, but he was alone on this smaller stage for the Kiddies' Show. She knew also that he was restricted out here: he couldn't operate the fireworks or the baby chickens, Philip said. Never mind, he was great. "He's great, isn't he?" she said to Thomas, who nodded solemnly while Perry made four colored handkerchiefs turn into a vase of flowers. He put the vase of flowers into a top hat on the table. Then he groped inside the hat He looked more bewildered than ever.

"Anybody lost a pair of ears—*long* ears?" he asked. Out came the rabbit. Everybody was yelling: Thomas was yelling and bouncing. Perry Potter blinked upon the rabbit and, as the noise began to subside, asked plaintively, "Anybody got a lettuce?" At once a shower of lettuces came down in his head; this was almost too much for Thomas, who didn't seem to have sighted them strung up on the wire, as she had.

Susie came to carry the rabbit safely away. Leo took the table and the props. Tubby removed the lettuces. Perry stood alone, bowing up and down, up and down. They were all shouting, "More! More!"

"I'm not supposed to do any more, you know," he said. "It's time for my tea. Isn't it?"

"No!" they all shouted.

For the first time he smiled. "Oh, isn't it? All right. You know best. One more." He came right downstage; he twitched a pack of cards out of his sleeve, played them like a concertina and put them into a side pocket.

"Cards are very clever things," said Perry. "Get up to all sorts of tricks. I want you to watch them for me. So I'm going to sit down right on the edge here—oops, that was a near one. Nothing to *laugh at*," he added severely as they screamed for the trick fall: now his silver-swathed legs and the little shoes with blue pompons dangled just above Rab's head. She and Thomas craned back their necks. The magician at this angle looked, she thought, like Humpty Dumpty. On the round face the make-up was beginning to streak with sweat.

"Who'd have thought it?" said Perry Potter. "They're at it already." He wriggled exasperatedly. "There's one got out of that pocket and it's climbing all the way up my back. Sort of thing they do." He scratched himself between the shoulder blades. "Here it comes. Don't know what card it is, but it's a card all right." He slipped his hand round inside the ruffles of his collar.

"It's the Seven of Hearts," said Thomas, so loudly that he made Rab jump. Perry Potter peered down at the front row.

"*What* did you say, sonny boy?"

"I said it's the Seven of Hearts," Thomas replied, in a voice that boomed a little less but was still entirely audible. Fascinated, Rab gazed at him. His profile was solemn. So was Perry's face, looking down.

"Did I ask you to guess?" said Perry.

"No."

"This card's inside my collar."

Thomas said nothing at all. Rab was aware of some rustling movements behind them: people standing up, or leaning forward.

"Well," said Perry, "you may be right, and again you may not." He was still acting Simple Simon. He drew the card from his ruffles. He blinked.

"The young gentleman in the front row is *right*." His voice went up into its highest squeak so far. More sweat trickled through his make-up. "For the benefit of those who didn't hear— this boy said the card crawling up my back was the Seven of Hearts. And so it is. See?" He held it aloft. Rab gave Thomas a violent nudge as the applause clattered. This was a lot of fun. It also explained why Thomas had chosen the front row. That Perry Potter should select him as a feedman was not, when she came to think about it, surprising. They had something in common. (Looks? Manner? She decided to use her mother's diagnosis: "They come out of the same box.") When had these two rehearsed the act? Over lunch, maybe.

Thomas, in answer to her nudging, gave her an irritated, professional frown. Perry Potter was asking humbly, "Mind if I get on with my trick now?"

"No, please do," said Thomas unsmiling.

"Thank you." Perry sat and twiddled his toes. Sticking up at the side of one little silver shoe, Rab saw the card. A second ago it had not been there. It was turned face inward. The magician gave Thomas an uneasy glance before he raised his head, saying to the audience, "Told you to *watch*, didn't I? You're not watching. Letting them get all over me, aren't you? See this?" He raised his foot. "Better get it out before it starts tickling." But he didn't touch it. He leaned down towards Thomas.

"You wouldn't, I suppose, happen to know what *this* one is?"

Thomas said, "Well, yes, I do."

"You do, eh?"

Thomas nodded.

"What is it, then?"

"Jack of Spades."

Perry looked quite beautifully scared. He pulled the card out of his shoe without another word and held it up. "The Jack of Spades it is. For the benefit—" he began but the applause was too loud to let him finish. Looking back and up around the audience, Rab saw how many were standing, craning towards the front row. Perry had drilled Thomas to perfection. He just sat there blinking, leaning forward, with his mouth a little open, never turning his head to the crowd.

"What's your name?" said Perry.

"Thomas."

"All right, Thomas. We'd better go into business, you and me. Hadn't we?" Just behind them Rab heard a child's voice shout, "Go it, Thomas!"

"Want to come up here and carry on?" Perry squeaked. This was obviously the next move; but Thomas shook his head: he was now rather red in the face.

"Quite sure?" Perry pleaded.

"Quite sure," said Thomas gruffly. He added "Thank you" and grabbed for a bull's-eye out of the bag.

"All right, Thomas. You'll leave me alone, eh?"

"*Don't* you go up?" Rab hissed at him, "*Why* don't you?" He didn't seem to hear. Perhaps something had gone wrong; he had missed some clue or signal. Perry, scratching at his silk skull-cap, was shooting pop-eyed glances towards him; he simply sucked away on the candy. Perry scratched again.

"You're all watching this boy; you aren't watching *me*—what's the good of that?" He looked and sounded quite desperate: "There's a card climbed right inside my cap." He gulped and rolled his eyes. "Shall we ask *Thomas* to tell us what card it is?"

"Go it, Thomas!" Rab heard again, but she thought she could feel the excitement dying down; it would; everybody must realize the act had been rigged in advance. Thomas was unmagicked; he didn't look as if he cared. His left cheek bulged as he stored the candy for better articulation.

"What's the card inside my cap?" Perry asked him.

His voice was muffled but confident, replying, "You haven't *got* a card inside your cap."

"I haven't?"

"No, you haven't."

"*Sure* I haven't?"

"Quite sure you haven't."

Perry said solemnly, "Would you believe it? The boy's right again." He untied the blue silk square and shook it out like a flag. There was no card there. His crushed, strawlike hair and the white top of his forehead above the make-up brought yells of laughter. As he bowed, the others came running back and Tubby began to thump the "Toys' Tango." Leo Clyde, wearing a cat's head, caught Gwen, still wearing her Dutch-doll outfit, around the waist. They began to dance behind Perry. It was in this moment that Thomas escaped. When Rab looked, he was vanishing out of sight at the end of the row, ducking through the side-screens. He had left the candy and his little box behind.

Rab picked them up. He was obviously going backstage. She would follow. The "Toys' Tango" must be the finale, or near-finale; the Kiddies' Show was timed to run for an hour and a quarter. Anyway, she had had enough. She wanted to be in on the meeting between Thomas and the magician. She snaked her way to the side-screens and ran round the corner of the built-up stage. Here she pulled up short. There was no sign of Thomas, but Philip, freshly powdered and painted, was drooping elegantly at the mouth of the marquee, waiting to go on. He wasn't looking her way and she was about to hail him when Perry Potter, mopping his face, came down the backstage steps.

"I say, Philip," he said and waddled up to the marquee. "I say, *Philip*," he said again. He looked distraught.

"What's wrong, old man?"

"There's a child," said Perry. He began to tie on his skullcap. "A *child*," he repeated.

"All right, old boy, what's it done? Thrown an egg? Thrown up?"

"No, no. No egg, no up. Most extraordinary little boy, quite plain, with white eyelashes, sitting in the front row—"

This was too much for Rab. Philip seized Perry by the arm and drew him inside the marquee. Giggling wildly, she darted towards it, flinging herself flat on the grass beside the guy ropes. She could only hear the collision of their voices, but she could easily imagine the talk, it took a Moonrakers turn in her head:

"That's my little boy."

"Your little boy?"

"I said my little boy."

"Well, he spoiled my trick."

"Spoiled your trick?"

"I said spoiled my trick."

She was utterly, beautifully baffled. This couldn't be happening. But it was. And now Leo Clyde, removing his cat's head, came down the steps just as Philip rushed out of the marquee. Philip waved him back.

"You're on," Philip called masterfully. "Give them 'Pussy's Gone A-Mousing.' "

"I just did," said Leo. "What's the matter with you?"

"Well, give them anything you like. I'm cutting Bye-Baby-Butterscotch. We'll go straight to the finale."

"We've got just three minutes—"

"Dammit," said Philip, "whose show *is* this?" Gwen the Dutch doll came down the steps and he shouted at her, "Crisis, ducky. Keep it going. I've got to find Thomas."

"Okay," said Gwen.

As Leo Clyde, swearing hideously and replacing the cat's head, followed Gwen, Thomas came in sight. Where had he been? Behind the marquee, perhaps. He was running. He passed within a foot of Rab and the guy ropes; he didn't see her. He didn't see Philip until he butted Philip in the stomach. Philip caught him.

With her head poked through the guy ropes, Rab watched the battle begin. Everything seemed to slow down. She saw Perry and Philip, the two silvery shapes, blue-topped, sweating and be-ruffled. The sun sharpened their colors, lit up the shimmer of their silks and threw their black wavy shadows on the green grass. Beside her shoulder the flap of the tent was rippling with the wind; it made a small hard, regular noise. The other noise was the music: Tubby's piano, the voices sounding from the stage.

She looked at Thomas, in his white shirt and gray knicker-bockers; the wind was shaking the back of his shirt too. It was lifting his touselled hair. He stood, square and small, looking from Perry to Philip. Suddenly, she realized, she had stopped laughing.

"I'm sorry if it upset you," said Thomas, his voice sounding even deeper than Sarah's, but more growly.

"Well—shook me a bit," said Perry Potter. "I mean, you can see how it would."

"Yes, I do see. But I didn't do it to make you angry."

"Nobody's *angry*," said Philip, sounding absolutely furious.

"Well, that's all right, then. Could I go and get my parcel? It's what I came back for. I left it—"

Philip cut him short: "Your parcel can wait."

Impossible to signal Thomas that she had it safe; Philip grabbed him by the shoulder, saying, "We'd like you to tell us how it's done."

"How you do it, he means," added Perry helpfully.

Thomas looked blank. Then he scratched his head. He said, "Oh well—" and no more.

"Come on, old boy, we're waiting. How did you guess what those cards were?"

"And how did you know there wasn't a card when there wasn't, if you follow me," said Perry, smiling at him.

Thomas frowned. "I don't know how it happens." He looked at his feet: Rab could see the back of his neck turning red: he mumbled something.

"What?" said Perry.

"Speak up, chum," said Philip. The music was growing louder on the stage. She thought Thomas said, "I saw through—" but she couldn't be sure. Whatever it was, the effect on Perry was different from the effect on Philip. The magician raised his fluffy eyebrows and gave a short sharp whistle. Philip snapped, "You mean you guessed, eh?"

"No. It wasn't a bit like guessing. It never is."

"*Philip! Perry! You're on!*" Gwen called from the top of the steps. She was giggling a great deal. "There's such a thing as going too far," she added. "And that's what we've gone, if you ask me. A finale's a finale, ain't it? One of the tots in the second row has just had an accident."

Philip made a noise like a sea lion; a kind of yawp. He moved toward the steps, with Perry. He turned back to shout at Thomas: "Not a word to Nanny about this, now," before he vanished. Thomas stood alone.

Rab wriggled out through the guy ropes.

"Here's your box. I rescued it. And the candy."

"Oh. Thanks awfully." He looked dazed, stuffing the box into his pocket.

"Better move, hadn't we? They'll all come back down any minute. And he'll start in on you again."

"Not till after tea, I shouldn't think," said Thomas. But he followed her briskly when she began to run; they cut through the formal gardens towards the far gate, and out onto the parade.

Here beside the railings they stood still and looked at each other. Thomas wore a sheepish grin.

"You're a surprise packet, aren't you, Mister?" said Rab. "What went on?"

"Oh don't *you* start," said Thomas, "please."

"But—"

"*Look*," he said, clenching a fist and stamping his foot, "*I don't know*. That's all. No point in going on about it, is there?"

"You *must* know."

"I *don't*, you silly cheese. It just happened."

"Oh phooey."

"And phooey to you," said Thomas, making a hideous face. She squared up to him, having hit plenty of boys in her time. An elderly man with a dog stopped to rebuke them and then she saw the Hispano drawn up on the other side of the parade. Miles was sitting on the step with his cap off, reading a paper.

"Mustn't fight," the elderly man said, "must we?"

"We can't," said Thomas gloomily, "because of not hitting girls." He began to walk away. Rab rushed after him. "Where are you going?"

"Home. It's time for tea."

"Want a ride home?"

"What in?" said Thomas.

"That's my car over there. And my chauffeur."

He blinked at her before he said, "Phooey." But Miles looked up and waved, so he had to apologize.

"Not my own car," Rab allowed. "It's Paula's."

"Who's Paula?"

"She's my mother."

He made no comment. When she told Miles to drive them to Roseclay he asked, "How do you know the name of our house?"

"Just the way you knew about those cards," said Rab. Delighted with herself, she leaned back. But he had lost interest in her again. He was opening his box.

"See what you think," he said. "A silver lion," he added unnecessarily after he put it into her hand.

"It's cute," said Rab. Holding it up, she saw that it had only one eye. Perhaps the other eye had come out in the box. She was wondering whether to mention it or not when Thomas asked, "What's your birthday?"

"March the eleventh."

He said a word she didn't know.

"*How?*" said Rab.

"Pisces. Your sign. The sign you're born under. They're *planets*," he explained impatiently. "Everybody's got one. Pisces. The Fish. Gwen's born under Leo. You'd think Leo Clyde would be, but he's Scorpio. It's Gwen's birthday next week. So I thought I might give her the lion." She was aware that he was watching her anxiously while she played with it, trying to make it stand up on her knee.

"Swell present," said Rab. "She'll love this."

"You—you do see it's lost one of its eyes," he mumbled, looking out of the window.

He sounded most unhappy. She said quickly, "Isn't it *meant* to be like that? Meant to be winking? That's what *I* thought."

"Did you honestly?"

"Sure," she lied. "A winking lion. Why not?"

Paula, she knew, would disapprove the lie. Her father, on the other hand, would say she had been kind. Anyway Thomas now looked happy again. He sat grinning at her.

"I'm *sure*," she told him, giving it back. "In fact, I *know*. Because I saw one just like it somewhere."

She had made the lie so good that she might as well make it better. "In San Francisco, it was. On Sutter Street. In a window," she improvised. Miles, slamming back the glass screen that cut them off from the front, called, "You're here, you two."

"So we are," said Thomas. "Why don't you come in and have tea?"

Rab looked at him. Then she looked at the house. It was large, red and forbidding. British as could be. She saw a turret, gables and a porch. In front of the house, the gravel driveway; the rose bushes, a monkey-puzzle tree. All very formal and belonging to itself, somehow.

Roseclay. The home of the Westons.

Miles said, "If you haven't the strength to walk to the front door, I suggest somebody opens a gate for me."

"Who's *there*?" said Rab to Thomas.

"Just Nanny. Oh, and Mrs. Gale. I don't know about Gerald and Sarah. They went out in a boat. With Mr. Evans."

"Who's Mr. Evans?"

"He was at the picnic. He's got fur on him. I think he belongs to Gwen."

"A dog called Mr. Evans?"

"No, a person."

"Well, but you said fur."

"All over his chest: you know. Quite a lot of grown-up people have it."

"It's called *hair*."

"*Some* hair is furry."

"You mean fuzzy."

"No, I don't."

"Have you," Miles asked, "decided to pay rent for this accommodation?"

"I don't believe I ought to come to tea," said Rab.

Now she would have to explain; and she couldn't explain. She was bogged down in shyness at the thought of the house and Nanny. She was suddenly aware of her own appearance: of her crumpled trousers, of her ugliness, of the "gawk" whom Paula deplored. All the magic fun of the afternoon went out in a flicker as she struggled for an excuse to make to Thomas.

Thomas, however, didn't seem to need one. He simply said, "Oh, all right," and opened the car door on his side.

"I'll come another day."

"Yes, please do." He jumped out. Miles said, "Just dropping the boyfriend? That the idea?" and started up the engine. But Thomas stood where he was, holding the door.

"Look—would you like to have the lion?"

"Oh, Thomas. You mustn't."

"*Yes.*" He held out the box.

"Goodness," said Rab.

"Please have him."

"You said for Gwen."

"Well, I've changed my mind. He's for you."

Nothing like this had ever happened to her. She took the box, saying, "Gee—thanks."

"Not at all," said Thomas. "Goodbye and thank you for the lift."

"Got yourself a beau . . . What did he give you?" Miles asked, backing the car uphill.

She said, "None of your business." She looked out as they turned. Thomas was standing watching them. He waved before he went up the gravel driveway towards the house.

V I

"N"anny."

"Yes, sir."

"Where's Thomas?" Mr. Philip stayed half in and half out of the sitting-room door; something had upset him: she could see the twitch at his cheek. When she said, "He's had his tea and the little Stevens boy invited him to play croquet," Mr. Philip said, "Oh hell . . ." and came right into the sitting room. Yes, he was obviously upset. He hadn't wiped off his make-up; small yellow-pink smears lingered at temples and jawline: the top of his collar was edged with the same stain. He gazed with apparent fury at her sewing machine, then with equal fury at Mrs. Gale, who was harmlessly mending one of Gerald's socks.

"Everybody seems very busy," he snarled.

"Did you want me to fetch Thomas, sir?"

"No, that's the last thing I want."

"Well really," said Blanche, "I mean to say."

Philip blinked, twitched, beckoned her and went out again. In the passage he said, "We'll go into the drawing room. Seen the new drawing room? Yes, of course you have," he added vaguely, running down the stairs ahead of her.

The late sunshine was in the new room, making all the rust and orange colors brassy bright. "Rather hidge," said Philip. "Isn't it? Sit down." He began to pace the carpet, pulling his pipe from his pocket and spilling tobacco from his pouch. "The devil of it is I've so little time. Got to be at the Marina by seven: those cads have turned up from Torquay. They would. Perhaps you'd better read it after I've gone," he suggested, making "after I've gone" sound like "after I'm dead."

"Read what—excuse me?" said Blanche.

"Oh—sorry. Letter. A letter from Thomas's headmaster. Quite appalling, it must have come second post." His walk brought him perilously near a little glass-topped table, rocking a pair of china figures on its surface.

"Is Thomas in trouble, then?"

Philip gazed at her: he held his pipe unlit. "Did *you* know he could do conjuring tricks?"

"I don't know about tricks. It was his grandmother who—"

"I don't want to hear one word about his grandmother."

"No need to be rude, is there?"

"No. There isn't. I wasn't. I simply said—" He had the letter in his hand. "Without this, I suppose I wouldn't have worried about this afternoon. Or so it seems now." He began to read it to himself again. There was, Blanche saw, a great deal of it, three or four typed pages. She waited, with her patience running out. He said, not looking up, "Sarah and Gerald had better not know. They've been out with Mr. Evans. Miss Richmond will tell us all about Mr. Evans. Coming to the picnic tomorrow, aren't you? Miss Richmond's picnic. Yes, well this is even worse than I thought."

"If Thomas *is* in trouble," said Blanche, "I'd like to know what sort. He's never been a naughty boy."

"Ha," said Philip. "Ha. That's a good one."

"No, sir, excuse *me*." She could feel her lips growing thin. "He gets over-excited sometimes, that's all. Never naughty, not what you could call naughty."

"Oh all right, *all* right: tell me I don't understand my own children—tell me I'm a bad father— Go on." He stepped back, bumping the little table handsomely this time: one of the china figures fell with a crack. "Blast it," said Philip, "My God, it's unfair. At this moment of all moments." Whether he meant the letter or breaking the ornament was hard to know. "*And* those cads from Torquay," he wailed. She had no idea who they were. Thomas's "states," she reflected, were easier to follow than his father's. He was dabbing at the pieces of china with a handkerchief.

"I'll see to that, sir."

"You can't. Nobody could." He picked up a shepherdess without a head and waggled it at her. "Glass cracked too. If I don't have a drink I'll die." He thrust the letter into her hands. On the way to the door he said, "I must say Perry Potter's behaved splendidly. Got three children of his own he tells me, not here, they're at Morecambe. With his wife till the end of August." Since he seemed to be awaiting a reply Blanche said, "Mr. Philip, I have no idea what you're talking about."

"No, have you?" he said and went.

Blanche put on her spectacles.

Puxford Preparatory School
July 22nd

Dear Weston,

It really distresses me to write this letter. Since first drafting it, I have read some parts to Thomas. He seemed to agree that they were fair, though I admit I always find it difficult to know what he is really thinking.

He worries us all very much. *Not* at work. Though extremely slow he is basically sound and intelligent. But out of class he is the most baffling boy I've had to deal with in all my years at Puxford. None of us can understand the source of his ungovernable rages.

He has definitely provoked a number of fights for causes so peculiar that I must go into some detail. The first arose after a Sunday afternoon walk. According to Thomas, the other boys had been offensive to an old lady who was mowing her lawn with a very blunt mowing-machine. The master in charge assured me (a) that it *was* a funny sight, which might be expected to cause mild giggles and (b) that the old lady couldn't possibly have heard, being well out of earshot. There was no "offence" involved. Thomas here tackled three boys and did a good deal of kicking which, as you know, we do not like.

The second occasion was an Eng: Litt: lesson. According to Thomas, somebody had "taken sides against" Sir Francis Bacon for trying to stuff his goose with snow. (You probably remember the story?) He refused to be more explicit and could see no reason to apologize.

The third, in which I am reliably informed that he went *quite* berserk, drawing blood, arose from a discussion on whether rabbits and guinea pigs had souls. The boy involved, whose father is a scientist, was as bewildered as I am.

But I'm afraid the fights are by no means all. Thomas has developed a most alarming habit of walking about all over the school at night, with an electric torch. Not only have some of the younger boys been scared out of their wits by his sudden appearances, but he has been foolhardy enough to climb up on the roof. Again he refuses all explanation. It has happened four times this term, despite warnings. I was obliged to cane him again last Tuesday. He was very plucky about it. He always is. Indeed, his stolidity and silence in the face of reprimand or punishment perplex us all. He seems to depart into a world of his own.

Lastly, though this may seem a small thing, I can't believe

you would approve of his buying *The Occult Review*. The
excuse he gives is that his grandmother takes it regularly.
Whether she does or whether she doesn't, I think it most
unsuitable reading for a boy not yet eleven. I confiscated the
three copies he was keeping in his locker.

Goodness knows, the last thing I want is to add to your
family worries. You and I are old friends and you have
plenty of trouble on your shoulders already. But after careful consultation with the rest of the staff I feel it my duty
to the school to tell you we don't believe Thomas is right
for Puxford—or Puxford right for Thomas . . .

For some minutes while she read, Blanche had been aware that
Mr. Philip was back in the room, pacing and joggling and oc-
casionally giving a small groan. She looked up over her spectacles.
His huge brown eyes were trained sorrowfully upon her face.

"Well?" he asked, and tilted down the last of a whisky and
soda that looked much too strong.

"Well . . . I haven't quite finished it."

"Go on, finish it. Finish it." He wheeled round with his back
to her as though this would make it easier.

On the other hand, I am by no means happy with the
thought that a son of yours should leave under a cloud. Perhaps when you have had a real talk with him, some solution
may emerge. Could we meet in London, early September?
I shall be taking my usual ramble next month, but a note to
my club will find me.

Yours always sincerely,
Ralph Appleby

Slowly Blanche folded the typed sheets and handed them back.
Philip loomed above her, but she could think of little to say; she
was neither startled nor wholly surprised by the letter, as Thomas's
father seemed to be. She felt almost as though she had expected
it.

"What the *hell* are we going to do?"

"There's no need for bad language. He hasn't been doing anything really wicked, after all. Just losing his head."

"That's right," Philip said, "take his side. I knew you would."

"Don't be silly—sir." When he tried to make her angry he could seldom succeed. "What I mean is you must have a talk with him: find out what makes him do these things . . ."

"Yes. And then?" His tone was acid.

"Well, perhaps we *ought* to try somewhere else. Mrs. Gale was saying the youngest Stevens boy goes to a very good day school in London."

"Remind me," said the acid voice, "to consult Mrs. Gale."

Blanche pressed on: "I've always thought Puxford was a bit what I call rough and ready."

"Oh you have—have you? Best prep school in the country—and that's what you've thought."

"If you're going to be rude to me, Mr. Philip, it's no good asking me to help."

"Oh Nanny, I'm sorry." He looked down at his feet. "Just when I was so happy," he moaned, like a child, and added, "so *much* to tell you."

"Yes, I thought you had something to tell me," she said.

The front door slammed and a chorus of voices sounded in the hall. "Damn," said Philip. "There they are—all of them."

❂

"Nanny—"

"Yes, M'm?"

"Got a minute?" Miss Richmond stood at the doorway of the kitchen, glass in hand. Blanche was surprised to see her still here; she had thought her gone already, with Mr. Philip, to meet those people over from Torquay.

"I'll get on with the supper, Nanny," said Mrs. Gale quickly.

"Sweet of you," said Miss Richmond, taking a gulp from her glass. "Let's go out, sit on the loggia; nice now the wind's dropped." She was wearing another new dress; much too short, like all this year's dresses, but pretty, with a pattern of brown and white leaves. She sang loudly

"But just for the minute
That's as long as we are in it,"

and skipped up on to the sill of the loggia, where she sat dangling
her legs: then she said, "Oh Nanny *dear*," and looked as if she
were going to cry. "I *must* talk to you."

"Will it take long?" Blanche wanted to ask. Her head was full
of Thomas and Puxford and Mr. Philip and the supper. There was
enough in the air without this sad, painted face gazing at her under the red curls: it didn't suit Miss Richmond to look so unhappy. Blanche sat down on the edge of one of the wicker
chairs. Miss Richmond went into a heavy silence; she finished her
drink. The evening sunshine made a halo round the red hair.
From the tennis lawn there sounded the rhythmic bumping and
the voices: Sarah and Gerald; with Thomas and the new Mr.
Evans. There was a pigeon crooning to itself in a tree somewhere
close.

"Have you ever been in love?" Miss Richmond asked. "You
must have."

There were two responses of memory: one could bring a
faint, jagged sense of shame and the other was like looking at a
picture in an old-fashioned magazine: the tall boy wearing his
black clothes for Sunday; the two of them coming down the
Berkshire lane on their way home from Evensong. The dimmed
face was still smiling at her across time.

"Yes, M'm. When I was engaged to be married," said Blanche.
"It's a long time ago."

"Why didn't you marry him?"

"He died. Gracious, there's no need to upset yourself; like I
say, it's a long time ago."

Miss Richmond blew her nose. "I'm not sure that's what I'm
crying about. I *think* it is. I dunno. First one cries because one's
miserable. Then one cries because one's cried. And after that anything makes one cry." She sniffed: "Did you love him terribly?"

"I don't know about terribly. We were very fond of each other,
and good pals, as the saying goes."

"That's frightfully important. Much more important than bed, really."

Everyone was behaving and talking oddly this evening: Miss Richmond would not dream of saying such a thing, as a rule.

"And you never fell in love again?"

"Well . . . I think I do remember being rather silly about somebody once. Just once, it was."

"*How* silly?"

Not to be told; the devouring, absurd devotion: to the children's father (of all people) in her first place: Captain Angus Hale. The name Angus kept its echo.

"I suppose you'd have called it hero worship, more. He never looked at me."

(Not quite true. There was that one time: still remembered: the pouncing and the struggle, the whisky-smelling embrace and the hands.)

"Us unrequited girls don't half suffer," said Miss Richmond, "even in bed. I don't mean you. I mean me. I'm out, Nanny."

"Out, M'm?"

"Out of the family. Out of the show. In September. Out of everything." Her vowel sounds were worse than usual. "I had to tell you before tomorrow. Everybody'll know tomorrow. Philip wanted me to wait—so this is between us, eh? You've always been so good to me, I'll miss you—I'll miss the children—*and how* . . ."

She looked as though she might burst into tears again. Then she jumped from the sill of the loggia and said in a loud voice, "I'm going to be married. Laugh that off!" before she began to twirl in a dance.

"*I'm going to be married, be married, be married!*" sang Miss Richmond. She added, "To Jimmy Evans. He's the little man down there on the tennis court."

From the hall the telephone began to ring. Thomas popped up his head suddenly between the pillars of the loggia, booming, "I say, I'm *frightfully* hungry." Miss Richmond went on dancing, all by herself.

❁

"That'll be your mother," said Miles. He went ahead of Rab to answer the telephone. She sat where she was, at the Corinthian Bagatelle board, making one more shot, since it was her turn. She played a private game along with Corinthian Bagatelle, though she never told anyone. She played it now. "If this ball goes into the five-hundred circle, I'll be on the Vineyard before Christmas." The ball just missed the gap in the pins. She heard Miles saying, "We're both very well and the hotel's remarkably good except for the coffee. We are all on the ground floor, with a very nice view. Except me. Your accommodation will be bed, bath and sitting room; Rab's room opens out of the sitting room and I am in a small cupboard looking out on dustbins. Your daughter has collected a boyfriend. I have no girlfriend. Here's Rab. You'll have to speak up," he told her. "It's a tricky line."

Paula's voice sounded faint and far away: "How are you, stupid?" "Stupid" was of pure affection and Rab loved it. "I'm fine: absolutely fine."

"Seen Philip? We had a gossip late last night and he said he'd call you today."

"Sure, he called. But he didn't *say* anything. He's to call again tomorrow. He sounded funny."

"Scared," said Paula. "Scared of Nanny. I knew how it would be. Not sure I blame him. I tried to get him just now and it was Nanny who answered. She could scare *me*." Then came Paula's sudden roar of laughter, quite loud in her ear. She knew why: Paula was never scared of anything. "You aren't lonely, darling?"

"Goodness, no. Miles and I swam all morning, and I went to the Kiddies' Show with Thomas."

"Thomas *Weston*?"

"Yes, Ma'am."

"Then you met them—" said Paula.

"Just Thomas. With Tubby and Susie and Leo. I only *saw* the others. Sarah's *beautiful*. Know what? Thomas does conjuring tricks *against* the magician. I thought it was an act but it wasn't. Philip gave him hell. I was hiding. He won't say how."

"I can't hear you very well, darling. Can you hear me? This is important. It's about Chester."

"*Chester?*"

"Chester. Can you hear? I found a letter from him at the American Express."

"On your trail, is he?" said Rab with a chuckle.

"On my trail. He may get to England before I do. If he comes through, *don't tell him.*"

"I won't. I won't tell anyone."

"Bless you, my darling; are you eating? Promise? Liar. Stupid. I love you. See you Thursday. Give me Miles again, will you please?"

"Hey. Would it be okay if I went to the picnic tomorrow? Gwen's picnic? With all of them?"

Paula said, "Ask Philip." Which was no help. Miles took over; for instructions about dress boxes and suitcases coming by train to Sawbridge Junction. He grumbled while they resumed their game. "You'd think she had enough clothes," said Miles, "wouldn't you?"

"She loves them. Says she could never have enough clothes or enough children. Six closets full of clothes and six little boys with fair hair. *You* know, you hear her say it." Miles played a ball neatly into the five-hundred circle.

"That Chester," said Rab, "on her trail. Wouldn't you know?"

"Some men are faithful."

"He's in for a shock."

"Life is shocks."

"Your game," said Rab resignedly.

"And time for my drink," said Miles.

"Can't I come to the bar with you?"

"No. Doesn't look right."

"Will you have an adventure?"

"Depends who's in the bar." He stood before the glass, straightening his tie.

"I'll miss you, Miles."

"I won't be long."

"I didn't mean that. I meant after Thursday. You're the last link."

He didn't ask what she meant because he knew. Nor did he make comforting remarks. He merely smiled at her and went. Rab wandered over to the window. She looked down to the rocks and out to sea: the sea was turning white now; the rocks were black and shiny. Any sea was better than no sea. And she was, she admitted, happier than she had been this morning. Some things had changed. She slid her hand into her trouser pocket and drew out the little lion: "That Thomas," said Rab to herself and grinned. She leaned on the window sill, watching the gulls. As far as she could make out they were all asleep on one leg, like small white torpedoes dotted about the weedy rocks. Very dull of them. She leaned further out, looking across the bay. The trees climbing up the hill towards the West Cliff hid the house on that road; hid the red house with the turret and the loggia.

Thinking about Roseclay and the Westons brought her to a puzzle. If you had to move around all the time because you were rich, and this was her experience, why did you have to move around all the time because you were poor? Did anybody really like moving around? She couldn't imagine it. She curled up on the sofa under the window and began to conjure back the Vineyard. She made herself sail into Vineyard Haven on a fine afternoon. Not difficult; she could see the harbor basin, the bright water, the little boats rocking: inland the gray frame houses and the brown church above the green trees. She took herself on, away from the harbor, to the left out of Vineyard Haven, walking the sea road towards Oak Bluffs. She saw the pond and the fishers. She saw the clamshells lying about the road at her feet. One of the big gulls swooped down to pick up a shell in its beak; folding its brown-flecked wings, then running across the road in front of her on its pompous, stilted legs. She grew wings like the gull and skimmed away up-Island, over the trees.

"Off we go, Gwennie," said Mr. Evans, rising from the table. "Thanks for the supper, Nanny. See you all tomorrow. Cheerie-bye." From the depths of her gloom, Sarah considered Mr. Evans. Lancashire accent, squinny little eyes, capable in a boat, friendly as a dog. Despite Leo Clyde's assurance that he was not the new backer, she thought he was. He was obviously rich (another car in the drive, a black Lancia with red wheels). He knew the show by heart. He had stayed to supper and he was nuts about Gwen. She made eyebrow signs at Gerald while Nanny, who seemed unusually remote for the first day, was directing Thomas to bed. "Because *I* say so," reached Sarah's ears, and Thomas's replying, "Oh well."

"You too, Sarah."

"Ten minutes."

"Ten minutes won't do that neurulgia any good."

"It's not too bad." She was dejected by the blow that had fallen to prevent her from seeing Shirley Ormonde again tonight. No good fighting. The sun, the sea, the wind, the date on the calendar, all had conspired against her. The pain was beating more slowly in her head, but it was there.

"You look quite green," said Gerald as the dining-room door shut behind Nanny and Thomas.

"I do not. I look pale, fragile—ethereal. I might faint. We *must* talk."

Gerald sat down on the window seat and plunked his ukulele.

"Gwen's tight," was his contribution.

"Not very. Anyway we were wrong, weren't we?"

"You were . . ." He played "Bye, Bye, Blackbird." He could sing in tune, which irritated her:

> "No one here to love or understand me—
> Oh what hard luck stories they all hand me."

"In my view, Mr. Evans-call-me-Jimmy has put all his fortune into Moonrakers and is about to marry Gwen," said Sarah.

"Well, why's everybody keeping bloödy trap shüt?" Gerald asked, imitating the Lancashire accent. "And what's biting Brigstock?"

"Father had a long brew with her in the drawing room."

"Breaking the news." Gerald made a Philip-face, dropped his chin towards his collar and murmured in a treacly voice, "Nanny, I want you to be the first to know that dear old Gwen has ceased to be my mistress."

"*Was* she?" asked Sarah, stunned. Gerald didn't answer that. He stood up and said violently, "I like Evans. I admire Evans. Admire him. Even if he *did* play tennis in his braces. Which I saw you notice and deplore, don't think I didn't." She was bothered by the sneer on his face, the sudden anger. Her head throbbed.

"Don't you see—" said Gerald, white and pointing a finger, "a chap like that, starting from nothing, earning good wages at fourteen—*is* to be admired? Better than trying to be ladies and gentlemen on other peoples' money, isn't it?"

"Well, all right."

"Weren't you listening to him in the boat? No, you weren't. I could tell you weren't."

He frightened her in this mood: so she lied, "Of course I was." She had missed the life story of Mr. Evans-call-me-Jimmy because she had been chasing a dream of silver lamé and roses.

"Well, then," said Gerald.

All she could remember was something about going to Australia in the cook's galley. And now he owned a chain of hotels and restaurants. The fury of Gerald went on: Ladies and Gentlemen: fakes and snobs: money and debts and money. All sparked off by Mr. Evans.

She said, "You're a snob yourself. You talk about oicks and cads and *you* noticed his braces or you wouldn't have mentioned them." Having scored this point, she decided to play her exit in Third Act fashion, murmuring, "Ah God, my head," on a cello note and contriving to reel as she went to the door. (Might as well make the most of what Brigstock called neurulgia.) Leaning back against the lintel she said, "If I die tonight, remember I have no regrets. I have laughed, I have loved, I have been happy with all of it." Gerald was paying no attention. He had returned to his ukulele, standing with one foot on the window seat, plunking "Bye-Bye, Blackbird." He looked lonely and grown-up: there was something of Philip in his pose, a Moon-rakers quality, the last thing—she thought—he would wish to hear. She shut the door on him, trailing across the hall.

"If I die tonight," she continued, clasping her head. It was a thing she often expected to do, though in the imagined event, she herself was there and watching from some corner of the room while the beautiful dead Sarah lay back on her pillow, mourned by all. (Miss Ormonde would linger by the bed, putting a red rose into the cold hand, saying, "How I wish I could have known her.")

❂

Thomas awoke and thought about the dream. On the whole, he decided, not. There had been a glimpse, a moment with the two theatres in it (and Perry Potter, surely), but he hadn't, in his own terms, got there. He was just conscious of a flavor, an echo. If he had really got there, he would remember.

It was quite dark. Despite his protest Brigstock had drawn the curtains at both windows. He groped on the chair beside the bed for his electric torch and promptly knocked it onto the floor. He heard it roll. Making as little noise as he could (although to judge by the feel of things it was late and everyone asleep) he crawled after the torch.

The battery was nearly dead. When he pressed the switch it brought a pale yellow ring of light, no more. He looked back in memory to the broad whiteness of the beam when it was new. But this was enough to guide him across the floor; to identify the window curtains. He pulled them aside. He saw the dark tops of trees and a starry sky. The sash window was open. He pushed it higher and leaned out. A light wind blew in the garden: the trees were moving. He thought he could hear the sea, though it was on the other side of the house and far down. Something sighed, anyway; went on sighing and the sigh beckoned him.

He could never say to himself, "Shall I or shan't I?" When this thing happened, this broad-awake and all-alone thing for which he had no name, he wasn't the decider; the thing was. Obedient to it, he began to dress himself. He put on everything except his socks and thrust his notebook into his blazer pocket. With infinite caution, he turned the doorknob. The light was out on this landing; he could see no light coming up from the lower floors, but he went warily. The thing, he had noticed, gave him a sense of direction. It halted his foot on the last step of any flight of stairs; it guided him past obstacles without letting him bump; it made him far less clumsy than he was by day.

Still, the stairs creaked too much for his liking. And when he reached the first-floor landing he was awfully aware of his father asleep in the vast new bedroom, three yards away. He took the longest possible steps. At least the darkness now was negligible; no curtains hung over the tall window above the last flight: he could see the outline of the banister rail. Safer to slide down, could he be sure of a soundless arrival at the other end. But he couldn't be sure. The stair carpet was helpful, thicker and softer than it used to be. (Why were Gerald and Sarah so certain that he had forgotten this house?)

Here came the last step and his instinct led him towards the dining room. The door stood open. The room was a shadowy shell with here and there a glint or a gleam: glass or china or polished wood. Thomas sniffed the room. Roses, food, a trace of tobacco and the slightly stuffy background-smell made by carpets and curtains and furniture at night.

He paused in the doorway, spying upon the room. It was Thomas's view that when there were no people about, things might well behave differently. Under cover of the dark, alone, they could do as they liked. A sudden light now could catch table and chairs hurriedly reassembling, getting back to their daytime positions. Couldn't it?

He decided against testing the theory. He moved towards the window seat; he knelt there, opening one casement laboriously, pushing it wide and looking out into the garden. The song, he realized, had been in his head for some time, though he hadn't noticed its coming. It was the night song. Only a rag of tune wrapped the words about:

I didn't go looking for gold and silver,
By the light of the moon, by the light of the stars.

He climbed up onto the casement sill and sat there swinging his legs. The wind was louder at this level. The garden was full of rustling noises. Leopards and tigers and deer and the unicorn going by.

"Look how the lovely animals come leaping," he said. He was content to watch for a while, becoming aware as he did so of the presence behind him in the room; not looking back lest he disturb it: they did not like to be disturbed. Besides, he rarely saw them; he simply knew them to be about. He could know this also in daytime, but that was his concern and seemed to have no interest for them. Like himself, they were different at night: the difference, in his opinion, being that now they knew he was here.

Thomas slid off the sill, down into the dream jungle which instantly changed back to the garden. There was a soggy flower bed underfoot: the leaves of the hydrangea felt cold as he brushed through. He crossed the gravel path and came to the grass slope that dipped towards the tennis court. He stood at the top of the slope, tilting his head far back to gaze at the stars.

When he was smaller, he had had no doubts that the place he called There was above the stars. "There" was up: he had climbed to it by way of a ladder. In these days he was more doubtful: entirely doubtful now, staring aloft into the hugeness of the sky with the unending, clustering, dizzying stars. And the notion of There, always hard to keep in his head, was becoming more elusive. When he tried to assemble the landscape it shredded away. Gloomily he wondered if he might soon lose track of it altogether. Certainly he got there less and less often. Didn't he? "Oh well," said Thomas, aloud and on a note of resignation. He went down the grass slope.

Here, where the tennis court was, the wild garden used to be. Brigstock had told him that: no need: he could remember the wild garden. It was one of those memories, however, that had too much of himself in it, blotting out the picture: himself crawling through green tangles that grew higher than his head. A game played with a wooden sword: not his own sword: it must have been given to Gerald or Sarah. The sword took over; there was a red silk tassel tied to the hilt and a voice, Brigstock's perhaps, saying, "Here's your wooden sword, come at last." Who had longed so much for the sword? Since this kind of thinking was for the day rather than the night, he let it go.

Striding over the tennis court, he reached another slope and this took him down. He had come to the trees. He was over his ankles in fern and ground ivy: the going became harder. That agitated rustle meant a rabbit. Flashing his torch he found the first long gnarled root growing out above the earth and moss: the root they used to call the Crocodile. This, then, was the big oak tree: all its huge roots spread out around it. Leaning his back against the tree, he slid down, to discover that the division of the roots still made a comfortable chair. Having proved this point, he got up again and slid down several times. Doing so, he dropped the notebook out of his pocket: hunting for it he grubbed up a handful of old acorn cups. He flicked them, one by one, off the top of his hand, into the dark.

> *I didn't go looking for gold and silver,*
> *By the light of the moon, by the light of the stars.*

What did one go looking for? Nothing in particular. Just the night, perhaps. He was done with the oak tree. Now he set off, back towards the house, by the side path that zigzagged upward and ended at the lily pond. The lily pond was different: not the pond that had made for his misadventure of yesterday: a round, darkened mirror, looking quite solid, glimmering faintly between the clusters of flat leaves. Thomas kneeled on the stone rim. He heard a delicious plop; that was a frog, but he couldn't see the frog. He leaned over to press the palm of his hand down on a large leaf until the leaf dipped under the water and the water rose to his wrist. He stood up, drying his hand on the front of his shirt.

He was just thinking, "That's all for now," instructed, as ever, that the night journey was ending, when a bird gave a single chirup from the lilacs close to the wall. Then the beginning of dawn took him by surprise. He stood on the flower bed under the open casement: he watched it come.

There was the lower crouch of the sky, the dimming of the stars. Over to his right, a gray-gold streak far down, the sky's rim seen through a gap. It all came on, the dark turning to gray, giving back the drowned, misty and private shapes of the trees. He grew colder and colder, but he had to stay here watching. He felt his teeth chatter: he could not leave the returning garden. This he had never seen before. One bird took the cue from another; the single notes shot up and sank and came again like signals through the leaves.

"My goodness," said Thomas. Shivering all over, he darted round the side of the house: here in a grayish hollow light were the rose bushes; the monkey-puzzle tree. Over the road he could see the pines and the place where the path began, the path leading down the cliff to the beach.

He had the knowledge that all this could belong to him, that if he crossed the road and climbed down, there would be splendor waiting at the edge of the sea. But he was cold: he felt his body losing power and will. He was growing heavier; stripped of his night armor, clumsy as the owl that blinked and flapped its way home. He was no match for the dawn.

VII

~~~~~~~~~~~~~~~~~~~~~~~

Philip Weston looked at the clock and thought, "It's not fair." Sunday morning was for sleeping late. The time was only a quarter past six; and here he lay, wide-awake, lonely in the large bed. All over his body he could feel the slight aching left by the party; too much whisky had been drunk with the cads from Torquay.

"Like Lord Byron, I wake in low spirits," he told himself. It was true. At this hour he failed in all his favorite roles: the Laughing Philosopher, the Gay Cavalier, the Regency Rake, the Lucky Fellow. He could not be any of these. All he could find in himself was an uneasy Puritan; whose predecessors had left behind them a sediment of worry and fear.

Nonsense. I am the happiest man in the world. All's well. I

have left the troubled waters behind. I am in love. Oh, my love, I love you. And I would love you if you hadn't a penny to bless yourself with. Wouldn't I? Oh, come back and prove it to me. Come quickly. When you go, you take yourself with you so completely: you take your dazzle and your magic most of all. I remember loving you and then I remember the shortness of your temper, the jarring note of your laugh, all your childish strength set against my will, because that amuses you. And I am afraid. And I go on thinking how rich you are.

But only five days to wait. And you will come as you truly are and exorcise your intimidating ghost.

So we may as well go on worrying, let worry take over, go to meet worry, drown in worry: let it all come. This is its hour.

He stretched out, flat on his back, with his hands behind his head, inviting the monsters to move in. Truth, he said to himself, the most important thing, as I always tell the kids: how can I admire truth so passionately and fall so short of it? Truth: integrity: living in the sun. Like Gwen. Dear old Gwen. Well, she is sad, but she says so. She isn't in love with little Evans, she still loves me, but she tells him the truth. And that common little fellow takes it like an angel, accepts it, knows he can make her happy after a fashion: devotes himself to picking up the pieces. Cards on the table for Gwennie and little Evans. And they will be good friends always.

I ditched Gwen because I fell in love. (That was integrity, wasn't it? Surely? Perhaps integrity is something one only sees in somebody else.) Damned if I see how I'm going to replace her in the show . . . *How good is Moonrakers 1926?* Magnificent. If those tired old Co-Optimists think they can do it again, they've got a surprise coming to them. Reopening at His Majesty's, August 23rd, eh? We'll be putting them out of business in September. Won't we? *Will you?*

Of course it's good: superlatively good. Magic, sophistication, beauty, wit: taste. *Who said taste? Granted, it's a lot less tatty than the other shows on the road. But how good is your taste? And your judgment?* I'm always right: what are you grinning at?

What *is* the thing in Gerald's pocket? That boy has too many secrets: Gerald, with the new sneer on his face, the withdrawal, the refusal to confide. What's his demon? What does he want from the world? Why won't he tell me? I'd back him up; he's like me. *But not like you.*

Well, we can shoot the worry straight away from Gerald (nice thing about worry is you can let it land anywhere) and we can turn it to Perry Potter: something wrong with his act, almost every time. He's a genius two-thirds of the way and then he fails to pay it off. What's the matter with him? *Would it be integrity?* No, sir. Don't tell me it's integrity that lets a top conjuror be thrown by Thomas.

Thomas, of all people.

". . . the most baffling boy I've had to deal with in all my years at Puxford."

God help me, it's Sunday and I've got to talk to Thomas. Not this morning, not oh not, oh never in the morning. This evening. (When the Laughing Philosopher, the Gay Cavalier, the Regency Rake or the Lucky Fellow would be in command again.) This evening, he thought, about six o'clock. Picnic over—drink time: *didn't you say you were going to Evensong?* Well, yes, I always do say that. Makes me feel better about not going to Matins.

What the devil do I say to Thomas? Somebody ought to have strangled the grandmother long ago. All her fault.

When are you going to tell Nanny? Today. She'll be pleased. Bless her. What would we have done without her all these years? Devotion, that is: selfless devotion: undemanding love. When Nanny dies I shall put in the *Times* "For years the beloved and devoted—" Ought I to ask her how much I really owe her in back wages? She'd be furious, wouldn't she? Better not ask. A check: a bonus: a birthday present. When's her birthday? *When are you going to tell her?* Oh, shut up; this evening sometime. It's Sunday.

You said you'd telephone Rab today.

So I must, poor little monkey. What a notion, parking her at the Rivermouth with Miles. Shady character, if ever I met one. Thank God he's going. Eunuch: how dare Paula compare him with Nanny? Blasphemy, that is.

I could go down and see Rab before lunch, just look in, make sure she's all right. No need for them to mix yet, the kids. As I said to Gerald, we all want a little time to settle down.

In Roseclay. Dear old Roseclay. *Back in the house you shared with your dead wife, paid for by Paula.* Oh, shut up. Last time we were here, it was paid for by Percy. *Well, is that a consolation?* Sort of, I don't know why. Poor darling Isobel wouldn't mind anyway. She knew me. She always said, "You're hopeless," but she loved me. And she knows I've done the right thing by the kids.

They can have a home now. They can have a dog. I've always wanted them to have a dog.

We've got a car.

Come on, Philip, sun's shining, you can't sleep again and you're king of the castle. *Because you've sold yourself.* Balls. We're going to make a mint this summer. Pay Paula back every penny.

He got out of bed, stretched all over and felt the ache again and cursed the cads from Torquay. But for them the term "cads" was an endearment; old comrades from the R.F.A.: his comrades in arms. They didn't look like themselves any more: but they brought their old looks with them. Floppy khaki caps, Sam Browne belts, the light-colored breeches and puttees. The swashbucklers from Mons and Loos and the Somme. (When I think about that, my cheek begins to twitch, funny thing.)

He put on his blazing new dressing gown. The little haunt, the war nightmare, went through his heavy head: a ritual dance of memory, bringing fear and bringing, sharper than the fear, the sense of astonishment: *I* was in that: *I* did those things: *I.* (With an M.C. and a gold wound-stripe to prove the facts: but you couldn't do it again and it felt as though the person who had done it wasn't you at all.)

He went quietly down the stairs. The Lucky Fellow was beginning to return. Thoughts of war had beckoned him. The lucky fellow, invalided out after the Somme: meeting Tubby Whittington (companion of a dugout in '15), working with Tubby on the first concept of *High Jinks.* The lucky fellow who had found the backers; who had somehow survived the bad patches every time:

whose talents had danced him out of trouble again and again. The lucky fellow finding Gwen: spotting her as a winner: making her as good as she was. *Meeting Paula?* Yes, that too, the last and the best.

He went into the kitchen. He smiled upon it because it was so new and white and opulent. While he boiled the kettle for his tea, the Lucky Fellow moved nearer; not wholly in possession yet, so Philip could still look at him with detachment, with a certain awe: with a glad, strengthening protest against any accusation of deliberate fortune hunting. There was sometimes a doubtful customer about, an adventurer whom he saw cashing in on other people's money, spending it with an air; and this character was privately christened Gentleman Jim. But I've never gone out after the good things, he thought; they've come to me.

I never knew Paula was rich. No idea of it: saw her across the dance floor and thought, "You're beautiful," and the thing began the way it always begins, the magic ripple on the air. I didn't know, when I asked her to dance, what I was finding. (And I'll always love that Folkestone hotel; its band playing "Ukulele Lady"; its Saturday afternoon *thé dansant,* where the lightning struck, all among the little tables and cakes and cucumber sandwiches. With a howling draught through the long windows, the east wind driving the rain across the Leas: the full horror of the English spring.)

"Will you dance with me?"

"Why—yes, Mr. Adair."

"You know who I am."

"I saw your show at the Pavilion last night."

"You did?"

"Does that surprise you?"

"I'd have thought you'd be bored."

"I was, some of the time." And the great shout of jarring laughter.

As he poured his cup of tea, Philip said to himself, to the threat of Gentleman Jim: "Well, there you are. I just happened to find her. I didn't go looking."

He drank the tea and found it delicious. Any minute now,

surely, Mrs. Gale or Nanny would descend upon the kitchen: he must escape, because the phrase "I didn't go looking" had brought some bars of music with it: beginning of a melody. He wasn't a composer in the true sense of the word, like Tubby, but the melodies came and he could trust Tubby to harmonize them, set them up.

> *"I didn't go looking for gold or silver*
> *I didn't set sail in a pirate ship."*

Nice, that. The pirate motif was exactly right for the Moonrakers. Humming the phrase, he refilled his cup, left the teapot on the kitchen table and went out through the baize door. The new drawing room, with the curtains drawn and the streaks of early sunshine between, the shadow-grouping of all the things in the room, was full of an unexpected gentleness. He wouldn't draw the curtains back to let in the blaring colors. He put his cup on the piano and sat on the stool: picking out the melody with one finger:

> *"I—didn't—go—looking—for—gold—or—silver*
> Te—*tum*-titty—*tum*—titty—*tum*—tee—tum."

Leaning back, using both hands now, finding a chord that was right, then another, sounding them out, becoming master of the melody, he was extremely happy. The words must follow. How did one rhyme with "ship"? A cigarette would help. As he crossed to the table where the china cigarette box was, he remembered breaking the china shepherdess last evening, talking to Nanny. He drooped a little. Oh, well: he could pay for anything now. At the table, he halted. On the plump sofa, shadowy but visible, there was something peculiar. A hummock: a bundle. Two of the fat cushions were dislodged and lying down, covering a shape; at least covering its head and feet: the middle of the shape could be seen. "What the devil—?" Philip began. The baffling structure heaved: one cushion fell on the floor; his son Thomas sat up and looked at him.

"What the devil do you think *you're* doing?"

Thomas gave a yawn, followed by a sneeze. He said, "Well, I was cold. So I put the cushions on top."

"Why are you down here?"

Thomas frowned. "Were you playing a tune" he asked, "or was I just dreaming it?"

"Answer *my* question, old boy, eh?"

Thomas looked at him warily and said nothing at all. He removed the second cushion from his feet. Exasperated, Philip plunged to the window and drew back the curtains. The room revealed in brightness was too much for him. So was Thomas, sitting fully dressed, tousled and blinking on the sofa, saying,

"Oh well, I went for a walk. Will that do?"

"No, it won't do," said Philip. "It won't do at all. Put your mind at rest on that point. You've been walking about all night? *Again?*"

"No, I haven't. I got up for a bit and then I saw the dawn: and I knew I'd make noises and wake everybody up, so I stayed down here." He added, "Why did you say 'again'?"

"I've had a letter about you, chum."

"Oh. From Mr. Appleby?"

"Yes. Mr. Appleby." Philip felt his hangover coming back. He was aware of himself, standing here, unshaven in the sunshine, with the hideous colors all about him, with the tune shot out of his head and a draught blowing round his bare ankles. He couldn't do Thomas now: not for anything. He said, "I want you to come to the study—"

"All right; can I pee first?"

"Don't interrupt, old boy, it's rude. I was going to say come to the study at six o'clock this evening."

"Right you are," said Thomas.

"And now go back to bed."

"Are *you* going back to bed?"

"Yes," said Philip. "Oh yes, I am. Oh indeed I am."

❀

The time, when Philip came downstairs again, was a quarter to eleven. He had shaved, bathed, dressed, had his breakfast in bed and lain low till they went. All should be quiet now, but was not, because of the church bells. Sawcombe, surely, owned more than its fair share of churches. He wondered where they all were. He had never seen more than one, the Parish Church at the top of Galleon Street: to which Nanny was now shepherding the children. (*Ought to have taken them in the car.* Shut up.) All the other churches remained unidentified, becoming wildly audible one day a week from seven fifty-five onwards. He stood in the hall by the telephone, hearing the assorted carillons reproach him with their pious discord. (Evensong? No: I have to talk to Thomas.)

With a groan, he picked up the telephone and asked for the Rivermouth Hotel. Having got it, he asked to speak to Rab. After a long time a voice told him that she had gone out in the car. A reprieve: he felt absolved and dutiful. Since she was in the car, Miles also had put himself blessedly out of reach. Unless, of course, Rab was driving herself which wouldn't, he decided, surprise him.

Here he realized that he had not completed the worry circuit. Rab was the next stop. Rab worried him profoundly in terms of past and future.

A child of twelve, who had never been to school: who was a world traveler and could mix a dry martini: a child of divorce: a child who had, despite these dooms, no appearance of sophistication and few graces. A wild one: *farouche* was the word that came to his mind. The worry tune skirled and screamed, "What will Nanny think?" He turned it off. Rab was a darling and all would be well.

He gave the telephone one more uneasy glance; he hoped Paula would ring before they came back from church. The telephone had become a guilt focus. It stood there on the hall table, with its black arm hanging in the socket, and its black mouth screaming, "*What will Nanny think?*" Why should it do this? Why should it seem to be on Nanny's side against him? Nanny didn't even like it. She was frightened of it. Her note, left for him last night, had read: "I'm sorry, but somebody seemed to be trying to get you from abroad. They will ring again. Hope I haven't been silly, but couldn't hear v. well." (Paula, at midnight, saying, "Hardly liked to leave my name" and roaring with laughter. No question: Paula thoroughly enjoyed this game of hide-and-seek they were playing—had played now for nearly two months. It was her idea of fun.)

I'll tell Nanny tonight. That's a vow. After I've done Thomas. No, she'll be getting the supper. After supper. That's a vow.

He went back to the drawing room, to the piano: he sat there trying to find the melody again: "I *didn't* go looking for . . ." No use. The words were still with him but the melody had blown away. It would come back. He strolled out through the hall and presently settled himself on the loggia, looking at the new car in the drive, feeling better about everything. In another hour the picnic party would be storming the gate, Gwen and little Evans, Tubby, Susie . . . Damn: General Stevens, a panama hat and two square shoulders in a gray jacket, was cruising past the hedge. Philip had begun to duck his head when the old man saw him. The old man (three generations of the Stevens family seemed rather too many) waved his walking stick and came up the drive.

"Good morning, Weston. What a perfectly glorious morning." Philip got to his feet: he adopted a threatening, majestic pose, grasping a pillar with each hand.

"I hope I don't intrude. I really have a most valuable word to say about the wireless." The General stood at the foot of the loggia steps. He took off his hat, revealing his narrow, silvered skull and domed forehead of papery tobacco-color. His eyes were pale blue and heavily pouched: the moustache hid most of his mouth: his neck narrowed down into a nest of wrinkles above the stiff collar.

He said, "Do *you* find you get a lot of interference from ships' Morse?"

"Do I?" said Philip. "No."

"Really not? When you're trying to get Two L.O., I mean? You're quite free from it? That's remarkable. I wonder why. Oh well, in that case you won't need my little tip. I had a word with the Post Office and they say the answer is to keep tuned to Daventry. It's quite usual at the seaside, this crackling. They have had a lot of similar inquiries, it seems. I must say I'm relieved. I was so disappointed; we all were. I was thinking it might be due to the lack of a loudspeaker. I insisted we should leave it behind, out of consideration for others, neighbors, I mean, and use the headphones. Then again, I thought it might be something to do with this business of the aerial and the window sill, height from the ground and so on. Now at home, at Kettering—I wonder if this is your experience—"

One would rather be anything than bored, Philip said to himself. Why don't I just tell the old fool I haven't got a wireless set? This was the truth but now he seemed to have left it too late. He had given himself an imaginary wireless set: idiotic. He could say he must go to fetch the children from church, but that would mean missing the Paris call. He settled for boredom: he found a crumb of happiness in reflecting that though Paula might exasperate, terrorize, or bring the thought of Gentleman Jim too close for comfort, she could never be a bore.

❁

Rab had adjusted the field glasses to perfection. This was a most amusing game: to bring one face after another into the glass circles, so near, so large, that it came as a surprise to lower the glasses for a moment and find the true picture. In the true picture she saw the picnic party, down there on the sands of the cove. She had crept between the trees like an Indian, tunneled through the high, tough grass, the gorse and ferns on the cliff, to make herself a hide-out at the edge. Here she lay flat, with the grasses arching up around her. A wigwam. Nobody looking up would see her, though the sun might reflect an occasional flash from the two round glass spy-holes.

In the matter of right and wrong, Rab knew herself to be pretty hazy. Either she was stupid about this, or somebody had failed to explain. Her mother's ideas of conduct had never tallied with her father's ideas. And she had never been to school to test any of them out.

Paula's program of good behavior was short and stern. It prescribed manners, telling the truth and, above all, being physically brave. The English books, Paula's choice, insisted upon courage. *Knights of the Table Round, Land and Sea Tales, The Book of Golden Deeds, Legends of Greece and Rome*, even *True Dog Stories* held the virtue high. Rab had learned their lessons. She could bear pain without crying and this pleased Paula. It meant nothing to her father, who was, in Rab's view, an engaging sissy. He was forever fussing about his health, about germs and dirt and draughts, about Miles driving too fast on corners. (He was also scared of dogs: with the result that they usually bit him; even a spaniel who never bit anyone had bitten Daddy.) Her father had told her with increasing frequency that the only important thing in life was to be kind: not to hurt other people's feelings. The meaning of this rule she had in time discovered. Paula was unkind and Daddy was the Other People whose feelings got hurt. When she added it up, her education so far consisted of Paula teaching her to be less like Daddy and Daddy instructing her to be less like Paula.

Neither of them had, in her recollection, said anything about spying on people through field glasses. It simply hadn't come up. But that it wouldn't square with the Golden Doers or King Arthur's Knights she now felt quite certain. Nor was she considering other peoples' feelings. The feelings she was considering seemed to be her own. Miles, shrugging and looking contemptuous had asked, "What's your worry?" He had been quite prepared to drive her to Roseclay and inflict her upon the Westons. He had argued the morning away while they drove and swam. "You are invited. You go," said Miles again and again, ending with, "*Tu es sotte, tu sais*," and departing in search of an adventure. She had been here, it seemed, for hours and hours.

The cove was a V-shaped strip of sand widening out towards the water where the rocks began. The slopes of the cliff were gentle and overgrown. You could make your way down by a choice of zigzags, through grass tussocks and sea pinks to the beach.

On the sand, the group had spread themselves and their belongings. Gwen's boyfriend had brought a large stripy umbrella and set it up for shade above the tablecloth. They had long ago finished eating. They lay around, a carefree encampment. She could hear the ukulele, Gerald strumming "Bye, Bye, Blackbird." She could see Thomas, a whitish head and a reddish face; a striped singlet: he was lying flat on his back. Leo Clyde had built a sandcastle over his feet and legs: he couldn't move without disturbing the castle. She had located Nanny: not the jailer of her imagination, but quite small and old, wearing a blue cotton dress and perched on a campstool. Rab brought Nanny's head into the circle of glass. It came, as they all came, ringed by a pale rainbow. There was nothing alarming about Nanny's face; narrow but cheerful, blue-eyed and pink-cheeked. She was talking to Tubby now: the voices echoed up with the music. Sometimes Rab could hear what they said; sometimes the words blew away.

She had heard Gwen and Gwen's boyfriend announce that they were to be married. She had heard the champagne cork popping. One sip had made Thomas sneeze. Cameras had come out, to take snapshots of Gwen and the boyfriend posing with their arms around each other. Tubby had sung "Who is Sylvia?"

Why didn't anybody swim again? The water was as she liked it, lively and loud, breaking into short waves on the rocks. Only Philip and Gerald had dived from the high rock. She considered the pleasing fact that she could swim as well as any of them, and better. She longed to swim. Though the air was cool, this endless watch among the dry grasses made her feel dusty, thirsty.

She brought Sarah close again, Sarah sitting up with her arms around her knees, talking to Philip. (How long ago yesterday was: yesterday with its image of the poor, dirty, starving Westons.) Sarah wasn't swimming. For the grown-up reason, possibly. Sarah's face, in the rainbow ring, gave her the utmost pleasure, so beautifully vivid and alight, with the dark hair blown and the mouth laughing. Her heart was given to Sarah.

Thomas sat up and sneezed. He sneezed very loudly. He had done it several times already, quite apart from the champagne. Nanny rose from the campstool to give him a clean handkerchief.

Well, thought Rab, time to be going. She couldn't watch them forever. She gave them all one last sweep with the glasses, taking in Gwen's bright blue sun hat, Tubby's orange cummerbund, Jimmy Evans' fuzzy chest, and a number of other fascinating details like the red-and-white-check pattern of the stuff that Nanny was sewing and Sarah's lemon-colored sweater, lying close to Sarah's hand. Wistfully, she shut up the field glasses in their leather case. When she knelt upright she was seized with cramp in the stomach and toppled over, backwards.

A fatal error. She had kicked the precious glasses, not hers but Paula's, and they slid inexorably down a long sandy funnel; down, down, coming finally to rest against a tussock. Peering from the wigwam, she could see them, ten yards below. Easy enough to climb down to their rescue. But she would then be entirely visible to the picnic party. "Wouldn't you know?" said Rab, kneading her stomach to get rid of the cramp.

There was the sound of voices coming nearer: upwards: Thomas's voice saying, "I don't feel ill *at all*. Not in the least ill. I feel rather nice and bubbly in the head. It's only one of my heavy colds. I always get one of my heavy colds about now. Nobody need worry. Sea water's good for colds. You said so. *Why* must I—?"

"Because I want to take your temperature. Besides, everybody's going home. The picnic's over."

"Oh *phooey*." They came past her lair. She had a glimpse of Thomas with a flaming red face; a glimpse of Nanny's blue cotton skirt, before other voices echoed up. Yes, the whole cavalcade: first Leo Clyde singing

> *"You want to watch me,*
> *I'm the one,*
> *One-one-one who's out for fun,*
> *One who likes the girls,*
> *Oh, oh, oh, oh, all the girls—*
> *You want to watch me."*

After him, Tubby came panting and puffing up the slope. Gwen toppled into view, halting suddenly to shriek, "There's a *wasp* in my whatsit!" Loud yells of laughter sounded. Crouched in her tunnel, Rab wriggled slowly backward, a few inches at a time lest they should hear the rustling. Now she saw Sarah's head and shoulders; almost on a level with her own face: Sarah must have come up by a nearer zigzag.

"If she looks this way—" Rab said to herself, "we're sunk." But Sarah was looking down. The deep, fascinating voice called, "Gerald. Would that be a pair of binoculars?"

"Where? Oh, I see. It would, Madam. It would indeed. Treasure Trove." Gerald's head appeared now. "A legacy from the sickening Stevenses, I make no doubt. Herewith impounded by Rabindranath Tagore." Swinging them by their strap, he went out of sight with Sarah. She could hear their voices fading away above her, through the trees, across the road.

Only Philip still to come. And this was surely an occasion, if not for a golden deed, at least for courage, for facing the music. (Gerald had Paula's field glasses. No solution presented itself. But why, oh why, had she not accosted Gerald and Sarah? That would have been much easier than this. "Slow-witted, that's me," thought Rab, "Paula says I'm slow-witted. She's right. She always is.")

She could still run after them, couldn't she? No. Here was Philip.

❀

"Hullo, Rab," said Philip. The sight of her added no more to a conscience already loaded. She had been on his mind all day: so she might as well be there, standing at the top of the cliff to confront him: Rab in the flesh, brown and dusty, with her short pale hair and her blue Breton trousers and the knife dangling at her belt. For once she wasn't slouching. She stood stiffly, with her arms at her sides and her chin raised. The pose conjured up firing squads, burning decks and Gallant Little Belgium. Did she expect him to hit her?

"May I have the field glasses back, please? They're Paula's, you see." Her face was as guilty as his own would be—if he let it.

"Field glasses?"

"Gerald has them. I kicked them down the cliff by mistake."

"Bird-watching?" he asked, knowing about Rab and birds.

"No," said Rab; her cheeks flushed through the brown: "Watching you-all."

"Why didn't you come down?"

"Are you mad at me?"

"No of course not."

"Paula would be."

"Why?"

She shrugged her shoulders. He saw that she bore him no malice for neglecting her; she now began to look happy. When he sat down on the grass she doubled up quickly and squatted beside him. He filled his pipe.

"It isn't that I want to leave you out," he said.

"That's okay. I'm okay, Philip. Better wait till Nanny knows."

He glanced at her sharply. She looked solemn, not impertinent.

"I shall tell Nanny tonight," he said, with dignity.

Rab scratched her head. "Know what? *I* wouldn't. I'd let Paula do the telling."

A disgraceful and acceptable notion. He blinked at it.

"She enjoys handling situations," said Rab.

"You're using very grown-up words, aren't you?"

"I got those two from Daddy: he knows her ways quite well."

Philip wasn't, he decided, in the mood for hearing about Daddy. He said, "So do I."

"I didn't mean to be fresh. I just thought it was more sensible for her to do something she'd enjoy than for you to do something you wouldn't enjoy."

"A logical approach," said Philip wryly.

"She'll do it fine," the child assured him, "because it's *new*. It's 'All Change Here.' Chester says that's her motto in life."

Philip wasn't, he decided, in the mood to hear about Chester. But Rab went straight on: "Chester told her she must have been born on the subway. She slapped his face. He only laughed. Chester always laughs. Does Paula slap your face?"

Feeling as though he were a disc being played on a gramophone at full speed with a scratchy needle, Philip said, "No.

And she'd better not try." Down the hill he heard a car's horn hoot three times.

"There's Miles," said Rab, getting up. "Goodbye, Philip. Maybe you can leave the field glasses at the Fundrome for me tomorrow?"

He cried despairingly, "You won't come in and meet them all?" and was relieved when she shook her head, saying, "Guess I'll wait for Paula."

VIII

"Moonrakers, moonrakers!
Masters of laughter, the melody makers,
Wandering minstrels, the givers, the takers!"

From her seat, a good one in the fourth row, Sarah watched them devotedly. It was her third visit to the Fundrome. There was wind and rain outside: all the lights on the silver and blue were the brighter for knowing this: she felt protected, here in the smoky dark, facing the cave of colors.

"I have eyes for only one," she thought. To love like this was to love all: to love not only the person but the silver dress, the red roses, the silver shoes. All were separate loves. She loved with her eyes. It was a savage ecstasy. Down below she was marvelously sad: still longing and hoping. Perhaps this afternoon would bring luck. She had prepared for it once again: putting on her best clothes and the red sandals, with a raincoat over the best clothes and goloshes over the sandals until she reached the magic place; the raincoat was now stripped off; the goloshes were on the floor beside her feet: the buckle on one of the sandals was working loose. Brigstock had said, "I shouldn't wear those." She had hurt Brigstock by refusing to wear the new red and white check overall. ("Oh Sarah—and I sat up late on purpose to finish it.") That made her feel mean, but one couldn't—could one?—risk wearing a homemade overall for Shirley. It was easy to turn her mind from the picture of Brigstock laying down the new overall disappointedly, because the adored image was right before her eyes.

Oh my darling, Sarah thought, I must meet you today: I have fought to get here. An exaggeration, but there was already a certain threat on the family air, a question mark for her devotion to *Moonrakers 1926*. She had set out for the cinema with Gerald and then abandoned him at the bus stop, saying airily, "Oh—I forgot. Wednesday's early closing: there'll be an afternoon show." In any case he was expecting to meet the inimical young man Morris and had no need of her.

Oh my darling . . . and now you shimmer away through the blue curtains and it is like all the lights going out and there are two long boring bits before I see you again. As Gwen and Philip took possession of the stage, she consoled herself with a piece of toffee, and presently with a fantasy wherein Shirley Ormonde was feeling faint, reclining on a sofa in her dressing room while Sarah bathed her forehead. There was another fantasy wherein she, Sarah, fainted in Shirley's dressing room and came to on the sofa to find Shirley bathing her forehead.

Since there was still no information about the husband in Bristol, she had been obliged to create him. He was tall and fair, with Lazy Blue Eyes and Finely-Chiseled Features. His name was Lionel. His nightly telephone call to the Wayne Court Hotel was an agony of love. The separation was agony to them both.

The city of Bristol had acquired an importance of its own. When Sarah read the word Bristol in the newspaper there was a halo round it. The Wayne Court Hotel wore a halo too. Yesterday she had contrived to take a walk to it. The hotel stood apart in its garden, up at the back of the town: a red stone building, tall

and thin and Gothic-looking. Not a magic place at all, but Leo
Clyde had said "far from cheap." Perhaps the rooms were beautiful. Or there was at least one beautiful room, white-paneled and
exquisitely furnished, smelling of Shirley's scent.

On the stage Susie was singing "Turn Into a Turnip."

One weekend Lionel would come over from Bristol: Sarah
would be invited to lunch at the Wayne Court. After she had
gone, Lionel and Shirley would talk about her endlessly. She
would become their best friend and they would be broken-
hearted when she died. She would die after saving Shirley's life
in an act of supreme, though unidentified heroism.

Susie sang:

> *"So in this smash-and-grab age*
> *Who wouldn't be a cabbage—*
> *Or a carrot or an onion or a bean?*
> *Though not, we think, a lettuce*
> *For a rabbit's sure to get us*
> *And we never have admired that shade of green."*

Leo Clyde advanced from the backdrop, singing:

> *"Now don't stand there and burn up,*
> *It's your turnip's time to turn up*
> *And we'll be the happiest couple ever seen."*

They took hands and went into the chorus:

> *"When we laugh and when we chatter*
> *Of some vegetable matter,*
> *I shall find your tops quite topping,*
> *I shall love you without stopping,*
> *In our tiny little turnip field for two*
> *In our tiny little turnip field for two."*

Susie wore a cylindrical white dress, stiff as cardboard, a kind of
round box slipped on over her silver uniform, and a small pointed
green hat. There were more changes of costume in *Moonrakers*
1926 than Sarah remembered in the earlier editions: a sign of
their new opulence. She had ceased to wonder where the money

came from. Love took priority over such mysteries, and anyway she had almost convinced herself that there was no mystery. The source was surely Mr. Evans. Sarah's thoughts came off duty for a minute, away from Shirley to the other smaller pang: no more Gwen, after this summer. That hurt a little, like the memory of hurting Brigstock. She would remember all the friendly, reliable moments, the I'm-on-Your-Side signals, Gwen saying, "Tell your chum," and opening her school report: the kewpie dolls and ribbons on the tea table. (Friday seemed to have happened years ago. And Sunday's picnic too.) Mr. Evans would carry Gwen off to live somewhere outside Preston, in the country, he said, though one couldn't imagine country near Preston. Did Philip mind? She couldn't be sure. Perhaps it was only her own marvelous sadness that made him too seem a little sad: the blazing happiness of the first afternoon was dimmed, wasn't it? He was in one of his "Bless you—I have to dash" zones: with old friends turning up to see the new show every night, parties, and the car coming back at what Brigstock called "all hours." Brigstock had snapped at Mrs. Gale for saying, "We don't see much of him, do we?"

But now she was back at her shrine, dazed and adoring.

> *"Are you afraid to bloom in cri-imson splendor,*
> *Lest someone come—and steal your heart away?"*

Absolute loveliness: absolute love.

❀

"Hullo-ullo-ullo," said Leo Clyde, at the door of his cubbyhole. "It's you again, so it is. Our best customer. Good house, I thought: not enough of 'em but the kind one can play to. All on your own? What about a cup of tea?"

Sarah refused it on the grounds that she had a message for Philip. Lies came easily on the wave of excitement. The next person she met was Perry Potter, carrying in each hand a beer bottle with a glass over the top of it.

"Hullo-ullo-ullo," said Sarah confidently. The fat little man peered at her in the dim light.

"Miss Weston, I believe. Miss Weston in person: our faithful fan."

"May I ask you something?"

"Yes. Provided it's something of no importance. Pray step this way." She followed him into the prop room. Perry dressed at one end of it, behind a curtain. The rabbit lived here in its hutch, and the baby chickens in their coop, with the rest of his paraphernalia, besides a good deal of communal equipment. Susie was hanging her turnip dress on a hook from a rail and Tubby was lounging about eating a pork pie.

Tubby said, "Hullo-ullo-ullo"; Susie said, "Hullo-ullo-ullo," and skipped away. Perry put the beer down on top of the rabbit hutch.

"What can I do you for?" he asked.

A joke: she had heard it often.

She said, "When will you do the mind-reading trick again?"

"Ah," said Perry, pouring out the beer, "that's it, is it?"

"I thought it was absolutely marvelous."

"You're a nice girl." He began to look almost as stupid as Thomas in one of his puddingy moods: he blew the froth off the beer while Tubby took the other bottle.

"Gerald says he knows how it's done."

"Gerald's a nice boy. How's your *little* brother? Thomas? Hasn't got a cold, has he, by any chance?"

"Well yes, he has. A very bad one. He's been in bed with a temperature. Did you know that by magic?"

Tubby gave a roar: "Like hell he did. He's been praying for it. Tomorrow's Thursday: Kiddies' Show, see? Poor old Perry, shaking in his shoes."

The magician's face remained expressionless: he said nothing to enlighten her. Tubby went on laughing.

"Thomas's cold will be gone by tomorrow, won't it, Sarah? Tell Perry it'll be gone by tomorrow, there's a good girl. Just to please me, tell him Thomas will be there, right in the front row, without the teeniest sniffle."

She looked from one to the other; Perry still solemn, Tubby still chuckling and rolling about. She said, "Well in fact Thomas's colds usually go on rather. This one has. He's still in bed."

"Oh that's all right, if you want to take that line—cheer him up," said Tubby, "cheer him up. Perry, I mean."

"I don't know *what* you're talking about."

"She doesn't know what I'm talking about. I say, Perry."

"I say, Tubby."

"She hasn't seen the program."

"I say, I say."

Sarah sighed. Sooner or later they would all begin to talk like this. From here back to *Hi Jinks*, she could remember the routine. There must be a law laid down for them that this was the way to talk to children. Perry seated himself on a large black trunk with *Moonrakers 1926* painted on it in white. You could see that the "1926" was newly added.

"Does Thomas ever back horses?" he asked.

"That," said Tubby, "will be the day."

"Not arf it won't," Perry agreed.

"He picked out the winner of the Derby in 1921," said Sarah.

"There you are!"

"There you *are*."

"Get the little chap a Pink Un in time for Goodwood, Sarah. And we'll have it on the nose. On the red red rose."

The words "red rose," even emerging from this welter of meaningless nonsense, made a small sharp pain pierce her ribs. She looked at herself in the big mirror that leaned against the wall, to see if she had turned pale. *The great tragic eyes, the face that kept its secret.*

"Not fair to tease you, is it?" said Tubby.

She had no time to answer. Shirley Ormonde's reflection had walked into the looking glass: she spun round quickly. It was happening: Shirley was here.

There seemed to be a long gap in time between seeing the face and knowing who it was: a whole silence in her head, a blindness in her eyes. Shirley came past her, carrying the red roses—now palpably artificial, though she wore two real roses pinned on her gray dress. She put down the bunch beside Susie's hat. Nobody said anything; or had she herself, Sarah wondered, gone deaf as well as blind?

Then the moment had passed: Shirley had walked out. Tubby was laughing.

"Her Grace the Duchess of Wapping," Tubby said, "the toast of the Waterloo Road."

Sarah had no sense of time between hearing these infamous words and being out of the prop room, running after Shirley. She might have been pushed down a well. She just woke up and found herself skidding to a half on the heels of the beloved. Her sandal with the loose buckle shot off and flew through the air: it struck Miss Ormonde's skirt, making her give a little startled jump. She looked round.

"I'm so sorry—so terribly, terribly sorry—"

"Did you *throw* it at me?" Miss Ormonde sounded both cross and incredulous.

"Oh no, *no*. The buckle's come off—it was loose, yes look, I mean it isn't, so it must—it doesn't matter." Her voice sounded like a raven croaking. Briskly she picked up the sandal and stuffed it into her pocket.

"I'm *so* sorry," said Sarah again. "You see, I wanted"— her throat dried: she gabbled—"Please may I have your autograph?"

"Why, of course you may."

"This page, please—and *will* you put 'To Sarah Weston,' please?"

"Ah. Now I know who you are."

It was enough.

"Better put on your shoe, hadn't you?"

"No, it doesn't matter."

"I really think you ought. This floor's all wet. People coming and going. Just slip it on."

(I must remember every word.)

"Hold my bag, dear, would you?" She stood under the light of a dim electric bulb, writing in the autograph book. The bag was gray suede. Cradling it in her arms, Sarah tried to think of something to say: something dazzling and memorable. She said, "I think you're absolutely marvelous," and it came out as roughly and abruptly as an accusation.

"How very sweet of you," said Miss Ormonde, still writing.

"Is it—is it nice, the Wayne Court Hotel?"

"The Wayne Court . . . It isn't bad." She sounded surprised. "Why?"

"I just wondered. Do you miss Bristol? I expect you do terribly."

This brought a look of anxiety. "I simply loathe Bristol," said Miss Ormonde. "What a funny child you are." She handed back the album. She took the gray suede bag. Sarah, impeded by the loose shoe, slithered along beside her. "Miss Ormonde, is there anything I can do for you? Shopping or anything? I'd love to."

"How very sweet of you," said Miss Ormonde again, "but it's early closing, isn't it?"

"I meant any time."

"Your taxi's there, miss," said the man at the door.

"Thank you, Johnny. Well, goodbye, dear."

Then an impossible thing happened. She unpinned the two red roses from her dress and held them out. "For you," she said and got into the taxi.

Sarah stood holding the roses, reading the inscription in the album.

> *A wise old owl lived up in an oak.*
> *The more he heard the less he spoke.*
> *The less he spoke the more he heard.*
> *We all should follow that wise old bird!*

Not Browning, not Byron, not Kipling, nor Rupert Brooke: not even Omar Khayyám. The thunderous disappointment lasted long. This must be erased in memory, like the Sixth Form idol's habit of saying "Pardon?" Sarah walked away through the rain. After a while she found herself pretending Shirley had written, *"So we'll go no more a-roving."* Presently she remembered having left her goloshes under the seat in the fourth row.

❊

"Carry your bag, Madam?"

"What? Oh—no, thank you."

Gerald touched his forehead, without rancor. He was already two shillings to the good, and she hadn't struck him as particu-

larly promising: just a long shot. She was the last passenger off
the local train. Another fifteen minutes to wait for the London
passengers; or as many of these as had traveled on from Sawbridge Junction: at this time of year there should be enough.

He stood, hunched against the rain. The high laurel bushes,
that grew beside the little gate at the foot of the steps, dropped
a rhythmic spatter on his head. He scanned the station yard.
The taxis had driven off. The Rivermouth Hotel bus sat drip-
ping and driverless. The driver was in the café. Gerald did not
dare follow him; the café was the haunt of the railwaymen, and
the elderly porter who had given him a dirty look was inside.

This game, more than any of the games, frightened him. Why
was he here? Morris Ward's telephone call had flattered him because Morris was twenty and a law student. But the greeting on
the telephone, "Hullo—is that Rudolph Valentino?" sent up
its danger signal and he had given only a half-promise to be at
the cinema. It was Sarah's decision to go the Moonrakers that
had made this happen. Oh, well: two shillings by way of result;
and a soaking. Should he give up now, not wait for the London
train? No. He would wait. Because, the detached mind informed
him, there was something enjoyable about being frightened for
money.

Action was beginning again; he saw two taxis whirl into the
yard, a car and three more cars; another taxi. The bus driver came
out of the café. So did the elderly porter. Listening for the
train, Gerald worked his way carefully under the skin of his act.
He didn't know why an act should help. It always did. He was, he
told himself, a Scottish boy, James MacBride, tramping over England, earning what he could to help his frugal, diligent father.
Father had scraped to send him to school in Glasgow. He was
now studying for a scholarship at Glasgow University. "It's a
wee bit difficult times, but I'm a plodder, forbye." He began to
get giggles about "forbye," relayed by Thomas as a word of old
McPhee's.

The great snuffle of the train echoed through the cutting, coming nearer. The smell of steam mixed with the rain. Gerald
turned up his collar and tousled his hair. The mackintosh was

not really shabby enough for the act, but he had taken off his tie.

First down the steps to the little gate was a large man with no luggage. Now a mother and father with two pallid children. No use: Mum and Dad were carrying what luggage there was. They were followed by a youngish woman who struggled with a big, shabby suitcase. Promising. She rocked, tilted and squeezed her way through the gate.

"Carry your bag, Madam?"

"Oh. Yes. Thanks ever so." The case weighed a ton.

"Taxi, Madam?"

"There isn't a bus, is there?"

"Where are ye bound for, may I ask?" said James MacBride.

"Sunnyside House. Marine Parade."

"Then you'll be best to wait on the corner there. I'll tak the case to the bus stop. Forbye it's no weather for a lassie to be getting her bonnie clothes wet."

"Pardon?"

He had perhaps overdone it. She was looking at him in a bewildered way.

"How much would a taxi cost?" she asked.

"Aweel, it's my opinion that their charrges are exorrbitant here in the south." (This was ridiculous, but now he had started he couldn't stop.) "Where I come from, they'd tak ye twice the way for saxpence." (*Oh, shut up; you'll be talking about "bawbees" in a minute.*)

The woman, looking a little frightened, said she would wait for the bus. She put up her umbrella. Gerald staggered beside her. She nearly lost the umbrella in the buffeting wind that struck as they came out of the station yard. She looked sadly up and down the wet seafront.

"How often do the buses come?"

"Aweel—" Another word, "aiblins," had come to his mind; he must try not to use it. He made a Hrrmph noise.

"You know I think I will take a taxi after all."

"Ye'll no be getting one for a wee while."

"Pardon?"

"There's none but a handful comes to meet the train at Sawcombe. At the Junction now they're as thick as the heather that grows on Loch Brittle."

"Lock *what*? I don't understand what you say."

"It's of nae consequence."

Obviously she distrusted him. She looked away to the taxis coming out of the yard.

"Are those all taken?"

"I fear they are, aiblins," said James MacBride. The woman wailed, "Oh do let's go back. I'll be under shelter there, even if it means a wait."

"As it will I mak no doubt," said Gerald sulkily. He picked up the suitcase again. What had she got in the damn thing—a full set of the *Encyclopaedia Britannica*? Canting to one side with the weight, he pursued her, back up the ramp into the danger zone. A small crowd waited forlornly outside the main exit.

"That's all right. Put it down here. You can go." She began to fumble in a purse, counting out coppers. Coppers, what a bitch. Here they came, penny by penny, into his palm. Over her shoulder he saw the elderly porter standing beside a loaded barrow. Sixpence. Then she put the purse away.

"Ye could no mak it a shilling, Madam?"

"Pardon?"

"A bonny shilling? The bawbees (there I go) mean a lot to a laddie with nae roof to his mouth." (Now why had it come out like that? He had meant to say no roof to his head.) "I mean nae roof to his heid," he added ineffectually.

"Go away," said the woman. "At once, do you hear?" The elderly porter took a step nearer, and revealed old General Stevens; wearing oilskins and looking straight at him.

"If you don't go away I'll call a policeman," the woman was saying.

"Gerald—" He jumped. A child in a black peaked cap and shiny black mackintosh was plucking at his sleeve. Its small brown face with the large blue eyes seemed vaguely familiar. Of course; he had seen it scrambling down from a chair outside the ice-cream parlor. An American girl, Tubby had explained: it looked more like a boy.

"My name's Rab. Would you and your friend like a ride?"

"Och, she's nae friend of mine, lassie, dinna heed her. Let's go," he added, coming out of the act. General Stevens, the elderly porter and the suitcase woman were all converging on him. He ran, with the child. There was a large gray car, a Hispano-Suiza, waiting; a chauffeur in uniform, holding open the door. As he sprang in, with Rab after him, he heard an outraged voice cry, "*There!*" Looking back he saw his enemies, all craning their necks after the Hispano.

"Where do you want to go?" Rab asked.

"Anywhere," said Gerald.

"Want to come to the hotel?"

"Yes, rather, that'll do."

"Home, then, Miles—" she said to the chauffeur, who removed his cap and threw it on to the seat beside him. The child Rab took off her cap. She scratched in her white-gold hair. An odd couple, this, Gerald thought, as he recovered his wits. The chauffeur was smoking a cigar. The Hispano was full of luggage and dress boxes. He took his tie out of his pocket and began to put it on.

"How did you know me?" he said to his rescuer.

"Seen you around. Why did you talk so funny to that lady? Why was she so mad at you?"

"Little girls must learn to mind their own business."

"That's right," said the chauffeur without turning his head: he drove fast: the cigar smoke blew back through the opened glass panel.

"Which hotel are we making for, Madam?"

"Rivermouth. That's where we stay."

"Who's we?"

"Miles and I."

"Miles and me," the chauffeur corrected.

"Is this all yours?" Gerald asked, looking at the luggage.

"Goodness, no. My mother's. It came from London and we went to the Junction to get it and they hadn't put it off, so we had to chase it to Sawcombe. Imagine."

"In the circumstances, I'm extremely glad you did."

She grinned at him. "How's Sarah?" she asked.

"Sarah . . . I think she's lost her head. She's taking a third dip at the Moonrakers."

"Don't you like Moonrakers? I don't either."

She puzzled him. He said, "Are you connected with it in some way?"

She shook her head: she didn't look him in the eyes. She said wistfully, "Sarah's so-o beautiful . . . How's Thomas?"

"Is *he* a friend of yours?"

She nodded.

"Well, your friend's in bed with what's known as one of his heavy colds."

"Oh *poor* Thomas. What could I send him? Would he like grapes? Miles—stop when we pass the place where you bought the greengages."

"They weren't greengages," said the chauffeur. "They were plums." While Rab was in the shop he turned back, friendly and conspiratorial. "Just got under the wire, didn't you?" he said. "What was the big idea?"

"The wire? The big idea? I am afraid I don't follow you."

Miles shrugged. "Okay, if that's the way you want it."

Rab came back with the large white box tied in pink ribbon. She whipped out a red fountain pen of a make that Gerald coveted and wrote industriously on the box. "It can stay in the car," she said, "till Miles drives you home."

"I call that very kind. Thomas will be pleased."

"He's welcome."

She stared at him with a mournful expression and lapsed into silence. After a while he said, "Not considered polite to pick one's nose."

"I know it," said Rab. She stopped, looking more desolate than ever. "I only do it when I'm nervous," she explained.

"Everybody does it," said Gerald, "but discretion is the better part."

"Better part of what?"

"Don't be fresh," said Miles. "And don't pick. I've told you before."

Sing for Your Supper (156)

They came to the harbor, to the old town, to the bridge over the estuary. The Rivermouth Hotel struck a note of grandeur. He caught a glimpse of wind-lashed palm trees and rhododendrons; misty green sward going up behind the long low facade. The hotel itself was built like a chalet. An expensive chalet, too, Gerald thought, looking at the cars in the drive. The lobby was gray-carpeted: the walls were white. There were flowers and a rich smell. A man in a white jacket came to help Miles carry the luggage.

"Are you the only person living in these palatial quarters?" he asked the child, who giggled and said, "They all go to sleep when it rains." She peeled off her mackintosh, becoming a small skeleton shape in sweater, trousers and gumboots. "This way," she said briskly, striding ahead of him. The gumboots left wet prints on the pale carpet. She shouted over her shoulder, "First floor—*you* say ground floor, don't you?" and opened a door with a flourish.

A private sitting room. A rich little girl indeed. Hispano, chauffeur, private sitting room. She pulled him to the window to look down on the rocks and the wild sea. "Like being in a ship," said Rab. "Only more birds. See the oyster-catcher? He's the one with red legs. Here they come with the stuff. In my mother's room, please," she said to the man in the white coat. She fished in her trouser pocket and took out half-a-crown. For a kid, and an ugly kid, she was now remarkably authoritative, grown-up, full of the aplomb necessary to these surroundings. When she tipped the man she did it as though she were well used to tipping.

"Two more to come," said Miles, "and that, *grâce à Dieu*, will be the lot."

"Guess I ought to take the dresses out, hang them up. They'll get all creased if they stay in the boxes till tomorrow."

"You do that," said Miles. He went.

"Would you like some tea?" the child asked.

Gerald didn't answer. His attention had been caught by the photograph on the desk. He stepped nearer to look at it. The man in the photograph was standing arm-in-arm with a woman. A beautiful woman, beautifully dressed. Two signatures ran across the corner of the mount—"Paula—Philip. June 1st, 1926."

❀

"Sarah! Hi! Sarah!"

Gerald's voice: she halted in her dreaming walk, coming back from far distances. She saw a large gray car with a chauffeur at the wheel; Gerald waving it away down the parade.

"That's luck, that is," Gerald said. He sounded breathless; he looked dazed and bright-eyed; just the way she herself was feeling.

"What's luck?" she asked stupidly.

"Finding you."

"Why? Whose car? Morris Ward's?"

He said only, "Got to talk to you." He had shed his pompous affectations; he was grabbing her arm, steering her back across the road. "In here," he said. "This'll do."

"It's the one Brigstock doesn't like," said Sarah.

It was the new ice-cream parlor painted in blue and yellow, patronized by the Moonrakers. Brigstock had naturally taken against the place where Thomas claimed to have eaten a fudge sundae on top of a banana split.

Inside, it was shiny and clean, quite empty and very cold. The tables were set along the walls in little booths. Gerald hustled her to the booth at the far end. A blue frilly waitress came to take their order. She gave them a menu each.

"Special today—Banana Royal," said Sarah, "V.N.T."

"V.N.T.?" he asked distractedly "What the hell's V.N.T.?"

"Very nice too. It's a code we used at school last term. I'll have the Banana Royal."

Gerald did not comment on the cost, an unforgivable one-and-tenpence. He said, "All right, two of those," and threw the menu down. Certainly he was not himself.

"Two nice Banana Royals," said the waitress. "Been to the pictures?"

"No," said Gerald curtly. Sarah raised her eyebrows at him, replying, "I've been to the Moonrakers."

The waitress said she didn't think much of *them*. She went

away: Gerald drummed his fingers on the table, watching her until she was behind the counter. Then he leaned forward, hissing, "Keep calm. Hold tight. Or you may drop dead in your tracks. Father's married an American heiress."

"*What?*"

"Listen."

Sarah listened. She searched among her various poses for one suitable to the occasion. She finally decided on the Mayfair sophisticate.

"Dahling—how unutterably peculiar. Where did he find her?"

"At Folkestone: at a *thé dansant.*"

"And this little girl's our stepsister? How excruciatingly tedious."

"Damn," said Gerald, "I left her grapes in the car."

"It's *her* car—? This woman's?"

"Yes."

"Why's he hiding her in Paris?"

"She comes back tomorrow."

"What on earth will Brigstock say?"

"I know. That's a thought, ain't it?"

"Will they move into Roseclay?"

Gerald nodded, scowled and ate his Banana Royal.

"Explains everything," he said bitterly, "doesn't it? Every damn thing."

"You mean the money. It's all her money."

"Well, of course."

"She's paid for Roseclay. And the Buick."

"And *Moonrakers* 1926, don't forget."

She thought about it, eating mouthfuls of cream, jam and nuts: staring a little vacantly at the two red roses beside her plate. That cue for ecstasy was suspended.

"But this makes Father a gigolo," said Sarah.

❀

Thomas awoke from a doze to see Brigstock coming round the door with a square white box tied in pink ribbon. She was wearing what he called her Sunday face and although she said cheer-

fully enough, "Here's a present for you," he knew something had
upset her.

"What's the matter?" he asked.

"Nothing's the matter. Don't you want to open it?"

He was deciphering the scrawl on the lid. He read "Love from
me and the lion get better quick. Rab." As he untied the ribbon
Brigstock said, "A chauffeur brought it in a car."

"Miles," said Thomas. "Didn't you like him?"

"I don't know, I'm sure." It was quite clear that she had not
liked Miles. "Who is he?" she asked while he unveiled a bunch
of grapes.

"He's her chauffeur. Look at these, did you ever see anything
so enormous? Lucky she didn't send them till today or I couldn't
have tasted them. Let's have some now."

Brigstock, dethroning an apple to a saucer on the washstand,
bringing the plate, said, "Who's *she?*"

"Her name's Rab. She's American. She sat next to me at the
Kiddies' Show."

"You didn't tell me about her."

"Oh well."

"How does she know you've got a cold?"

"I can't imagine. Have a grape."

"Just one." She looked at him sternly: "Was it Rab you gave
that lion to?" she asked.

He nodded.

"Why did it have to be a secret?"

"I don't exactly know." Nor did he. Something about Rab herself had suggested that she would rather be kept a secret. He
said, "What about a game of Snap?"

"Not now. I've got too much to do. And your father's coming
up to talk to you."

He sighed. His time was short. The cold had been a mercy in
its way, postponing this hour. Brigstock plumped up his pillows,
gave him a comb and removed some lead soldiers fom the blan-
ket. She also straightened the notebooks and pencils on the bedside table.

"Do you really *like* Puxford?" she asked. It was the first time she had mentioned it, though he knew his father must have shown her Mr. Appleby's letter.

"Ho," said Thomas. "Ho." It had never occurred to him to ask himself whether he liked Puxford or not. It was just the thing that happened to him between holidays.

"I mean, would you be sorry not to go back?"

He blinked at her. "But I've *got* to go back. There's an awful lot more."

That made her laugh, for some reason. Then, unexpectedly, she kissed him. "Remember what I used to tell you when you were a little boy?"

"I expect so. Which one?"

"So long as you tell the truth there's nothing to be frightened of. Ever."

He nodded again. He could not quite see how this applied to the moment. He would have to tell the truth because there was no point in doing anything else: Mr. Appleby had written it all down. Nor was he afraid. The reason why he dreaded the talk was that he would be asked to explain. "And I'm worse at explaining than anything," he thought, in heavy gloom. "I do wish I'd still got a temperature."

After Nanny had gone he lay, rigidly anxious. His window framed the tops of two chestnut trees and he watched their fight with the wind, a movement like the movement of the sea, pouring and continuous. The wind had blown away the rain. The clouds had gone over: there was a clear sky and a gold wash of sunlight. Presently the trees began to quiet down. He heard his father's footsteps coming up the last of the stairs, along the passage. "Here we go," said Thomas.

○

Now the evening sun was bright, the tree tops green and almost still. Philip, with his back to the window, became a silhouette, the detail of his face less and less visible. Thomas wondered if he himself was tired. He couldn't be sure. "You're tired" was an accusation from adults when he behaved badly; it

was not a feeling he recognized as a rule. Legs could ache after
a long walk: sleepiness could come down like a shutter at bedtime. But this sensation, of wanting everything to stop, of muttering, "Oh don't," inside his head and feeling slightly dizzy, might
be the true state of being tired. Surely Philip must stop soon.

"No more fighting, no more kicking. Just say to yourself, 'I
know it's wrong so I won't ever do it again.' You can say that,
can't you?"

"Well, *no*," said Thomas and added, "Can anybody?" He
played with a leaden Highlander who had got left behind in a
fold of the sheet.

"But you'll try."

"Oh yes, I'll try."

"Good." The voice was gentle. "And you still won't tell me
why those particular things made you so angry? The old lady and
Francis Bacon's goose—and the guinea pigs or whatever they
were?"

"*Somebody's* got to stick up for them," he said.

His father sighed. "Stick up for anything you like, but don't go
bashing people—all I ask. And no more prowling at night, eh?
If you can't sleep properly I shall have to send you to a doctor."

Thomas blew his nose. "Hasn't it ever happened to you?" he
asked.

"Listen—prowling around at night isn't a thing that happens
to you. It's a thing you *do*: quite deliberately, even though you've
been forbidden to do it."

"Well, but it doesn't feel like that, you know."

"I shall *have* to smoke," his father said suddenly. "I told Nanny
I wouldn't, but it's no good. If I open a window— Not in a
draught, are you?" The near-silhouette moved agitatedly to and
fro, lighting its pipe. It came closer, standing at the end of the
bed, blocking the sunlight.

"This card business. You said, 'I saw through.' That's right,
isn't it? That's what you said?"

"Yes."

His father put one foot on the lower bed-rail, jogging the bed
up and down: the pipe smoke shimmered.

"All I want is for you to tell me what you mean by 'seeing through.'"

"Oh *crumbs*," said Thomas. He slipped further down among the pillows and lost the Highlander. The best he could do was, "Well, it's the same as ordinary seeing except the thing you see needn't be there—I mean visible."

His father went into a long silence. The bed went on jogging; the smoke went on shimmering.

"Thomas, listen to me. Everyone has hunches now and again. Most hunches don't come off. We only like to remember the ones that do—you'll find that out in time. What happened with those cards was just a hunch. You guessed right. You *could* have guessed wrong."

Thomas decided to say nothing. His father sounded happier with this mistaken view.

"You've got a terrific imagination. Family gift—nice thing to have. But it *can* run away with you—make you think all sorts of odd things are happening."

"What would you call odd?" Thomas asked cautiously.

"Anything that hasn't a rational explanation. By a rational explanation I mean one we can all understand. Everybody. Nanny: Gerald: Sarah: me: Mr. Appleby—"

"And the grandmother?"

"Your grandmother isn't here. Never mind about her for the moment." Mercifully Philip took his foot off the bed-rail. He went over to the open window, shook out the pipe and came striding back to put his hand on Thomas's shoulder.

"Now—next time anything odd happens—anything you can't explain—you'll come straight to me and tell me, d'you see?"

He saw.

"*That's* easy enough, isn't it?"

"Well, no."

"Why not?"

"If I can't explain, how can I tell you?"

"Oh *Lord* . . . Look. Suppose you thought you'd seen a ghost—well, you couldn't explain that. But you could come and

tell me, couldn't you? All right. That's what I want you to promise. On your honor."

Thomas looked all round it and all over it in his mind. He was
not happy. It wouldn't be wrong; but it would be a mistake, he
knew."

"Will you promise? Please."

"Oh well . . . all right."

"*Good*," said Philip. "On your honor now. We'll shake hands
on it, eh?"

Thomas grinned and held out his hand.

"And now I'd like to put all this out of your mind—not think
about Puxford or anything else, start afresh from today—just be a
good boy and we'll—we'll—" He seemed to have difficulty in
finishing the sentence. "We'll see how we go," he said, and went.

❂

Mr. Philip was taking a long time: a very long time indeed.
The prescribed half-hour was past. "Over forty minutes," Blanche
said to herself as she looked at the dining-room clock. She disapproved of worrying in front of the children; worry always showed.
But Sarah and Gerald were paying her no attention. They were
locked in some private game which involved making faces at each
other and limiting their talk to a particularly silly exchange.

"Well, *well*."

"Just fancy."

"Who'd have *thought* it?"

"Fig-u-ray *voo*."

"Stap my vitals."

"Rabin-bin-bin-dranath Tagore."

"Tagore or not Tagore, that is the question."

"Ah lackaday."

"Ah day of wrath and dreadful burning."

"Mute the camel."

"Labors with the heaviest load."

"Or toad."

"It's the last toad that breaks the camel's back."

Then, "I say, Sarah," and "I say, Gerald," in imitation of the
Moonrakers: followed by long hooting whistles. Blanche let them
be. She was preoccupied in more than one direction: with Mr.
Philip and Thomas upstairs: with that dreadful foreign chauffeur,
driving the great car, bringing the grapes, calling her "Nanny"
and grinning at her: oddly, with the absence of Miss Richmond
from this supper table, where she had been an institution for so
long.

A great deal seemed to have happened in five days. But when
she reviewed the actual events, she could find only Miss Richmond's engagement to Mr. Evans, the letter from Puxford and
Thomas's cold. "Well, quite enough for the first week," Blanche
thought.

Five more minutes and she would go upstairs. Mr. Philip—as
usual—was leaving himself no time to eat before the evening
show, he hadn't seen Gerald or Sarah since breakfast, and
Thomas would be tired out.

She was aware of silence: so unusual in the family as to seem
like a noise. Sarah and Gerald sat gazing at each other; their
plates were pushed aside. She had chosen one of their favorite
suppers: cold ham, baked potatoes, bananas and Devonshire
cream. Neither of them had noticed: neither had an appetite.

"What's the matter with you this evening, I should like to
know?" said Blanche. "Doesn't anybody want any more?"

"No thank you. It was lovely, but I simply couldn't."

"Nor could I."

"You haven't been off eating ices at that place?" She could
now be sure they had, because Sarah blushed and Gerald, with
his father's rapid turn of the head, his father's smile, said, "*Ices*,
Brigstraw? What a suspicious mind you have."

"Well why were you so late back?"

"There wasn't a bus," said Gerald.

"*He's coming down*," Sarah croaked. She sprang from her chair.
Gerald said crisply, "My advice to you, Madam, is to let sleeping
dogs lie. And I mean *lie*," he added, knotting up his face and
leering. Blanche had no time to wonder why they were both behaving like this, because Mr. Philip rushed in; he looked dazed,

battered. If Thomas had been too much for him, then he had, most certainly, been too much for Thomas.

"Hullo, all," said Mr. Philip. Blanche felt his hand on her shoulder, a quick, caressing pat. "Went quite well," he said to her out of the side of his mouth and then aimed for the sideboard where the whisky was. Sarah blocked his way. She stood in front of him, pale and shivering, with her head at an extraordinary angle. Mr. Philip didn't seem to take her in. He said, "Mind if I give myself a drink, darling? Got to dash," and still she stood there, in his way.

"Sarah dear," said Blanche. "Sarah—" Mr. Philip gazed downwards. "What's the matter with *you?*" he asked.

"You owe us an explanation." The words came out as though she had a very sore throat and Mr. Philip gave a gurgle of laughter. "What the devil are you *as?*" he asked. "Let me guess. Would it be Lindsay in A *Bill of Divorcement?*"

He was wrong, Blanche saw. Sarah was really in a state; she wasn't only acting. The shivers went all through her, so that her head jerked up and down.

"You've married again," said Sarah. "Why haven't you told us?"

Startled into silence, Blanche could still hear herself saying, "*There* . . ." alone in her mind. She kept her eyes fixed on Mr. Philip, who said nothing for what seemed a long time. He was smiling now: but he didn't speak. Before the smile, Sarah wilted: she croaked, "Well, it's true, isn't it?" and muttered to Gerald, "Why don't you back me up, you cheese?"

"Do you think," said Mr. Philip, "that you could be a nice kind girl and let me get myself a whisky and soda?" As Sarah moved from his path, Gerald gave a mischievous grin.

"Who blew the gaff?" he chirruped. "I, said Hawk-Eye, the great detective. At the Rivermouth Hotel."

Blanche said, "What were you doing there, I should like to know?" just as Mr. Philip said, "What were you doing there, I should like to know?" and Sarah shouted, "Oh for heavens' sake what *does* it matter?" Blanche found herself giving the automatic response: "There's no need to be rude." Out of the corner

of her eye she saw Mr. Philip drink the whisky and soda straight
down, without seeming to swallow. It was a wonder he didn't
choke. He didn't. He put his empty glass on the sideboard and
then dazzled at them all, looking gay and young as he used to
look in the old days when poor Mrs. Weston was going for him.

"Reluctantly I see what Sarah means," he said. "First things
first. Too bad I've so little time. But if you will go digging out
people's secrets behind their backs, you two, you've only yourselves to blame. Incidentally you've seen to it that poor old
Thomas doesn't get a chance to share the news—haven't you?"
He looked from one to the other.

Sarah said furiously: "Well *really*—I call that—" Her father
interrupted: "Don't call it anything now, ducky, please. You
asked me for an explanation, remember?" He loped across to the
white mantelpiece, where he stood with his hands in his pockets.

"My very dear Nanny—my rather *less* dear Sarah and Gerald—
just for the moment, that is, just for the moment, I have the
honor to announce . . ."

○

There was the sound of the car driving off. Silence stayed in
the room. Blanche sought for a formula and found none. This
was without precedent: no glance over her shoulder to any past
situation, with Hales or Mattingleys, could instruct her here.

Sarah sat playing with two tired-looking red roses on the tablecloth. Gerald had walked to the window: he stood there with his
back to the room. She could no longer judge their behavior, good
or bad. She saw only the strange door opening for them; opening
on to a future neither she nor they could imagine.

Instinct told her to leave them alone with it. She trusted her
instinct. She said, "Well now, I'd better take Thomas his Bovril.
If anybody wants me, they know where to find me. I'll be back
directly."

Not a word.

In the kitchen Mrs. Gale was putting out Playmate biscuits on a
plate for Thomas. "Only two, please," Blanche snapped. Mrs.

Gale, taking away the surplus, leaving the elephant biscuit and
the giraffe biscuit, asked, "Something wrong, Nanny?"

"Gracious no, why should there be?"

"You seem sort of upset."

"No, indeed I'm not." She managed to smile. Mrs. Gale said,
"Well, that's good. I expect they've finished in the dining room.
Shall I clear away?"

"Oh—I think you'd better leave it till I come down. I shan't
be many minutes."

"Very well, Nanny."

*Paula: beautiful nice as she is beautiful Paris home tomorrow
Rab who's twelve Married under name of Weston to dodge the
publicity.* These words clicked in her head as she carried the tray
upstairs. Only words. There were no thoughts yet.

Thomas, writing in his notebook, looked flushed and heavy-
eyed.

"Here comes your supper," said Blanche. Then she sniffed.
"Has your father been smoking in this room?"

"Oh. Yes—he did smoke." Thomas put the notebook aside.
"You know," he said, "it's quite difficult to judge what would
count as odd and what wouldn't. So I'm trying to make notes."

"Well, you needn't bother with difficult things now. Drink
your Bovril."

He floated pieces of toast, stirring them around with the spoon.

"Having *promised* makes it so tricky," he said. "Now I've a
person on my mind. She just came walking in. Does that count
as odd, I wonder?"

"I shouldn't think so."

"I've never *met* her, I've only heard of her."

"Who is she?"

"Rab's mother. Her name's Paula."

"Well, didn't your father just tell you about her?" Blanche
asked, but she knew the answer before it came.

"Oh no. It was Rab who told me her name was Paula." He
put his head on one side and screwed up his eyes. "She gives a
shallow light," said Thomas.

Part Two

AUGUST

IX

"Now, the plan for today," said Mrs. Philip. As always, she looked Blanche straight in the eyes. One would have said (wouldn't one?) that it was a usual practice to look people straight in the eyes. It was polite; it was a sign of frankness and friendliness: Blanche herself had always taught the children to do it. ("Sarah dear, we look at the person we're speaking to, remember?") Why then should this habit of Mrs. Philip's remain so persistently noticeable? It had the power to distract Blanche from the business in hand. She would meet the brilliant blue stare and lose track for a moment. She lost it now: thinking how very young Mrs. Philip seemed and finding again that fleeting look of poor Mrs. Weston. She had remarked upon this to Mr. Philip himself, the first day. Mr. Philip, suffering from loss of head and several glasses of champagne, had replied, "See what you mean. There *is* a certain likeness between a Pekinese and a lion." By the Pekinese he had meant poor Mrs. Weston: Blanche knew that because he used to call her "my little Pekinese-face" and poor Mrs. Weston never minded; being fond of Pekinese.

A lion . . . Blanche couldn't see the resemblance to a lion. She saw the extreme of fairness ("Nordic type unlike yours truly," said Mr. Clyde). She saw the soft, gentle hair, cut short and brushed back from a square white forehead: the brilliantly blue eyes: upward lines of a face that was very nearly the sentimental angel face on the lid of a chocolate box. Very nearly. Not quite. Something else showed through. Something blunt, strong and reckless: perhaps the effect of the bumpy bones. The same bones were to be seen—exaggerated—in the face of the child Rab.

"Now—the plan for today. *I'm* going to take the children. Mr. Philip's lunching with Mr. Marshall and Leo Clyde." She paused, still looking Blanche in the eyes before she said, "There's trouble, you know," and then laughed: which was her way, Blanche had observed, of saluting trouble.

Mr. Marshall being the lessor of the Fundrome, it was only too obvious what this trouble was. Now Mrs. Philip rose abruptly from the armchair and stood before the mantelpiece, where the bronze animals fought their battle. The daily conference always took place in the little study.

"Marshall wants them to take a week out at the end of the tour, put in some damned operetta, I forget its name. Anyway, you can see what that does to Philip, can't you? Doesn't *matter* . . ." She gave a quick frown and a laugh. "He might have known. Except he never does know, does he? *I* knew." She fitted a cigarette into her long amber cigarette holder. She stood, looking light and defiant.

"I'm sorry," Blanche said. "Mr. Clyde told me the receipts were bad seeing it's August."

"Show's a flop," said Mrs. Philip, sounding as though she didn't care. "Where were we? Oh yes—I'll take the kids—drive them

over to Mortehoe, give them lunch and keep them out till tea-
time. If you want to go off before lunch, please do."

"Thank you, M'm. But I think I'll have my lunch here. My
friend isn't expecting me till three o'clock and the bus only takes
fifty minutes."

"As you like." She began to prowl, another regular habit. Mrs.
Philip, besides looking young, looked elegant, even when wearing
a plain dark-blue sweater, white skirt and none of her copious
jewelry. It was hot, Blanche would have said, for a sweater, but
Mrs. Philip was always cold. The scent she used hung in the
room. It was still strange, after three weeks, to have a feminine
presence here in authority: strong as the scent and all over the
place. The half-remembered details, like the dressing table with
its equipment of jars and bottles, or the clothes in the wardrobe
or the flowers, bought in abundance and beautifully arranged,
still seemed to shout, "Here she is." And still seemed oddly temporary; an invasion that was happening to them all for a little
while; that would end, with everything as it was before. Why did
it feel like this? Blanche didn't know. Perhaps it was simply hard
to realize that she was back with the regime of husband and wife.

"You did tell Violet to leave the vacuum cleaning till he wakes
up?" (Violet, known to Blanche and to Mrs. Gale as "the girl,"
came every day now instead of twice a week.) "There's no *need*
for him to worry, that's what's so crazy," said Mrs. Philip and
laughed again. "Told him so half the night. It's his ego taking
the rap, of course." She clenched her thin muscular hands. "So
silly. What the poor darling doesn't get is the fact that he's a
fellow with good, small talents and mighty little taste. Give him
his head and what do you have? *Moonrakers 1926.*"

"It's disappointing for him."

"Oh sure," said Mrs. Philip, and came swiftly to pat Blanche's
shoulder: "Don't be sad. I've got it all taped. With the right kind
of producer—" She moved towards the desk. "Get down to
these," she snapped; she could interrupt herself as easily as she
could interrupt somebody else.

Had they chosen the London house yet? Blanche could see the

house agents' letters lying there, the sheaf of rainbow-colored prospects in black and white, scarcely to be believed.

Mrs. Philip was diverted from the desk.

"I want you to tell me something, please. Something important." She stood before Blanche, looking her so straight in the eyes that Blanche was obliged after a moment to blink: "Did he always worry this way when times were tough? Or is it just because he's spending my money?"

Here was innocence. What Mr. Philip had told her about the past, Blanche couldn't imagine. The answer in her head was "Goodness me—'been spending other peoples' money all his life." The answer as she spoke it was a tactful, "Well—he gets these worrying fits. Sometimes it's one thing, sometimes it's another. The shell shock, they say." Then she added deliberately, "Of course he *does* worry about the children; he always has."

There was an impulse of accusation behind the words. Mrs. Philip was, in a sense, wonderful to the children. She played with them, seemed to love them and took pains for their pleasure. But never for a moment did she worry. They might be a family of puppies, except that puppies would possibly cause her more concern. She would let Rab and Thomas go off alone together; she would allow three swims in one day: she was a great one for plans but she had no regard for rules. Imposing a discipline of her own (which included wholly admirable matters such as cleanliness and politeness) she sailed over the long-established laws. So that Sarah was allowed to wear her scarlet chiffon dress at supper, "time for bed" was no longer a fixed canon and nobody was forced to finish the food on the plate.

She had certain childish qualities herself. She was, in her own idiom, "a sucker for a story." She would sit still and listen to Blanche's reminiscences, to Sarah's tales of school, to any of the Moonrakers harking back. It was the only time she sat still, listening to stories. She would often side with Rab or Thomas, pleading "Not yet, Nanny," against the clock.

That was one aspect of her. There was another aspect. Although she deferred to Blanche as final arbitrator in any crisis,

Mrs. Philip could throw out a tiny, but disturbing hint that she,
Blanche, was inclined to take an "old-fashioned" view.

"About the *children*," Mrs. Philip repeated, drawling now: the
American drawl. There were times when Blanche forgot that she
was American. "A true cosmopolitan," Mr. Philip had said; familiar with European backgrounds; loving Europe, England most
of all. She had also introduced Blanche to the startling notion of
an American aristocracy, who had not only made their millions
but knew how to behave; who mixed with titled playmates and
with royalty itself. The extent of Mrs. Philip's acquaintance was
astonishing. She had illustrious friends everywhere: headline people, people whose names were in the gossip columns. London,
Paris, that place in Venice where they wore pyjamas—called the
Lido; the theatre, and the paddock at Goodwood seemed full of
Mrs. Philip's friends.

"About the *children* . . ." The dazzle of her smile was like
Mr. Philip's, a sudden switch-on of endearing light. "Well, thanks
to you, he never really had to worry. And thanks to you and me
together, Nanny, *together*, he never will."

The plucked eyebrows lifted; the voice sharpened. "Think I'm
doing it all right? All of it? You must tell me if you don't. Please.
Terribly important. Tell me every time. You must."

Too frank, somehow. (If there was such a thing as being too
frank.) And yet, unforgivably in oneself, the sense of an act, a
suspicion that deeper thoughts were concealed.

Blanche smiled back at her. "Well, M'm, you must remember
you're so much younger than I am—we're bound to see things a
bit differently now and again. It's not for me to interfere."

"Thomas," said Mrs. Philip and stopped.

"What about Thomas?"

"Feel he sort of hates me sometimes." And now the laugh.

"Good gracious, what an idea to get in your head. Of course
he doesn't."

The level, challenging look showed that Mrs. Philip had not
accepted this. Why should she think Thomas hated her? Blanche
said briskly, "It's nice for him to have Rab to play with—good

for him too. He was getting to be rather the odd man out. Always happens when the older ones move up, like."

Mrs. Philip shrugged. "Well—among your miracles, Rab's at last beginning to eat," she observed as she went to the desk. "I'll just do these bills before I go down to the beach, Nanny."

It was one of the changes in this time. Bills were no longer dooms to be dreaded, but trifles to be paid.

❁

"Can I come in?" Paula asked and walked in without waiting for the answer. It was a trick Gerald found disconcerting: at least he had his trousers on. The new invader was unselfconscious about degrees of nakedness—other people's or her own.

She stood in the doorway, still wearing her bathing dress, a small black sheath with a white belt. He found himself frequently spying on her beauty; upon the fair head, the brilliant blue eyes, the body and the legs. (His father, with his obsession about long, beautiful legs, would never of course have married a woman with short ones.)

"You didn't have much time on the beach," said Paula. "Going some place?"

"I have to meet Morris and Poppy."

She was an inquisitor, though the inquisition was not of the adult kind. There was no judgment here: rather, the innocent prying of a child, wanting to know all.

"You can't come to Mortehoe, then? I'm taking the bunch in the car."

Paula's use of the word 'bunch' was extensive. She could mean the family: she could mean the Moonrakers with whom, astonishingly, she was on back-slapping terms: she could mean unknown clusters of friends in far places. ("I was in Newport with the bunch": "I had to join the bunch in Salzburg.")

This time, he assumed, she meant Sarah, Rab and Thomas. Not Philip. Philip was to be left in peace, though "peace" was hardly accurate. The *King Lear* atmospherics were abroad in the house and Gerald, like everyone else, knew why. Decline of Moonrakers—poor old Moonrakers. He stood before the glass, shaking a few drops of brilliantine onto his brushes. Paula watched keenly while he dealt with his hair.

"If I didn't know your age, I'd put you at eighteen," she observed. (Morris Ward said much the same.) He murmured, "Permit me to return the compliment, Madam," and drew her uproarious laugh. This had embarrassed him with its loud suddenness at the beginning: after three weeks he was used to it, though not yet used to Paula. She still gave him the odd impression that she came from nowhere, having had no real existence until now. All the odder when he thought of her world-wide journeyings, of Rab, Rab's father, and the various homes in America. (Not to mention the retrospective Bunches.) Every time she talked of America, of the California ranch or of New York City, she could make these places shine for him—adventurous and desirable as Samarcand. She had an agreeable trick of saying, "When you come to America."

"I thought you didn't like Morris." She came right into the room and sat down on his bed.

"I don't."

"Then?"

"He amuses me. Besides inspiring a certain envy in this otherwise calm bosom."

"Envy? 'Cause why?"

He turned from the glass to meet her level stare. The habit of looking people so straight in the eyes diverted him: it was his own, when lying.

No need to lie now: "I envy anyone who's out of school."

"Well why not quit?"

Innocence again. She said, "I've always quit when I wanted. Always will. It's best. *Why* do you have to stay on at school?"

"You had better ask my father."

"I will," said Paula with a kind of light emphasis that could be taken as a hint of authority. It set him wondering. Uncle Percy, he supposed, was no longer expected to pay the school fees. "What time can you get back?" she asked.

"I don't know." He glanced at his new watch. She had given

watches to them all, describing these as her moving-in presents. All three watches were different. His was gold, with a square face, and a strap made of plaited leather thongs: a beauty.

"Try to get here around four: then we can play some tennis." She beat him regularly, by the narrowest margin, but she still beat him. She was a remarkable performer in many fields. He saw her always doing something; compelled to swim, ride, to cook (over Mrs. Gale's dead body as you might say), to paint, to play the piano. Failing these, she would corral a partner for backgammon or bezique. She liked every moment filled.

Putting eau de Cologne on his handkerchief, he agreed to be back at four. She had not, naturally, sat still for long. She was at the window.

"Here they come," she said, "Thomas last, as usual." Leaning beside her, looking across the road, Gerald saw Rab waiting for Thomas while he blundered through the high grass and fern.

" 'Love the shape of his head," said Paula.

"When visible through the idiosyncratic coiffure, the head is quite a good shape," Gerald allowed.

"What do *you* think about this Puxford problem? Philip isn't looking a yard beyond his lunch with—what's the fellow's name?"

"Appleby. God-and-Games Appleby. The problem won't arise if he persists in crossing in front of that bus," said Gerald. He watched Rab deflecting Thomas. Paula said, "And what happens if Appleby refuses to take him on?"

"He can go into the Navy when he's sixteen." She hadn't recognized the quotation: she never did recognize quotations: she chuckled as if at a spontaneous wisecrack.

"Such an odd little customer, isn't he?"

"A screw loose, would you say?" Paula looked startled, as he had intended. "We've debated it," he went on, "Sarah and I. Our final conclusion is no. On the other hand he may be illegitimate. Or perhaps one of those cradle mix-ups that happen in hospitals." She wasn't amused: she said, "At least Puxford does get him away from Nanny."

After a calculated pause, he replied, "That is, admittedly, one function of our school life." She got it. She began to plead: "Ah,

don't . . . I adore Nanny; I'm her slave." (A lie, Madam, if ever
I heard one.) "But I do think Thomas depends on her too much
—for a boy of his age. His whole life centers around her." (And
does this, perhaps, make you jealous?)

"You *must* see that," Paula was saying.

Gerald shook his head. "Old Thomas doesn't depend on anybody. It would never surprise me if he went off to the North Pole
one fine morning, leaving a note. Sorry, Paula, I must go now."
Still she lingered: Sarah, Rab and Thomas would be waiting long
before she was ready. "You know," he said at the door, "if you
asked the old boy, I think you'd find it's the other way round;
he regards himself as Brigstock's keeper."

"That sounds crazy."

"He worries about her," Gerald said, "but then he worries
about everything."

Paula looked completely baffled: "Well, I guess you know," she
murmured. "He doesn't talk to me."

"Thomas doesn't talk much to anybody."

"Except Rab."

A note of jealousy there, too? Perhaps. Walking down the hill,
he had the puzzle of Paula on his hands. She was so little like his
wild imaginings—and Sarah's. They had expected her (hadn't
they?) to change all, dominate all: the high-powered American
stepmother, with the millions.

She was humble, curious, wanting friendship and confidences,
wanting to be wanted.

She might not be rich at all.

Oh, there were glimpses: her clothes, the emeralds described by
Gwen as "too big *not* to be genuine"; the Hispano nudging the
Buick in the garage. He knew the bills were paid regularly, when
he scanned the envelopes on the hall table. The talk of a London
house was rich talk. (A house of all things; a home, the thing
that other people had, a place that would stay. Hyde Park Gate
seemed to be the chosen address.) He could, he was certain, look
forward to reasonable pocket money this term.

Here the words, "Why not quit?" came back. Was she serious?
"I've always quit when I wanted. Always will."

*Well, well, Madam . . . How does this philosophy go down
with the new bridegroom, we ask ourselves?*

❧

"Now I saved these for you," said Mrs. Dalley, "though I expect you've seen them." She laid a small collection of newspaper
cuttings on the rustic table between her and Blanche.

The garden, though small, was as neat as the white cottage
with the brown thatch. Mrs. Dalley was neat too, plump and
pink and smooth. She was dressed smartly in black, with a lace
collar: a small gold cross, hung on a chain, gleamed in the middle of the lace. Mrs. Dalley had always ranked high on Blanche's
landlady list, though she dated back ten years. The friendship,
since Lyme Regis in the wartime summer of '16, had kept itself
alive more by letters and Christmas cards than by their few meet-
ings.

Here was another proof of Mrs. Dalley's fidelity to that one
summer. She had cut out all the nonsense from the local press:
most of it concerned with Miss Richmond's wedding and the
secret marriage of Philip Adair. One paragraph was headed
Honeymoonrakers' Week! and several said *It can now be revealed.* There were pictures. Here was Mr. Evans wearing a
boater, with Miss Richmond in a bathing suit.

"It's a pleasant face—" said Mrs. Dalley. "I remember her in
Hi Jinks at Redcove as clear as if it was yesterday. *He's* not much
to look at, is he?"

Miss Richmond, said Blanche, seemed to think the world of
him. (*"I'm going to be married, laugh that off . . ."* But one
had to say these things.)

"When you put those two next to *these* two." Mrs. Dalley had
the picture of Mrs. Philip at the wheel of the Hispano and Mr.
Philip dazzling from the running board. "He's handsomer than
ever: and she's quite beautiful; looks rather like that Tadoodle
Bankhead. Is it *her* car, Nanny?"

"Yes. She's a very good driver," said Blanche. "They had a
chauffeur with them on the Continent but he's been sent pack-

ing." She could hear the overtone of relief in her own voice: she would not quickly forget her glimpse of the dreadful Miles.

"What did I do with the party one? *Torquay Trumpeter*—Here it is." Blanche hadn't seen the party one. Mr. Philip had groaned about the party, with its double-wedding motif: Mr. Evans' idea. The photographer at least appeared to have enjoyed himself. Moonrakers Make Merry occupied a full page. She looked upon Miss Richmond and Mr. Evans bursting a toy balloon: Mr. Potter doing a trick with cakes: Tubby Whittington falling down. The picture of Mrs. Philip, with Leo Clyde, had caught her laughing. Mr. Clyde was laughing too, the rest of his features dimly grouped around his teeth. Shirley Ormonde wore a flower behind one ear and simpered from a staircase.

"Silly," said Blanche.

There was a moment's silence from Mrs. Dalley before she held out one last press cutting; she had kept it stored under her plump hand.

"*This* was in the Devon and Exeter *Gazette*."

Blanche knew what it was. She had read the paragraph; so had Mrs. Gale, whose comment had been, "Plenty of bad men in the world, eh Nanny?"

Mrs. Philip Weston obtained a divorce from her first husband, Mr. Herbert Lee, in America last year.

"I understood," said Mrs. Dalley, "that she was—A Widow." She made the word "widow" sound high-ranking, like the word "Duchess." And there was about her, was there not, something of the same superiority that emanated at times from sister Mary? As if the status of being a widow must never be forgotten. Blanche could feel its familiar impact on the air. Here in the cottage garden as there in Ramillies Terrace.

"It must make you very sad," Mrs. Dalley intoned. "I thought of that first." She fingered the little gold cross at her neck. They had gone to Early Service together at Lyme Regis: one of the bonds between them.

But this, being an attack on Mrs. Philip, was therefore an attack on the family. Blanche assembled her somewhat inconclusive weapons:

"Her husband was an American," she said firmly.

"Well, so's she," said Mrs. Dalley, with a sniff. "What difference does that make?"

"They were *children*. She was only eighteen," Blanche temporized. It was her private conviction and consolation that though English marriages were made in Heaven American marriages were made in America and didn't, therefore, count.

"It's not just a predijuice. No divorce can be the proper thing in the sight of God," said Mrs. Dalley. "Can it now?"

"Well, we don't know the rights and wrongs, do we?"

"I must say I'm surprised at *you* taking that line."

Blanche felt her cheeks growing hot. "Mrs. Philip has been quite frank with me, Ellen, and I don't think we need say any more about it. Except she's had her sorrows out of this and one of them was not being able to marry Mr. Philip in a church. *And* she's been to church with us all three Sundays." She had scored a point. Mrs. Dalley looked less grimly righteous. "And if you ask *me*, though Mrs. Philip didn't say it in so many words, that American young man wasn't quite right in the head."

"Even so," said Mrs. Dalley, "I know what my Fred would think. I can just hear him."

It would be unkind to raise a doubt as to whether Mrs. Dalley could in fact hear her Fred think after fifteen years. Blanche said, "Well now, suppose we change the subject."

"Do the children know?"

"I said we'd change the subject, Ellen, didn't I?"

"Very well."

They sat in complete silence. Mrs. Dalley picked up the big orange-colored cat who had been rubbing against her skirts and began to talk to it rather foolishly, calling it Mother's Own Boy. Blanche looked about the garden. The flower beds were almost too tidy; rigidly spaced hollyhocks against the fence; small ranks of roses: little hard clumps of color lined along the borders.

"Well, I'll put the kettle on," said Mrs. Daley: she sounded forlorn, though there was, surely, no reason why she should. "I expect you're ready for your tea. Shall we have it indoors? Turning a bit chilly now, isn't it?"

"Gracious, I'm hot."

"Oh—well then—let's—"

"No, no, whatever you say."

"I'll bring it *out*."

"Let me help you."

"I'll call you—"

The smart black shape, followed by Mother's Own Boy, went up the path under the pergola. Blanche gave a moment to wondering whether it was really an advantage to have had a husband and lost him, like Mary and Mrs. Dalley. Both women would tell her it was. The idea that she could pity them would never enter their heads.

Had she been unkind? No. Insincere? She thought not. Her views on divorce were the same as Ellen's, but Ellen couldn't look at the situation from a family point of view: nor had Ellen heard Mrs. Philip talk about it, seriously, sadly, looking her straight in the eyes.

She began to search for a peace-making subject: the coal strike: the Prince of Wales: Sir Alan Cobham: Suzanne Lenglen turning professional: the pyjamas on the Lido. She was satisfied with none of them and it was good to see Ellen bustling back, calling cheerfully, "If you'll just help me lay the cloth," and then saying, as if she too had worked at this, "What I *meant* to ask you was about the little girl. How does it feel to have another baby on your hands?"

"She's a bit of a Turk," said Blanche: realizing, as she said it, how fond she was of Rab already. (Of any child? Every child? Perhaps: it was a question she had asked herself before.) "More like a boy than a girl, really."

"Have the others taken to her?"

"Oh yes. She makes us all laugh. She's Thomas's *friend:* she looks up to Sarah and Gerald, more. Specially Sarah. Funny," said Blanche as they carried the plates from the kitchen, "to think of that little monkey traveling all over the world. School next term won't do her any harm. She's looking forward to it. Going to

Sarah's school—in a lower form of course: as Mrs. Philip says, it's about time."

(To be kept hidden: her reservations about Rab's upbringing: about the endless pocket money; the adult world made plain to babyish eyes; about Mrs. Philip letting her wear boys' clothes—and come into the bathroom when Mrs. Philip wasn't wearing a stitch. It was a wonder Rab took so kindly to the Roseclay regime. And yet it wasn't: all children throve on steady, sensible treatment.)

"And *now*," said Mrs. Dalley, when she had given Mother's Own Boy his saucer of milk, "How are they doing at the Fundrome? One hears all sorts. It's quite a different type of show, they say."

"It is different."

"Joe—you wouldn't remember Joe—that's my cousin's boy—came over on his motor bike last week, he's wonderfully regular, Joe didn't think much of it, to tell you the truth. But Netta—that's his wife, he said she thought it was wonderful. Attendance very poor, though, that night. Shame . . ."

It was now solidly reassuring to think of Mrs. Philip and of this morning's talk: to grasp the fact of the money, the safety: not to feel, as in the old bad days, that the floor was cracking beneath their feet. She could drink her tea and answer comfortably. "I'm afraid they're *not* having a good season, no good saying they are." She wasn't going to say more than that.

"What do you think of the show yourself, Nanny?"

"Well—I don't know that I care for this one as much as I've liked some of the others. But then I suppose I'm old-fashioned. I liked them in their white—with those black bobbles—and not so many—well—London-y kind of songs and jokes, if you know what I mean."

Mrs. Dalley knew what she meant.

"Joe and Netta both thought the little conjuror-man was the best. Quite specktular."

"He's very good, Mr. Potter: some talk of his leaving us, though. I don't know why. What's funny, Ellen?"

"The way you say 'us.' I declare you still talk as if you were in charge of them all. You always did. Any news of their grand-mother?" she asked suddenly. Mrs. Dalley had never met the grandmother.

"What put *her* into your head?"

"I suppose the conjuror."

"She won't be with us this summer. Thank you, Ellen, I would like another cup."

X

"Well, there we are," said Leo Clyde as Marshall moved out of earshot. "We've got him by the orchestra stalls, by the marble halls." He watched the stubby, complacent shape in gray flannels until it was lost among the crowd on the parade. "Teach *him* to try tricks with one of his own race. Marshall, my foot. His name's no more Marshall than mine's Clyde." Taking Philip's arm, a habit which Philip hated, Leo turned him west, away from the Marina. "Mind you, if there *had* been a loophole in the contract he'd have been out and through it fast enough. For all his pretty prattle about 'a gentleman's agreement.' Puzzle-find-the-gentleman eh?" He laughed.

"You said that," Philip reminded him, "at lunch."

"Well I know I said it—what's the odds?" asked Leo plain-

tively. "Anything good's worth saying twice. Look here, you're
not worried are you, old man?"

Worried, Philip reflected, was scarcely the word. He was hurt in
his soul. Though Marshall couldn't, in terms of the agreement,
evict *Moonrakers* from the Fundrome a week early, the unbearable fact remained: he wanted to. He had produced solid enough
reasons for wanting to.

"The hell with him," said Philip, disengaging his arm. It was
too hot. He had drunk too much wine, eaten too much food;
the brassy lowering afternoon pressed on his head and his eyes.

"What about a dip?" Leo said. "Let's go down to the huts—
take a dip—sleep it off."

"Not for me. I had a rotten night. I'll go home if you don't
mind." They had come to the corner of Galleon Street. "Car's up
here," said Philip. "Drop you anywhere?"

Though Leo refused the offer, he came on up the street, past
the toy shop and halted before McPhee's window. A poster
stuck on the glass announced, OUR ANNUAL HOLIDAY: NO BUSI-
NESS WILL BE DONE FOR TWO WEEKS BEGINNING MONDAY AUGUST
30TH. WE ARE GIVING YOU PLENTY OF TIME TO DIGEST THIS INFOR-
MATION.

Leo groaned. "He couldn't just say 'This shop will be closed
for two weeks from August 30th,' could he? Not if it was ever
so."

"I like old McPhee. He's—"

"—such a character," Leo finished for him. "Well I *don't* like
the old bastard. But I do want that garnet tiepin. Think I'll go
in and have another crack at Jewing him down. Before I take my
shut-eye. See you tonight, Maestro." He saluted and plunged into
the shop.

Philip, relieved of his presence, at once felt better. He climbed
into the Buick and drove back up the hill, singing capably,

> *"But just for the minute*
> *That's as long as we are in it,*
> *We are walking, you and I,*
> *On our way to by-and-by"*

and he thought of Paula as he sang so he dropped the couplet

I'm your burden, you're my load
In the middle of the road

and whistled the tune instead. There was no burden; love was here and money was here. There was no load, except his own hurt vanity. As he reached the gates of Roseclay he was already reconstructing the situation so that the end of *Moonrakers 1926* had nothing whatever, but nothing whatsoever, to do with box-office receipts. The show had come to its natural end.

True, surely . . . Gwen was off the boards next month, to become the chatelaine of Mr. Evans' mansion at Bamber Bridge. Shirley Ormonde, the amateur, must return to Bristol and her dubious husband. The cryptic Perry Potter had a doctor's certificate advising a long rest.

That left the hard core, remnant of the old guard, Tubby and Susie, Leo and himself: and there were winter jobs beckoning for all except himself. This, not by failure (he was Philip Adair, wasn't he?) but by his own decision. He didn't need to go looking, planning. Philip Adair was safe. Under Paula's starry influence, the wide, gold-paved paths opened up. He could be another Jack Buchanan in musical comedy: he could steal the scenes —and the notices—in the next Cochran revue.

The Gay Cavalier had moved back into residence.

Strolling from the car to the house, he was happy to be alone because at the end of the loneliness (sometime after five o'clock, knowing her disregard for Nanny's tea-at-four-thirty rule), there would be Paula. And all the children tumbling out of the His-pano to tell him about their day. Odd that his fast, unconsidered image of the children should always bring them as younger than they were: a chubby gaggle of six-year-olds and seven-year-olds, not in the least resembling the truth of Gerald, Sarah, Thomas or Rab. Why was that? He stopped to think about it while he took two aspirin with a glass of Bromo-Seltzer.

" 'And then, feeling rather sick,' " Philip quoted, " 'he went in search of some parsley.' " He gave an enormous yawn; the kind of yawn that irritated Paula. It was comforting to be able to yawn without reproach. Having stripped and put on his bathing suit, he swaddled on his toweling bathrobe and slid his feet into rope-soled sandals. He ran downstairs, feeling the lightness and emptiness of the house. Consoled by the trace of Paula's scent hanging about the air, he paused, listening to the silence.

Nanny's afternoon off: Mrs. Gale upstairs and inaudible: not a person, not a sound: and the sense, after words and people, of snapping back gratefully into oneself, restored, complete, untrammeled. Why did he like it so much? And why—this was one for the book, he said, meaning a point to be observed, studied— why did Paula like it so little? A thing he had learned early on was that she could not bear to be alone. Not for ten minutes. The only thing, he thought, that frightens her.

He opened the front door.

He went past the Buick, patting its nose because it was, would be always, a triumphant toy, perhaps the first of many triumphant toys; who could tell? He went out of the gate and over the road and under the shade of the pinetrees; he took one of the zigzag ways down the cliff to the cove.

Not a Stevens in sight. The cove lay empty. The tide was high: the sea was flat; only the smallest lace of bubbles fringed the rocks. The brassy light had turned suddenly clear and kind. He saw the dry white sand, then the rim of black seaweed rags, and broken shells, then the shimmer of the wet sand. He kicked off his shoes. He dropped his robe. The air pleased his body. It would be good to swim naked, and why not? He had swum here naked with Paula in the early morning: always putting the robe on a strategic point of rock, to be grabbed in emergency, standing waist-deep, though she laughed at him. He followed the procedure now. With the robe held about him, he shed the bathing-suit. At the water's edge, he heaped the robe on the rock-point and climbed higher. Then he plunged.

It was so good that he could have no thoughts at all; he was just a body, freed in a blink from heaviness and headache, claimed by the sea, the darling of the sea. He plunged again, he swam underwater, he came up and struck out lazily; then turned on his back, feeling clean and adored and ready to quote Rupert

Brooke. He looked up at the wide sky. He looked toward the cove.

His mother-in-law, the children's grandmother, was standing at the foot of the cliff.

Oh, no.

Oh, yes.

She took a few paces across the dry sand; slowly, delicately, gazing about her. She wore a buff-colored coat and skirt and a kind of cowboy hat. She was using a red parasol as a walking stick.

She ought to be in Scotland.

Treading water, Philip shut his eyes, hoping that when he opened them she would not be there. She was. Hell. It was not so much that he disliked poor Isobel's mother as that he knew himself to be quite incapable of handling her. When Percy and Flavia were about they took the impact. His sister-in-law, Flavia, the pale carbon copy of Isobel, had developed a passive technique of not answering. Percy could be briskly rude.

Why had they let her loose? What was she doing here?

She had come to his bathing suit that lay abandoned; she prodded it with her parasol. Then she took off the cowboy hat. She placed it on top of the bathing suit. She stood gazing out to sea, chin lifted; the carriage of her head and shoulders was very fine. Straight, statuesque: the carriage of a tall woman: she was not tall. Her figure had a kind of squat neatness. Her yellow hair looked almost white at this distance: she used to dye it.

"Philip! Philip!" He could only hear half of what she was calling to him. The last words were "Come out—quick! Hurry up!" Her voice was shrill. The effect was that of a bosun's whistle or somebody calling a dog.

Resignedly, he swam to the rocks. She came down the wet sand, branching right, to meet him.

"Why do you take *that* way?" she called, most audible now, and most visible: the broad round forehead, the glittering eye, the lipstick: a face of ravaged beauty. "Surely it's the longest," she continued as he halted waist-deep in the tongue of water behind the rocks.

"I've got nothing on."

"Oh I see. What do you want me to do about it?"

"Turn your back, like a lady, while I get into my bathrobe."

"If I must, I must," she murmured in a faint, faraway voice. She went on chirping, "The genitals. The genitals. Not visually attractive. Nor, I suppose, designed to be. It's of no significance," she added as though he had contradicted her. Lashing the girdle of the robe around his waist he said, "All right now." She turned. "Well," she said, "*there* you are. How nice."

"My *dear* Marion—" (Had he managed to turn the protesting My-dear into the warm welcoming My-dear? He hoped so.) There was laughter in her eyes and she was giving him a good pearly grin; she had remarkable teeth. The whole face, shiny between patches of powder, was a forceful edition of Isobel's face.

"Dear Philip. How nice," she repeated.

"How on earth did you get here?"

"By bus," she said. "They're very quick."

"By *bus*—? From Inverness? Whatever time did you start?"

She shrieked. "I'm staying at *Ilfracombe*. Only for two nights. I'm going to visit the Carmelites in Cornwall."

"The who?"

"Don't look as if you ought to know them, they're nuns," she said. "Percy and Flavia are quite cross with me. They had decided to take me abroad and I asked for a check instead. I will say Percy sent it. But not with pleasure. Dear Madam I have much displeasure in enclosing my check." She had begun to walk up the beach towards the cliff, purposefully leading: Philip said, "I want to smoke," and she said, "Smoke, dear, smoke; who's stopping you?"

"I want to smoke *here*." His voice sounded as peevish as a child's. He sat down on the sand (a mistake in a wet bathrobe). Marion promptly found the only flat stone of comfortable size to sit on. She stretched her short legs out in front of her, holding herself upright with a hand at each side, pressed down.

"Well? Where are they all?" she asked.

"Paula and the kids?"

"*And* Nanny—"

"They'll be back."

"When?"

"Nanny's afternoon off. She doesn't usually come home till supper time. Paula and the kids—well, not before five."

"Oh that's all right. I'll get a glimpse—a glimpse. I'm coming to see the Moonrakers, so I'll get a glimpse. I really ought to have let you know I was coming, but I didn't trust you not to find an excuse. An excuse. Any excuse."

This repetition, he and Isobel had decided long ago, was due to a swerve of absent-mindedness leaving her with the conviction that something remained to be said, though she had forgotten what, and would meanwhile give no one else a chance to speak until she remembered. It was an exasperator.

"I sent Perry a postcard. So he knows. He knows."

"Perry Potter? A friend of yours?"

"Don't sound so surprised. I have friends. Happy?" she asked abruptly.

He nodded. He found difficulty, as always, in meeting the fiercely kind eyes: gray-blue fire.

"Good. Good. Good. Now tell me all about the children." He didn't want to. Her most damnable characteristic was that she could get anything out of him, anything. He was powerless against the dragnet. He had often tried to persuade himself that he was not afraid of her, but this must be the reason why. No secret that would not be yielded up; she sucked the secrets out. Though the compelling wave of authority was warm and charitable, it could still make a demand like a Customs Inspector's "Have you anything to declare?" He might stall it for a few minutes, but not longer.

He stalled: "Where did you meet Perry? And why's he never said a word about knowing you?"

"He knew me as *Lucille*," said Marion with enormous emphasis. "We have kept in touch. In touch. Not regularly, but still in touch. That's all. Not quite all. I had a pathetic letter from him —pathetic. In the spring, it was. Poor Perry—I hope he has made his decision by now. Tell me about Thomas. And Gerald. And

Sarah. And the new one, whatever its name is—her one, *her* one."

"Wait a minute. I want to hear about Perry."

"Why do you?"

"Why shouldn't I? What's wrong with him? I knew something was, but what's this decision?"

Marion sneezed. She sneezed like a cat in tiny little spasms, almost soundless. She sneezed three times. "It's the seaweed," she said. "Come along." She rose clumsily, but when she was on her feet he saw the straight, beautiful carriage again. She pointed her profile at the cliff. She said in her faraway voice, "To be given up. Given up. Given up."

"*What* is?"

"One can't, of course, give up the gift. There simply comes a time when one has to stop using it. Stop using it. I did—didn't I?—give it up."

Grumbling inwardly, he said, "I know you did."

"Well, so must poor Perry. That's all. Simple—Simple—Simple. How's Thomas?"

❀

Marion's trick of repetition was never indulged while she was in full spate. And she was in full spate now. With Paula's devotion to a story the spate had become inevitable. From the loggia, Philip kept watch for Thomas; being determined that Thomas shouldn't hear a word of this.

For the moment all seemed safe. Thomas and Rab were playing some jungle game in the trees, down and away below the tennis court. A lone Stevens, the youngest boy, appearing wistfully, had been allowed to join them. Sarah had done a vanishing trick. Gerald was in attendance, remotely amused.

"I began to accept fees from time to time. Special clients. Long sessions. Visits to private houses. And that is what one must not do as a clairvoyant. Better to starve, one is kept by others. I suppose I am a remittance woman. Luckily my son-in-law can afford me. I've never had much sympathy with those who go on saying, 'The Lord will provide,' until somebody gets up and passes the butter from sheer exasperation. In my case, the Lord does not provide; Percy does. Though of course you might argue that it's the Lord who provides Percy."

"I call *that* a libel on the Lord," said Gerald.

"We are inclined to misunderstand Percy. What he likes is to be consulted, to be allowed to organize, and *then*," said Marion, with italics at the full, "*to pay*. Where was I? Oh, yes: the journalist. This little fellow who wrote the series for the *Sunday Star*. He was out to expose fraud; or so he said. He went the rounds: séances, fortunetellers, spiritualist societies—all of it. And in due course he got himself invited to Lady Chudley's. A distinguished gathering. 'And I with my harp was there,'" said Marion. "I don't know if you recognize the quotation, but it's relevant."

"Over to Philip," said Paula. "I married into a dictionary of quotations."

Gerald, to Philip's annoyance, got ahead of him.

> " 'The Derby Day sun glittered gaily on cads,
> On maidens with gamboge hair,
> On sharpers and pickpockets, swindlers and pads,
> (For I with my harp was there.)' "

"Precisely," said Marion.

"But don't you make it sound as though—"

"Precisely," said Marion again. "There were some notable fakes present. Among them Zoltan and his wife—she wasn't really his wife, who was she? can't remember—in their thought-reading act. Poor silly Lady Chudley was completely deluded and so were the guests—such guests I mean as weren't planted by Zoltan and—what was that damn woman's name?—doesn't matter, for the purpose of the act. The little man from the *Sunday Star* had no difficulty in spotting *them*. This ball was for charity, by the way."

"You didn't say it was a ball."

"Didn't I? Well, it was."

"Tiaras?" Paula asked.

"There were some tiaras, I remember."

"Bobby Chudley plays good golf," said Paula.

"He wasn't playing that night," said the grandmother, on a note of rebuke. "I was asked to read hands; really rather a childish exercise. I used to look on palmistry much as the baccarat player looks on roulette. Still, I obliged. I was given a room to myself and some caviar sandwiches. Champagne, too. I never drink it, but it's the thought that counts."

"They were all very easy hands. Rather dull, as you might expect. The only interesting palm was Judy Harrison's—the Hon. Judy."

"Saw Judy last month. She's living with a Negro on the Left Bank," said Paula.

"I have no views about miscegenation," said Marion. "I didn't know who she was at the time. None of them gave their names and I was curtained off in case I recognized their faces. This hand, the Hon. Judy's, came through the curtains and the first thing I said to her was 'You've died twice.' I'm afraid I always put some cheap drama into the diagnoses at that kind of function—it was what they liked. The Hon. Judy told me she'd twice tried to commit suicide. Which of course accounted for the breaks in the line, though they might just as well have been dangerous illnesses.

"The journalist came in for a reading, but I don't remember anything about him. When his article appeared on Sunday it completely exposed Zoltan and—if I don't remember her name I'll go mad. . . . Then he did a piece about me. He claimed to have been charged three guineas by Lucile. The fool spelt it with one 'l' and nearly got himself a writ from Lady Duff-Gordon. He implied that the money was for my benefit and not for the charity's. And —very stupid of him, he obviously hadn't done his homework, he gave a report on my career, saying I made my living out of gullible women. It was virtually an accusation of cheating. So I brought the action. Percy was dead against my doing such a thing, wasn't he?"

"He and who else?" Philip murmured.

"The *Sunday Star* offered to settle out of court, but for a miserable sum. So off," said Marion, "we went. What made the case spectacular was my witnesses. A dazzling cloud of witnesses, one might safely say. Most of them well known, all absolutely delighted to be in the box talking about themselves. Some extraordinary revelations. It was a very great show, a positive circus. I enjoyed every minute."

"What did you get?" asked Paula.

"Not as much as I should have. The difficult point of law was to decide—*not* if I was genuine, that was proved to the hilt. But since I'd chosen never to earn any regular income by my gifts (my lawyer, I always thought, made rather too much of that, he was so anxious to establish my integrity) well, then, how could the libel cause me to suffer materially?

"Quite a point. The jury stayed out for three hours. They were all for me, but they found difficulty in assessing the figure. The Judge had done his best to help them—not a very good best in my view. I remember his warning them against regarding me as a martyred saint. I got fifteen hundred. Very nice, while it lasted."

Marion stopped speaking: Paula stayed in an attitude of rigid expectancy. As always when he looked at her suddenly, Philip felt the possessive pang, part pain, part pride.

"And then?" said Paula.

Marion chirped, "Then—then—then," and stared into space. "What the devil was the name of Zoltan's mistress?" she asked irritably.

"You *can't* stop there," Paula pleaded. "I have to know what happened next."

"I hope," said Marion, "that Rudy will get over this operation successfully."

"Rudy?"

"Rudolph Valentino. I always call him Rudy, don't you?"

Paula uncurled regretfully and stood up. "Would you like a drink, Mrs. Murray? What can I offer you?"

Philip studied Marion studying Paula. He could see that one of those quick, unnerving summaries went on inside his mother-in-law's head. If Paula too could see this happening, she gave no sign. She was without self-consciousness as ever, looking beautiful and scratching her back between the shoulder blades.

"A drink?" she repeated.

"I gave it up," said Marion.

"Well, would you like lemonade? Ginger beer?"

"I'll have a gin and It, please."

Paula now looked as baffled as Rab could look when Sarah quoted Browning.

"You asked me what happened next. Next. Next. I was trying to think what did. And that did. No more professional magic *ever*. My mind moves on two levels," said Marion, and Philip could see she was laughing at Paula who, undisconcerted, laughed back. "The moral," said Marion, "is Magic Doesn't Pay."

"I'd have thought the moral was magic pays fifteen hundred quid," said Gerald.

"You would, would you?" It was his turn for one of her demanding, devouring looks. She kept it up while she took her glass from his hand. "I brought you a present, Gerald—don't let me forget. The presents—"

"But Mrs. Murray—"

Marion stopped speaking at once and gave Paula a regal glare for the interruption. It didn't take. "I still don't understand," Paula went on, "*why* you gave it up."

The rustle in the hydrangea bushes made Philip look to his left. Yes, it would be. Thomas came swarming through the bushes and scaled the side of the loggia with a scramble instead of coming round by the steps. His head appeared over the sill just as Marion said, "My dear young woman—nobody possessing the gift can afford to monkey with it. It must be surrendered. Simple. Simple. Simple."

Thomas threw one leg over the sill and jumped down among them. Philip said, "Hullo, old boy—like some lemonade?" and snapped his fingers at Paula for a warning signal. Paula was lost to him. Glass in hand, she was gazing steadfastly at Marion. "I'm the least psychic person in the world," she said. "So maybe

I'm just being stupid. But *can* one stop like that? Give up magic altogether?"

Thomas's voice boomed, "No. Magic just gives *you* up." He added, "I want an apple and so does Johnny Stevens," before he marched away into the house. The tail of his shirt was hanging out.

"Funny little boy, isn't he?" Marion remarked to the silence.

❖

Blanche got off the bus at the end of the parade, and walked up the hill. As she reached the gates of Roseclay, she recognized the twinge of anxiety; anxiety, the regular pursuer. Any afternoon off could bring him running at her back. It was not, she told herself again and again, that she expected things to go wrong in her absence; it was more the sense of having left all that was important here—for the sake of what? Tea with Ellen Dalley. "You're getting old and you're getting very foolish, if you ask me," said Blanche to Blanche. She pushed open the gate.

She saw the children's grandmother, with Mr. and Mrs. Philip, standing beside the car. She saw Gerald, Sarah, Thomas and Rab; picking up each with her eye and finding all well, nothing wrong, as Mrs. Murray came away from the group to greet her.

"What a lovely surprise, M'm," was the truth. This person was the beginning of all of them (with that first interview in the house at Bickley, Kent, 1912) and the sight of her brought its old reassurance. She was positive, masterful and palpably, despite her queer ways, a lady.

"Dear Nanny. I'd almost given up hope. I'm off to the Moonrakers, you see, and then I'll be gone—gone—gone. There's a present for you, I left it on the hall table. I left all the presents there. Labeled. Best way to give presents—just leave them—in case people aren't really pleased with them." She tucked Blanche's arm through hers and led her away towards the monkey puzzle tree. "Do you *like* her?" she asked, rather too loudly, and followed it up at once. "I can see *you* feel as *I* feel. It's all right—quite all right—quite all right. For the moment. Might have been much worse. Walk up and down, don't stand still, less obvious. Suits him to have some money to play with. Question *is* how long will it suit her? She's an innocent, that always softens one's heart. Americans usually are. Efficient—a good manager. And the house—" she began; then she stared past Blanche at the monkey puzzle tree. She went on chirping, "The house—the house—the house"; her usual habit.

One minute she was doing this; the next, she looked pained and puzzled, repeating, "The *house* . . ." Blanche glanced towards Roseclay, helpfully trying to see what was wrong with it, if anything. "Oh but they aren't in the house," Mrs. Murray said. "They're going."

"Mr. Philip likes to get there about twenty minutes before the performance," said Blanche.

XI

She had written, "These were your grandfather's and they come to you with my love. Marion." The oblong leather case was battered and old: the three pearl studs rested in a shell of fading violet plush. Gerald took out the tiny paper with the handwriting upon it, laid this aside and then took out the studs, one by one; turning each in the sunlight. It had become a regular performance: nine days divided the grandmother's visit from now.

And still he could not make up his mind.

Ding-dong, the doubts went, ding-dong. Yes, no? Yes, no?

Today was Saturday. Were it nor for old McPhee's damnable notion of shutting up shop from Monday onwards, he would have more time.

What was the point, after all? What did his private hoard mean to him now? We're rich, he said to himself, we're rich.

There was a tapping on his door. He called, "Come in."

"Another fine day. Gracious, you're early." Brigstock, come to draw his curtains, surprised to find him awake and dressed. He smiled at her, not attempting to shuffle the studs out of sight.

"Still admiring them? I'm not surprised. . . . How soon will you have a dress suit to show them off, do you think? Christmas, perhaps?"

"Perhaps."

"And what are you all going to do with yourselves today?" There was a twinkle in her eyes; she could be having a secret laugh at Paula's craze for program-planning. This now included two free afternoons for Brigstock instead of one. More for Paula's benefit than for Brigstock's, he thought. Things were all right between them; the rhythmic wail of "*Don't* be cross with me, Nanny," meant little and was familiar to him from his mother's day; still he had the feeling sometimes that Paula bucked against Nanny's rule: not like a grownup competing for authority but like a fretful child.

"Only one more Saturday after this—*hasn't* it gone quickly?"

"It always does, my darling."

"Your father seems in better spirits, don't you think? About the show, I mean?"

"Rising above it and on to the next thing, whatever that may be."

"Oh there's always something," said Brigstock. "I mean there always has been. Besides, Mrs. Philip's got a plan."

"She *has?*"

"Don't be naughty. And of course once we're in London—" she broke off, looking dazed with pleasure. "Wonderful to think about, it is . . . a house. What he's always wanted for you. But of course," she said, "we'll miss them all, won't we?"

"Some of them," Gerald corrected her. "I can't truthfully say I'll miss Ikey-Leo: *or* the telephone doll. As to which I can guess what Sarah will be doing with herself today, can't you?" Brigstock's Sunday face came upon her at once; as he had known it

would. "Well don't you let her, now. It's getting quite beyond
a joke. She must have seen it twenty times at least."

What would she say, he wondered, to the poem he had found
on the lavatory floor yesterday? Since it was obviously an abandoned draft, he had flushed it away; with a shudder. It was
headed SHIRLEY: the first line read, "*I have your roses and I still
remember.*"

"Not let her go to that silly matinée, now," Brigstock was
saying. "You take her with you—go somewhere nice this afternoon."

This afternoon? Ding-dong.

❀

Sarah saw Gerald rise from the luncheon table on the loggia,
with a quick glance at his watch and a reminder of his date at
the tennis club. She envied him. He might not be lying, but he
wore that all-of-a-piece look suggesting some secret adventure
ahead.

Had she the same gift she could, even now, spring up with a
thundering lie. She could be out of the house and away, killing
time, unseen, till the matinée began. But lately she had lost her
nerve; she was self-conscious; her fidelity to *Moonrakers 1926*
had become a joke. (Except, of course, to Brigstock, who had no
patience with passions; who always identified the object of worship and disapproved it.)

"My beloved—" said Philip. When he looked at Paula, he
looked like the great actor in all the love scenes. Philip and
Paula were a reflection of her constant image: the two, the
romantic two; and it was strange to have the mystery in the
house. She could not help thinking about their embraces, following them in her mind beyond the bedroom door.

"What's the guilty face for?" Paula was asking Philip.

"Forgot to tell you I invited Shirley and Rupert back here
after the last show tonight. Rupert's only staying till tomorrow—
felt I ought to do something about him."

Sarah abandoned her helping of stewed plums. This was a
miracle. Several decades of adoration had gone by, it seemed,

since discovering that Shirley's husband was called Rupert; not as fine a name as Lionel, but dashing in its association with Browning's Cavaliers. She knew also, and thanked Heaven for it, that the surname was Miller. Rather dull, but neither shaming nor ridiculous. Mrs. Rupert Miller.

Leo Clyde's original estimate, "Keeps herself to herself," had never been disproved. (Oh yes, Shirley had attended the double-wedding party, but what was the use of that? One had not, oneself, been present.) Never a word beyond "Hullo, Sarah," had come since the day of the roses.

Here, tonight. Imagination leaped to its task, first painting a picture of herself in her scarlet dress closeted with Shirley in a corner, then richly ornamenting the scene she could not share, the lovers reunited in the bedroom at the Wayne Court Hotel.

"May I," she croaked, "stay up for the party?"

"Party—who said a party?"

It had become a party in her head. She tried to sound *distraite*: "Didn't you say—tonight—after the show?"

"Only Shirley and Rupert," said Philip, "old Gwen, possibly. No one else."

"Yes, well—could I stay up?"

"Why not?" said Paula.

"Better ask Nanny. We'll be late."

Paula said, "Oh, honestly—" and then changed gear, which, Sarah had observed, she could do with some speed. "You can put on that delicious dress of yours and say hello to them, darling. If it turns into an all-night session, then of course you go to bed."

Sarah said, "Thank you," feeling her heart thump. She went back to the sonnet:

> "*I have your roses and I still remember.*
> *I have your smile to comfort me at night.*"

These lines had come without effort. A certain amount of cudgeling had produced,

> "*Though sad my heart as any bleak December,*
> *I need but think of you to find the light.*"

This image was unsatisfactory, somehow suggesting a hurried search for an electric switch on the wall. She must improve it. Two more rhymes for "remember"?

"My love glows constant like a rich red ember"

was not too bad: and then something about *"a promise bright."*

"De-dah, de-dah, our parting in September,
And after that, though you forget me quite—"

"Wake up, Sarah, Paula's talking to you."

"I'm sorry."

"I said have you got any plan for the afternoon? Want to come for a run in the car—take a swim somewhere new?"

Here it was; the thing she and Gerald noticed all the time. Paula, unlike other adults of their acquaintance, hated to be alone. She must have company and she couldn't stay still.

Sarah was dubious about the drive. Her head felt a little cold and achy after this morning's swim. She would rather lie on the sands of the cove in the sun, dreaming of tonight and working at the sonnet.

Coward always, she said, "Yes, that would be lovely."

"Fine. I'll just run Philip down to the theatre and come back for you."

The Buick was having one of its frequent medical inspections, Sarah remembered. ("If it isn't his watch, then it's his car," was Brigstock's comment.)

"I can walk down, darling," Philip said. "The garage will have it ready by six. Rab, Thomas, up to rest now."

"I don't *want* to rest." Rab's voice was loud and plaintive: "Nor does Thomas—do you, Thomas?"

"Thomas," said Paula, "does what he's told instead of yelling his head off."

"Not always," Thomas said thoughtfully, giving her his absent-minded smile.

One again, Sarah saw, he had put Paula off her stroke. Thomas, of all people. Since he always meant exactly what he said, no more, no less (indeed on a boring level of simplicity), why should Paula look puzzled and almost rebuked?

Philip leaned over and ruffled Thomas's hair, saying, "Well, you do now, eh? Just as you're told. Upstairs and onto your bed. You too, Rab. You'll be asleep in ten minutes after all that swimming."

"I will *not*."

"Whether you will or whether you won't, out of here and quick," said Paula.

Rab said, "Hell's blasted flames and pouring buckets of blood." This drew a giggle from Thomas while he placidly collected his treasure of stones and shells from beside his plate. They went, Thomas plodding as usual and Rab slouching deliberately. Paula shouted, "Hold your head up, Rab, for Heaven's sake! Walk properly. You look like a niblick."

Then she laughed.

"I could *kill* her when she goes into that act." She sounded loving, all the same. "It *is* only an act, you know. And she only puts it on for me, have you noticed?" This was addressed to Philip. "Never for Nanny, I mean," said Paula. "When Nanny gives orders around here, Rab takes them."

"Who doesn't?" said Philip.

"Well, but I'm interested. Rab playing at being a proper child interests me. 'Comes out in defiance of me and total submission to Nanny—see? She's not herself these days, she's a changeling."

Sarah considered this. Rab did in appearance conform to her notion of a changeling: bony and brown and big-eyed. She and Gerald had long ago dismissed the likelihood that Thomas was a changeling, simply because of his shape.

Her father's silence was studied. Not in front of Sarah, said the silence, not discuss Nanny in front of Sarah. Paula got it, turning to her after a moment.

"How d'you think she'll get on at school?"

"I'll keep an eye on her. She's bound to find it rather be-musing at first."

"I like 'bemusing.' Your children do have such splendid vo-cabularies." Philip looked more gratified.

"If she finds it *too* bemusing, I'll take her away." Philip looked shocked by this. Paula got that too. "Why not, if it doesn't work out?"

"She'll be all right," said Philip.

"Can't know, can we? What's the worst of it, Sarah, would you say?"

"My worst was being different. But one learns. If one's differ-ent, then it's no good pretending one's not." She had Paula's whole attention: the square-set blue eyes were trained upon her face. "Go on," said Paula. "Expand on that, will you?" It was as though an equal, somebody of her own age, were asking.

"*Well,*" Sarah crooned in her darkest voice, "I believe it's a question of finding oneself."

"You *are* introspective, aren't you?" It was said admiringly.

"Whether she is or whether she isn't," said Philip, rising from his chair.

"Oh darling—must we? I'm fascinated."

"Then you stay and be fascinated, my love, my love."

"No. I'll drive you down. Be back, Sarah. Wait for me, we'll go on with this."

Philip kissed the top of Sarah's head, murmuring, "*Think* you'd better ask Nanny about tonight, don't you?"

"Oh honestly—" said Paula again.

Alone at the table, Sarah helped herself to a banana. There seemed to be something in the air: a ripple of summer light-ning, an uneasy excitement stirring all about them. It had come with Paula and it stayed. What was the word she wanted? Precarious, perhaps. These days were bright and brittle and chasing on: on to the end of the summer, the end of Moon-rakers, goodbye to Shirley forever, falling leaf and fading tree, lines of white in a leaden sea. "I am myself," she thought. "My heart may turn to stone after September (a possible line for the sonnet). But I would rather be me heartbroken than anybody else." She finished eating the banana, rose from the table and stood looking out through the pillars of the loggia. She saw the

younger members of the Stevens family trooping across the road:
a purposeful caravan, swishing through the grass and going down,
out of sight, to the cove. She could not imagine how it felt to be
a Stevens, nor did she want to. She smiled pityingly upon the
last of them. *The still, graceful figure, the dark hair with its
coppery glints, were draped in sorrow like a cloak.*

"Who am too wise in all I should not know!" she cried, flinging out her arms.

"Hello," said Rab, slouching, and scuffling with one foot.

"You ought to be resting."

"Who were you talking to?"

"It was a cry from the heart."

"Got a misery?" Rab asked, and added, "I do hope not."

"You go to bed, now."

"Oh I will. I just wanted to say hello. I waited till they went."

Rab looked at her as Philip looked at Paula, as she herself
looked at Shirley Ormonde. It was flattering: why should it make
her feel guilty? She said, "Would you like to have the bird book
to read while you're resting? It's in my room."

"Gosh, yes. Can you spare it? I'll take the greatest care."

The vast bird book, the grandmother's gift, meant nothing to
Sarah. She did not know why the grandmother should have
chosen such a thing. It was always disappointing to receive a
present that set up no sort of a glow inside. Here she glanced
at her wrist, at the present whose glow was still strong: Paula's
present, the silver watch with the square face and the gray suede
strap.

"Tell you what," she said to Rab, "you can have the book.
For your own."

"Gosh, you mustn't."

"Why not? You know about birds. I don't. It shall be yours."
She had to fight free from a throttling hug. "Only one thing—
don't let Brigstock know I've given it to you. She's against that
sort."

"She's gone," said Rab. "I saw her walking down the hill.
Why didn't they take her in the car?"

"She'd have said no, thank you."

"Why would she?"

"You go to bed now."

"I love you so," said Rab.

❀

Having made his escape, Gerald was in no hurry. He strolled, at ease and not at ease. The lull of early afternoon lay on the town; with the parade deserted, little traffic along the sea road and a few picnic parties scattered across the sands; the majority were all inside their hotels and boarding houses, eating solidly. Gerald observed their backs at the open windows of Elgin, Rockcliff and Sunnyside House. Sunnyside House, with its echo of the cross woman who had given James MacBride sixpence in coppers, made his wary thoughts warier still. (Lucky to get away with that one. General Stevens, wuffling, "Didn't I see you giving an—ah—*impersonation?*" had been fobbed off with the story of doing it for a dare. Appeal to the General's sporting instinct had succeeded: the General wouldn't tell Philip.)

Coming to the corner of Galleon Street, Gerald loitered, less fearful of a possible spy than of himself. He was still unsure. He fingered the contents of his left-hand pocket: his silver watch, Uncle Percy's present last Christmas, still in good running order: the old Eversharp, likewise down-graded: and the source of doubt, the small oblong leather case.

The hazards were all too obvious. A query about his age: ("Now why would a laddie like yourself . . . ?") A suggestion of stolen goods. ("I'll be obliged to ask how you came by these.") Recognition. The last was unlikely: he hadn't set foot in the shop this summer. But it could happen: old McPhee might have seen him going past, with Philip.

Ding-dong. Yes—no?

One had to: and one didn't know why.

Old McPhee was there, in his low dark cavern, looking puffy, sleepy and rather cross. The crossness was a help, a challenge. Gerald heard his own voice, sounding light and clipped. "How much—for these? The studs are really good."

McPhee stared at him under his tufty eyebrows before making

a Hrrmph noise. He picked up the small leather case first. He fitted the microscope into his eye to look at the pearl studs. He kept it there after he had abandoned them: he pressed open the back of the watch, examined its works and then shut it up again. He didn't touch the pencil at all. His silence was disheartening. He took the glass from his eye, polished it, and made another Hrrmph noise.

"How much are ye asking?" he said at last. It was a strong temptation to answer him in his own parody of an accent: with an effort, Gerald refrained. "Lord—I don't know," he said. "What are they worth?"

"Verra little. They are worrth verra little. To me, that is. I could no put them in the window: they would have to go in the tray and tak their chance with the small stuff."

"Even the studs?"

Mr. McPhee said there would not be much demand for them in a place like Sawcombe—he must see that.

"All right I see that. How much will you give me?"

Behind him, he heard the door clack open. He didn't look round.

"Now the watch would be worrth at the most fifteen shillings. I could offer no more than one shilling for the pencil. And these—now these—"

Was it guilt that made him so deeply conscious of the person standing just at his back? He had to turn.

"Hullo, Gerald," said Leo Clyde.

Winded, Gerald stood silent, letting the picture come in: the black silky hair, the nutcracker face with the sharp sad eyes. Deplorable suit, his mind registered automatically: a dazzle of gray, pink and white checks, worn with a pink shirt: the color made a most unhappy contrast with Leo's complexion.

"Don't mind me, Gerald."

"For these—" McPhee repeated. "Now, I would be prepared to offer a pound for each stud. Three pounds in all."

The right thing to do was to say no and get out of the shop. He couldn't say no. Not to three pounds, sixteen shillings.

"Very well," he said loftily. "That'll do."

Mr. McPhee raised a majestic finger. "Aha—aha—one minute, please. You did not observe that in all these offers I was using the conditional?"

"I beg your pardon?"

"I said 'I would' and 'I could' throughout, did I not? Did you once hear me say 'I *will*'?"

The moment was mixed up; he saw the tufty brows, the stretching smile: he felt the great, downward jolt of his heart under his ribs and a swirl of panic fury in his head.

"You," said McPhee majestically, "are a minor: and I do not do business with minors."

Through the mist of rage he heard Leo Clyde's thick, smooth voice: "Mr. McPhee, supposing I told you the studs were mine."

"I would not believe you."

"Of course you wouldn't, old boy. But would you offer *me* three quid? If you tried it on, I'd tell you just what you could do with it. Bye-bye." Grabbing Gerald's arm, Leo steered him out of the door: and now Gerald found himself trapped, linked arm-in-arm with Leo, dazed and sick with anger, unable to speak.

"Old So-and-So," Leo said. "For a dirty deal I'd back the Scot against the Jew any day. They're nice studs. Sure you want to sell them?"

Dry-mouthed, still speechless, he saw what was coming.

"I'll give you six quid," said Leo. "Can't make it more on my salary. But I saved two on the garnet tiepin. That's what I went in for. Old McBastard lost himself a sale." He halted outside the toy shop. "What about it?" he asked, grinning.

Not Leo Clyde. Anybody but Leo. Anybody. They were pretty things: he could see them on a curved white shirt-front, worn with an off-the-peg dinner jacket: worn by Leo.

Philip might notice them there. Would Philip remember? Even though he had barely glanced at Marion's present, these were from long ago. Philip might.

And in any event, no matter what the danger, the answer was Not Leo Clyde.

"All right," said Gerald. "If you'd like to have them." He

handed over the little case, hurriedly, looking out for spies. With the same quick secretive gesture, Leo whipped out his wallet. Something practiced and abominable here; from himself as from Leo: the feeling that it had been done before, would be done again. He disliked this very much.

They walked on in silence. He had no wish to walk along the parade with Leo and he had no energy left for escape. He whistled "Bye, Bye Blackbird." They came past Sunnyside, Rockcliff and Elgin. It began to be better. (Six pounds, six pounds, six pounds: and the sense of shame drawing off, blowing away.)

"Could we keep this transaction private?" he asked in a stiff, unnatural voice.

"Philip not to know, eh?"

"I'd rather nobody knew."

"Look, Gerald, I won't wear them till the show folds. And that ain't long now. And meanwhile I promise not to say a word. Good enough?"

"Thank you."

Leo halted again. "You aren't in a real fix, are you? Money jam? *That* isn't why . . . ?"

"No, it isn't."

"I wouldn't feel right about it, you see. You see how I wouldn't? I'd tell you to go straight to Dad."

"I can assure you—"

"We don't need assurances. What we need," said Leo, "is a little job done for us. Won't take you a tick."

"What sort of little job?" Leo had caught the sharp, suspicious note in his voice before he caught it himself. Leo looked wounded.

"*Not* playing a fast one, Gerald. I don't do that sort of business with minors." (He means me to laugh now; I can't laugh: I can't laugh his laugh any more than I can talk his language. Why is that?)

Leo said, "I'm cutting it a bit fine for the matinée: which I don't imagine you're patronizing—correct? Then if you'll just pop to the post office and send this wire for me? That's all. Here's the bob for the wire. Get it off right away, won't you? Gee-Gee."

"I beg your pardon?"

"Gee-Gee. A cert. I only bet on certs. Bonus for you if it comes in at anything over fives. Bye-bye Blackbird."

Gerald stood where he was, cooling down. He read the telegram, addressed to a London bookmaker, whose advertisements he had seen above the slogan, "Duggie never owes."

Five pounds to win seemed a heavy investment, on Leo's salary. The horse was called Sandblast. Gerald found this service somehow distasteful, but it might have been worse. He turned back in the direction of the post office and he had just passed Sunnyside for the third time when Morris Ward loomed up in front of him, thrusting out his can to make a barrier: Morris, pussy-faced and smiling.

"Mr. Valentino, in person . . . oh, mustn't call you that now he's dead, must I? Poor Rudy. Gerald, I've got the car—Father's let me have it for the afternoon. Like to come to Redcove? Oh, excellent. Make speed, though—I'm dodging Poppy. Swore I'd take her to the cinema tonight and enough is enough."

"I have to send a wire."

"Well, send it from Redcove, can't you?"

"All right," said Gerald.

※

Thomas awoke from his short afternoon sleep. He looked at his watch, the new possession. It had a squat gun-metal case, luminous figures and a shiny brown strap. Only three o'clock. Had it stopped? He raised his wrist to his ear and heard the reassuring tick. For the first few days of ownership, he had done this so often that Rab laughed at him.

Was Rab awake? Undoubtedly: she hadn't eaten enough lunch. No Brigstock to make her eat, that was the trouble. Anyone who refused to eat at mealtimes surprised him. But someone who ate for Nanny and for nobody else was especially interesting. Yesterday she had even drunk some quite beastly milk at Nanny's request. ("It's *not* sour, Thomas, don't be ridiculous, drink it up." Why, he wondered, was Brigstock always on the milk's side?)

He got off the bed and began to dress himself, slowly as always, though he was eager to find Rab, the valued companion. He had never imagined being friends with a girl. He remembered having mistaken her for a boy at their first meeting. She looked like a boy; she behaved like a boy. She could swim better than any of them, better even than Gerald. She played all the games like a boy. Hard and fearless, she never cried. She never fussed about her clothes.

Though she talked little when they were with the others, seeming in awe of Sarah, she would talk when the two of them were alone. Her stories hypnotized him. It was hard to realize that somebody only a year older than he should have traveled so far and seen so much. He had come to put the island called Martha's Vineyard first on the map of her journeyings, because she put it first: to see it as a magic place because that was how she saw it. She kept postcards of the island. He had drawn its odd outline in his notebook.

Were it not for Rab, thought Thomas, hunting a shoe under the bed, these last weeks would have been—what? He gave up the search for the shoe as he searched instead for the right word, sitting back on his heels on the floor. He never could do two things at once.

These last weeks had been . . . no, empty was the wrong word. Surely they had been full; full of newness; ever since Paula and Rab arrived. (That was Thursday, July the 29th: today was Saturday, August the 28th.) Try as he might, he could only see Paula and Rab as two sudden new sisters, one larger than the other. He told nobody this. A stepmother was a stepmother; and those in books were always cruel, whereas Paula was kind. "But she doesn't feel true, somehow," was his bumbling verdict.

He went after the shoe again, having failed to find the word. Perhaps "empty" was right. No newness could compensate for the thing that was gone. It left a bewildering gap. Without Rab he would miss it even more. But he missed it very much.

For the first time ever, the days were just days, the nights just nights and that was all. He was here and nowhere else. Somebody, something, had shut the doors on his other world: his dreams were ordinary dreams: never a hint of having been There; There might not exist. No waking to the call of the night-walk, and no more seeing through: the friendly invisible shapes were gone from the air.

And how much else was lost as this steadily different time went by? He was, he feared, forgetting a great deal. Always it had been difficult to grasp the memories, even when they were a moment old: now they had completed their vanishing trick. Nor was it any use trying to restore them by re-reading his notebooks. Such records as he had made from year to year were utterly meaningless: his observations on the landscape of There, for example.

He found one comfort: forgetting completely, he would cease to miss the past. You couldn't (could you?) miss something you no longer remembered. But even that thought had a horribly final and mournful flavor. "Magic gives *you* up," he had said to the grandmother, in the hope that she, of all people, would sympathize. She hadn't answered him. Or were her parting words, perhaps, meant to be an answer? Hard to tell with the grandmother. She had patted him briskly, saying, "Shield and buckler, Thomas, shield and buckler. As the day is, so shall thy strength be." This he had written down.

Her present, unwrapped after she had gone, as she wished, was a black bone elephant with ivory tusks; magnificent, but too big for the bedside table. It stood on the mantelpiece; to be paid regular homage. He now said, "Shield and buckler," twice to the elephant before he went to knock on Rab's door.

"Come—" said Rab.

Since her bed was high, and the foot of it pointed towards him, he saw two flat bare soles with their fringes of toes and immediately beyond them the back of a huge book standing upright. It was a funny perspective and he began to laugh in the doorway. Rab let the book go down on her stomach, becoming visible.

"I didn't sleep a wink. So there," she said.

"Well don't 'so there' me. It isn't my fault we have to rest."

"Bet *you* did. You look all owly. Want to see a Great Tawny

Owl? This is the finest book—" She slammed it shut in his face
as he came to see the owl. She jumped off the bed. She was naked
to the waist; her ribs showed. She was wearing only her shorts,
boys' shorts with flies. (None of the other girls in Sawcombe
wore these and he had noticed Brigstock's Sunday face coming
on when she looked at them.)

Rab pulled a blue jersey over her head, strapped her belt round
her waist and hung the big knife on the belt. She made a half-
hearted stroke with the hair brush, kicked her feet into a pair of
plimsolls and said, "Let's go have an adventure. We'd better take
supplies." Opening the top drawer of her dressing table, she took
out three apples and a lot of money. "You can stow the apples,"
she told him. He paused only to set the silver lion upright on her
bedside table where it had fallen over.

In the tradition, they both crept close to wall and banisters,
dodging their way down and out through the front door. There
was no real hazard today. Paula, even if she caught them clear
of the house, would never dream of stopping them. Brigstock
would. But it was her afternoon off. There had been arguments:
sometimes Brigstock gave in, sometimes Paula. The arguments depressed Thomas and he was soothed to know there were none
ahead.

Still playing their game, they crept across the garden, doubled
up and keeping a lookout. Beyond the gate they began to run.
Halfway down the hill Rab stopped running.

"Okay," she said, "they lost the trail."

"And they were savage customers," said Thomas. "What shall
we do now?"

"The tide's way out. Let's get a bus to the harbor and go on
the Rivermouth rocks." As they waited for the bus outside the
Fundrome, she said, "Unless you'd rather go to the Kiddies'
Show." (She was always hoping he would do what she called his
trick with Perry Potter again. But she knew she wasn't allowed to
mention it.)

He said doubtfully, "Would *you* rather?"

"Silly old Thomas, why won't you ever choose between things?
I asked you."

He circled round her chanting, "I asked *you*—Lyturgum-Lytoo—"

"Lyturgum-Lytoo doesn't *mean* anything."

"Yes it does. It means all sorts of things."

"Well what?"

"It's a secret password; you simply wouldn't understand about Lyturgum-Lytoo."

She aimed a blow at his head.

"Here's the bus," said Thomas.

Side by side in a front seat on the open top, they soared grandly along the parade.

"Tell the one about the Vineyard hurricane," he suggested.

"No, I'm playing. Watch out: they've got outposts down there." She unhooked her knife. "Their plan is to board the bus and kill the driver and commandeer the bus and get us back across the frontier."

"I'll dissolve them," said Thomas.

"How?"

"With my powder. A secret formula." He stood up and leaned over. The conductor, coming to collect their fares, told him to sit down. There was once, according to the conductor, a little boy who did just that and fell straight off the top of the bus.

"Was he killed?" asked Thomas.

"What do *you* think?"

Taking a cue from Brigstock, Thomas said, "Well, I don't know, I'm sure. What do you think, Rab? Think he was killed?"

"*And how.* A truck was coming right behind and squashed him flat. So flat they had to peel him off the parade."

"Then they rolled him up to take him away, just like a doormat," said Thomas. "What was his name?"

The conductor said crossly, "Same as yours. Now where do you want to go?" and, having collected their pennies, departed.

There were two ways to approach the rocks. "Want to go by the jetty or through the grounds of the Rivermouth and over the private beach?" Rab asked. She dug him viciously in the ribs with her elbow, adding, "*You choose now, see?*"

"Ha, I have it," said Thomas after a moment's thought.

"Have what?"

"It's an expression. People in books, old books, often say, 'Ha, I have it,' when they've decided something."

"Well Ha what do you have?" she asked.

"We'll go there by the jetty and come back by the River-mouth."

It was a longish walk from the bus stop, but downhill all the way; by slanted narrow streets paved with cobblestones and full of smells. "Like France," Rab said, "except the colors of these houses are paler."

"It's the poor part of the town, according to Brigstock. Has everywhere got a poor part, do you suppose?"

"I wouldn't know."

"It's jolly nice anyway," said Thomas. He examined the dark caverns of doorways, and chased the scouting cats; he stopped every now and then to consider the thin gutters at each side of the cobbles, full of bright green weed.

Suddenly it ended, coming out on a parade unlike the parade further west. He saw humped cottages with white-washed faces; boats drawn right up on to the road; nets spread out to dry. A man with gumboots on was mending a barrel.

To his left there was the jetty, coming up tall as a castle out of the green rocks, running on toward the great fan of the sea that lay out, silken and colorless, far off. He could not tell where the wet sand stopped and the sea began. The smells had turned to a mixture of salt and fish and tar. Overhead the gulls were screaming.

They decided to walk all along the jetty to the end. The steps were high, requiring a stretch of the leg each time. Rab went faster than Thomas. At the top they stood looking down on the eastward side: onto the huge spread of weedy rocks, pools and sandribs. Thomas stared up at the colored cliff towering above the hotel in its hanging garden; the garden hung down to the dry white part of the sand where the rocks were plain gray like elephants. From here it looked as though the garden were stuck to the cliffside: in fact there was a dip between; the channel where the river ran out. Beyond the dry white sand, wet rocks piled up again and the sea met the river.

"Come on," said Rab. "Let's get there."

Thomas paid no attention: his progress along the jetty was designedly slow. The crevices between the stones were deep, full of weeds and water: he kept stopping to put his hand down a crevice and fish for treasure. He tugged at rusty iron rings stapled into the stone, pretending he could lift the jetty up in the air by doing this. Rab was far ahead now. The crevices yielded no treasure except a small tin lid and two shells of a kind he already possessed. When he caught up with her she was sitting dangling her legs. "What a time you take. How's about an apple?" she said.

❀

Rab had settled for Thomas. Though she longed for Sarah as friend and companion, this was a dream, could never become reality. The facts that he was a year younger and distinctly babyish, appointed her the leader in all their expeditions.

She had led him a long way, she realized, returning from the estuary, crossing the dry white sand, aiming for the tall pointed rock. It was one of her favorite rocks, although it stood back so far from the sea. It had a commanding, lighthouse presence; she shinned up it like a monkey. Miles had taken a snapshot of her doing this. Where was Miles, she wondered? Only one pink French postcard declaring JE PANZE À TOI had reached her. He belonged to the past and it shocked her to find how little she missed him.

She could not link past and present. The time before now was sealed off. Now meant Roseclay, Brigstock and the Westons. After Sarah, Brigstock claimed her most devoted attention: there was no reason why Brigstock should wring her heart; except, perhaps, that she was used to adults having fun. Miles, in memory, had fun. Nanny, never.

Clinging to the rock spire, she looked for Thomas. There he was, still squatting by the biggest of the weedy pools a hundred yards off. Armed with the white, twisted branch of wood, whose discovery had given him pleasure, he was dragging the pool. He raked up a swathe of seaweed, then laid the branch aside and examined the seaweed carefully. She didn't know what he expected to find. Left alone, she thought with a giggle, he might well stay there doing that until the tide cut him off. It had turned now. From this exhilarating outpost she could see the estuary filling, the cross-wave curling and breaking, and from east to west the long silken sweeps of water advancing over the sand. Where were the giant rollers of South Beach, the surf that roared, the high mountain walls of green marble coming up, riding in? Lost. But not so sadly lost as they used to be. Thomas had conjured them back. His most endearing aspect was his thirst for information about the Vineyard; about all her private magic. Sarah, she guessed, would not care. Sarah had private worlds of her own.

Ah, but the best adventure still lay ahead, school in England, the adventure through which she would walk in Sarah's shadow. Thinking about it was too much for Rab. She jumped wildly from the rock and began turning cartwheels. All her money fell out of her pockets, half-crowns and shillings and sixpences were sprinkled on the sand. She collected them and piled them on a stone. Then she walked on her hands and turned more cartwheels until she was dizzy.

"I do wish I could do that," said Thomas, appearing suddenly with his white branch sloped across his shoulder like a gun. Rab lay with her eyes shut, saying, "Everything's going round and round and round."

"Are you going to be sick?"

"I am not."

"If you *were*, the sick would only be that one apple, wouldn't it? Wouldn't it?" he repeated in his maddening way: "That's all it would be. You didn't eat any lunch and your breakfast must have gone down too low by this time." He added, "I'm starving."

"You always are. Know what? We'll have tea at the hotel."

"I've only got—"

"—one-and-nine," said Rab. "We know all about your old one-and-nine. Didn't you find any doubloons or pieces of eight with all that fishing? You're a lousy treasure-seeker. All I have to do is lie on the sand—look around and there it is." She pointed to the pile of silver on the stone. Thomas grinned and asked, "How do *you* see pieces of eight? I see black metal eights that have got broken. Moidores are oysters shells. Doubloons now . . ." He sat down, presumably to think this out. She hauled at his collar: "You're starving, remember?" She dashed away from him up the sand, shouting, "Follow me—follow me— follow me!"

They crept up the steps, through the gardens on to the lawn of the hotel, playing their game. Rab said, "We have to get to the glass porch before we're safe."

"Why do you call it a porch? I call it a veranda," said Thomas. "I say, are *all* these people hostile tribes?"

"Every one of them."

She led him briskly among the garden chairs and the snooty British families having their tea outside. Tea was happening inside also: through the glass she could see the waiters in white coats, the flowers, the heads and shoulders.

"Can't we have tea out here?" Thomas asked.

"I don't see a table empty, do you?"

"There's one over there—beside the weeping willow. It hasn't got a cloth on—does that matter?"

Rab looked where he pointed. Round the green tent of the willow, a man came strolling; he carried a book under his arm. He halted beside the rustic table, glancing about him before he decided to sit. There was no mistaking that height, that flaming red hair, those fancy sports clothes. Chester.

She grabbed Thomas and tugged him. "Inside—quick! quick like a fox!" she hissed.

"Are you playing?"

"*No.* Come on."

She dragged him after her: up the three steps to the glass porch, through the swing-door. "Keep going," she muttered as he bumped into her from behind. She tore along between the tables, dodging waiters with trays, saying, "Excuse *me*," and scurrying off the porch by the far door that led into the lobby. The lobby, with its gray carpet, white paneling and huge Chinese pots of flowers, was deserted. Now she had lost Thomas. She danced from foot to foot, waiting for him to follow her through the door. "Oh, honestly," said Rab. She dodged back to peer in through the glass panels. She saw him standing beside a table, having something wiped off him by a waiter. The waiter was grinning as he wielded the napkin. The people seated at the table, two old ladies, looked cross.

And now—doom—here came Chester. He had seen her after all. He strode past Thomas and the waiter; he pushed the door open; he seized her up and swung her around in the air.

"Rab, darling! Gosh, I'm glad to see you. Where were you running to?"

"Running away from you," said Rab.

He yelled with laughter. As usual. There he stood, as she always remembered him, large and highly colored with his head tilted back, laughing.

"What's the idea, baby?"

"Got bad news for you," she said. "I hate to bring bad news."

"Let's have it," said Chester.

"Paula's married."

He laughed again, uproariously. Shock, perhaps. No. He said, "Well, I knew *that*. I heard from her. Married her Pierrot—acquired three stepchildren. I'm here to visit your new family."

"You *are?*" She saw past and present mixing most indigestibly. Now Thomas came butting through the door. There was an enormous brown stain on his shirt, beginning at the shoulder and spreading down the front.

"Look at you," said Rab.

"It was my branch. It whacked their coffee pot. They were frightfully angry. I had no idea people had coffee for tea."

"Introduce me," said Chester. He was nice to Thomas, interested in the branch, pleased to hear that Thomas was hungry; he whipped them back to the porch; he annexed a table and ordered tea. "On a mammoth scale," he explained to the waiter.

"What do you do?" Thomas asked courteously.

"I'm in show business. Like your daddy."

"We call him Father."

"Sorry, pal. Like Father."

Two waiters came scurrying. This was Chester's effect always: Rab had seen it operate in New York and in California. Perhaps because he was so big and blazing, perhaps because he was so rich. King Organizer, Paula said.

"Then, when we've eaten ourselves stupid I'll run you home," said Chester.

Thomas, putting out a cautious hand for a scone, turned suddenly crimson. He drew his hand back.

"Change your mind?" Chester asked, pushing forward the plate of sandwiches instead.

Thomas sat quite still.

"I've remembered," he announced despairingly.

"What? Bathroom?"

Thomas blinked. He said, "We can't do this. At least I can't; I'm sorry." He slid off his chair and began to tug at his branch; this had now got caught between the chair leg and the wall.

Rab groaned, "Gosh, Thomas, *what?*"

"I must go home," he explained to Chester. "Rab can stay and have tea with you but I must go home."

" 'Cause why?"

"Mrs. Gale has made splits."

"Splits?"

"*Devonshire* splits. I saw her making them and I clean forgot."

"Oh who cares?" said Rab. She was unprepared for his look of blind fury. So, it seemed, was Chester, who extended a gentle arm to bar his way. "Splits can wait, can't they? 'Sure they can, though I wouldn't know what they are."

"They're just old scones, like those," said Rab, pointing.

Thomas stamped his foot. "Don't you *see*—she made them specially. It's important. *Somebody's* got to eat them. My goodness I'd think you could see that." He struggled against Chester's arm: "Let me *go*, will you?"

"Steady, Mister. How'll you get home? Long way, isn't it?"

"Doesn't *matter*— Let me *go*." He dropped his branch and began to pummel Chester. He put his head down and struck out with flailing, furious blows. At once he became the center of attention. Behind her Rab heard somebody making the "Tht-tht" noise expressing British disapproval. Somebody else cried, "Good Gracious!" A child's excited shriek came up: "Look at him, look at him, *look at him!*" and a grumbly throaty voice cut through the shriek, saying, "That's the one who upset Mrs. Seton's coffee."

Thomas changed his tactics all at once; he stopped punching, doubled up and ducked away under Chester's arm. He ran. By some miracle he avoided a waiter carrying two teapots. He dashed out through the garden door and across the lawn.

Chester went on laughing.

XII

Sarah tried to discount the flickering headache and the shivers that still stayed after the swim. The sun was warm now; but here on the cliff the wind blew strongly: she stared obediently towards the sea, while Paula said, "That's how I want you, with your chin up. Hold it." Nobody had ever sketched her portrait before and she should, she knew, be enjoying this mightily. Aware of a blur at the corner of her left eye, an odd little flutter like gray feathers, she blinked. The feathers were still there.

"Nice to have a long neck," said Paula. She added, "I've always wanted one," as though a neck were the sort of thing one could be given for one's birthday.

A yawn took Sarah by surprise; it was followed instantly by an-

other and the little stabbing headache came again. "Hungry?"
Paula asked. "Tea time, would you say?"

It was, of course, long past tea time. Another of the oddities
about Paula was her indifference to the clock: not, in Sarah's
experience, an adult sign. Nanny, Philip and all schoolteachers
might well carry clocks inside their heads. Under their rule it was
always time to stop something or start something. But Paula believed her when she said it was nowhere near tea time yet: the
reason being that she could no more eat than fly. "Never have I
felt so peculiar," Sarah thought, blinking through the feathers at
the sea. She prayed, "Please let it stop soon, because of tonight,
because of Shirley."

"You frown like Philip," said Paula laughing. "It's a distinctive
frown. Something on your mind?"

"Not really."

"Are you sad about *Moonrakers?* I think you are."

"I'm sad for Father," Sarah said cautiously, then braced herself to swallow the next yawn.

"Don't be, darling. He's liable to have a splendid surprise coming to him."

Terrible to feel so unresponsive, to think of nothing to answer.

"Forget the bad times, sweetheart. No more bad times and
that's a promise," Paula said.

It was not only the headache that confused Sarah when she
tried to see the past as a series of "bad times." Paula had made
this kind of observation already; she found it puzzling. Nothing
had been so very bad, surely? Their mother's death, yes: but this
was long ago, and this was not what Paula meant. She meant the
later years, the lodgings and the landladies and not enough
money: the whole pattern of their life before she came. She
didn't know, couldn't know, much about it. She knew nothing
of the fun and the adventures; nothing of the peak moments;
Nanny meeting the school train; Philip shouting, "*That's* more
like it!" as he ran to them.

"Not cold, are you? Two minutes and I'll be through." The two
minutes became five. Paula said, "It's wrong somewhere—don't
quite know where. Hold it." Five more minutes; then the gay,

absorbed voice: "Only making it worse, that's what I'm doing. Come and see."

Sarah looked down upon the likeness of her own face in black pastel lines with scarlet for the lips. It seemed to have infinite beauty and infinite importance and, because of the pain in her head, her blurred vision, to be many miles away: a gift withdrawn, made tantalizing. She said, "It's wonderful. I love it."

"All yours," said Paula."

She tried to think of showing it to Shirley tonight: of Shirley asking if she might keep it. The deadness of response was here too. She could only put her hand over her eye and yawn. "Sorry —sleepy," she muttered.

"That's the swim. Better not tell Nanny about the swim, eh?" Paula laughed. Then she said sharply, "Are you all right? You're not. 'Take you home."

On the way to the car she made one comforting observation: "When I feel ill, I don't want to be touched and I don't want to be talked to." Then she drove, fast but smoothly. Sarah kept her eyes shut: it was better now, just a little. But tonight?

"Nearly there," said Paula's voice. Opening her eyes, she saw that they were at the top of the hill road; they came under the tunnel of trees and down towards the gates of Roseclay. Paula braked the car gently.

"Out you get."

The pain in her head changed as she stepped from the car. It jumped up and down. She could feel the weight of it, the shape of it, a round jumping pellet: when she began to walk, the feathered blur on her eye was shot full of sparks. She could only see half the loggia. Was that Thomas sitting there? She thought it was: at the end of a dancing white shimmer that resolved itself into a tablecloth. Why was he there all by himself? Whose was the car roaring into the drive now and who was yelling, "Hey, Paula!" in a loud American voice? She neither knew nor cared. She went blindly in through the hall, side-stepping to avoid Mrs. Gale who was saying something about Thomas and a taxi, and whose face was cut in half as she spoke.

"Perhaps I really am dying this time," thought Sarah: it would

be a miserable waste to die when Shirley was not here to see it happen. She steered herself up the stairs, holding tightly to the rail.
The stairs were in her head, thumping upward one by one, a
staircase of separate pains going up. She must remember this and
write it all down. If she lived. The landing seemed to be covered
in thick black stripes. Then more hurting stairs; then the door of
her room. The room was too full of brightness, too much sun and
no strength left to draw the curtains across the window before she
fell onto the bed.

❀

It was idiotic, Gerald told himself, to be worrying over Leo
Clyde's bet. Anyone who talked about a "cert" was in for trouble. The horse Sandblast was bound to lose. He would, he argued, have done Leo a kindness in not sending the telegram at
all. But the words "Get it off right away," were nagging him as he
strode up the hill. He had sent it off at twenty minutes to four, by
the Redcove Post Office clock. He tried to put the blame on
Morris Ward.

Once he could get at this morning's newspaper, he would be
out of at least half his trouble: he would know what time the race
was. Four o'clock, he said, Sandblast for the four o'clock. Sandblast winning by a neck, losing by six lengths, objection against
Sandblast for bumping and boring, Sandblast falling and rolling
on its jockey, Sandblast crossing its legs for a Tom Webster
cartoon, Sandblast doing anything it damn pleased, provided it
hadn't run earlier than four o'clock.

He streaked in through the gates of Roseclay. Another new car
in the drive, an American car, nudging Paula's. He was diverted,
hearing a man's loud voice on the loggia. He went that way.

The first thing he saw was Thomas, up at the far end of the
table, which was laid for tea. The silver teapot and tray were at
the nearer end. Removed from them, Thomas sat with a plate of
Devonshire splits and a glass of milk before him. His face was
scarlet; his mouth was full. He had managed to upset something
over his shirt. Above him there towered a stranger, with flaming red hair, dressed in extravagant clothes and laughing heartily.

"So these are the splits," the stranger was saying. "Do I get one?"

Thomas nodded and shoved the plate towards him.

"No hard feelings, Thomas?"

Thomas shook his head.

"Boy, you can certainly land a punch."

Thomas eyed him in silence.

"You ought to challenge Dempsey. Wouldn't that be an idea?"

There was a longish pause; then Thomas said, "We don't box until we get to Form Four," and the stranger's laugh resounded. Who he was and why he was teasing Thomas (always an unprofitable exercise), Gerald could not imagine. Nor was he much interested. The only matter of importance was that abandoned *Daily Mail*, lying on the floor just beside Thomas's chair.

As he moved to pick it up, several things happened. Rab appeared at his elbow, saying, "Sarah's got sunstroke"; Philip—driving the Buick in through the gates—hit the bumper of the visitor's car with a loud clunking noise; Paula strode out to meet Philip, the stranger ran after her and Thomas upset his milk straight across the tablecloth.

"How life does continually unfold," Gerald murmured as he picked up the newspaper. He stood, turning to the sports page while the milk dripped beside his foot with a small noise. He heard Rab groaning, "She just can't talk, it hurts her so," and Thomas replying, "Neurulgia, I expect," before his eyes found the list of runners at Gatwick. Sandblast: Nemesis, he said to himself, the three-thirty. (Might have known it. But that doesn't mean it won.) *Sandblast Doped—Scratched—Gatwick Sensation.* His mind went on writing the headlines.

❀

"Well, thank you very much, Nanny, I've enjoyed myself," said Mrs. Dalley.

"They do one quite well there, I always think," said Blanche. She had returned Ellen's hospitality at the Landslip; which specialized in farmhouse teas. Now they were waiting for the buses that would take them by their different ways home.

"It's gone quickly," Ellen said, "the summer, I mean—I suppose as one gets older . . . You'll send me a postcard once you're settled in?" And then the bus came and bore her away.

The words "settled in" stayed on Blanche's mind. The homeward bus pottered down through leafy lanes. Looking out of the window she saw the hints of autumn: stacked corn with the sharp gold furrows running between: the apples growing big: the pale green fruit of the chestnuts among their darkening leaves. She was aware of the shorter twilight, a bloomy dusk coming over the hill. The end of August. Hard to realize there was no longer the old threat upon the air.

"Settled in."

She thought of the new house waiting: the house that was, said Mrs. Philip, larger than Roseclay: the house where she would, said Mrs. Philip, be run off her feet. This prospect suited her well. Holding on to it, she skipped the twelve chilly weeks of the winter term lying ahead: this would be a different autumn and a warmer winter. Far off but certain, there glowed the Christmas tree in the new house. And all of them together again.

(Thomas? Puxford? These question marks remained. According to Mr. Philip the problem had ceased to exist. This was, of course, a way Mr. Philip had with problems; he treated them as he treated bills in the middle of the month; when they were quiet they weren't there. Certainly, Mr. Philip said, Thomas would go back. It was possible that the headmaster would explode this theory. And then? The day school in London?)

"Settled in."

Tomorrow she must write to Mrs. Latham and Mrs. Fothergill. She began to arrange in her head the words she had not dared try out on paper. "Now that Mr. Weston has remarried, I shall have a permanent position as housekeeper." After this, what? "Sorry not to come to you again," would be polite, must be said in all its insincerity, together with the sincere hope that both employers would find somebody suitable. Mrs. Fothergill would accept in good temper. Mrs. Latham would write a moan, begging to be "fitted in on odd days." Well, perhaps: later on.

The road dipped down steeply and the sea fanned out beyond

the crinkled roofs of Sawcombe, silver ridges under the beginning of a fiery sunset. Blanche got off the bus at the pier.

◈

Thomas stood up, leaned against the oak tree and slid down again into the enclosing chair back made by the roots. Rab said, "Why do you go on doing that?" She was carving slices of moss from the crocodile root with her knife. He said, "Well, why do you go on doing *that?*"

"Because I'm so miserable."

"It's taken *years* to grow and you're just spoiling it."

"Carve *you* up," said Rab, "any minute."

"Phooey," said Thomas.

He stared at the garden terraces; the shadows were growing longer; evening advanced upon it all. The trees, the roses, the hydrangea bushes had begun to look heavy and velvety. The red walls of the house were turning to violet; the windows were turning to gold. Listening carefully, he could hear two kinds of noise: the bird notes growing lazier through the leaves, and from the loggia the echo of grown-up voices laughing faintly, on and on.

"Why don't they get a doctor for her?" said Rab.

"You don't need a doctor for neurulgia."

"Neuralgia."

"Brigstock says neurulgia."

"Well, she's got it wrong."

"She'll be back soon," said Thomas, "and everything will be all right. Except," he added, "it feels like the end of a phase."

"Huh?" said Rab.

"Well—you know. Suddenly everything gets to look different. You were *in* it—and now you're remembering it—do you see?"

"No," said Rab.

"Perhaps it's just that Chester person making it feel different."

Rab didn't answer. She shot up suddenly: "They're all going. Down to the show. No, too early . . . Somewhere else for a drink first. That's what. Listen."

"Well *you* don't want to go, do you? Besides, supper hasn't happened—"

"I'm going to sit with Sarah."

"She won't want you. She doesn't want anybody when she has neurulgia. And Brigstock will turn you out as soon as she gets back, mark my words."

But Rab went up the garden with enormous strides. When she reached the top terrace she ran. Thomas began to collect the rags of moss she had stripped from the root and try to press them back where they belonged. It was difficult. He gave it up and wrote "End of a phase" in his notebook. He added a question mark. He was tempted to write "It bodes ill" which would be impressive as a statement, but cheating, because he couldn't know those things any more. He was merely downcast. "A chapter of dooms" he wrote. There was the row at the Rivermouth, the coffee on his shirt, the beautiful white branch left behind: hitting Chester: spending his one-and-ninepence on the taxi, but this had been the only way to get home in time for the splits. He sighed. The money was not exactly wasted. He had achieved his purpose. But he needn't have bothered. Bursting in triumphantly upon Mrs. Gale, he had found her with her feet up, reading a magazine. She had failed to understand his frenzy. The splits, her pride and joy while she was mixing the dough, appeared to have lost all importance for her. "Mrs. Philip didn't say anything about tea," was a grumble and she had brought out the splits most grudgingly from their tin.

It was also a mistake to have let the taxi drive right up to the door. Mrs. Gale, having spotted the taxi, was shocked: and would undoubtedly tell Brigstock. Then there was the milk upset on the loggia. Thomas took refuge in, "Oh well," and remembering Gerald's comment, wrote "How life does continually unfold." He was impeded by the spelling of the word "continually," which he tried several ways. Where had Gerald gone, he wondered? Dashing off again . . . having been out all the afternoon. Gerald's pursuits always seemed to him most enviably exciting and mysterious.

He shut the notebook. Tired of himself, he left the trees and wandered up to the house, skirting it on the loggia side and settling down on the front doorstep to wait for Brigstock. He had timed it well. Here she was, at the gate, her best hat a little crooked from the day out. He rushed to meet her.

"I *am* glad to see you. It's been one of those days," said Thomas.

"What do you mean by that?"

"Well, Sarah's got terrible neurulgia for one thing."

One thing seemed to be enough: she scurried past him and away up the stairs.

As he had surmised, it was only a few minutes before Rab came down. She came slowly and slouchily, passing him on the step without a word, slouching as far as the monkey-puzzle tree, where she threw herself on her face. Here she lay, shaking and snuffling. It took him a little while to realize that she was crying. He had never seen her cry, not even when she shut her finger in the door of the Hispano.

Cautiously he moved towards the fallen figure, saying, "Don't cry." She looked small and flat, with the shorts hitched and wrinkled up the backs of her skinny brown legs. He felt very sorry for her and very fond of her.

"Poor old Rab. Don't cry."

He heard a muffled gasp: "Why not?"

"Well, because it worries me."

The noise she made might have been a giggle or another sob.

"Shall I get the chocolate peppermint creams? I happen to know where they are."

No answer. He sat down on the grass, hugging his knees. Presently she rolled over on her back. Then she sat up. Her hair stuck out all round her head. Her eyes glittered.

"Who do *you* love best in the world?" she asked furiously.

"I don't know. I don't do it like that. It's too foxing," said Thomas. "I've got them all standing in a row. Like they are in my prayers," he added. She looked so miserable now that he added, "You're there too," hoping to please her by this truth.

She said, "If Sarah died, I should die."

"Nobody *dies* of neurulgia."

"Know what you are?" she said. "You're a great big lump of nothing."

"There couldn't *be* a lump of nothing, don't be ridiculous," said Thomas.

Her eyes still glittered with rage and tears.

"Do you say your prayers every morning? And every night?"

"What a mood you're in. Yes of course I do."

"Does it *have* to be morning and night?"

"I don't know if it *has* to, it always is."

"Could you pray for Sarah's head to stop hurting *now*?"

He considered this: he said, "Why me? Why don't you do it?"

She said, "You believe it all. I don't. I think it's just one of those old Santa Claus jobs."

He could not have heard her correctly. He said, "You mean— you think God's an old Santa Claus job?"

"Yes, I do."

"And Jesus?"

"Yes."

Thomas shouted, "You stupid, silly, cheese-faced ass!"

He had never thought Rab would make it happen, but here was the surge of fury, the blind thing. Twice in one day, too. As he rushed upon her, he heard Brigstock calling from the steps: "Rab! Thomas! Supper!" and this took him off balance so that Rab dodged his blow and hit him squarely on the chin. His teeth clashed. He got one in, hard on the side of her head before she tripped him and then they rolled over together, clutching, kicking and punching. Not for long. Now Brigstock had him by the collar and he was strangling, hearing her worst voice of all— "*Thomas, how dare you* . . ." Whosoever was in charge on Judgment Day would, he guessed, use that voice.

He got up.

"I began it," Rab was saying. Quite untrue, but kind enough. He grinned at her, knowing it wouldn't work. The rule about boys not hitting girls was inexorable. This meant bed.

XIII

~~~~~~~~~~~~~~

Rab had slept in spite of her vow to keep awake. Keeping awake was meant to be a vigil for Sarah and she had lit her bedside lamp as the room darkened, reading desperately, with the weight of the bird book crushing her stomach. She must have gone to sleep with the book still there. Now it slithered to the floor with a bang; she found herself blinking at the unexpected light. This hurt her eyes: one side of her head was hurting too; the bruise on her temple made by Thomas. Rab sat up, fingering it with care. It was quite dark in the room, beyond the lamp. The time, she saw by her watch, was half-past nine. She got out of bed, and switched on the top light, to examine the bruise in the looking glass.

It was enormous. She bore Thomas no grudge. She couldn't imagine why he had got into such a state about God and Jesus, but he was her comrade in arms. Besides she had fought with boys since she could remember: too bad, Nanny showing up just at that moment. But for this they would have gone on until they were tired, and shaken hands afterwards. Tough on poor old Thomas, she thought. She hadn't done him any good by pretending it was her fault and electing to be sent to bed with milk and a biscuit (Nanny would have let her off). Still, that was the only way you could stand by your comrade in arms.

She was just wondering whether she dared climb the short flight to the turret room and peek at Sarah when she heard the sound of a car in the drive; the brakes; the slam of the car door. Looking out, looking down, she saw her mother crossing the arc of light on the gravel: alone and in a hurry; she was carrying a great box in front of her: a carton that looked heavy.

Warily Rab waited. Yes; footsteps coming up the second flight of stairs: along the passage, stopping at her door. Paula darted in: she looked different suddenly, bright-eyed and electric; no, not different: it was a familiar look forgotten; a party look, an American look. She was wearing the dress of peacock colors bought in Paris; all her emeralds picked up the blue-green dazzle of the dress.

"Don't you look beautiful," Rab greeted her. "How's Sarah?"

"Sound asleep, Mrs. Gale said. I know those headaches, I used to have them at her age. Nothing to worry for, stupid." She fondled Rab's hair. "Well, well. How did you get your great bruise?"

"I ran into the door."

Paula said, "I seem to have heard *that* story quite often. Who were you fighting?"

"It was the door."

"Liar. Who hit you?"

"A very old man with a beard," said Rab. "He hit me with his beard."

"Thomas?"

"I hit him first."

"Well, fair enough. But he seems to be in a slugging mood," said Paula. "Were you there when he hit Chester?"

"Chester began it."

"There are times," said Paula, "when you go too far. Cut, now. Cut the Counsel-for-the-Defense act. I'm not going to take it out on Thomas."

Rab was silent, studying the rule of Paula and the rule of Nanny in collision. "Though I daresay," Paula observed to the looking glass, "I'd knock him cold if he ever tried it on me. Much as I love him." She was powdering her nose—putting on more lipstick.

"Do you love him?" Rab asked.

"Can't help it. Always one to make myself cheap. Did you put something on that bruise?"

"Witch hazel: Brigstock gave it to me."

"And it doesn't hurt too much?"

"No—I can't even feel it."

"Fine. There's a party coming up. So you can stop going to bed and begin getting ready."

Stop going to bed . . . that meant Paula knew nothing of the disgrace: Brigstock had not told her. And Paula was away on a rainbow, for some reason. "Chester's bringing them all back here after the show. I ducked out at the intermission and collected some supplies from the Rivermouth." She swung the wardrobe door open: "What d'you want to wear, stupid? And don't say 'pants'—I know that already."

"What's so exciting?" asked Rab.

"What do you mean, what's so exciting?"

"You're all sparky—aren't you?"

Paula smiled at her. "A little, maybe. Just a little."

"Is it Chester?"

"Why do you think it is?"

"Well, he can give Philip a job, can't he?" said Rab.

"Did he tell you so?"

"No. I figured it: figured it was your plan. You wouldn't want him back as a beau—would you?"

"Don't be fresh," said Paula, hunting through the dresses in the wardrobe. "The white? Or the yellow—which do you hate least?"

Rab squirmed. She decided on courage: why was courage always such a stinker? "Guess I won't come down to the party," she said. She added, "Excuse me, please."

Paula was onto it faster than she had expected.

"Are you thinking Nanny wouldn't like it? Because if you are—"

"*Look* . . . I'm being punished. I wasn't *starting* to go to bed, I was *sent* to bed. Hours ago. I got out because I woke up."

Paula's laugh came with a roar, then she turned off the laugh in a hurry. The face was a stone face now.

"What are you being punished for, may I ask?"

"Fighting," Rab muttered. She added, "Oh hell, why not? She doesn't like us to fight." But Paula, in one stride, was out of the door.

❀

From the dining room Blanche heard Mrs. Philip returning, delivering something with a brief instruction to Mrs. Gale through the green baize door. Blanche put the sandwiches and the fruit on the dining table. Then she stood looking about the blue-and-white room, ostensibly checking that all was in order, but knowing this to be an excuse for not facing Mrs. Philip yet. She didn't trust her own temper. Her mind went on repeating its angry grumbles: "Letting Sarah swim again, sit up on that cliff getting cold: ought to know by now: isn't as if I hadn't told her: always gets her neurulgia just *before* or just *after* . . . giving her *aspirins* . . . I mean to say. As for Thomas, there's not going to be any more going off together, him and Rab; thoroughly over-excited. Somebody's got to take a hand. Irresponsible. If that's the way they do things in America, well we're not in America now." She took a second syphon from the sideboard drawer and placed it beside the whisky bottle. Was Mrs. Philip coming to find her? No: the footsteps retreated across the hall, up the stairs. Blanche went back to the kitchen.

Here Mrs. Gale, looking a little dazed, was confronting a carton dumped on the table, a carton the size of a packing case.

"What's all that?"

"For the party, Mrs. Philip said."

"I understood there'd be just Miss Richmond and two more—didn't you?"

"It's been changed. They're *all* coming: something to do with the American gentleman."

"Well really," said Blanche, beginning to unpack the carton. Over the years she had grown used to parties erupting suddenly: for no reason except that Mr. Philip, or Miss Richmond, or both, or somebody else, had so decided. At times the reigning landlady had rebelled; the adjective "racketty" had been called into use. More than once the landlady had left her all the washing-up to do, with Mr. Philip and Miss Richmond giving her a hand.

No reason to feel so put out by a party, was there? No reason why the lavish stuff in the carton should be irritating; but it was: bottles and bottles, a cold chicken wrapped in waxed paper, slices of ham, rolls: "Lucky Sarah's up in that top room," said Blanche. "You'll have to bring the other plates."

"I'd better slip into my black, hadn't I?"

"Gracious, no."

"I mean, handing things and all."

"They help themselves, that's the way they like to do it. We just lay it all out on the dining-room table."

They were doing this when Mrs. Philip shot through the door. "Oh not the dining room, for Heaven's sake—mind?" The "mind?" was obviously an afterthought, a dabbing attempt at apology: "Let's make it a picnic on the loggia." As she picked up two dishes she snapped at Blanche:

"What's all this *nonsense* about sending Rab to bed? You're an old monster, Nanny, that's what you are," and the loud laugh following; the eyes that shone strangely above the laugh: shone with anger? It was hard to know that, because of her own anger rising, rising.

Thomas began to ask himself if he were staying awake on purpose. Surely not. In the first place, this was most difficult to do: he had tried often, on Christmas Eve or on the night before his birthday. In the second place, there was no reason to stay awake. There was nothing enjoyable to occupy his thoughts: on the contrary. He touched the bruise on his chin. Rab can certainly land a punch, he said to himself, in the idiom used by the Chester person: "First girl I ever hit, too. Oh well."

Why this urgent, prodding conviction that he must not sleep because there was something to be done? What was it? He had drawn the skull and crossbones in his notebook, final comment on today: he had wound his watch; said his prayers. " 'Can't be anything else," said Thomas, threshing about in the bed. He could only connect this urgent, unrestful feeling with the lavatory, which he had visited twice to make sure.

He sat up on one elbow, for a blink at his watch; the pale green luminous hands pointed ten minutes to ten. Nearly three hours since he had finished the punishment ration of milk and biscuits. Certainly he was hungry. "But there's more to it than that," he thought and this manner of thinking gave him a sudden clue. It belonged to the lost days, to the time before his second world shut its doors in his face.

"I wonder," said Thomas.

He got out of bed. He went to the window and drew the curtain back. He stood waiting, listening, watching the dark sky.

As he took his dressing gown from the chair, he was appalled. What was he up to? Bound to be caught; and steeped in disgrace to the eyebrows already. He put on his slippers: he put his torch in his dressing-gown pocket and opened his door upon the passage that was still brightly lit. Waiting for more precise instructions, he looked down over the banisters. He could see the first-floor landing; nobody there; up from the hall came voices, Paula's loud laugh, a sound of rattling china; footsteps and a door that banged. All much too near, lively and dangerous. Thomas turned back; he slipped past Rab's door, his own door, and onto the small twisting staircase that led up to the turret room. There was no light on this staircase. Here it began. He glided up through the dark, not knowing, but sure all the same.

Before he turned the door handle, he could hear Sarah's voice: she was moaning, "Still there, it's still there." In the new darkness he could just make out the line of the bed and the ominous white glitter of the basin on the floor.

"Who's that?" asked the moaning voice.

"It's me."

"Oh Thomas," she said, "it's still there. I thought it would be gone when I woke up."

"Poor Sarah."

"It hurts me so."

"Poor Sarah."

He came to the bed and sat down on the side of it, hearing the springs creak. "Don't," she said. "Don't come near or touch." He put out his hand with assurance and found hers, lying clenched on the coverlet. He clasped it lightly, stroking her fingers until these unclenched and their two hands lay palm to palm. A sigh came welling up inside his body.

"What are you doing?"

"Be quiet," said Thomas.

The sigh had set the pace for a way of breathing he did not know, a rhythm like an exercise: in, out, in, out. It was happening by itself; no will of his own made the rhythm. At first his hand lay quite still upon Sarah's; then he drew it forward and back and a prickling sensation came into the tips of his fingers.

The breathing went on, slow and strange: in—out, in—out; this made his head swim after a while and all thoughts vanished with the swimming sense, leaving one word repeated to the rhythm: "Please, please, please, please." In—out; in—out. "Please, please, please, please." Was he going to sleep? He seemed to be shrinking away.

Now he felt the prickle draw up over his hand like a glove until his whole wrist tingled and then his arm. The tingle burned in, becoming a pain like toothache; a zigzag lightning pain. He felt it flicker from his shoulder down to his fingertips and back. *In . . . out. In . . . out . . . Please, please, please, please.*

Cloudy-headed, he knew only that he was in charge: in charge of his arm that ached, that stretched out aching and raised his hand a little way above Sarah's, steady in the air.

The pain came up too. He was in charge of the pain. He drew it safely off into his own power, away from Sarah, as he bent his agonizing arm and nursed it.

He sat there silently nursing it while his breathing changed and all became ordinary once more. There was his ordinary voice saying, "It's gone, hasn't it?"

"What did you do?"

"I don't know," said Thomas. But he knew she must not touch him. He stood up quickly, beyond her reach, and groped through the dark to the door, nursing his arm as if it were treasure.

❁

Six fives make thirty. Six-to-one winner, thirty pounds: I owe Leo thirty pounds. The words went on and on, like the film whose sequences he saw and missed, saw and missed, staring inward. He was alone inside himself with the horror, yet talking, laughing; there were two Geralds. One sat between Morris Ward and Poppy, the black-haired girl, down in the ninepennies, sweaty and smoky, shoulder to shoulder. Poppy leaned close, too close; she had grabbed his hand when the murderer on the screen loomed up suddenly through the fake fog; he had patted the hand briefly, condescendingly, before he gave it back to her. This amused one of the Geralds: the waiting, brooding atmosphere of Morris amused him too. But the other Gerald, alone, lashed and furious, cursing himself, predominated.

Why didn't you? Why didn't you? Why didn't you? "Get it off right away." That's what he said. Six fives make thirty. Thirty pounds. How could you have been such a fool—you of all people? That's what you want to know.

Think of a lie, think of a lie, think of a lie. There isn't one. If there was you'd have got it by this time.

He looked back on his last moments of happiness: sitting on the loggia with Chester Groves, with Paula and Philip. He could

not now remember being troubled. Perhaps the smallest of worries, quickly pressed down. The crackling, laughing American had
diverted him, with his Broadway background, his foreign quality
that called out a foreign quality from Paula, transformed in a
blink with his arrival. They might have been two strangers, visiting Roseclay, visiting Philip; making noise and excitement come
from nowhere. Paula vanishing, returning in a dress he had not
seen before, wearing all the emeralds. The four of them driving
in two cars: the drink at the Rivermouth because Chester wanted
to get back there, to put on a tie for the Moonrakers. Amiably
crazy, all of it and he had been at ease, feeling adult and involved,
delighted that his line of talk could make the American laugh.
And then he had stopped the clock, killed the moment, while the
three ordered their drinks.

He could see himself from here, loping out through the gray-
carpeted lobby, finding the hall porter. He could hear his au-
thentic-sportsman's voice asking, "What won the three-thirty at
Gatwick?"

Sandblast at six to one. ("Bonus for you if it comes in at anything over fives.")

If you hadn't asked the porter, you still wouldn't know. And
what good would *that* be?

To pretend not to know: to pretend: to meet the grinning Leo
(When? Where?) with outraged innocence. "But, look here, you
said 'Get it off by four o'clock, latest.' " He had rehearsed the act.
He had rehearsed it into the ground. He had begun rehearsing
it as he returned from the lobby, smiling and making his agile
excuses to the group of three. He had rehearsed it on his blind
walk, all the way from the Rivermouth, over the bridge, back into
the town: to find Morris and Poppy, because a cinema was a
dark place for sitting shut away and hidden.

It was ending, the short safety: lights going up.

"I *knew* it was the detective—said it was, didn't I?"

"It always is," said Gerald languidly.

"What shall we do now?"

"I'm going home." He saw the face of Morris turn sulky, the
eyes heavy-lidded.

The cinema had been better than walking alone. Now it was the other way; this was better, walking fast along the parade on the seaward side, gulping the salt air after the smoke. Across the road he saw the loops of light spangling the Fundrome gardens: the deserted place, show over now; they would be out by now. If he met Leo, walking, grinning—No, don't, he said to himself, you'll make it happen. He was relieved when he reached the end of the parade and crossed into the shadows. He walked uphill under the trees.

Paula, I'm in trouble. I don't want Father to know. Could you possibly help me? He plunged on into the fantasy. In the fantasy he asked her for the whole thirty pounds; and got the whole thirty pounds, leaving the hoard untouched. He could not bear to think of the hoard. (Made up to eighteen pounds, four shillings and sixpence, by Leo today: the riches of Gerald Weston. To vanish like fairy gold and still leave him in Leo's debt.)

He began to slow down as the hill mounted and the house came nearer. He could not, he thought, face anybody. There must be nobody. Chester Groves might (might he not?) have taken them to the Rivermouth for supper. Yes, on reflection this was most likely; he saw Chester Groves entertaining the whole company at the Rivermouth. The house would be dark; Brigstock waiting up for him, perhaps. For Brigstock, whose antennae would tell her at once that there was something wrong, he must invent a lie: borrow from Sarah and claim a headache. She might not believe him but she would let him alone.

Back into memory there rattled the shilling he had taken from the shopping money, to buy a water pistol—how long ago? He had confessed to Brigstock. There was a lecture, he remembered, with talk of God seeing people when they did things like that; and a small accolade at the end: "But at least you owned up. That's why I'm not going to punish you. Always own up."

A taxi chugged slowly past him. He saw it stopping at the gate. That was Tubby, getting out with Susie and somebody else: Leo, bound to be Leo. No, it was Perry Potter. Warned, Gerald stood still. He let them go on and in. He came to the gate. They were well ahead of him. He saw the cars, he saw the lights on the loggia and heard the voices before he turned quickly, running for the back door. He was safe now, on the other side of the house; safe as the door yielded to his hand.

"Who's that?" Brigstock came to meet him. Over her shoulder, in the white kitchen, he could see the signs of the party; bottles, glasses and plates. Was it this moment of frenzied guilt making her look sad, cross and quite pale around the temples? Surely it must be.

She wore her gray silk dress: below its hem there were the flat black slippers with the single straps and the cut steel rosettes. She had tied her frilly evening apron over the dress.

"Well—where have *you* been?" The beginning of a smile. "The back door, like a tradesman," she added. "Really . . ."

"My darling. What is going on?"

"A party," she said. "You'll find them all there. Be kind and get me down the big coffee pot, will you, dear? I can't reach that shelf and Mrs. Gale's quite—" She stopped abruptly: "What's the matter, Gerald?"

He stretched up for the coffee pot, wincing and frowning: "Headache. A splitter. My eyes—the cinema. Don't worry, I'm going straight up to bed."

"Oh, my dear."

"Don't worry," he repeated; and kissed her and said, "Headache day in the Weston family."

"Is there anything you'd like?"

(I would like to be dead. Or I would like it to be this morning and none of it to have happened. Nothing else will do.)

He went up by the back stairs. The sound of the party still reached him in his room. He locked his door. He sat on the bed for a long time, counting over the hoard and wanting to cry.

❊

"Hullo, Nanny. How's Nanny? Had to come and say hullo to Nanny."

Mr. Leo Clyde this time. Mr. Whittington and his wife had already found their way through the green baize door; bringing with them the little fat magician: who had disarmed Blanche by asking after Thomas. Mr. Clyde could not disarm her, ever, though she hoped he remained unaware of this. It was what Ellen Dalley called a predijuice. She mistrusted him. Why? He did none of the things she disapproved and therefore gave no name to. He was jolly, friendly, thrusting: he was shiny and eager, wanting to be in everything; but by the look behind his eyes, he knew he was out: and exactly what she meant by this she could not have explained: it made her sorry for him without helping the predijuice.

"You look very fetching tonight, Nanny."

She couldn't master more than a response of thin politeness. Mr. Clyde didn't seem to care. He swung to and fro in the doorway with a dancing step, as though about to sing "*You want to watch me.*"

"None of the kids about. Why's that, Nanny? Packed them off to bed, have you?"

She looked at him suspiciously; deciding, after the look, that he was innocent, not cued by Mrs. Philip. She contented herself with, "Well, it's getting late."

"Oh come. Tonight's a farewell party, ain't it? Only one more week to go. No more Moonrakers. Does that make you as sad as it makes me?"

"I'm sorry, of course," said Blanche.

"Me too," said Mrs. Clyde somberly. For a moment his profile sagged into deep and gloomy lines: then he perked up again. "Not that I've much to be sorry about today. I'll say not. I'm laughing. Where's Gerald got to? Can't be *his* bedtime yet."

When she told him, he looked disappointed. "I was waiting for him. Got a little present for him. And a great big thank you. He's earned it." Mr. Clyde winked, then stood with his head tilted back, the grin widening and widening until he said, "No. On second thoughts, no. Definitely no. Something tells me you wouldn't like it, Nanny." And he waltzed away from the door.

This disturbed her. But it was in line with tonight. She moved about the kitchen, the place that made its own sense for her, waiting for the coffee to run through the percolator a second time: they liked their coffee strong.

She must try to feel quiet inside; not to be angry nor resentful; not put herself into opposition; above all not allow herself to feel victorious because Rab had refused to come downstairs. This wasn't the way she wanted things to be. And Mrs. Philip was young (remember that; she's young; she flies out at you like a child, she doesn't mean it: she didn't mean it). But the set of her own lips warned her. The pinched sensation at her nostrils warned her. "Can't go on like this" were the words in her head. She tried not to hear them.

Mrs. Gale came to fetch the coffee. (All in her black silk and beaming; prepared to stay up, so silly; she would be fit for nothing in the morning.) Now Miss Richmond, in a mood to hug her, and help with the washing up and talk about the dear old days. She tried not to record, even with the part of her mind that would remember, Miss Richmond's reddish, rolling eyes and the things said twice.

"Who's this great giggling American chap, Nanny? Or don't we care? *Lor*, that piano needs tuning, doesn't it? Ah well, on with the dance," said Miss Richmond, butting out through the baize door.

There was nothing more for Blanche to do. She lingered, thinking that Mr. Philip would come to tell her this and say good night. She had not seen him since the morning. Unlike him not to come. Against her will she was reminded of another kitchen, of a clock that ticked on; the young woman she used to be, inventing small chores for herself until she heard the sound of a footstep in the hall. Captain Angus coming home. And then the moment, horrible yet splendid; the door shut behind him, the whisper and the struggling. Why think of that tonight? Because in fact one sometimes liked to think of it, shameful as it was.

"Nanny darling." Mrs. Philip looking positively luminous now, the fairness of head and skin luminous above the greens and blues that dazzled together. "Go to bed, there's a good girl."

"I'm going now, M'm."

"We'll do all the clearing up."

She didn't answer; untying the apron strings behind her, folding the apron.

"Something the matter?"

"I'll say good night, M'm," said Blanche, making an effort. She met the blue stare. The smile was still on Mrs. Philip's mouth.

"What's that face about? The party?"

"We've always had parties," said Blanche, speaking with difficulty.

"Then don't glare like a tiger. Like Medusa, more." The loud laugh shot up. "You just look at yourself in the glass. . . .

"Ah go on," said Mrs. Philip, "tell me what it's all about. Can't still be angry with Rab, can you? Or me? You won that round." To the silence she pleaded, "Sarah, is it? My letting her swim again? . . . You do fuss, you know. They aren't babies any more . . .

"Nanny, I can't *stand* sulks and silences. They depress me. And everything's so fine tonight I refuse to be depressed, see?" She dropped her cigarette ash into a clean saucer, then added, "Can't stand people who do that, either," and laughed again, snatching the saucer away as Blanche put out a hand for it.

"Now darling, cut the family tyrant, please. While I'm around at least . . . Is that a deal?"

She carried the saucer to the sink and ran the tap.

"Rod of iron—that's what you rule with. . . . Isn't it? A rod of iron . . ." Mrs. Philip dried the saucer. "Okay, but you must give me a break sometimes." She turned. The smell of her scent was sharp on the air. Below the skin of the laughing, near-angel face there showed the strong bones.

"Try not to be an old spoiler-of-the-fun *every* day—wouldn't every other day be enough? So tired of saying, Don't be cross. . . . Always cross . . . Why? Is it *me*? If it is for God's sake say so. I mean that. *Please* . . ." And the laugh.

Blanche heard a grinding, creaking voice that was her own. The voice said, "Good night, M'm," and no more. Turning, she saw Mr. Philip in the doorway. He must, she thought, have heard some of it. The muscle on his cheek had begun to twitch, and for this she had time to be sorry.

"What's wrong, Nanny?"

"You'd better ask Mrs. Philip, sir. Good night."

As he stepped aside, Mrs. Philip went out to join him; they barred her way to the back stairs. She would not face them and go past them. The sounds of the party came to meet her: the piano hammering "Charleston, Charleston" from the drawing room: plunking music of the ukulele from the loggia. She was walking into a blurred, warm tunnel, shot full of voices: she was crossing the hall. Somebody called, "Good night, Nanny." She hoped she answered. Nothing mattered except getting up the stairs and away. She held the banister rail. She kept her eyes down all the time, seeing the hem of her gray silk dress, the shiny black slippers with the cut steel rosettes, moving, moving.

A hand touched hers on the banister rail. It was Sarah's hand. Sarah stood in front of her, dancing and twirling. She wore her scarlet chiffon dress.

"I'm cured," Sarah was saying. "It's gone. I'm coming down."

Still able to react swiftly to this sort of crisis, Blanche said, "That you're not," and made a grab. Sarah twirled out of reach. "It's all right, Brigstock. Paula said I could. Just for half an hour. Oh *don't* be cross."

The word weakened her; put her off guard so that in the seconds of saying to herself bewilderedly, "Cross? Am I always cross?" she let Sarah slip past. Sarah danced on down the stairs. Standing still, looking down over the rail, Blanche saw her run to meet Mr. Philip, with the scarlet dress flying. Now they stood hand in hand. Mr. Philip looked up and she thought he called something to her for reassurance, but she did not hear it. She turned away, moving more slowly.

XIV

Sarah was past the first horrifying impact, past the unbelieving
"Oh no" that shouted inside her head. But she could not help
staring regularly at Rupert Miller, husband of Shirley. The need
to stare took her every few minutes. It was easy to indulge. From
the far corner of the loggia, where she sat with Gwen and Philip
and the highly colored American, she could glance over her
shoulder. Shirley and her husband shared a low stool, drinking,
eating sandwiches from the same plate. Above them, leaning
down towards them, was Leo Clyde; with whom Mr. Miller
seemed greatly, noisily, at ease.

For one happy moment she had taken Chester Groves to be
Shirley's husband. Would that it were so. He was tall; he was
broad-shouldered; he had chestnut hair and beautiful teeth. He

was paying attention to her, asking kindly questions about her stage career; warning Philip not to try to talk her out of it; saying he had two daughters, both set for Broadway: "What would be your favorite part to play, Sarah?"

She said, "Iris March in *The Green Hat* and Lady Macbeth," before she stared again at Rupert Miller. Back on the floor of her mind the image of a fair-haired six-footer with finely chiseled features lay shattered to bits. The wrecker sat there, ten yards off. A bulky red man with a snub nose, a little black moustache and too much face for his hair: an ugly, lumbering Jumbo: common, too, and shiny with sweat. (How could Shirley, how could she?) The wrecker glanced up and caught her staring; he stared boldly in return: she looked quickly away. She watched Philip leaning towards Chester; Philip as radiant as she had seen him on the first day here: she had forgotten that flash and herself measuring the difference in him, wondering about it.

"You mean that?" Philip was saying.

" 'What I'm here for," Chester Groves told him. "If I can get the star, I can get the production: that's what I'm here for."

"Anybody tell me what I'm here for?" Gwen asked sleepily. "I was supposed to be dancing with that little runt, Perry. Where's Perry?" Without Mr. Evans, Sarah supposed, Gwen would be rather sad and drunk like this. And now she was drawn to stare at Rupert Miller again. To her shame, he was ready for it, glass in hand, his eyes meeting hers. Behind him the exquisite figure of Shirley rose with a ripple and went off the loggia, escorted by Leo. The lights sank down. Not a word had Shirley spoken, beyond, "Hullo, dear," and, "What a pretty dress." Which, Sarah said to herself, is not enough. To have awoken, free from headache and sickness, *full of a wild surmise*, to have dressed in rapture, and run downstairs on winged sandals: surely such a beginning could not end here. "Half an hour" her father had said: ten valuable minutes were gone already. Worse, there was the creeping conviction that the sight of Mr. Miller did something to damage the goddess figure itself: that she would not feel quite the same adoration for Shirley again. It was sad beyond belief.

Gwen's voice cut into the sorrowful reverie. "Where's Perry? Where's everybody? On with the bloody dance, I say." She moved out of the corner, past Philip and Chester talking low-voiced, heads close together. Sarah leaped to her feet, crying, "On with the dance!" At the same moment Mr. Miller rose from his solitary position on the stool. He confronted Sarah, bulking and towering. She stared up into his huge face; at the wet forehead, the bright dark eyes, the serious set of the mouth below the horrid little moustache.

"On with the dance," he said, not smiling at all. "Want to dance with me?"

She was disarmed by the adult treatment. She said, "Thank you, I should like to."

Still he didn't smile; nor move. He said, "Quite sure? I thought I'd offended you somehow."

"*Offended* me?" That he should address her in this grave, grown-up way was diverting and she felt no approach of a blush, no guilt for having stared. Somehow he turned into a person for her, standing here: a large, peculiar person; solemn Jumbo.

"Well, you were shooting looks at me, weren't you? Or was it my wife you were shooting at? I'm used to that," he said, smiling a little now, "people looking at Dorrie, I mean."

"Dorrie; you call her Dorrie."

"Why not—it's her name. Don't know where she got the Shirley from. *Did* know, but I've forgotten."

Dorrie was dreadful. She couldn't stand it: she said strenuously, defensively, "She's so beautiful."

"Well, so are you," said Rupert Miller. "That's an ideal color for you, that red. Ideal. Come and dance. Just let me finish my drink. Want a sip? Tiny sip? Better not;" and now he was a kind uncle; his laugh was endearing; he gave her shoulder a little squeeze. She walked beside the kind uncle.

It was Paula who played the piano in the drawing room, while the others danced: Tubby with Susie, Gwen with Perry, Shirley with Leo Clyde. Paula had a new radiance tonight. This was more the stepmother whom she had imagined, the rich American coming from Paris, beguiling and glamorous; visitor from the unknown, the desirable world. Tides of romance rose in Sarah's mind, as she looked on the fair head and the face that laughed, the green jewels, the hands flickering over the keyboard.

> *"Pack up all my cares and woe,*
> *Here I go, singing low*
> *Bye, Bye, Blackbird."*

Gerald's tune. Gerald's absence puzzled her. "Gone to bed," was all she knew. Would he not like to be here? She pitied anybody who was not here, who was not dancing. Because, and this came as a most happy surprise, Rupert Miller, despite his disheartening bulk, danced like a professional.

"You're good—" he said to her, looking down, the dark eyes serious, the mouth solemn. "You're *very* good."

"I love it so," said Sarah.

"So do I. Lord, so do I. Oh don't stop. Why does she have to stop?" He stood, still holding her, poised and ready. But Paula was asking for a drink and a cigarette: into the air without music a voice said, "It's quite late, dear." Shirley's voice, sounding sharp and suburban, addressing Rupert. She doesn't look at me, Sarah thought; I don't exist for her. "We ought to be off."

"Not yet, Dorrie."

(*Her name is Dorrie.*)

"I'm tired, dear. Two shows today. And you've had enough too."

"Enough what?"

"Come along, now, I'm tired."

(I should mind her being tired, I should feel my heart touched and wrung; shouldn't I?)

> *"Moonlight and starlight above,*
> *You with your hand clasped in mine,"*

sang Tubby's wooing tenor. He was at the piano now, Paula leaning beside him as he began to play the Moonrakers' Waltz. Rupert Miller said "Wonderful" and swept Sarah across the floor, away from Shirley. She did not care: this was what she wanted,

simply to be dancing, to go on and on dancing. This for the
moment was ecstasy. It had nothing to do with Rupert Miller
himself: he was not the wrecker any more: not even the kind
uncle. Lightly held against his warm bulk, she neither saw him
nor knew him. He was the dance and he was the music. ("And I
am beautiful, I am all the sad, beautiful women there have ever
been, waltzing in London, in Paris, in New York, in Vienna.")

He was waltzing her out of the door: they were waltzing
across the hall. "This," she said to herself, "is the most grown-up
thing I have ever done," and then the music stopped.

"Alas for it," said Sarah, standing still.

"You're a wonderful little dancer. Thank you. Bless you."
They stood by the half-open door of the study. One lamp was lit,
on the Buhl desk. "Do I see a drink in there?" Rupert Miller
asked. "I declare I do." She walked in ahead of him and he shut
the door. But he didn't take the drink. He gave a great sudden
sigh and leaned his back against the desk, staring at her.

"A wonderful little dancer," he repeated.

From the drawing room she could hear the Charleston music
begin. Rupert Miller smiled at her and held out his hands: she
thought he meant to dance her away out of the room but when
her hands met his, he turned her round with her back to him
and drew her close to his warm stomach.

"You're strong, aren't you? Awfully strong."

"Am I?" She did not know why he should say so: his voice
had dropped, sounding a purring note as he repeated, "Awfully
strong. Lovely strong little body. Lovely and strong." Holding
her close with one arm, he switched off the lamp. Then both
arms held her again. He began to rub himself up and down
against her back. At first it was only strange and silly.

"Lovely and strong."

Now Sarah did not like it. She tried to pull free but the grip of
his hands tightened and he murmured "No, no." The rubbing,
the pressing went on: the murmuring went on: she was afraid,
ashamed and guilty all at once, hating it, not daring to struggle
again, until a high hard voice from the hall shouted, "Rupert!

Rupert! Where are you?" The hands relaxed their grip. He gave her a violent push. The door opened and the lights went on. Shirley stood there looking at her husband.

"Thought as much," said Shirley. "Out of here now, and quick. Hurry up. *Get out.*" She spoke as if he were a dog. Sarah saw him go; huge, heavy, sullen, slinking past his wife and saying nothing at all. Shirley slammed the door behind him.

"Did he hurt you?"

"No."

"What did he do to you?"

"Nothing. Nothing at all."

"Sure? Quite sure? He didn't—"

Could this person ever have been the beloved, the maker of the rain and the fine weather? Mercifully the hectoring voice ceased upon its unbearable words.

"Goodbye," said Sarah abruptly.

"Sarah—" Shirley caught her by the elbow, "Don't tell. Not your father, not anybody. Promise not to tell."

"Why should I?" was the best retort she could achieve; she said it gruffly, furiously, before she ran. She raced up the three flights of stairs as if the devil were after her. In the dark of the turret room, alone, she stood still; shaken, confused and profoundly interested.

❂

Finding himself suddenly awake, Thomas consulted the pale green figures of his watch. A quarter to one. There were no dreams to go chasing, there was no echo of a journey, but he felt most happily all-of-a-piece. He thought about this.

"I cured Sarah's neuralgia. Didn't I? Yes, I did."

Staring at the unlikely event, he saw it perform a familiar trick: it simply vanished. The harder he tried to play the adventure back in his mind, the less he could remember. His arm hurting, Sarah's pain going—that was all.

Then he understood. The vanishing trick proved it. Magic had returned at last.

He sat up to switch on the lamp and make the record. Any

old sign would do. Grinning, excited, he feathered back through the pages of the notebook to find one suitable. Nothing: nothing: nothing: just routine symbols; a star; an occasional skull and crossbones; a humdrum question mark. It was of course a long, long time since the other world went away. August the Second: August the First. Now he was back in July. He turned the July pages and came upon two lines that stopped him cold.

He had printed them in block capitals. They read, TELL AT ONCE NEXT TIME SOMETHING ODD HAPPENS PROMISE and the date was written below: July the twenty-eighth.

Yes, indeed. The bed jogging up and down, the pipe smoke curling on the air, his father's voice. This memory performed no kindly vanishing trick. It was all there in his head. "Anything you can't explain," was there, too.

A promise was a promise.

"Better get it over," Thomas decided, "that is, if they aren't in bed yet."

He got up and put on his dressing gown. He opened his door onto darkness. He could hear nothing, but the house felt awake and lively: downstairs, he decided, there were still people about. He hoped only Philip and Paula, though on a Saturday night one could never be sure.

He set off, treading cautiously. As he came down to the first floor landing, he saw that all the lights were on. He could hear the piano. He crossed the landing and squatted, poking his head between the banister rails. Nobody in the hall. He would go down and take a look. He went.

Gazing about him, he saw two glasses on the oak chest, with a plate holding some sausages, and a single white glove lying beside the plate. He sniffed the air. Yes. The strongly familiar smell of a party, any grown-up party: smoke and scent and food mixing: on the air also, the suggestion of people no longer here, but having left a kind of hot echo behind them.

Thomas was tempted by the sausages. But the sound of Gerald's ukulele deflected him: Gerald on the loggia was playing a tune. Thomas went to look for him.

In the light from the roof lanterns he saw flowers, a trail of plates and glasses, all the cushions flattened and squashed; the ends of cigarettes piled high in every ashtray. On the seat that swung, the seat in the far corner, Gwen was lying back among the pillows; she seemed to be asleep. The person sitting on the floor, with his back against a low stool, playing the ukulele, was not Gerald but the magician, Perry Potter. He looked small and round. When he saw Thomas he stopped playing his tune.

"Hullo," he said. "Bit late for the party, aren't you?"

"I didn't know there was one."

"Well it's over now, chummy. We're waiting to go home. 'Nice American gentleman said he'd drive us."

"And Gwen's gone to sleep."

"That's right," said the magician. "Have a sandwich? Or a sausage?"

"I'll have both, please," said Thomas, "and then I've got to find my father." He roamed around, helping himself from the plates.

"Your father's in the study, with the nice American gentleman."

"Where's Paula?"

"Playing the piano."

"I see. Well, I'd better get it over."

"Get what over?"

"Just a thing."

"Come and talk to me first."

"All right." Carrying his provisions, he took a seat on the stool. He was diverted because Perry Potter was wearing red socks with white sand shoes, rather dirty sand shoes, on his funny little feet.

"Haven't seen you for a long time," said the magician. "You don't come to the Kiddies' Show any more."

"No," said Thomas, munching.

"Given it up?"

Thomas hesitated. There was, he supposed, no reason why he should take the words to have a special meaning. Perry Potter was looking at him quite innocently, benevolently, wearing his babyish smile. All the same, he asked, "Given what up?"

"Seeing through," said Perry.

"Ho . . . I thought that was what you meant." A light, trustful feeling followed. "*You* know all about it, don't you?" he asked.

The magician scratched his head. He scratched as Rab would, until Brigstock intervened; making a thorough exploration of his untidy fair hair.

"All about it," he said at last, "is rather a tall order. I don't suppose anyone knows all about it."

Thomas took another sausage.

"You'll find it comes and goes," said Perry.

"Oh yes, I know that."

"You do, eh?"

"Certainly," said Thomas.

"Well, it's to be borne in mind," the magician said, sounding rather gloomy. He then shot his feet straight out in front of him, grasped his toes and rocked to and fro on his bottom. Thomas, who had seen a brown bear at the zoo behave in this fashion, watched him with interest.

"Swing-door," said Perry Potter thoughtfully.

"Swing-door?"

"You don't know why it swings, why it shuts again, why you should be the one to get a look through before it shuts. Or do you?" he asked, letting go of his toes and peering up at Thomas. "Perhaps *you* do."

"I don't think I've ever thought about why."

"Your grandmother would say it's a privilege. One that mustn't be abused."

Thomas looked all around the words. They were familiar, from Puxford: where a framed motto in one of the recreation rooms announced, *Remember: People Who Abuse Privileges Often End By Losing Them.* He had had it explained to him on the first day. This got him no further with the present conversation, so he went on eating.

"I'm grateful to Lucille—to your grandma—" said Perry. "One knows it all along inside, but when the minute comes—when the door *does* swing—well, it's jolly hard to avoid the temptation.

That's what I find. So—of course—does everybody else. She says 'occasion of sin.' That's how she puts it these days. Know what she means?"

Thomas shook his head.

"Well, I'm a conjuror from now on. Just a conjuror. Nothing else. Plenty of jobs, with the winter coming. As long as I can look after my wife and my kids—pay my way—I've no worries, have I?" He shot Thomas an anxious glance. There was an appeal in his round blue eyes and this was baffling. Did he mean that to pay his way would make all worries end? Perhaps. Adult worries, as far as Thomas could grasp, were chiefly concerned with money.

"What's on *your* mind, Thomas?"

Sudden voices in the hall brought Perry to his feet. Gwen sat up and said, "Oh, hell, what?" in a thick, sad mumble. She rose and stretched herself. Paula, Philip and the Chester person came crowding onto the loggia.

The clattering voices, to Thomas's relief, took no account of him. So long as he stayed sitting on the stool he was hidden by Perry and Gwen. Now they were all sweeping away, saying good-bye many times in the adult tradition. Somebody switched off the lantern lights: he was alone in the dark. He helped himself to another sausage while the car outside lit up, started up, slid roaring to the gates and was gone. At first he could hear Paula and Philip talking in quiet tones. Then Paula's voice lifted, sounding furious, saying, "As for Nanny—" Thomas rushed out of the dark to confront them at the foot of the stairs.

Paula's reaction was a loud and friendly laugh. His father said, "Good Lord, what are *you* up to?" and then groaned: "Oh don't tell me you're at it again."

In a sense, Thomas reflected, this was exactly what he must tell Philip: but only in a sense: he was not, after all, prowling on the condemned night-walk.

"Nobody need worry. Or get cross," he said firmly. "I came down to see you because I promised I would."

"You *did*?" said Paula, still amused and friendly, smiling at him. He did not return the smile: those three sharp words had made him wary. He addressed himself to Philip.

"You said I was to tell you at once next time something odd happened. Well, it has. What *you* call odd," he added scrupulously.

"Oh God," said Philip, "*What?*"

"I cured Sarah's neurulgia."

It was Paula who gave a peal of laughter: "That was *very* clever of you, darling. But it's quite late. Suppose you tell us all about it in the morning?"

Thomas looked at his father for confirmation. Philip only nodded at him and waved a hand vaguely while Paula said, "Up to bed, now. Quick! Quick like a fox!"

He could still hear her laughing as he climbed the stairs.

XV

Blanche came downstairs as the clock struck seven. She made herself a cup of tea and set about the work; admitting, while she feathered from the drawing room to the kitchen, from the kitchen to the loggia and back again, that she had seen much worse in her time.

The glasses, though unwashed, were all stacked beside the sink; the plates too. The ashtrays were emptied of butts, leaving only their thin grime to be rinsed off. Certain disordered groupings of the furniture needed attention, but someone had plumped up all the cushions with care. The party smell lingered in every room; Blanche opened window after window to the misty sunlight. Then she began to wash plates, glasses and ashtrays.

She was not angry now. She felt merely dazed and miserable, glad of work to do with her hands.

She was above all bewildered: because there was no precedent. From time to time she had, in her own phrase, had words with each of her employers; with Mrs. Hale, Mrs. Mattingley and with poor Mrs. Weston. There had been misunderstandings and reconciliations, flyings-out and apologies, all to a routine pattern. Nobody had ever before said impudently cruel things in a voice that laughed, going on and on: attacking the face she wore, the rule she kept, the person she was. (Like being slapped again and again, standing quite still to receive the slaps.)

"She'll be sorry. That's the first thing she'll say when she comes downstairs: 'I'm sorry, Nanny,' and then I must just try to forget all about it. Like I say, she's young."

It was childish to feel as if the world had broken to bits and could never be mended. It was more than childish to feel the approach of tears all the time. "Sticks and stones may break my bones, but words can never hurt me," she reminded herself sharply: an old stand-by, less convincing than usual. The worst of it was the rhythmic return of a dreary, helpless wonder, asking, "Am I really like that? Is that really how I seem to other people?" and no stern, sensible denial could keep it from coming. Every thought led to there. She could not even complete her censure of Mrs. Gale ("Told her she'd be fit for nothing this morning.") without finding herself reproached by the words "always cross." The words might have been written up all over the kitchen.

She had finished the washing and drying. She had laid the dining-room table for breakfast. She would go up to the children now. At the sound of feet above, at the shadow interrupting the moted sunshine that hung across the staircase, she stood still. She kept her eyes lowered.

"If it's her," Blanche thought, "she must speak first." She was dimly aware that yesterday Mrs. Philip had been Mrs. Philip and was now "she" or "her" in the authentic rechristening made by hostilities.

"Hullo, Brigstock."

The chirp was out of Gerald's voice, nor did he smile at her.

He came hurrying down with his shoulders hunched: his face looked yellow.

"You're very early," she said. "Has the headache gone?"

He snapped, "What headache?" then appeared to remember: "Oh, yes, thanks. I'm all right."

"You don't look very all right to me."

He gave her a wan smile. He said, "Mute the camel. I'm going out."

"To Early Service?" she asked hopefully. Gerald looked down at his shoes. "Wouldn't do any harm, would it?" he muttered, sounding ashamed, most unlike him. Then he tried to swagger it off. "I'll grab some tea now, please. 'May be late for breakfast."

She followed him into the kitchen, saying, "Gerald, what's the matter?"

"Nothing, my darling. Not a thing in the world. I have an invitation to go pig-sticking with Sir Rabindranath Tagore." He gulped his tea. After a minute he said, "Don't *eye* me, Brigstock, it makes me feel nude," and even this had power to hurt her today. "I'm sorry," said Blanche and went out quickly before he could see her face.

❀

From his bed, Philip lay listening to the bells and pursuing his routine reflections on the number of churches in Sawcombe. Blithe and relaxed, he faced the morning. No trace of the uneasy Puritan today. The Lucky Fellow and the Regency Rake joined forces, with a blessing on the side from the Laughing Philosopher, who had known all would be well. There were only two minor clouds in the air, to be dispersed after breakfast.

Where was breakfast? Had Paula—still in a temper—gone off to church without telling Mrs. Gale to bring it? No, no: he was magnifying the first of the small clouds: Paula might snarl for a moment, but she would never carry a temper through to the next day. Last night he had quenched the turbulence by the simplest means in his power. This was not, of course, an enduring solution. No woman was the same in bed as out—a fact he had established over the years. (Gwen had come nearest to being the same:

embarrassingly the same on occasion: he had never been one for
knockabout comedy between the sheets.)

Oh, all was well. It had to be. Love was here, money was here,
he told himself again, and in proof of his laughing philosophy,
Chester Groves was here too: the American ringmaster, with the
London production pending. Wide open, the Golden Road to
Samarkand, by way of Shaftesbury Avenue.

Here came Mrs. Gale, with the breakfast. No, she didn't.
Paula, without the breakfast.

"Awake, no less," she said.

"I thought you'd gone to church."

"Not this morning."

She looked beautiful, perhaps a little sporting for Sunday,
wearing a white sweater with her primrose-yellow suit; flat
brown-and-white shoes.

"I'm off to the Rivermouth," she said briskly. "Will you join
Chester and me for lunch as soon as you're through with that old
devil."

"I beg your pardon?"

"With Nanny, I mean."

"You mind your manners. Please don't call her names. Where's
my breakfast?"

"She *is* an old devil. She won't say a word this morning: just
looks at me as if I was slow poison and talks to the kids. What's
she expect me to do? Tell her I'm sorry I had to *beg* her not to be
such a bitch? *Beg* . . ."

"I'm going to have my bath," said Philip, leaping out of bed
and grabbing at his dressing gown.

"*Listen.* I can't stand her gloom-and-doom act another minute
and I don't intend to. You let her get away with everything. If
you'll only—"

"Please ask Mrs. Gale to bring my breakfast."

"If you're content for her to restrict and retard your children,
that's fine. But she isn't going to do it to Rab. See?"

"Tell Mrs. Gale black coffee, fruit and toast. Just what the
Prince of Wales has for breakfast."

"Damn you," said Paula. "You've about as much spine as a

cream puff. You make my ex-husband look like Tarzan. I'll leave *you*, d'you hear?"

"All right, you do that," said Philip. He shot into the bathroom and locked the door, turning on both taps full blast.

The hammering on the door was so long and so loud that he had to turn them off. "*Stop* it, Paula. Have you no consideration for my shell shock? Not to mention my hangover?"

"I only wanted to tell you," said a crisp voice, "that Mrs. Gale is in bed with a bilious attack. Everyone else is at church. You'll have to get your own breakfast."

When he came downstairs, the quiet was comforting. He made himself some rather nasty tea in the kitchen. The kitchen was tidy, free from all party traces; signs of orderly preparation for lunch; he wondered whether this was Nanny's work, since Mrs. Gale was out of action. It might, of course, be Paula's. Certainly not Nanny and Paula together. He groaned. The last thing in the world he wanted was a situation developing between the two.

Not feeling strong enough to make toast, he put a biscuit in the saucer. He carried his tray onto the loggia. Here again there were no stale reminders of the night before. "Wonderful woman," he thought, meaning Nanny and not Paula. He sat down in the most comfortable chair. When he had drunk the tea and eaten the biscuit as far as the softened crescent where the tea had slopped, he lit a cigarette. He played back in his head some words spoken by Chester Groves. These soothed his mind as the look of the late roses in the garden soothed his eyes. He went on being soothed until the thought of Thomas came; Thomas in his dressing gown at one A.M. He flicked Thomas away at speed. Thomas had been dreaming: that was Paula's verdict.

The gate clicked. Oh, *not* General Stevens. No. Leo Clyde. Bad enough. Leo could only be here to talk business, to mourn over the returns, perhaps: certainly to embark on some dreary matters; the winding-up of contracts, the niggling details which Philip found intolerable even when times were good. (How often had he told Leo he loathed talking business on Sunday? How often had Leo retorted, "Then you shouldn't employ a Jew as company manager"? Oh well, hell: it was the last time. Make an effort; do it pretty.)

"Mr. Clyde, I presume? In a very alluring shirt," he added. Leo's clothes were always so terrible that he felt himself obliged to say something about them. He got no traditional response. Leo merely groaned as he came; not one of his Jewish-joking groans, either: no "Oy-oy," no hands flung upward. He said, "Philip, I can't take this." He threw an envelope down beside the cup and saucer. It was a fat envelope; a great many pound notes were sticking halfway out of it.

"You can't?" said Philip. "I could."

"It's no joke."

"Well, naturally not. If there's anyone hereabouts who finds money a joke, I've yet to meet him." Looking up into a ravaged, hostile face he dropped the act. "What's wrong, old boy?"

"Your idea, was it?"

"Was *what* my idea?"

"Making him push it under my door."

"*Eh?*"

"Oh my God," said Leo. "Read the letter."

Gerald had used writing paper with the public school crest and motto.

DEAR MR. CLYDE,

Since unforeseen circumstances prevented me from sending your telegram in time to back Sandblast, I owe you an apology and thirty pounds. Enclosed you will find the sum of fifteen pounds, which is all I have in my possession at the moment. I hope you will allow me to pay the rest in installments, which should not take me very long.

Yours regretfully,

Philip read it again. Above his head, Leo was wailing, "How could I take it? From a boy his age? What sort of a kikey trick would that be? . . . Why couldn't he send it? Fifty yards from the post office. Why can't he call me Leo? Never been Mr. Clyde to *one* of your kids—have I?" He collapsed on a white wicker chair.

"Have a drink," said Philip.

"I never drink before lunch, you know that by now, surely."
He sat bowed forward, with his head in his hands. "What do you
all take me for?" he said. "A bloody Shylock?"

"I know nothing about this, Leo."

"But you gave him the money. He couldn't raise that much on
his own, stands to reason."

"I did no such thing."

"You *didn't?*" said Leo, suddenly returning to life. "Well,
well . . . where did he get it? He's a deep one, Gerald. Thought
so for a long time. Thought so yesterday." He stopped, looking
away.

"Why yesterday? What happened yesterday?"

Leo said, "Oh, nothing special. Ran into him in the town.
That's why I gave him the wire. Here's your gang."

The church party, in its Sunday clothes, carrying its prayer
books, came through the gate. Philip watched it come. He saw
Nanny's mauve muslin and rose-trimmed hat. He saw Rab, more
grotesque in white embroidery than she could ever look wearing
boys' clothes. She had taken off her hat and was swinging it furiously. Beside her, Thomas plodded against the handicap of white
serge knickers a little too tight for him. Sarah came last, walking
alone. There was no sign of Gerald.

❂

"*I thought when love for you died, I should die.
It's dead. Alone, most strangely, I live on.*"

Sarah intoned from the book on her knees. It meant nothing to
Rab. Obviously it meant a great deal to Sarah; who had repeated
it twice already. Rab found it hard to believe that any of this was
happening. The only flaw in the moment was her Sunday dress,
not merely uncomfortable but ridiculous. The dash to her room
to change after church had been halted by Sarah's descent from
the turret, Sarah carrying this poetry book and most unexpectedly noticing her existence, wishing for her company. Here they
were, far down among the trees. Sarah sat with her back against
Thomas's pet oak tree, crooning lines from the book. Rab's mis-

trust of poetry was in suspension. She watched the leaf-shadows on Sarah's face.

"It's true," said Sarah and shut the book, "absolutely true. *Most strangely I live on.* Me, I mean."

"Why do you?"

"Oh I couldn't tell you why."

"Couldn't you?"

"No."

"Okay," said Rab.

"Of course if I saw her again suddenly I might feel the same . . . He doesn't seem to have written a poem about that," she added, consulting the book and then laying it down. She hugged her knees, staring ahead. She murmured, "Feet of clay."

"Feet of clay?"

"Wouldn't that be a wonderful title for a story?"

"Zowie!?" said Rab.

"But of course *she* hasn't changed. It is I."

"How have you?"

"Completely changed. I have grown up. I thought about it all through church. I couldn't stop thinking. I can't now. I'm still thinking about it."

"About what?"

"About the thing I can't tell you about."

"Oh."

"One keeps going back in one's mind to a terrible thing," Sarah told her, "as though one liked it because it was terrible. I remember doing this after a motor accident we saw."

Rab nodded her head in violent, uncomprehending approval.

"Ah well . . ." Sarah stretched her arms. "*Who am too wise in all I should not know!*" she cried upward to the leaves.

"You said that yesterday, didn't you? You were saying it to yourself when I came into the dining room."

"Was I? Perhaps I had a moment of clairvoyance. I must read *The Rape of Lucrece* again, remind me."

"Gosh, I'd like to read it too."

"Hardly fit for you."

"Why not? Who was Lucrece, and what guy raped her?" Meeting Sarah's look of startled astonishment, she said, "I'm sorry, but I don't have any education."

"You can't *possibly* know what rape is."

"I do, too. 'Means men doing it to women when women don't want to. Not only women. Quite a young girl was. At Sausalito. There was a trial."

After a long, frowning silence Sarah said, "But you're only twelve."

"It wasn't me who got raped," protested Rab, "it was this girl at Sausalito."

For the first time ever, Sarah the idol was looking at her with fascinated interest. She felt wonderful.

"Who told you?" Sarah asked.

"It was in the papers."

"I don't mean that—I mean all of it. What happens—you know."

"Sex? Paula did. Quite a long time ago. She explained with some drawings. But I'm not very interested, are you? It sounds kind of embarrassing."

❂

Philip looked at his watch, the exquisite gold thing, Paula's first present: the time was a quarter to one. Since Leo left, he appeared to have wasted at least twenty minutes sitting here on the loggia, wondering what to do about everything and which to do first. He stared at Gerald's envelope, Gerald's money, lying beside his hand. He was still dumbfounded. But his brief, pitched battle with Paula kept thrusting its shape into this immediate worry and was followed hotfoot by the voice of conscience telling him he ought to speak to Nanny. He reminded the voice that he was waiting for Gerald. "*In that case, you must ring the Rivermouth and tell Paula you'll be late. Go on. What,*" it added nastily, "*are you going to say to Gerald anyway?*" "Oh shut up," said Philip. In a sudden masterful burst of decision he solved all problems. He would take a quick drink and go off to the Rivermouth. Everything could wait till after lunch.

Striding through the hall he nearly ran down Thomas, who

was proceeding from the kitchen, head lowered, like a small preoccupied bull.

"Sorry, old chap—do try and look where you're going."

Thomas said, "I wasn't really going anywhere." He had
swopped his white serge for a pair of gray knickerbockers. He
was kneading a lump of red and yellow plasticene in both hands.
"You *are* out to lunch, aren't you?" he said. "Brigstock wants to
know because it's only cold, she says, and she's all behind. Mrs.
Gale can't keep anything down."

"Don't be disgusting."

"Well, that's what was said."

"No need to say it again, is there? Yes, I am out to lunch. I'm
just giving myself a drink. Then I'm off."

"Can I talk to you while you're having your drink?"

"Yes, if you make it snappy."

Thomas came slowly after him to the sideboard in the dining
room. He stood there working at the plasticene.

"About Sarah," he said. "Paula didn't pay any attention, did
she? But *you* wanted to know. That's why I came to tell you."

Conscious of a shadow falling, Philip put too much vermouth
in the gin; he added some more gin: "Well, you had a dream,
old boy, didn't you? It woke you up, so you came downstairs."

"No, certainly not," said Thomas. "It had happened ages before that. It was about ten o'clock when it happened. It wasn't a
dream. I went into Sarah's room and cured her neurulgia. I took
the pain away."

"You what?"

"Took the pain away. Into my arm."

"Oh no," Philip said, "oh no."

"Oh yes."

"How *could* you?"

Thomas shrugged. Philip tilted the drink straight down his
throat. "Am I going mad?" he wondered—"or is he?" Puxford,
Appleby, Perry Potter, the accusers of Thomas, clamored together with the slow, deep voice of the child himself. It was impossible, he thought, looking at his youngest son, that these
Gothic shapes and darknesses should frame him about. In such a

frame there should be someone of bizarre significance. All he saw was Thomas: the bleached head, the stocky shape. He noted the knickerbockers bunching above a belt with a metal snake for a clasp. He saw that one gray sock was coming down. The square hands went on kneading the plasticene.

"Thomas," he said heavily, "I'm surprised at you."

"I was surprised too. Nothing like that had happened for such a long time."

"You're not trying to tell me you've done it before."

"Well, not that exactly. But it's all part of the same thing, isn't it?" Below the absent-minded smile, Philip saw the heavy bruise on the chin. This was disarming and he did not mean to be disarmed.

"You're making it up," he began and then clashed his empty glass down on the sideboard. "I mean I know you don't *think* you're making it up, but you're imagining it."

"No," said Thomas, "truly not. You can ask Sarah."

"I can't ask her now. I'm late for lunch. Yes, I can, I will ask her now. Where is she?"

"Down under the oak tree, with Rab."

"All right, come along." He grasped Thomas by the shoulder. "Let's get this out of the way. Hurry up." He had to accommodate his stride to the short, plodding legs. "I could be quicker," Thomas said, "if you'd let go of me."

Under the oak tree, Rab and Sarah rose to their feet; Rab scrambling awkwardly in her white dress, now streaked with green; Sarah with graceful nonchalance.

"Run indoors, Rabby please. I want to speak to Sarah for a minute."

"Okay."

Sarah, acting her head off, turned upon him a face that looked as though she found him a trivial intruder; she gave him her most languid smile.

"Come out of your trance, darling," he snapped. "Go on, Thomas."

"Thought *you* were going to ask her."

"Shut up, and tell Sarah what you just told me."

"I can't do both."

"Both what?"

"Shut up *and* tell Sarah," said Thomas.

There were times, Philip thought, when one could murder him. Perhaps he realized this, because he added, "Oh well, sorry," and at once began to gabble. "Curing your neurulgia, he means. I did, didn't I? I came in and you said it was still there so I sat on your bed and took it away into my arm. That's what happened, isn't it?"

Sarah put up a hand, to stroke her hair reflectively.

"Well?" said Philip, "Well? Is it true?"

Of course she glanced at Thomas, with the conspirator's glance, asking, "What do you want me to say?" But Thomas wasn't, apparently, out to conspire. Having delivered himself, he returned to his plasticene.

"All I can remember is the pain going," said Sarah.

"And Thomas was there?"

"Yes, he was there."

"What did he do?"

"He just sat."

"Please look at me, Sarah. How many times have I told you to look people in the face when you're speaking to them?"

"Paula always does, doesn't she?" said Thomas. He added, "Hyptonists do it—that's wrong, hyptonists. Hyptonics, hyp—"

"*Will* you be quiet?"

"But she doesn't remember. I can see she doesn't. Oh well."

"I am sorry." Sarah spoke in her most unnerving contralto: "Very sorry indeed. But you see—something so devastating happened afterwards." She shuddered: "Nobody could blame me for forgetting. Truthfully, nobody could. Nobody in the world."

"All right—what happened afterwards? Oh don't be silly," said Philip, catching up with it. "You put on your red dress and came down to the party."

"*That* was where it happened."

"Where what happened?"

"I can't tell you in front of Thomas."

"Want me to put my fingers in my ears?" asked Thomas cheerfully.

"No, no," said Sarah, "far better I should never tell."

Philip shut his eyes. He felt as if he were trying to catch two kittens with one butterfly net: or trying to stand upright in a hammock. He shouted, "Run *along*, Thomas! Tell me *at once*, Sarah!"

Thomas replaced the lump of plasticene in his pocket, put his fingers in his ears and moved with incredible slowness away from them towards the tennis lawn. Sarah watched him go. Then she said, "I was raped. By Mr. Miller."

XVI

"Now," said Paula, "I'm bored. Bored. Bored."

Nobody answered. There was nobody here to answer, except seagulls. She had had a nice time with a picnicking family: the children had joined her in throwing stones at the empty beer bottles bobbing beyond the line of surf. She could still see the bottle; it was drifting with the current. She threw one more pebble after it. No fun, alone.

Nothing was ever any fun alone. Driving the car could give her the illusion of company for a while. But she didn't want to drive any further. She felt as though she had been out and away for many hours. She had no exact idea where she was. One coast town led to another, one more cliff road looped on and up and over: a sudden deep chine had beckoned her down to this small bay. At the top there was a whitewashed inn, where she had bought the beer; and a whitewashed cottage belonging, it was said, to the coast guard. The inn was undoubtedly shut by now. She wondered if the coast guard, lonely and sea-girt, were dying for a chat with somebody. Failing him, she must head for home. Where she trusted to find Philip frantic.

She remembered doing this to Herbert, after one of their earliest fights: on their honeymoon in South Carolina; with the highly satisfactory result that Herbert had called the state police, though he had revenged himself later by running a temperature of a hundred and two. From Philip, she was forced to admit, she expected less. There was something implacably adult about the Englishman compared with the Californian. Philip could behave like a baby when it suited him. Herbert couldn't help behaving like a baby even when it didn't suit him.

Paula gave a gigantic yawn; the kind of cracking, hideous yawn she forbade herself and all around her. It was rather good. She did it again.

She wondered what the time was. The clock on the Hispano's dashboard had stopped in Cannes during February. She was without a watch. She loved watches; she gave them as presents always, and she had a pretty collection of clocks in the New York apartment. Strange, then, that any watch living on her wrist would begin to act up, would keep nothing recognizable as time. She had tried all sorts. Frightening, somehow.

"Oh, pooh," said Paula. She retrieved her damp swimming suit from a rock, rolled it in the towel and stuffed both into the canvas bag, which was initialed E.Q.M. in red. Miles had left the bag behind at the Rivermouth. She wondered whether Miles would consider a job in London: the next question was whether Philip would consider Miles: she thought not. To Philip, Miles remained a sinister conundrum. For Paula the only puzzle was his ancestry: could anybody really be half Spanish and half Swiss?

It was Chester, coming home from the war, who had imported him. Valet, chauffeur, cook and houseboy; a paragon with comedy value. Everyone was mad for Miles. At first. Then the cumulative sins, mostly indulged in bed or on the bottle, began to catch up with him. Fired by Chester, he resorted to one highly doubtful deal with a check. It was Paula to whom he turned for help. Paula rescued him, simply because he made her laugh. He had been her slave—and an honest slave—ever since. Miles was the one solid pillar of her shifting household. Or had been . . .

Picturing Miles and Nanny in the same retinue made her feel she was developing a squint.

She decided to test her temper by prodding at those things which had caused her to lose it. Walking uphill was a strain on her temper anyway, so she might as well use the strain.

She began with Blanche. What more could one do, for heaven's sake—go on one's knees? She had done it, by her own standards, so well. Pleading, but never crawling. She had been gay, light and friendly, with just the necessary balance of good-humored teasing. Why had it not worked? Servants had been her speciality since childhood. She had started in charming them at the old brownstone house on Sixty-fifth Street, and never yet failed. She saw in devoted procession a Dantesque butler, a Scottish cook and a cherry-cheeked parlormaid. Colored maids, French maids and a Swiss housekeeper went by. They were followed by a string of personal maids (and she would have had just enough of life without one by the time they settled into Hyde Park Gate, so she would). She saw servants in other people's houses going out of their way to look after her. She saw Miles. She saw Rab's own nurse, twenty-three, imported from Ireland and a perfect sweetheart, who had cried at leaving her.

So what the hell was the matter with Blanche Briggs?

Nothing mysterious, Paula decided: maddening but not mysterious. Blanche was old-fashioned to a point of antiquity, probably having change of life, and certainly suffering from too long a reign as the boss. No wonder the children were such a peculiar mixture; a fascinating mixture, but still bafflers, every one.

Her mind stopped on Thomas: it was always stopping on Thomas. Her dream, when she married Herbert, had been a lot of little boys with fair heads, those special little boys' heads with rather too much back to them. Thomas's head looked like that, though his body was below the dream-standard; he should have long legs. And he should *not* be a baffler. Her dream sons were all tough little guys, sprouting into keen sportsmen. Simple chaps, with truth and courage shining in their faces. Thomas remained woolly; opaque; unapproachable. As for his magic . . . Philip had pleaded with her not to "encourage him." Of course she had disregarded the plea, more than once: after reading the letter from Puxford; after meeting Perry Potter by chance on the parade; after the grandmother's visit. All she got from Thomas in return were some owlish stares and murmurs of, "Oh well." Despite the family jokes on the subject, she had her moments of serious wonder about the state of his wits.

Gerald, though more promising, was another baffler; a blend, she said, of the public schoolboy and the gigolo. A cold fish, with charm on the surface. The hint of some steel-plated quality gave her a hunch that he would go far in the world. A congenital winner. Bored with school, and understandably so: more of an adult than he knew. "If he wants out, well he can have out, any time," she said, "why not?" (Memo, convince Philip formal education isn't a sacred cow.) Up to her, wasn't it, now the uncle was no longer holding the purse? (Purse. Percy. *Prissy old Percy*, she said, not having met Percy. Philip was a little shocked, though perhaps relieved as well, that she showed no enthusiasm for meeting her in-laws. "Only in-laws-in-law, after all . . . I might as well insist he meets Herbert.") "You can quit, Gerald, I'll fix it," she said to the boy in her mind.

Sarah . . . Sarah was the simplest of the three; drowning in dreams. "Though she might (mightn't she?) have chosen to adore *me* instead of the hop-pole with the fake roses . . ."

Oh, I love them all. But they do make me feel so damned inferior because I don't know any quotations.

And they *do* get my goat the way they all bow stiffly to the Briggs regime.

By now she was almost at the top of the slope and reviving her rage about Rab. Rab going overboard for the Briggs regime and turning against her . . . fine thing. But in justice (and one was a stickler for justice) there was an excusing factor. The obsolete punishment inflicted by Nanny had condemned Thomas and Thomas was Rab's pal, so she had elected to suffer with him. An act of loyalty; Girl Scout stuff. (Okay, Rab should have been a boy, you knew that already Stop there, before you get to the fierce little jealousies.)

As to Philip, the beloved exasperator, he liked to keep his head in the sand. And this was masculine. Heaven knew one needed them to be masculine. Not another Herbert, oh no. Philip's gay, ostrich act was less trouble than his agony performance. The agony performance was rarer, but it kept her awake. King Lear: just the actor in him. Nanny said shell shock, but Paula thought just the actor.

The thought of the actor led straight to Chester Groves.

❀

She went back to this morning, to Chester's bedroom at the Rivermouth. She could see now that she had been overconfident, riding high and believing she had fixed it all. She had arrived too early for once, because of the flight from Roseclay. Chester was half-dressed, his luggage half-packed and the bedroom chaotic.

There were times when Chester could make his smooth, easy-going face appear to jut; like the face of a ruthless man. He liked to assume this mask and it suited his symmetrical features better than it suited the character who lived inside. (If I ever met a really ruthless man head on, one of us would drop dead, that's for sure, but which?) He jutted at her while she made her opening speech. He had called her a natural hijacker.

"But you mustn't try to hijack me yet, darling. Unless I get the star I want—and I'm not telling you or anyone else who that is—the whole plan for a London production goes out of the window."

"But you said last night—"

Chester had interrupted her. (Every time somebody interrupted her she could see how annoying this habit was, but she always forgot before she herself did it again.) "What I said last night holds good. *If* the production cooks, I can use Philip. In a smallish part. Told him just that, no more. And that's the way it's got to be. Now go downstairs, like a good kid, order yourself a drink and let me finish up here."

"You're stalling. You weren't stalling last night."

"Want me to throw you out of the window?" was Chester's reply. She had gone raging down to wait, without a drink. He had not kept her waiting long. Not nearly long enough, as things turned out. The words spoken on the lawn under the willow tree were still here for hatred. Even the innocuous start was to be hated now:

"There's one thing strikes me about your Philip—first and foremost, offstage or on. He's a hundred percent the English gentleman. He's every *American's* idea of the English gentleman. That's why I believe he'd go down better on Broadway than he ever would here. Surely the home market's glutted? Philip's for export."

Towers had shot up in her mind. The flash of quick thinking had fired her into her favorite game of All Change Here.

Then: "You're right, Paula, he's talented. He can sing and dance and waft a little charm across and I can see him doing just that quite successfully for the next twenty years—with a toupee towards the end of the cycle. 'Have to peel him out of his Pierrot union suits—you're right there too. White tie and tails and a red carnation. *And* that accent. Never let him lose the accent."

It was here that she slapped his face: a ringing, satisfying slap. In the old days Chester would have seen it coming and dodged it; not this time. She could still be pleased, in retrospect, with the look of the slapped face. But he had taken refuge in his enormous laughter.

"Honest to God, Paula—you asked me, didn't you? You wanted a professional opinion." He had said inevitably, "I don't understand you." This was an old cry; family cry, friends' cry, lover's cry. Despairing, furious or resigned, it echoed after her down the years.

"The lioness . . . I attacked your cub." More laughter. "I didn't, you know, but that's how you see it. I'd forgotten the lioness. Know what your real trouble is?"

Ah, the hell. All who protested "I don't understand you" would immediately set out to explain her as though they did.

She had leaped up from the chair under the willow tree and left Chester sitting there.

He had, she supposed, expected her to come back. For a while, anyway.

It was likely (wasn't it?) that he and Philip had had a wonderful time over lunch telling each other how impossible she was.

❋

Was she impossible?

Certainly not.

Hating self-analysis as much as she hated analysis from anyone else, she went no further than Certainly Not; a lid shut down.

It was time, besides, for pure concentration at the wheel. Paula got lost very easily, having no sense of direction. People with what was called a bump of locality were mysterious in the extreme; almost as mysterious as people with accurate, recording memories. Maybe the two gifts were connected; why not?

The coast road, with its arbitrary crinkles, its inadequate and misleading signposts, took her on a zigzag version of the correct route. How she came to take the right fork for Sawbridge Junction instead of the left fork for Sawcombe, she could not imagine. An attempt to remedy matters with a short cut led her into a lane signposted for somewhere quite different. The lane was too narrow for turning. Finding a gate in the hedge, she got out and opened the gate, preparing to back the Hispano through the gap. But at once a whole troop of small red cows, hitherto invisible, came plunging across the field. They charged from all directions, with a kind of hey-diddle-diddle gallop; nursery-rhyme cows. She remembered this happening when she and Herbert were on a trip through the Lake District. (Larger cows, there, and fuzzier. Herbert had been terrified; he climbed a fence.)

The cows swept up to the gate and she just managed to drag it shut before they engulfed her. After that they all stood together and glared at her, most reproachfully. She drove on uphill.

At last the road went down. A signpost read *Sawcombe* 1½ *miles*. She came through the outskirts, by the back streets, into Marine Square.

Oh, dear . . . The church looked, in its way, as reproachful as the cows had in theirs. Without the safe, near-smug sense of having been to church, Paula was conscious of guilt and disorder standing only a little way off. The church clock pointed ten minutes past four. She drove down Galleon Street onto the parade. Sudden reluctance to face Philip came with the British-Sunday depression: a killer. She had sampled New York depression, Paris depression and San Francisco depression. Each was as recognizable as a scent when you took the stopper off the bottle. All of them frightened her.

In a two-way panic, wanting to be back with Philip and not wanting, she braked the car at the pierhead. Strains of brass throbbed from the pier, muted because the bandstand was at the far end.

There would be people to talk to on the pier: children anyway. Maybe some of the company, strolling or sitting still. She found in the Moonrakers the reassuring warmth that came from any chance community: the crowd, the gang, the bunch. No matter what its origins, she was the better for it. Walking up to the turnstile, she looked back wistfully on the fun and games of this departing summer, and then shut off nostalgia. (*All change here.*)

As she swung the turnstile she heard a voice say, "There's Paula." It was Gerald's voice. She saw him halted beside the outgoing turnstile, three yards away. He was with the pale young man Morris Ward and the black-haired girl. Seeing her come through, he left them and hurried to meet her.

"Hullo—ullo—ullo," he said in Moonrakers convention.

The blend of schoolboy and gigolo, she thought: the cold fish perhaps less cold today. There was something precarious about the wayward smile and no sparkle of secret amusement in the eyes.

"Hullo, Gerald."

"All by yourself?" he asked.

"All by myself."

His two friends had gone out through the turnstile: they were waiting for him on the other side, but he waved them goodbye. "Enough," he said, "is enough. Are you looking for me? A search party of one?"

"Lord, no," said Paula, "I was coming to hear the band."

"Don't. It's terrible. Do I take it I've not been missed?" He sounded relieved.

"Missed? Have you been running too?"

Some of his swagger returned at once. He arched his eyebrows, saying, " 'Too,' Madam? I know not too."

"Pipe down," said Paula. "The Weston quote-voice puts me off. Just where are you going?"

"Home . . . I suppose."

"Want a ride?"

"Yes, please."

He walked beside her dejectedly. She had not seen him in dejection before. As he slumped into the car, he kept his face turned away from her.

"Miserable?" she asked.

"No. Yes."

"Can I help?"

Silence. They drove past the Fundrome.

"Ah, come on, Gerald."

He gave her a shadowy smile. All the way up the hill she was aware of him struggling. That he wanted to tell her she was now quite sure.

"You're in trouble?"

"Yes. No. Yes."

"Have you told Philip?"

"I haven't told anybody. Mute the camel. I'm a shareholder in Mute-the-Camel, Limited."

"Don't know what you mean. I presume there's a quotation hidden somewhere. Come clean now. Sex or money?" she snapped at him. He blushed and she had not known he could blush. His olive skin was turning near-purple. She brought the car to a halt outside the gates.

"I'm waiting," she said.

"Money," said Gerald.

"How much?"

"Fifteen pounds."

"Right. How soon must you have it?" He looked so much ashamed that she added quickly, "Look, it's easy, but it's in my bureau drawer upstairs."

"B-but—any time—today or tomorrow—any time," he muttered.

"Oh you can have it tonight. But wait till I give you the high sign. We're going to find all hell ripping loose around here," she told him as she drove through the gate. He sprang out, kissed her frenziedly on the forehead, and rushed away. His act was off. He ran like any excited boy, with great leaps, waving his arms. He went plunging round the side of the house. Paula sat at the wheel, wondering about him. Then she climbed out of the car. Since there was no Buick in the drive she looked for it in the garage. The garage was empty.

In the hall she stood listening, waiting. Not a sound. Only the silence and the sunlight. She went from room to room: nobody here. Nobody on the loggia. She looked down the garden terraces. Nobody there either. Even Gerald on his drunken war dance had vanished from view. Paula walked up the stairs.

Philip, in the Buick, was obviously combing highways and byways for her. She began to feel awful. Where was everybody else? Had he the sense to keep his anxiety to himself? Would she find Rab, Sarah and Thomas in the playroom, white-faced, huddled around a grieving Blanche?

Mrs. Gale, looking remarkably well and pink, appeared to wish her a brisk "Good evening."

"Hello. Better?" Paula asked and interrupted the answer: "Where's everybody got to?"

"They're all having tea on the beach."

"Not Mr. Weston?"

"Yes, Ma'am, he's down there. And Nanny."

"Then where's the car, I'd like to know?"

Mrs. Gale said Mr. Stevens had borrowed the car to take the General over to his golf game: at Woollacombe, she thought it was. Would Mrs. Weston like a cup of tea here or would she be going straight down to join the party?

"Here, please," said Paula. "I'm very tired and I'm going to have a hot bath."

Mrs. Gale made the error of saying a dip in the sea would be nice now, wouldn't it? She rather fancied a dip herself, but perhaps better not after her little upset.

❁

"Hullo, darling," said Philip. He looked tanned and hearty, still in his robe and swimming suit.

Paula was out of the bath. She had taken pains with her face and she was lying on the bed, wearing her Paris pyjamas. Philip leaned down to kiss her. "Had a good day?" he asked her. "Mine, by and large, has been exceptionally tricky."

"Rat," said Paula, "rat and rat and rat." She added, "Not to say louse. I suppose Chester put you onto it."

Philip stood, making a Spanish Grandee face, mainly with his eyebrows.

"Onto it? Onto what, my love?"

"*Cut*," said Paula.

"Apart from anything else, I haven't seen your friend Chester," said the Spanish Grandee, stark naked now and rubbing himself with a towel, but making the most of his eyebrows.

"You . . . Come again?"

"I couldn't get to the Rivermouth." Philip put on his undershorts: "There was far too much happening here." He wandered into the dressing room, calling in a warm, reassuring voice, "Chester quite understood; I telephoned him." He came back with a shirt and a pair of trousers.

"And he told you I'd gone?"

"That's what he told me." Philip pulled the shirt over his head. Always sensitive to the look of shirt tails and legs, he put on the trousers very quickly before he gave her the dazzle treatment.

"Well then naturally," said Paula, "he told you there was no need to worry. I'd be back just as soon as my temper was. 'That what he said?"

"He may have hinted at something of the kind. Just a hint, you know. And he rang up again after lunch."

"To ask if I was home?"

"Not precisely. To send you his undying love." Philip lingered over a choice of ties. "I think it was 'undying,' he said. Nice fellow."

"*Philip* . . ."

Her husband chose the Gunner tie and knotted it impeccably. "Oh, he asked me to say goodbye to you, too."

"Goodbye? . . ."

"He'd finally got in touch with that star he was chasing. She turned him down flat, so the London production's off." Philip sounded uncannily blithe about it. "Chester decided to drive straight to Southampton and get on whatever boat it is that sails tomorrow."

Paula lit a cigarette. "And did he by any chance tell you you were for export?"

"Ah, that was one of his observations last night. I liked it: made me feel like the best kind of Scotch tweed." He turned from the looking glass. "Beloved, would you mind if I talked about my *other* children first?"

"The hell—" said Paula. "Told you before we married I was a case of arrested development, didn't I? Didn't I? You knew what you were getting."

"I knew what I was getting. And I love what I've got," said Philip. "But there *are* times for stopping and counting ten."

"There are. Oh, there are. I always know that when it's over. Sometimes I know it when it's still going on," she added handsomely. She came out of the embrace saying, "Sorry—sorry—sorry. Tell me what happened . . ."

"Well—" Philip paused. "I don't really know how I'd have got through today without Nanny."

Part Three

========

SEPTEMBER

XVII

The children were in the dream; in a strange house that seemed
to consist of one enormous room. There were endless trunks to
be unpacked, and she had lost the keys. But they were there, all
of them: Gerald, Sarah, Thomas and Rab. So it was all right. "I
told you it didn't *have* to happen," said Thomas. The pang of
joy was too sharp: it awoke Blanche instantly. Sitting up, still
credulous, she saw today waiting for her: September the Twenty-
fourth, Nineteen Twenty-six.

Blanche got out of bed. She pulled the blind and twitched
aside the lace curtains. She saw thin, tentative sunlight on the
roofs of Ramillies Terrace. She had slept later than usual: downstairs she could hear Mary's thumping progress and the bathroom
noises meaning Frank already roused.

No hurry, Blanche thought: she was not due at the hotel

before eleven o'clock. There she would supervise the last of the
packing, have an early lunch with them all and leave in time to
reach Mrs. Latham by two-fifteen. Mrs. Latham had said, "Oh
you *angel*—" and added, "I expect you're terribly disappointed,
though," which was silly of her. Some words at this time had a
new power: the word disappointment was one of them.

There sounded a rattle of china, next a bump against her
door. Mary staggered in with a tray.

"I've brought you your breakfast in bed," she announced, unnecessarily and triumphantly. She stood in the doorway, smiling,
waiting to be thanked. "For a treat," said Mary.

"Oh—thank you." Her voice was nipped, not pleased enough.
"That's very kind of you," she added. She could not remember
having her breakfast in bed since the one time she went to
hospital, years ago. She looked doubtfully at the tray. The teapot
wore a knitted jacket, trimmed with wooden beads, and the
egg a knitted cap.

"I thought—" Mary began and left the sentence unfinished.
Having settled the tray on Blanche's knees (the feeling was one
of imprisonment rather than luxury) she walked to the window.
She stood looking down at the parcels. She had seen the presents last night: Gerald's tie, Sarah's silk stockings, the notebook
for Thomas and the pocket compass for Rab. ("Funny thing
for a girl to want.")

"What pretty ribbon," said Mary. "You always make nice bows.
What's the other parcel?"

"Just a petticoat of Sarah's. I brought it home to wash and
iron. That hotel iron's no good, dreadful old thing, I was
surprised."

"You know," said Mary turning from the window, "I've the
funniest feeling you'll go out there—that he'll send for you. I
can't get it out of my head, the feeling. Funny . . ."

"I don't know what I should do in New York, I'm sure."

"They say it's wonderful."

Blanche drank some more tea. Mary came back to the bedside.
"About this evening—" she began. Her fair face with its crumply
lines looked almost frightened.

"What about this evening?"

"It's the Whist Drive. I shan't be late, not to say late, but I won't be here to get your supper."

"Well good gracious, I hope I'm capable of getting my own supper," said Blanche, and laughed.

"Frank won't be in, either."

"No, he told me," said Blanche briskly: "What do you really think about this young lady?"

"Haven't had a chance to think much. She was only in the house ten minutes. Pretty hair. She giggles all the time: never stops looking at him. Did I give that egg too long?"

"No, it's just right, thank you."

"They're *driving* down to the boat." Mary's emphasis suggested that they might be flying, or swimming. "What about the luggage?"

"Some went yesterday. The rest goes in the two cars."

"*Two* cars?"

It was, Blanche reminded herself, the last of the painstaking questionnaires.

"I should have thought there were enough cars in America, from all one hears, wouldn't you?"

"Mr. Philip's fond of that Buick, being the first."

"He drives the one and Mrs. Philip drives the other—is that it?"

"No," said Blanche. "She's got her old chauffeur back. I don't mean he's old. He's—" She really could not bring herself to describe Miles.

"Nice, is he?"

"I've hardly seen him."

Was this the end? No. Mary said, "I suppose they're all very excited, the children," as though she hadn't said it before.

"Too excited," said Blanche, "I told you. All over the place yesterday, I couldn't get on with anything."

"Oh *dear*," said Mary, "I think it's awful. I can't help it. I *do* think it's awful. Taking them away from school, too."

"There are plenty of schools in America."

"Why couldn't he—oh well. Blanche, Frank says please listen

to his wireless if you'd like to. It says what to do on the bit
of paper."

"That's very kind of Frank."

It was a relief, when Mary had gone, to be able to escape the
imprisonment of the tray on her knees. She would leave the
house as soon as she was dressed: nothing else would stop Mary
talking. When she came downstairs, she said, "I forgot. Mrs.
Philip asked me to get some chemist things. Start now, I'd
better."

"Got your umbrella? Your best hat . . . They say it's going
to rain."

"Oh I don't expect so." She listened to *chops in the larder I'll
make a sponge pudding shouldn't be much after eight got your
key?* Now she was in the hall, with the sad plant on the table by
the hat stand: now she was going down the three steps and
across the red tiles: now she was opening the stiff latch at the
gate. Now she walked along Ramillies Terrace, between the little
houses with their sooty laurels and their lace curtains. The old,
silly song came back:

> *"But just for the minute
> That's as long as we are in it."*

She had, of course, made it come back. Just for the minute
she was on her way to them.

●

Merritt's Hotel was in Dover Street. Blanche drank a cup of
coffee at Lyons in Piccadilly, reading her newspaper more thoroughly than usual. She went from the Misery-Making Antics of
Mr. A. J. Cook, the miners' leader, to a French railway accident;
from there to the Dempsey-Tunney boxing match; past the
story of a bridegroom killed on his wedding day, to a picture of
some Siamese kittens poking their heads out of stockings that
were hung on a clothesline. Silly. Pet dog at a wedding: nasty:
nothing to do with the dead bridegroom, of course, but unpleas-
ant in this conjunction. She read the advertisements. *Make your
cold enjoyable by using Pyramid* was just nonsense.

And now it was only twenty-five minutes to eleven. She paid for her coffee and went, carrying her string bag with the parcels, leaving the newspaper. There was no reason, surely, why she should not get to Merritt's Hotel ahead of time. Yes, there was. *Her,* thought Blanche.

The skies had turned gray: reaching the corner, she saw the first spots of rain on the pavement. Mary had been right. She went into Merritt's, out of the rain. She would sit on a chair down here in the lobby, until eleven struck. Not looking to right or left, because this hotel intimidated her, she aimed for a chair in the corner.

A commanding voice said, "Nanny." A gloved hand shot out to grasp her arm. She looked into the eyes of the grandmother.

Mrs. Murray, wearing bottle green with a felt hat, square as a cake, of the same color, said, "I'm delighted to see you. Are you just going up? Up? Up? You're early. How nice. Come and talk to me." She pushed open glass doors leading into a room full of paneling, tapestry and chrysanthemums. She steered Blanche towards the fireplace.

"You would think they'd have a fire," she said, avoiding the armchair and choosing the embroidered stool that faced the cut-steel fender. "But of course we are not in Scotland now." She placed her bag and gloves beside her on the stool. "You knew I'd left Inverness? No, naturally, they would forget to mention it in all the excitement. My sweet old landlady died, so my son-in-law had to move me. All very quick—very quick—very quick. Here I am in Onslow Gardens. A bed-sitting room, so far. You wouldn't like to do a little work for me, I suppose? Not that I could afford to pay you anything, hardly anything, hardly anything at all."

Blanche explained about Mrs. Latham and Mrs. Fothergill. Mrs. Murray sat regally, but with a wandering eye.

"Is it necessary, I wonder, to depart at such speed? You have none of you had time to turn round."

"Well, I understand they're beginning rehearsals very soon," said Blanche. "This is the only boat that can get them there in time."

"I don't know anything about this play, in New York, do you?

The play? I understand it's a small part, a very small part. Why do they say it will lead to something? What will it lead to? Another very small part?"

"I couldn't say at all, M'm."

"*Why* is there always supposed to be a future in America? Has any country the monopoly of one tense—one tense—one tense? She's a very restless nature, I saw that immediately."

There seemed nothing to answer to this; but Mrs. Murray never insisted on answers.

"Uprooting," she observed, "is bad. But then they have never really had roots, so one cannot look upon it quite like that. I enjoyed my glimpse of them. Butterflies. Butterflies."

Blanche waited for explanation. "Gerald and Sarah, butterflies," said Mrs. Murray. "That makes two butterflies . . . And one"— she paused, smiling as if at a picture on the wall—"Funny little boy," she murmured. "It's never worried you, has it?"

"Excuse me, M'm?"

"Thomas and all—Thomas and all."

"All what, M'm?"

"Ah, what indeed? True or false, true or false. It *was* you who moved the ginger fox, wasn't it?" Mrs. Murray asked; she sounded entirely serious, though she could not be. Blanche knew who had moved the toy fox: Mrs. Murray herself: she had played that game with the children, making them cover their eyes and then hiding the toy animals for them to find. An old game. Mrs. Murray had called it Magic, so they called it Magic too and were happily convinced that the animals moved of their own accord, until they grew too big to believe it.

Mrs. Murray must be joking when she said, "Own up now— it was you."

"Oh no, M'm," said Blanche, beginning to laugh. "How could it have been me? I was getting the coal." She remembered going to fill the scuttle for the sitting-room fire; leaving Thomas upside down on the sofa, with his head buried in a cushion. The grandmother was reading, at the other end of the room. She remembered coming back with the scuttle, and Thomas shouting that the fox had moved itself over to the window sill. The grandmother had glanced his way for a moment, before she returned to her book.

All this was most clear in her mind, perhaps because the ginger fox was quite new and she herself had bought it for Thomas.

"I never touched the fox," said Mrs. Murray, staring at her. "He was playing that game all by himself. I didn't even know he *was* playing."

"But . . . I mean . . . You never said anything."

"I've said something now. So have you."

Mrs. Murray must have forgotten. Or else she was imagining things. Or else . . . what? Blanche saw that she looked competent and satisfied, picking up her possessions from the embroidered stool: rather as she had looked at the end of their first interview. ("Well, Miss Briggs, I think you're just the person we have been waiting for. I am going to call my daughter.")

"The best of luck to you, Nanny. Here's my address. And my telephone number. You may need them. One never knows—knows —knows. . . ." She marched out, square-shouldered, into the lobby, where she wheeled and stood quite still, saying in her clarion voice, "As the day is, so shall thy strength be." An old gentleman in morning dress, passing through the lobby, jumped and dropped his pearl-gray gloves.

Blanche went up in the lift, thinking about the fox. She came to the second floor and turned to the right, down the passage with the pale carpet. She came to the two doors, with the brass numbers on them.

The first door was opened at once by Mrs. Philip, dressed for the street, but carrying her hat. All in almond green today: the diamonds: long thin shoes of light-colored suede.

"Hello, Nanny darling. Just going to get my hair done. Everything's under control, at least I think it is. Sarah seems to be losing her mind about a petticoat. Thomas *would* have breakfast in bed, so he's way behind with everything. ("Breakfast in bed, the idea . . .") Sarah's going to drive with Philip and me in the Buick. The others go with Miles." Mrs. Philip was nervous, smiling too much, gazing too straight, chattery as a child. "I'm sure you'll—oh, there you are, darling." She moved away as Mr. Philip came through the door. He was wearing a new gray suit. He gave Blanche a hug, while his wife walked on to the lift.

"Here's the plan," he said, smiling and twitching a great deal. "We're going to lunch out, so you'll have them all to yourself. The lunch is ordered. For half-past twelve sharp." He dropped his voice. "Paula's idea: she thought you'd like it."

❀

Sarah stood in front of the looking glass. She leaned back her head, pressing a hand to each cheek. She murmured, "The death of a whole past life—the birth of a whole new—were struggling in those magnificent eyes, choking in that magnificent throat." (Some years now since she had read *Westward Ho!* and she could not be sure the quotation was correct. Still it would do.)

Behind her in the room, Rab made one of her consenting 'Ug' noises and then returned to her slow monotonous chant. "Vineyard—Vineyard—Vineyard." The dirge refrain went on. Sarah turned from the glass saying, "Oh do stop." The setting, with its gilt and tapestry and dark panels, made for splendor. So did the last of the luggage, sprouting the bright labels of the shipping line. Rab, crouched on the second bed, looked like an orphan, somehow. Her latest haircut had left her very little hair. Her new dress had lost all shape, rucked up above her brown, bony knees. "Vineyard. Vineyard. Vineyard. It's a talisman. As long as I go on saying it, I don't mind going back."

"Mind going back . . ." Sarah echoed.

"Vineyard. Vine— But we won't get there till next summer. Maybe not even *then*," grumbled Rab. Meeting Sarah's eyes, the truculent boyish face softened. She grinned. "Anyway I'd rather be in America with you than here without you, see?"

It was, in this new pattern of days, consoling to be loved. It was not so much fun as loving, but—like the Kingsley quotation —it would do. It helped the lingering sense of shame. Even with this colossal adventure ahead, shame could still return. For the past, for the summer of Shirley Ormonde, above all for the rape that was no such thing, the brandished lie.

All over, Sarah reminded herself angrily: all over: Outward Bound: Salute to Adventurers:

> *"Ah, outward bound! The words beget*
> *A dream of mosque and minaret*
> *And golden dalliance."*

Anything could happen, in America. Couldn't it?

Interesting face, said Cecil B. de Mille to his secretary: I believe we could use that girl in the new Ronald Colman picture. See she has a test tomorrow.

Sarah drew a comb through her hair and told Rab to get a move on. "Your flannel and sponge and everything are still in the bathroom, did you know? And you'll forget your lion if you leave it sitting there."

Rab stretched a listless hand for the silver lion on the bedside table. She tossed it up and caught it. She giggled.

"What's funny?" Sarah asked.

"Thomas getting breakfast in bed. Paula wouldn't stand for it from anybody else. I never knew anyone as *bored* as Thomas. Except me," said Rab.

Certainly, Sarah reflected, he had gone through this intoxicating time with the utmost nonchalance. He wasn't excited: he wasn't anything. He would not even admit to pleasure at leaving Puxford, saying, "Oh well," and shrugging. He had remained politely unimpressed with the stage box for the "Co-Optimists." According to Gerald, he had declared a preference for *Moonrakers 1926*: though this seemed unlikely, reluctant as he always was to declare a preference for anything. He had been quite noisy and cheerful at Madame Tussaud's, and at the ensuing tea; Brigstock's treat. Once back in the hotel he had muffled himself again. Yesterday, while she was here packing, he had behaved like a gay lunatic, reverting to stolid silence only after she went. True, she had heard him gabbling away to the grandmother just now. But he always talked to the grandmother.

Rab gave a loud yawn and climbed off the bed. Gerald

strolled in, wearing his new paisley silk dressing gown. He stood posing for them.

"Oh take it off and pack it for Heaven's sake," said Sarah. "Mine eyes dazzle."

"I only put it on to show Brigstock," said Gerald. He added, "*Mesdames sont servies.*"

"*Mesdames sont* what?"

"Tables have come sliding in. Chafing dishes are ablaze. White-coated minions on noiseless feet—"

"You mean lunch is ready."

"That," said Gerald, "is what I mean." He strolled away whistling: Gerald's nonchalance, unlike that of Thomas, was transparent. He was, she knew, as wildly excited as she. Half-past twelve. Less than two hours to wait. But the awful hurdle of saying goodbye to Brigstock was in the way. Sarah shut her eyes. Whereupon Rab asked, with tireless solicitude, if she was feeling ill.

"A little faint. It's the excitement," she murmured.

Though on a far grander scale than ever before, this could be any lunch on any last day, with the school train ahead. There had been so many that Sarah, recalling them, felt quite old: boarding houses, furnished rooms, Elmo Court, a little hotel in Bloomsbury. September was made for this: with the rain falling outside the windows; one's thoughts a jumble of new clothes and luggage; it was the all-packed-up-and-here-we-go feeling; the familiar features persisted: Brigstock at the head of the table, smiling determinedly, Gerald showing off and Thomas having lost something. (His blazer, this time. *In the bottom of the big one, no need to make a fuss, I remember distinctly.*)

The same as ever: even to the wrapped parcels beside their plates. Now they were all undoing the presents, gloating separately. Gerald took off his tie and put on the new one with a flourish. Rab rushed around the table checking compass points. Sarah decided to emulate Gerald and put on the silk stockings.

"Not now," said Brigstock.

"After lunch, then. *Immed*iately after lunch."

"No, you must save them."

Thomas, gazing at his notebook said, "I've never had anything with my *initials* on it before. Crumbs, crackers, onions, owls."

"I knew it would have to be a notebook," said Brigstock, laughing at him. "It's got loose leaves, for a change."

"There's a present for *you*," said Rab sounding suddenly gloomy.

"I'm too old for presents. Come along now, you're letting everything get cold."

"I don't want to eat," said Rab.

"Oh yes, you do. Everybody's got to eat properly. Look at all these lovely things."

Only Rab continued sullen with despair. She did not, of course, understand the rule about last-day lunches. One had to do them as well as one possibly could. One ate everything and behaved uproariously; Gerald, twining his discarded tie round a long, crusty roll, was obeying the tradition. So was Thomas: with an enormous helping on his plate, telling Brigstock about the Indians. The Indians, who were maharajahs and maharanees, lived in the next suite. "*Rings* in their noses," said Thomas, "like pigs. Ha—*ha*. Just like pigs. You can't see how the rings stay in. I stood next to one of the ladies in the lift and I looked right up her nose and I still couldn't see."

Brigstock, trying to sound stern, said that was not nice. "No, it wasn't very, as things turned out," said Thomas. "But I had to look, didn't I?"

"Sarah dear, don't you want one of these rolls?"

"Madam is banting," said Gerald.

She was staring on, ahead, to the picture of the ship at the quayside. Rab had described it, looking like a high wall full of portholes: gangways with canvas covers, sloping down steeply to the dock. When you had climbed the gangway, Rab said, the ship became much like an hotel inside.

"By Easter," Gerald was saying, "we'll all have American accents. 'Say, bo, I'm mighty glad to get acquainted.'"

"Americans don't speak that way," said Rab wearily. "You'll learn."

By Easter . . . It was tossed about, this promise, this theory that they would all be home by Easter. Philip's promise? Paula's? Sarah was not sure who had made it, but they kept it going. She looked at Brigstock. (The straw hat with the roses: beginning of the holidays: Paddington Station: no, don't go back to there. She looks so cheerful, smiling away. Perhaps it is true; perhaps we will come home at Easter.)

Thomas took two meringues, arranging them neatly, one each side of his fruit salad. He then laid down his spoon and fork. "It's a lie," said Thomas placidly. "About Easter, I mean. I don't know why anybody bothers." He picked up his spoon and fork again.

❂

"It's perfectly possible, Nanny, perfectly possible. In fact I should think more than likely." Mr. Philip's smile was desperate, and his eyes.

"Well, then, perhaps somebody could explain that to Thomas. He likes everything what I call cut and dried," said Blanche. Mrs. Philip, hovering at the other end of the room, half-listening, called, "Don't worry, Nanny. I'll take care of it." And then, "He looks quite grown-up in the tweed suit, don't you think?"

Blanche, who had reservations about the tweed suit, looked past Mr. Philip to the gilt clock on the mantelpiece.

"Well, I'll say goodbye now," she said. She might be a little early for Mrs. Latham, but this was the moment, she thought, feeling finality: feeling the presence of two people who had nothing to do with her any more.

"Did you like your present?" Mrs. Philip kept up the straight blue stare to the last: "Pretty stuff, I thought. Sarah helped me choose it." Then the light kiss and the scent and her own voice saying, "I hope you'll all have a good voyage. I'll be thinking of you." She gave Mr. Philip a little pat as he broke away from hugging her, but she did not look at his face.

Outside the door, she was, astonishingly, tempted to go on down the passage to the lift: not to open the other door again. She opened it. She saw one bright glimpse, caught in a bubble forever: the four of them standing still: Gerald, Sarah, Thomas and Rab.

"Have to be off now," said Blanche. She managed to glare. "We don't say goodbye, remember. We say *au revoir*."

They came at her in a rush, all trying to hug her at the same time. "*Au revoir*," the voices said, "*au revoir*." They came with her to the lift, Gerald holding her arm, the rest all mixed up and clutching until the lift doors slammed back. She stepped inside. They were waving, shouting as the doors shut them away. The lift went down.

Blanche came out of Merritt's Hotel and walked slowly towards the tube station. She stopped for a moment, blinking her eyes, to look in a shop window. This proved to be foolish, because it was a dress shop, one of the expensive sort, with a single evening dress of flame-colored taffeta posed beside a long, oval looking glass. She saw her reflection. She looked funny and small and old in the glass. Her best hat was crooked, getting spoiled by the rain, too. She saw the wisps of gray hair sticking out, her nose all red, and the tears at last spilling over. She got out her handkerchief.

"It's good for them," she told herself, "good for them. They're going to have a lovely time. Not like the bad old days, not a bit. And there'll be letters coming."

She straightened her hat and walked on through the rain.

XVIII

"Make speed, Madam," said Gerald. "Come away from that looking glass, now. Father and Paula are losing their little minds. At least, Father is."

Sarah turned. She said with violence, "Wish I was coming with you in the other car."

"So do I." (And I know what's hurting you, because it's hurting me.)

"*Outward bound!*" she cried and swept past him to the door, a tragedy queen. He said to her back, "I feel bloody about Brigstock, don't you?" She halted, looking at him, her eyes wide for the forbidden adjective. "Bloody," he repeated, "bloody, bloody, bloody."

"*Sarah!*" Paula's voice rang from the corridor.

"Coming," said Sarah and stayed where she was. "Keep remembering the overall," she muttered.

"What overall?" (But I don't want to know.)

"My red and white one. She sat up late to finish it and then I wouldn't put it on."

"There was a check, with the dress length," said Gerald. "Paula told me."

"Like a tip."

"Meant to be kind."

"I *hate* kindness."

"So do I," said Gerald and gave her a hug. "*We* know," he added, though he could not have explained what he meant by that. But she said, "Yes," hugging tight. "Yes. We'll always know."

"Sarah!"

"On my way."

"Cheer up. After all," he told her, "it's really only the same as going back to school." Then he began to laugh because the great and glorious adventure had suddenly shrunk down to this.

Beside the lift, his father, who had turned military and masterful, as might have been expected, fussed him about the hotel rendezvous in Southampton; next about the tickets, the passports and the cabin numbers: "Miles has everything. You do just what Miles says. If by any chance—though there *isn't* one—we *aren't* at the hotel, then you all go straight to the boat with Miles. If—" Paula interrupted him, looking maternally amused, "Cut, darling, will you, please? Miles is in command. Okay, Gerald, see you later. *Don't* let Thomas leave his new cap behind, that's all I ask. 'Bye now."

As the lift doors shut, the doors of the twin lift opened and Miles stepped out. He sprang to attention, saluting Gerald, grinning like a skull. He wore gray uniform, with a pink carnation in his buttonhole. He smelled of musky scent.

"*En avant, grenadiers de France*," said Miles. "Luggage in. Three morons who haven't done a hand's turn waiting for tips. Got enough silver? I hope," he added, "that you had a better lunch than I did. Maybe there's still good coffee in America. If there ain't I'll shoot myself. Where are the kids?"

"I'll round them up."

"In fact," said Miles, "we're allowing far too much time." He grinned still more: "That's your father's influence. I've known the lady catch the Berengaria with just three minutes in hand. Better take a look around. She usually leaves something." He wandered into the first suite, whistling "Rose Marie." Gerald followed.

"How d'you like her?" Miles asked, opening drawers and shutting them.

There was no way of snubbing him: perhaps one would discover a way. Gerald tried, "Who?" and tacked on, "may I ask?"

"Stockings; let's see if they're laddered. Yes, they are. Who? Why, your stepmother, who else?"

"We are friends," said Gerald, doing his best to sound lofty. It was true, wasn't it? Paula was a good friend. She had not betrayed him to Philip. Throughout the angular little row, conducted in her presence, she had taken his side most vociferously: "Let's cut, Philip. Gerald did the right thing in paying Leo. Leo did the right thing in refusing to be paid. Your only grouch— as I see it—is that Gerald's somehow managed to save fifteen pounds. Now *honestly*—darling—"

Here Philip had burst into laughter, saying, "See what you mean," and going to get a drink: the moment of danger had taken a most unexpected turn, with Paula saying, "I'm right, aren't I, Gerald—you would rather he didn't know you asked me for the other fifteen?"

"I would—please."

"I'd have done as you did, chum. But let's remember Leo didn't *lose* thirty pounds: he just didn't win it. And he's a nice guy. If I sent him a check now, he'd be bound to send it back."

She was an innocent. She thought he had been straining to pay Leo the whole debt. The simple truth that his agony had been concerned only to replace the hoard was still his own secret.

But since then, oddly, he had not wished to look too closely at himself: a new pattern persisting through these days that were all new. (And, remembering the pearl studs, he had felt most unhappy with the grandmother today.)

Miles said, "Friends . . . That's good to hear. She needs friends. Though you might say she has plenty friends. You might. You'd be wrong. I doubt they'd stick with her, most of them, that is, if it wasn't for—" he shrugged. "Let's get going, shall we?"

Gerald found Rab and Thomas seated each on a bed. Thomas, in his porridgy tweed suit, hunched up, with his back to Rab, was writing. Rab was reading.

"Can't be time yet," she said.

"Yes it is. Step on it, now." He glanced at the enormous book. "Couldn't you have packed that?" he asked.

"It's my *bird book*, dopey. *I'll* carry it, you don't have to carry it."

"Wake up, mate—" said Gerald, addressing Thomas's back. "Where's your cap got to?"

"Packed."

"He doesn't want to wear it," said Rab.

"Everybody wears tweed caps on boats, you'll see."

Thomas said, "Oh well," and unearthed the cap from his hold-all. He crushed it down, pulling at the peak and making hideous faces at Miles. Miles turned up the whites of his eyes, putting out his tongue and waggling it.

"I have to go to the bathroom," said Rab.

"Oh, lord, couldn't you have thought of that before?"

"It's all right," Miles told him. "Like I said, we've lots of time."

Gerald groaned. "That's the *last* thing to tell these two. What about you, Thomas?"

"Well, what about me?"

"Lavatory?"

"No thanks." He picked up his hold-all. He stood ranged beside Miles, who stared down at the tweed mushroom with apparent fascination.

"You want to sit in front with me?" Miles asked.

"Yes, please, I do," said Thomas.

The rain was letting up, and the sun came through, making a watery blaze across the street. The gray Hispano glistened all over with raindrops. Thomas swung himself in beside Miles. Gerald let Rab go first while he dealt out the last of the tips. As the car moved, Rab said, "You didn't give the doorman anything."

"Well why should I? Father will have tipped him."

"You had enough left," she went on. "A florin was it, or half a crown? I saw you put it back in your pocket."

Looking at her with a new exasperation Gerald saw that she was no longer peevish and sullen, but leaning back at ease, one arm resting in the gray loop that hung beside the window: giving an impression of the experienced traveler.

"Little girls must mind their own damn business," he snapped, "mustn't they?"

"That's right," said Miles, not turning his head.

Rab winked at Gerald, then settled the bird book on her knees, placed her detective story on top of it and began to read. He felt ruffled and—for a moment—most unhappily alone. As the car turned into the Piccadilly traffic, he knew he would have liked Sarah beside him. This was the adventure. This was going. And there was no one with whom to share it. Thomas in front was just a pair of ears under the tweed mushroom. He tried to unroll some suitable poetry in his head, but all that came was the opening chorus:

> *"Moonrakers, moonrakers!*
> *Masters of laughter, the melody makers,*
> *Wandering minstrels, the givers, the takers . . ."*

The summer was in the tune: the tune would bring it all back for a while: Sawcombe parade; old McPhee behind the counter: Mr. Evans playing tennis in his braces: the cliff path down to the cove: Morris Ward and the black-haired girl: the loggia: the Fundrome gardens: the woman whose case was carried by James MacBride: and Brigstock coming into his room to draw the curtains, telling him it was another fine day.

❀

"The Chief Inspector's heavy jaw set. 'The Dower House?' he snapped. 'Right. We're on our way.' He put back the receiver and

there was in his tired eyes a look that Carstairs had seen before. He gave a dry, mirthless laugh."

Rab glanced up from the page. She looked out of the window. She saw two shops on the corner: a greengrocer and a tobacconist's. Shabby little shops: it was a shabby little street. She had no idea where they were. Thomas was taking forever, wasn't he?

"Thomas takes longer to pee than anyone I know," she remarked. Gerald didn't answer. Gerald was sour with Thomas and sour with her; Miles, by the set of his shoulders, might be sour too. He had had to turn off the main street to wait for Thomas.

"Rab. You've got the lion." Why should the words linger to trouble her? He was always fussing about the lion. Exactly like Thomas to stop and fuss about it when in urgent need of a bathroom. She returned to Scotland Yard.

" *'You mean—he's struck again,' Carstairs said grimly.*

'Looks like it. Throat cut. No sign of a weapon.' "

"Takes his time, doesn't he?" Miles, turning back from the wheel, proved not to be sour at all; he was laughing.

"Probably out hours ago: just mooning in front of a shop window. I'll go and get him," said Gerald crossly.

"I'll come with you," said Rab.

"You can't come into the Gents."

"You just said he'd be out hours ago."

"Don't *you* two get lost now," said Miles. "Lost, kidnaped, stolen, strayed," he added merrily. Gerald outpaced Rab to the corner. *"Wait,"* he snapped at her as he plunged across the tramlines. She sauntered to and fro, spying for Thomas at one of the shop windows, though they were surely not exciting enough to absorb anyone's attention for long: they were cut-rate shops, cheap tailors and jewelers. She turned to watch for Gerald. The public lavatory was set on a concrete surround in the middle of the street, where the trams stopped. It had two tiled entrances, marked LADIES and GENTLEMEN. She saw Gerald come out, alone. He had to wait for a gap in the traffic.

"Not there?" said Rab.

"He may have dodged back to the car by now."

"He couldn't. I'd have seen him."

"Anything he wanted to *buy*, d'you know?"

"Why'd he choose to buy it here?"

Miles came strolling to the corner. He pushed his cap to the back of his head. He stood with his hands on his hips, looking from one to the other.

"Well, well," said Miles. "What do we do now?" The tilt of the cap, the grin and the ample air, gave Rab a clue (as if, she told herself in sudden misery, a clue were needed after he said, *You've got the lion*). She watched Miles hand the note to Gerald, who began to swear before he took hold of it. Miles cut him off: "That's no good, swearing. This was stuck way down between the cushions. He must have been sitting on it since we started. I only just saw—came to get you."

Gerald snatched the note and unfolded it. There were two single sheets, loose leaves from the new notebook. Peering over his elbow, Rab read the painstaking print:

NOBODY NEED WORRY AND NOBODY PLEASE MUST TRY TO STOP ME DOING THIS. I KNOW TELEGRAMS CAN BE SENT TO BOATS SO YOU WILL BE ABLE TO HEAR THAT I AM QUITE ALL RIGHT. ON PAGE 2 I HAVE WRITTEN DOWN THE ARRANGEMENTS. I HAVE PUT THE BUS-ROUTE DOWN TOO, TO STOP ANYBODY WORRYING ABOUT THE FIRST BIT.

YOU SEE, I HAVE THOUGHT IT ALL OUT AND SOMEBODY'S GOT TO—

Gerald whipped away from her. He kept his back turned, reading on. Then he crushed the paper violently in his hand. He stood quite still in front of the tobacconist's shop, his head down, his shoulders bowed, looking furious and alone.

She was aware of Miles, winking at her. "One thing I *did* see," said Miles. "Thomas took that bag of his when he went."

"You saw? So you didn't do anything?"

"So I didn't do anything."

Now Gerald turned abruptly, saying in a gruff voice, "Drive on." He said nothing else.

"Better so," Miles observed, "ain't it, really? Got to catch that boat, haven't we?"

Nobody answered him. As he drove the car back into the

main road, Rab pushed the books onto the floor. She began to dig in her small suitcase until she found the silver lion. She sat squeezing it tightly between her hands: she was quite unable now to cope with a sudden enormous sob.

"What's *that* for?" Gerald asked.

"He was my friend."

"Is, not *was*. He hasn't died."

"Could go and get him, couldn't we?"

"No."

"*Why* couldn't we?"

Gerald said, "I've always expected Thomas to do something like this, sooner or later. And the old boy somehow manages to convince me." He read aloud from the note on his knee: " 'It isn't as if I was really needed in America.' "

Rab burst into tears again. She went on crying.

After a time Gerald said peevishly, "Oh, do stop. At least *you* haven't got to do the explaining."

"But he won't get to the Vineyard now. Not ever," she sobbed.

"Anybody like a piece of nougat?" Miles asked. "It's good. I got it in Montelimar."

❂

"Quite a fine evening it's turned out, hasn't it, Blanche?"

"Yes, M'm, it's nice now."

"And *what* a change . . . the room, I mean. It looks almost human," said Mrs. Latham.

"I've only done the tops. 'Give it a proper turnout tomorrow. What I say about these girls is they never go in the corners."

"No they *don't*, do they?" Mrs. Latham billowed about in a new tea gown, stopping occasionally before one or another photograph, twitching at curtains, leaving half-smoked cigarettes in ashtrays and then with a sudden air of generalship, bringing a little watering can to water the ferns.

"There's a whole mountain of mending," she said guiltily.

"So I saw."

"Could you bear to take some home with you? The nightgowns? I haven't *one* fit to wear."

"Yes, M'm."

"You're an angel. It's nearly six o'clock, you know."

This needed no telling. They were on board. It was difficult to imagine the inside of so large a ship; neither Rab's descriptions nor the plan shown her by Mrs. Philip conveyed much to her mind.

"Would you like a glass of—"

Blanche never knew what precise drink Mrs. Latham was offering her because she always said, "No, thank you, M'm," at this point. She said it.

"Sure?"

"Quite sure, thank you."

Mrs. Latham's oil painting of the Solent had its uses this evening: looking at it she could imagine the ship sailing down that treacly blue-green surface. Behind her, from the sideboard came the squish sound of the syphon.

"Shall I put up the card table, M'm?"

"Oh *yes*, please. Just the table. I'll do the cards and the markers."

"This leg's got worse, surely."

"I *know*." A note of agony in Mrs. Latham's voice, as though nothing whatever could be done about a card table with a rickety leg.

"I suppose," she said, "I might treat myself to a new one. But I'm so terribly hard-up at the minute." She tilted the drink down her throat and lit another cigarette.

"You must go, Blanche. I'm sure you're tired."

"Nothing to be done about supper, M'm?"

"No, no. We're just going to play a couple of rubbers here and then go over to the Club. The food's quite good these days—a new chef. It was *angelic* of you to give me the afternoon. Have you something to put the mending in?"

As usual she stood in the kitchen doorway while Blanche put on her hat and coat: glass in hand, anxious to talk up till the last possible minute. "Anyhow, you *did* have the whole lovely summer, that'll be something to remember."

Blanche refolded the silk nightgowns, stuffing as many as would go into the string bag with the parcel from Mrs. Philip.

"I'll never forget how I felt when Muriel went to Canada. Never. Not if I live to be a hundred. *Sure* you won't have a glass of—"

"No, thank you, M'm." She picked up the bulging bag. "I'll take the rest tomorrow. That's all I've room for now."

"Bless you. Going back to your sister's?" (Where else would I be going?) "I expect she's glad to have you, isn't she? *Nice* to have a sister. Brothers aren't the same."

"Well, I'll say good night, M'm."

"Good night, Blanche dear. Try not to be sad."

Silly. She meant to be kind, of course, but she was really silly.

Waiting for the bus, Blanche tried again to make a picture of the cabins on B deck—Gerald sharing with Thomas; Sarah with Rab. But one came to a full stop. When they went back to school it was different. Having seen the schools one could always make the picture, and there was something about no picture that made one feel as if they were nowhere; nowhere in the world. Which was ridiculous. On the bus to Marble Arch she kept her mind away from such foolishness, answering her neighbor, who was rather a peculiar lady convinced that the end of the world was due next week. On an ordinary day, Blanche reflected, she would have moved to another seat.

"It's been a pleasure to talk with you," the peculiar lady said to her at Marble Arch.

Now the wait for the Battersea bus. The sky was turning pink above the trees in Hyde Park. She began to wonder how soon the sea grew rough, convinced as she was that the Atlantic went on being rough all the way to America. "They'll get their sea legs: everybody does," said Blanche to Blanche.

Here was the bus: and a seat by the door. These seats were much too high: her feet barely touched the ground. After she had paid her fare she pushed her handbag in on top of the nightgowns and the parcel: one thing less to carry. As she sat nursing the fat burden, she came down to the sober sense at the bottom of her mind. *It was always going to happen and you knew it. 'Come a bit sooner than you expected, that's all.*

It had happened before. She remembered driving away from

the Hales' house in a hansom cab. She remembered Mr. Mattingley taking her to Ludlow Station in the pony trap. Five years with the Hales: seven with the Mattingleys: and fourteen years with the Westons.

Adding up the years, trying to reckon the years as nursemaid that came before them, Blanche felt herself growing sleepy, stupid in the head: not able to mind very much now. "Just about ready for bed, I am. Would Mary be offended if I didn't cook the chops? Just boiled myself an egg and went to bed?"

The bus jogged over Battersea Bridge: the sky was a deeper pink behind the chimneys of the power station. The pink sky was in the river. She looked at her watch. She saw the liner going down the Solent; and now the Solent was no longer the blue-green treacle in the gilt frame above Mrs. Latham's mantelpiece: it was as still and silken as this river, reflecting this pink sky. She saw the funnels smoking, as the chimneys of the power station were smoking; with orderly plumes of purplish gray.

The bus stopped. Here it all was again, the avenue with the people hurrying home: the corner: here was the last of her own road home: Ramillies Terrace waiting. Was that Mr. Dalbrook's Morris-Oxford outside Number Fourteen? Surely Mr. Dalbrook should be at the Whist Drive. Disappointing for Mary. Best to cook the chops; not give Mary two disappointments in one evening . . . (Though in time she would be likely to find that Mary hadn't cared about Mr. Dalbrook's absence and would have welcomed the chops saved for tomorrow.)

Shipping the string bag onto one arm, she prepared for the assault on the gate of Number Twenty-Four. The latch was stuck fast as usual. A shower of raindrops from the laurel bush came down on her gloves and still the latch did not yield. As she pressed it again, she glanced over the gate and up the red-tiled path to the steps.

Thomas was sitting on the steps, with his arms round his knees and his canvas hold-all beside him. He had taken off the new tweed cap and this lay on top of the hold-all with some magazines. His hair was very untidy: he looked as though she had just woken him up. And of course this must be a dream, or tiredness giving her hallucinations. That was the word for it; hallucinations. Thomas, squatting on the steps in his new tweed suit, could not be here. Thomas was gone to America, sailing down a pink river under a pink sky.

He didn't move. Nor did she. They were caught in a silence, staring at each other across the gate.

"Hullo, Brigstock," he said at last. "I suppose I was asleep." He got up slowly, stretching and wriggling. "I've been here simply ages. I rang and rang. That latch," he added, "isn't difficult if you take it by surprise." He rubbed his bottom. "Pins and needles," he said, "all over."

The latch went down under her hand: the gate burst open. Something bumped against her feet. It was the string bag falling, rolling away across the red tiles, spilling everything as it rolled. Well, it would. Her arms had gone up, flying into the air; flying wide.

About the Author

PAMELA FRANKAU is a third-generation novelist; her grandmother, "Frank Danby," and her father, Gilbert Frankau, were both best-selling authors of their time. She wrote her first novel at eighteen and has been writing ever since. She is miserable when not writing and her only regret in middle-age is that the ideas come more slowly than they used to.

Work is Miss Frankau's favorite recreation; other recreations, less important, are travel, cooking and gambling. She lived in America for ten years and describes herself as a sufferer from trans-Atlantic schizophrenia, since she is often homesick for England when she is in America, and vice versa.

Seventeen of Miss Frankau's novels have been published in this country, among them *The Willow Cabin*, *To the Moment of Triumph* and *A Wreath for the Enemy* (which last incorporated her famous story, *The Duchess and the Smugs*). In *Pen to Paper*, a novelist's notebook published in 1961, the author summed up her thirty-year apprenticeship to the craft of fiction with a study of technique, some hints that would be valuable to younger writers, and a self-portrait on the side.

For many years Miss Frankau has wanted to write a sequence of novels covering the life story of a single human being, and in 1960 she began work on a trilogy called *Clothes of a King's Son*. *Sing for Your Supper* is the first of the series; the second, *Slaves of the Lamp*, is already in progress.